THE BLACKHOUSE

Carole Johnstone grew up in Lanarkshire, Scotland, and in her twenties relocated to Essex to work as a radiographer. She has been writing as long as she can remember and is an award-winning short story writer.

She now writes full-time and lives with her husband in an old farmhouse outside Glasgow, though her heart belongs to the sea and the wild islands of the Outer Hebrides.

Also by Carole Johnstone:

Mirrorland

THE
black
house

CAROLE JOHNSTONE

THE BOROUGH PRESS

The Borough Press
An imprint of HarperCollins*Publishers* Ltd
1 London Bridge Street
London SE1 9GF

www.harpercollins.co.uk

HarperCollins*Publishers*
1st Floor, Watermarque Building, Ringsend Road
Dublin 4, Ireland

First published by HarperCollins*Publishers* 2022
1

A catalogue record for this book is available from the British Library

HB ISBN: 978-0-00-836143-3
TPB ISBN: 978-0-00-836144-0

This novel is entirely a work of fiction.
The names, characters and incidents portrayed in it are
the work of the author's imagination. Any resemblance to
actual persons, living or dead, events or localities is
entirely coincidental.

Set in Minion by Palimpsest Book Production Limited,
Falkirk, Stirlingshire

Printed and Bound in the UK using 100% Renewable Electricity
at CPI Group (UK) Ltd

MIX
Paper | Supporting
responsible forestry
FSC™ C007454

This book is produced from independently certified FSC™ paper
to ensure responsible forest management.

For more information visit: www.harpercollins.co.uk/green

For Iain

'No man chooses evil because it is evil;
he only mistakes it for happiness, the good he seeks.'
                                        Mary Wollstonecraft

            'Whisper her name,
            she is island,
            sheep-littered, stone-wracked
            she cries the wild Atlantic
            to her door;'
            'Na Hearadh' (Harris)
                                        Shirley Wright

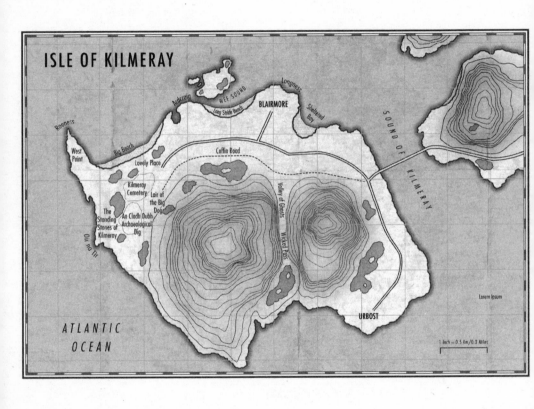

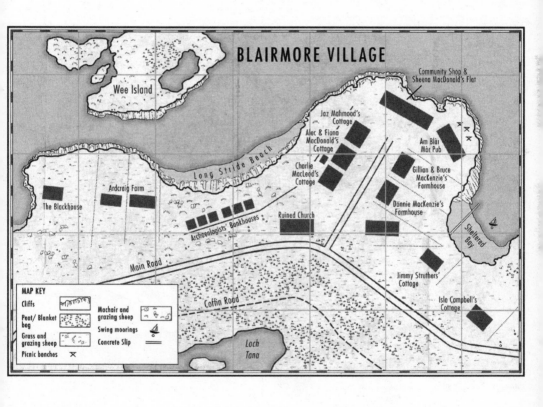

PROLOGUE

It wasn't the screams he remembered most, although they crashed to shore inside the howling, furious wind and ricocheted for hours around the high cliffs above the beach. It wasn't the storm or the roaring, foaming waves that carved great snaking wounds through the wet sand and stole its shape from under his feet.

It wasn't the dark or the flashing torchlight. Or the frantic hours of men pushing boats into the wild surf: motorboats, fishing boats, even old wooden *sgoths*. All to be smashed into the bay's high headlands or hurled back onto the shore like stones from a slingshot.

It wasn't the long, tired wails of the women whose silhouettes stood in a clifftop vanguard ahead of the silver-starred inland sky. Nor those waving white arms out on the rocks, which became slower and less frequent as the screamed chorus grew quieter. And it wasn't the wondering about which of those arms, those bobbing heads that disappeared and sometimes reappeared, belonged to his father.

It wasn't even the eerie silence that came after. The exhaustion of energy and grief and hope. The exhaustion of wind and rain and thunder and sea.

It was the tide bell out on those rocks. Its low, heavy ring growing ever more muffled under the weight of water and all that time.

And it was the black tower casting an invisible shadow over the sand and bay and calming waves.

They were *always* what he remembered the most. Sometimes they were all he could think about.

The tide bell. And the black tower.

And knowing that every man on those rocks would never come back. Because of him.

Because of what he'd wanted. Because of what he'd done.

CHAPTER 1

Thursday, 14th February 2019

Maybe it will be all right. Maybe I've just become too used to it *never* being all right. It's possible. That the angry, fearful dread living inside my stomach for the last three months is less an ill omen than old ballast that's just become too familiar. Maybe.

The pub is busy. Absolutely packed. And loud. Way busier and louder than I'd been expecting; it makes me feel more anxious. More off-balance.

'You've missed the riveting monthly meeting, at least,' Jaz says, with a smile.

Ever since he greeted me at Stornoway Ferry Terminal – *You must be Maggie, I'm Ejaz Mahmood – Jaz – welcome to the Isle of Lewis and Harris!* – tall and slim, with a round face, neat goatee, soft Scottish accent, and a wide grin, he's treated me like a lifelong friend instead of a complete stranger. Throughout the following forty-mile car ride, he kept up an endless scattergun commentary that was at first unnerving and then a welcome distraction. *There's actually a pretty big Pakistani community round here – always surprises folk. Kelly says you're from down south? I'm English too, Berwick, but keep that to yourself – think I've got away with it so far. Word is you don't know how long you'll be staying? Best thing about this place is it's home to anyone just as long as they want it to be.*

We travelled south along a coastal road of occasional hamlets – white houses with twin dormers and slate roofs – and then west across flat empty lowland that made me shiver in the gold dusk, the Range Rover buffeted by whistling winds. On into claustrophobic corridors of flanking rock walls, and then a landscape of green hills and glassy lochans; moorlands of fiery heather and moss framed by high craggy mountains.

And every change from A road to B road to single-track with the occasional passing place and few if any houses, made me feel further and further away from the bustle of Stornoway, never mind London. That was when the weight inside my stomach began to get heavier. Even before we reached the west coast and I heard the roar of the Atlantic. Before we crossed the last loch, and were rattling over the cattle grid and then the causeway across the sound. Before the last fans of sunlight lit up the sign on the other side:

Fàilte gu Eilean Cill Maraigh
Welcome to the Isle of Kilmeray

My teeth started to chatter as Jaz drove us west along the only road. Away from the lights of Urbost on the southeast coast, population sixty-six, and towards the only other village on this island of two and a half by one and a half miles. Older and smaller, and on a windy headland called Longness, population less than twenty. Blairmore. Goosebumps broke out on my skin as we turned into its only street, Jaz finally stopping outside this pub – long and white with black-painted eaves strung with fairy lights. Too many people moving around inside its bright windows. Its white sign grey in the rapidly fading light: AM BLÀR MÒR.

'*Blàr* means "battle" and *mòr* means "big". No one knows much more than that, but that's the islands for you. Mystery is the mother of exaggeration.' His grin was as oblivious to my chattering teeth and the weight in my stomach as my sudden and desperate urge to say, *I know. Because I haven't just been here before, I've been having nightmares about this place my whole life.*

And that was when I stopped trying to distract myself with what little I actually knew about the island – its geography and demography – and started trying to tell myself instead that maybe it'd be all right. Maybe no one would remember me. Maybe I could somehow do what I was here to do without them finding out. I didn't believe it for a second then, either.

The crowded bar lounge is a cosy space with a vast open fire, red walls, dark wood tables, and cushioned stools. I feel both weary and uneasy as I look around, trying to avoid catching anyone's gaze. Jaz nudges my elbow, making me jump. He nods towards a large group of people on the other side of the room. Most of them are young, the tables around them crowded with half-empty glasses and crisp packets.

'Archaeologists from Glasgow Uni,' he says. 'That was me many moons ago. Came over as a student to work on the Cladh Dubh burial site out near West Point. Was only supposed to be there six months, and here I still am.' He laughs, shakes his head. 'They're reopening the dig. So you're not the only newbie.' Another grin. 'Why don't you have a drink while I go get Kelly? She'll be upstairs in her flat.'

I don't want a drink. After three train journeys, a delayed flight from Stansted, an eleven-hour bus ride from Glasgow, and a ferry from Ullapool, I'm so knackered I feel like I could sleep standing up. Drinking, never mind socialising, feels completely beyond me.

'Thanks for picking me up, it was really kind of you.'

'No worries. A taxi would've skinned you alive.'

He gives me one last smile before he heads towards a door marked STAFF ONLY. I turn around reluctantly. The bar itself is relatively empty. Two men in fishing gear – yellow bib and brace trousers over thermal vests and safety boots – sit hunched on stools at its other end.

'Hello. I'm Gillian MacKenzie,' the woman behind the bar says. Her face is tanned and freckled, her smile warm, her accent local, but with the faint traces, perhaps, of something else. She tucks long dark-blonde hair streaked with silver behind her ears before reaching out a hand to shake mine. 'And you must be Maggie.'

'How—'

'Oh, everyone knows about you.' A barman turns from the optics at the other end of the bar. Until I see his easy smile, I take him literally, and my heart briefly gallops. Just like it did when Jaz asked me if I'd ever been to the islands before and I left too long a pause before shaking my head.

The barman sets two whiskies down in front of the fishermen before turning back to me. He's short and lean, his eyes a startling dark brown. 'You're Kelly's first booking. She danced about this place like the Road Runner on speed when she got your email.'

'My husband, Bruce,' Gillian says. 'Ignore him. Anyway, what can I get you? First one's on the house. We're doing strawberry daiquiris and pink G and Ts in honour of Valentine's Day.' She pauses for a moment, and then leans towards me. 'Are you okay?'

No, I abruptly want to say. *My mum just died.* It's like a very specific and sudden form of Tourette's. I lasted less than ten minutes on that Stansted plane before saying it to the poor woman sitting next to me, soaking up her sympathy for the whole journey to Glasgow. Where presumably she imagined my mum had just died. Three months ago isn't *just*, even if it feels like it is. And no matter how much I'd like it to be true, Mum not being here any more isn't the cause for that ballast in my stomach, the nightmares I can't stop having, all those *maybe-it'll-be-all-rights*. It's not the reason why, less than two weeks after being discharged from the Maudsley, I've travelled seven hundred miles to this place – this village – in the middle of nowhere. Even if it's easier to pretend that it is.

'Sorry. I'm just tired,' I say. And try to smile. 'Could I have a white wine, please? Whatever you have. And thank you.'

I pretend to be interested in the photos crowding the red wall next to the bar as Gillian takes a bottle of pinot grigio out of a fridge and starts pouring. Some photos are framed, some laminated; colour, sepia, and black-and-white landscapes of sea and cliff and beach; portraits of men and women and children. Above them is a mounted piece of varnished driftwood carved with black-painted words, *The sheep will spend its life in fear of the wolf, and then be eaten by the shepherd.*

'A cheery sentiment,' Gillian smiles, handing me the wine. 'But it's been here longer than I have; bit like most of those pictures. Lot of the folk in them are here tonight.'

'Maggie!'

I recognize Kelly's gap-toothed smile and sleek brown bob from her online photo. She rounds the bar, throws her arms around my shoulders and squeezes hard.

'I'm *so* glad you're here.' She lets me go just long enough to flash another big grin before hugging me again. 'I was beginning to think I'd imagined you. How was your journey? Awful, I'll bet. It's probably easier to get to the North Pole. Gillian, can I have my usual?'

Kelly climbs onto a stool next to me and turns to face the lounge. 'Ah, I missed the monthly mass moan,' she says. 'What a shame. Complaining is a full-time job to some folk around here.' She hands over a fiver as Gillian sets another large glass of wine down on the bar. 'Thanks.' She looks at me and winks. 'So. Would you like a quick rundown of the great and the good since you're going to be living amongst them for the foreseeable?'

'Sure.'

'Okay.' Kelly leans her elbows back against the bar, crosses her legs, and then points to four men squeezed around a small table. 'Wank, Wank, Good Guy, Wank.'

When I start to laugh, she squeezes my arm. 'Oh, thank God. Someone who finally gets my jokes. Please tell me you're under

8

thirty. That's probably really rude. I mean, you *look* under thirty, obviously. It's just that people around here have a habit of buggering off as soon as they leave school, and they don't come back until they're about ready to draw their pensions. Personally, I'm all for an invasion of archaeology students.'

I laugh again. She's pretty much exactly how I imagined her. 'I'm almost twenty-five,' I say. 'You didn't leave?'

'Mum and Dad moved to North Uist when I was like three, so I never really lived here at all until now. Most folk here tonight are from Urbost for the meeting, and in the summer, there's always tourists. But the population of Blairmore is, like, seventeen. A grand total of seven are under thirty – and three of those are under ten. Including my five-year-old son.'

'You have a son?'

'Fraser.' Her smile returns. 'He's partly why I came here. I left the islands when I was eighteen, met his dad in Glasgow. We had a pretty ugly break-up just over three years ago.' The shadow that crosses her face is so brief I almost miss it. 'A very long, very depressing story that would require more than one glass of vino to tell. But I'm going to go back. To Glasgow, I mean. Just as soon as I've got enough money to rent a flat, restart my training. I want to be a paediatric nurse. Oh my God, that's such a fab necklace. Where did you get it?'

I look down, realise that I've pulled the long silver chain out of my jumper to rub the cool quartz of its pendant between finger and thumb. A nervous tic that I've never managed to shake. I think of Mum's big open smile, the light in her eyes that always scared me. And how much I missed both the minute they were gone; the day she found me in the garden to tell me it was time to take her to the hospital. She'd have told me not to come here. That light in her eyes would have told me too. *I know you can see the darkness. I know you can.*

'You okay?'

No. My mum just died. 'Yes. Sorry.' I look away, back towards the lounge. 'So . . . the great and the good?'

'Right.' She looks over at a couple sitting alone at a nearby table. 'The old guy is Charlie MacLeod.' His grey hair is wild, his stubble patched silver, his skin the colour and texture of someone who has spent a lifetime outdoors. 'He's like a hundred and fifty years old. Has an opinion about everything and everyone.'

The woman next to him is small and smiling. Her silver hair sits over her shoulder in a long heavy plait; her hands are big-knuckled with arthritis.

'That's Isla Campbell. Lives outside the village at Sheltered Bay. She's a cool dude, tough as old boots. Basically, I want to be her when I grow up.' Kelly nudges me. 'Her son, David, lives in Glasgow. Single and hot as fuck. I chickened out last year, but I'm going to make my move when he comes back over for the peat harvesting.'

She points to a younger man playing pool on the table behind, sandy-blond and stocky. 'And that's Donnie MacKenzie. Gillian and Bruce's son.' She snorts. 'Donnie's Gillian with a Y chromosome. Don't think there's any actual MacKenzie in him at all.' She ducks her head as Bruce turns towards our end of the bar. 'Long-running island joke. Not everyone finds it funny, obviously. When they first took the pub over from my parents—'

'Your parents used to own this place?'

'Leased it. I mean, everyone in the village has always helped out here or at the shop – I work at least a couple of shifts a week behind the bar – but there's always been someone in charge, you know, on the paperwork. And it used to be my parents. Dad had this crazy idea of becoming a farmer once, but thankfully that didn't last long.' She rolls her eyes. 'Can you imagine? I'd have had to buy *wellies*.'

She glances along the bar. 'Donnie was just a kid when his parents took over running this place. They own the next-door farm and croft. You'll have seen it when you arrived: two cottages, huge stone barn, outbuildings, acres of land. Another long-running joke is that the MacKenzies own the "right" half of the village. Donnie manages the farm full-time now.' She shrugs. 'He's all right. In the under-thirty club, at least. Divorced. Two part-time kids. You know, if you're in the market for being a farmer's wife.'

She talks so quickly, it's hard to keep up, but I don't mind. Even if that weight in my stomach is unchanged, the anxiety that's been sitting inside my chest since London has begun to unspool.

'If there's going to be some kind of test after this, I'm not going to remember names, never mind anything else.'

Kelly arches a brow. 'Listen, after a couple of days you'll know how many bowel movements they all do in an average week.'

My laugh is loud enough to attract the attention of one of the fishermen on the other side of the bar. Tall and broad-shouldered, with jet-black hair and a Roman nose, he shoots me a strange long look through narrowed eyes.

'Jimmy Struthers,' Kelly says. 'He gives good angry Scotsman, but he's all right. Likes his whisky a bit too much, I guess, but who doesn't? Actually, me. It's fucking gross. He lives next to Isla. Runs a prawn boat out of Sheltered Bay.'

While he goes on looking, I turn round in my stool to face the lounge.

'Last ones, I promise,' Kelly says. 'See the sulky-looking guy in the plaid shirt over by the piano?'

I follow her gaze. Tall and dark-haired, he looks a little older than Jaz, maybe mid-forties, but his expression is that of a teenager: belligerent and persecuted.

'That's Alec MacDonald. He and my dad go way back. Don't ask me why. Look up *crabbit* bastard in the dictionary, you'll get Alec's mugshot. The woman next to him with the big hair is his wife, Fiona. I've come to the conclusion she must be one of those women who gets off on being miserable – can't be any other reason she'd choose to stick it out here with him.' Kelly's tone is almost cruel, but her cheeks are pink, and I remember the shadow that crossed her face when she mentioned Fraser's dad.

'Their daughter, Sheena, lives in the flat above the community shop and post office. She's crabbit *and* miserable. And – uh-oh.'

She turns abruptly back to the bar as a man in his late sixties, bald-headed and dressed in a grey tweed suit that's at least a size too small for him, crosses the lounge towards us.

'Euan Morrison,' she hisses in my ear. 'His family used to own the whole island. Just shake his hand and smile, don't speak. Otherwise we'll be stuck here until *we're* drawing our pensions.'

'You must be Maggie Anderson,' Euan says, smiling broadly with very white dentures.

'Yes.' I glance at Kelly and shut my mouth. Shake his hand.

'Welcome to our wee island,' he says. 'Hope you don't find it too boring after the glitz and glamour of the Big Smoke.'

'I'm sure I won't.'

'Can I buy you two girls a drink?'

'Sure.' Kelly beams. 'We'll have two more—'

'Get me a Ballantruan,' a man says, pushing his way between Euan and my stool to get to the bar. It's Alec, the angry-looking guy in the plaid shirt. 'A double. Now that it looks like we're going to have non-stop noise and hassle for the next Christ-knows-how-long.'

'Ach, don't worry, it'll be fine,' Bruce says, pushing a glass against the whisky's optic lever.

'This place'll do good business anyway,' Alec scowls. He rounds on Euan. 'And you'll clean up renting out all the bunkhouses at Long Stride, I don't bloody doubt. While the rest of us have to put up with bulldozers, diggers, and university twats traipsing about the place day and night.' He pokes a finger hard into Euan's chest. '*You* said you'd do something about it.'

'And I've already told you there's nothing I *can* do about it,' Euan says, as Bruce puts the whisky down on the bar. 'Anyway. We have another visitor here. Maggie Anderson, a journalist from London.'

'I'm just a writer for a mag—'

'And we don't need you bellowing the place down, Alec,' Euan booms, 'Showing us up.'

'A journalist?' Alec ignores Euan and swipes up the whisky, sloshing it over his fingers as he looks me up and down through narrowed eyes. 'And what the hell is it you're here to *journalist* about? The dig?'

'No.' I can feel my face heating up. 'Just a story about something that happened a long time ago.'

'Oh, really?' Euan says. 'Sounds very intriguing. And what—'

Alec lurches towards me, shoving Euan aside again. His eyes are wet-bright and heavy-lidded. There are sweat rings around his armpits. He's quite a bit drunker than I thought. 'Wait a minute. Wait a wee fuckin' minute.'

I can feel Kelly bristling beside me, but for the moment, I'm frozen motionless, staring at Alec staring at me.

'Jesus Christ. Ah, *Jesus Christ.* I'd recognise those eyes anywhere.' His laugh is like a bark. 'It's *you.*'

It's just my left eye. Permanently dilated after a car accident when I was four, and perhaps not noticeable at all if my eyes were browner, darker. Fitting, I suppose, that's what finally obliterates all those *maybe-it'll-be-all-right*s. Because I know exactly what's about to happen. What he's about to say. That ballast in my belly knows too. I'm almost relieved.

'Alec,' his wife says, tugging on his arm. Up close, Fiona MacDonald's face, tight with anxiety, is liberally covered in tiny freckles. She shoots me a nervous glance, and then another. I can't tell if she knows who I am or not.

'Don't mither me, woman.' He shakes her off, downs his whisky, thrusts the glass back at Bruce. 'Another.' And when he looks back at me again, the disgust is still there, the hostility, the recognition, but there's something else too. Something that makes me feel worse. I think it's fear. He turns round to the rest of the pub, throwing his arms wide. People are already looking over. 'You don't recognise her? None of you? You don't recognise little *Maggie?*'

'What the hell are you talking about, man?' Euan asks, now more confused than angry, one hand held up between us like a boxing referee.

Alec's smile is icy cold. 'Andrew MacNeil.' He lunges close enough that I can smell the sour whisky on his breath. 'You're Andrew fucking MacNeil. I'm right, right? *Right?*'

I can hear mutters and exclamations from the lounge behind us. Loud and getting louder. Absolutely everyone is now looking at me.

'D'you want to get out of here?' Kelly mutters in my ear, just as I realise I'm squeezing her hand, digging my nails deep into her skin.

When I manage to nod, she jumps off her stool, drags me off mine, and marches us both towards the door. The squeal of its hinges makes me flinch, and Alec's still furious shouts chase me outside, where the deserted darkness is as welcome as the headland winds blowing wild against my face and my too-hot skin. I should never have come here. And now it's too late to go back.

CHAPTER 2

'So, left takes you back to Urbost and the causeway, via Sheltered Bay – *Bàgh Fasgach*. Ben Donn's maybe five hundred yards that way, over a thousand feet high, a good day's hiking, if that's your thing. But that beast up ahead is Ben Wyvis. *Beinn Uais*. "Terror Mountain". *Not* such a fun hike.'

Kelly barely stops talking to draw breath as we fast-march past the old red phone box at the junction out of Blairmore. The evening air is bitterly cold. I can hear distant waves. I can smell the sea and the distinctive heavy sweetness of peat fires.

'*Gleann nam Bòcan*. The Valley of Ghosts.' She shines her phone light over the road and into a shadow between the mountains so dark it's just black – flat and impenetrable. Her snort puffs white ahead of us like fog. 'Wouldn't recommend a hike there either.'

I nod in the darkness, watch her bright light bouncing off the tarmac as we turn right onto the main road west. I think of Alec's

Jesus Christ. It's *you*. All those looks of shock and anger. It was worse than I expected. No. It was *exactly* what I expected.

'There's a torch in the house,' Kelly says. 'And if you have to give way to a car, make sure you get onto the grass over this side, especially at night. The other side is nothing but bog. Oh, and the old Coffin Road, where folk used to carry their dead to the cemetery in the west.' She flashes her torchlight over an old stone building, and I realise that it's a ruined church, its roof collapsed and windows boarded up with wood.

'Those lights out towards the beach are the bunkhouses where the archaeologists are staying. They're absolutely teeny; just looking at them makes me feel claustrophobic.'

There are no lights anywhere inland, I realise. The whole island must live on this narrow coastal strip between mountain and cliff. And up ahead, beyond the small line of bunkhouses, there's nothing but more darkness. No people, no distant squares of gold. I shiver, pulling the lapels of my coat tighter against my throat. *You're Andrew fucking MacNeil. Right?*

'Welcome to the Outer Hebrides in February.' Kelly laughs, briefly blinding me with her torchlight before turning it back onto the road. 'Hope you packed some thermals. Oh, hey, and before I forget, there's a ceilidh in the pub tomorrow night. I know, bit tragic, but they're usually pretty fun. You should definitely come. We can get ready together in my flat and preload on vodka Red Bulls like we're eighteen again.'

'Sounds good,' I lie. Because I have to go. Despite what just happened, I can't forget why I'm here.

Eventually, a long stone barn looms out of the blackness

alongside the road, and next to it a smaller two-storey cottage, stone-built and blazing with light.

'Will Morrison's farm,' Kelly says, her torch swerving wildly again as she thumps her palm against her breastbone. 'Sexy Will Morrison's farm. I mean, it's slim pickings obviously, but still. *Very* Sexy Will Morrison's farm.'

She guides me off the road and up onto the grass alongside it. The wind picks up, and I can smell the sea again, see the faint shadow of another building up ahead. 'This is Ardcraig. Means "high cliff", but it's actually pretty sheltered for a headland this far west. Most of it's grazing land, but Will tends to take the sheep in on cold nights. And . . .' She turns onto a narrow paved path. 'Here we are! I can't wait for you to see it in daylight. I mean, I know there were photos on the website, but they don't really do it justice. Jaz took them, and he's no David Bailey. When Mum and Dad moved to North Uist they sold the land back to Euan and then pretty much left this place to rot. Folk do that a lot around here, but it's madness – these days, holiday homes are like gold dust.' Her light stutters over a large wooden door with a small inset window. 'They weren't keen on me coming here at first, but when I offered to do the work and Airbnb it, they eventually caved.'

She turns the handle, pushes the door open with a creak. 'There are keys on the kitchen counter, although the lock's a bit iffy, I keep meaning to get it fixed. But don't worry, no one locks their doors around here anyway.' She steps over the threshold. 'Welcome to An Taigh-dubh.'

Inside is a small mudroom and three closed doors.

'Bathroom, box room, and . . .' She pushes opens the left-hand door, flooding the big room beyond with light. 'Everything else.'

On one side of the room is a living-dining-kitchenette panelled entirely in pine, even the ceiling. On each wall are tiny quarter-barred windows with tartan curtains. Facing an open, tiled fireplace and long mantelpiece made of driftwood sits a large brown leather sofa covered with Harris tweed cushions. A double bed dominates the opposite wall, alongside a pine wardrobe and chest of drawers.

I set down my suitcase. 'Kelly, it's amazing.'

Her cheeks, already pink from the cold, flush pinker. 'It's a replica of a traditional blackhouse. That's what *An Taigh-dubh* means. The Blackhouse. Before I forget, the Wi-Fi password's on the router. Four-G hasn't quite reached this far west yet, and the HebNet's data allowance is abysmal, so no downloading porn, or you won't be able to check your email for a month. There's no mobile signal out here, no landline either, but there's the phone box in Blairmore and a payphone in the pub.' She nods towards the fireplace. 'No peat, just coal and logs. And there's no mains gas supply. Although the walls are like over two feet thick, so it doesn't get too cold. The bathroom has underfloor heating. And you've no idea how much *that* bloody cost. I ran out of cash after about two months. Have debts coming out of my eyeballs.'

'What's down there?' I say, pointing to a large trapdoor in the floor towards the corner of the room.

'It's an earth cellar. Kind of an extended root cellar, I guess.' Kelly makes a face. 'I've been down there like once, gave me the proper creeps.' She goes over to the kitchenette, opens the fridge. 'There're two bins round the side of the house: general waste and recycling. Just wheel them down to the road every Thursday night, and keep your fingers crossed someone turns up to empty them. I've left you coffee, milk, butter, eggs, bread, some lamb chops that were going cheap at the shop. I can only eat them this time of year, when they aren't bouncing about outside the window begging me to give them names. Oh, and to warn you, everything comes to a standstill on a Sunday, I'm afraid. Nothing will be open, no public transport. Most folk'll either be going to the church at Urbost or one of the others on Lewis and Harris. D'you go to church? I mean, it's not a rule or anything, but there's plenty of choice: Church of Scotland, Wee Free, Catholic—'

'I don't go to church.' I think of Mum's funeral. A twenty-minute slot in Hither Green Crematorium.

'Me either; we can be heathens together. Oh, and I got you this as a Welcome-to-the-Blackhouse.' She pulls a bottle of fizz from the fridge and sets it down on the counter, waves away my thanks as she opens a cupboard and takes out a bottle of whisky instead. 'But, I got this for emergencies.' She finally pauses, finally draws breath. 'And I'm completely knackered pretending nothing nuts just happened back there.'

'I thought you said whisky was gross,' I say, playing for time.

She pours it into two glasses, hands one to me. 'It is.'

I take a sip, even though I can't stand whisky, particularly not the island kind, malted over peat fires. 'Don't you need to get back for Fraser?'

'Jaz is looking after him.' She grins. 'Listen, this is the most interesting night I've had in weeks. Minute I go back to the pub I'll find out – or more likely be told – what's what. So quit stalling. Spill.'

I don't say anything, and it's a mistake. I did that too often in the Maudsley; it gives weight to silence, to the thing you're trying not to talk about.

Kelly drops her smile. 'God. I'm sorry. I do this. Mum says I'm nosier than a tabloid journalist. It's the Hebridean in me – no question too personal; no secret a secret for long. But you don't have to tell me anything. I mean, it's just because you don't look . . . you know . . .' Her cheeks get pinker. 'Like you were . . . once an Andrew. Shit. That's not—'

'God, no, it's – I'm not – okay.' I sit down at the dining table, press cool palms against my face. 'Okay.'

Kelly sits too.

I drain the whisky. I probably shouldn't be drinking at all, but Dr Abebe isn't here to see me, and so I decide it doesn't count. 'I'm originally from Croy. It's a village northeast of Inverness. And when I was five years old, I came here. To this island. Mum . . .' My voice manages not to break on the word. Progress. 'She brought me.'

'Why? D'you have family here?'

I have a sudden and very unwelcome flashback to us running along the beach at Shoeburyness, screaming with laughter as we battled to hold on to the flying lines of a diamond rainbow kite that swooped and rose under wild gusts of wind. I remember secretly worrying that it would snatch me up and carry me away.

'No.' I watch as Kelly refills our glasses; force myself to wait a couple of breaths before I pick mine up again. 'I said that I was a man called Andrew MacNeil.'

Kelly's brow furrows.

Shadows and rock and grass, the howl of the wind. A nightmare so familiar, so unforgotten, it's just another memory.

'I *believed* that I had once been a man called Andrew MacNeil. And . . .' I watch Kelly's eyes grow wider. 'That one day . . . I died – drowned – and when I woke up, I was Maggie.'

'No. Way.'

I make myself put the whisky down. 'And apparently, I was so insistent about being Andrew and not Maggie that I told anyone and everyone. At some point, a documentary filmmaker got involved. Offered to foot the entire bill if he could come with us – I doubt Mum could have afforded it, and Dad had already remarried and pretty much forgot he had a daughter – so . . . I don't know.' I shrug. 'That's what we did.' I'm leaving out a lot, but this feels like enough for now. More than enough.

'But why here? Why did you come *here*?'

'I don't remember this, but Mum said around the same time I also kept telling her "Kill Merry" over and over again, like she should have known what I was talking about.'

Kelly's mouth drops open, and I can feel the heat climbing up my neck. 'I know. Pretty creepy kid, right? And then she found me freaking out over some Scottish travel show about the Isle of Lewis and Harris on TV. She looked at a map, and there was Kilmeray.'

'Wow.' Kelly closes her mouth. 'So you came here – and then what?'

'I don't remember much of being here either.' I pause. Shadows and rock and grass. And sobbing the way only a child can – too hot and wild to breathe. 'Brief flashes mostly. But Mum said it was a circus. She regretted bringing me. She regretted bringing the film crew. I was traipsed around the whole island to see if I could find my house, or where I was supposed to have died. The director even had his researchers knocking on doors, stopping people in the street.'

I think of Alec's glacial smile. *You don't recognise her? None of you? You don't recognise little* Maggie? All those mutters and exclamations from the bar lounge.

'Wow.'

'He was desperate by then, I reckon. Because they hadn't found any record of an Andrew on Kilmeray, never mind an Andrew MacNeil. I think he'd gambled on the fact that island parish records are notoriously unreliable, and just the spectacle of it, you know? Of me. Apparently I was scarily convincing.'

'*Did* anyone find anything?'

'No, at least, I don't think so. Mum said the locals didn't exactly make us feel welcome, and we ended up leaving within days. Afterwards, I had nightmares about the whole thing. Mum said I cried for weeks. She never forgave herself for taking me.' I shrug. Mum not being able to forgive herself pretty much defined my childhood. 'About six months later, she said I stopped saying that I was Andrew MacNeil. And within a couple of years, it was like it had never happened.' Apart from the nightmares.

'Huh.' Kelly looks at me, swills the remains of whisky in her glass. 'So why are you here now? In your emails you said you worked for a women's magazine and were writing a story. Is that what it's about?'

I nod, take a surreptitious breath. Get ready to tell my carefully prepared lie, even if I can't quite look Kelly in the eye while I'm doing it. 'The magazine got a new editor-in-chief a couple of months ago, and he basically said, if the most interesting thing about you is interesting enough, I'll let you keep your job.'

'Bell-end.'

My smile feels fake. 'And I think this is the most interesting thing about me.' That much is true at least.

'Well . . .' Kelly blinks. 'Why didn't anyone here recognise your name? I mean, I've been talking about your booking for *weeks*.'

'I was Maggie MacKay back then. Mum got married again when I was ten. Anderson is my stepdad's name. We moved to England before I went to high school.' I don't mention that the marriage lasted less than one school year. 'I've lived in London more than half my life. I have an English accent. I'm betting you told everyone that I was English.'

'Yeah, okay. But, I mean, *why* was everyone so pissed off? And why the hell are they *still* so pissed off?'

I reach for my glass, look at that instead of Kelly. 'Because, when I came here, I didn't just say that I'd died. That I'd drowned.' I drink until the whisky's gone. 'I said that I'd been murdered.' I look out at the night through one of the small windows. 'By one of them.'

'*Wow.*' And in the following silence, I realise that Kelly has finally run out of things to say.

*

After Kelly leaves, I make myself eat a few slices of toast, drink some water. I take the pill bottle out of my rucksack, and my fingers only hesitate for a few seconds before they twist open its lid. Also progress. I swallow the pill with the last of the water, sit on the sofa. There's no signal on my phone, not even one bar, and it's something of a relief. I can't phone Ravi even if I want to. I look down at my ring finger, absently rub at the nearly faded white line. I know what he'd think – what he'd say – about all this anyway. I might not have seen or spoken to him in months, but I still know. I can always hear him as if he's sitting right next to me.

What are you doing, Maggie? What if something happens?

I think of the sharp angles of his cheekbones; how I'd loved to look at him. Even the frown lines on his forehead and around his eyes that I had put there.

'There's a GP in Stornoway who's agreed to see me, do all the tests,' I say, staring up at the ceiling. 'I'm not on the moon. I'm not on my own.'

Because I *am* scared something might happen without him. I'm always scared. But after what happened in the hospital with Mum, and after what happened inside Hither Green Crematorium after Mum, I feel different. The flying lines of that diamond rainbow kite did snatch me up and carry me away, and it was more frightening than I'd ever imagined it would be. And I can't let that fear stay. I can't live with it any more. It's why I'm here. Because, of all the things Mum hated – and she'd hated a very long list of things – she'd hated cowards the most. And Ravi had always made it easy for me to be a coward.

I pull on the long chain around my neck, rub the warmed pink quartz pendant. Think of Mum kneeling by my bed. *Pick a hand.*

And me picking the right one because I never guessed wrong.

The box had been pink. The bow, white. The chain inside so long, its silver links caught the light as I pulled and pulled it out. Found the quartz pendant at its end.

You've been carrying that thing about for months. It's a miracle you haven't lost it already.

You said it was just an ugly stone.

The light in her eyes as she shrugged, cupped my face in her hands. *It's your ugly stone.*

And then suddenly the memory fades. Mum is lying in another bed. Her smile is gone. The light is gone. The room is in darkness, except for a thread of silver stretching thin across the floor between us. I can hear scratching taps and a low whistling breath, too close. A man's face looms suddenly out of all that darkness, his smile lopsided, lips hidden under a Dick Strawbridge moustache. He touches me with cool fleshy palms, and I flinch as Mum rears up from the bed to throw her bony arms around my neck. I can feel her heartbeat fluttering against the thunder of my own. The wide dark of her open mouth, the black beads of her eyes.

Trust nobody. They all lie. You know it's true. You **know***. Please, Maggie. Please.* And then that awful serene smile I always hated more – so much more – than her pain.

There are people behind me. Breathing, waiting. Watching. Expectant horror muttered in low rising whispers that prickle my skin, make its hairs stand on end.

And then I'm outside, in yet another place, another time. The silver Lexus comes out of nowhere, ripping Mum's hands out of mine, yanking me up into the air. A silver-black grille. A windscreen and a face, its mouth a perfect round O. A cliff face of rock and grass, the wind roaring like the sea. And then I'm dropped like a stone, like a diamond kite without any wind.

And I see it. Squatting on the glass-littered road next to Mum's bed. Next to Mum's coffin. Bald and grinning with big, crowded teeth. Claws tap-tapping at the ground, scratching black wounds into the tarmac.

*Maggie, make it go **away**!*

I jolt awake, nearly fall off the sofa. When I open my fist, the pendant has left indents in my skin, and I push it back inside the collar of my jumper, take long, deep breaths. Massage my aching head. *I'm okay.* I should meditate. Or do one of Dr Abebe's breathing exercises. Instead, I get up and retrieve the whisky from the dining table. Swig straight from the bottle as I wait for my heartbeat to settle again. I look across at the clock on the mantelpiece: the cartoon face of a ginger Highland cow. Five minutes past midnight. *Happy birthday to me.*

I hear a sound outside. Far too loud in the otherwise quiet. It's an almost welcome distraction until I'm standing next to the front door and peering out of its small square window. I can see nothing except the silhouette of my head framed by the windswept frizz of my hair. I jump when the door rattles against a sudden gust of wind, and this annoys me enough that I find the courage to open it.

Even though I know there are no streetlights, the blackness of outside is so opaque that it's a shock all the same. There's no moon, no stars. I imagine the stone path and the grazing grass immediately ahead. The single-track road and the blanket bog beyond. The vast loom of Terror Mountain; the darker shadow of the Valley of Ghosts. Perhaps it's the childish, *who's-afraid-of-the-Bogeyman* nature of the names – or more likely that I *am* afraid – that makes me step out of the blackhouse without going back for either my phone or Kelly's torch.

The wind howls around me as I stand on the path. I turn towards the welcome lights of the farm on the other side of the headland, and something shifts suddenly under my foot, making me lose my balance. I stagger backwards against the open door, grab hold of its frame. I stare down at the ground as I catch my breath, but the light from the mudroom isn't strong enough to see anything but shadows.

I go back for the torch because I can't just shut the door and leave whatever is out there on the path. I can never leave anything alone. I always know it's still there.

The torch is bright. It exposes what I stood on, in alarmingly stark relief against the stone path.

'Jesus.'

It's two dead birds. Big dead birds. Crows. I creep closer and hunker down. They don't look like the kind of dead bird you see lying by the side of the road. Their wings are stretched out, heads turned to one side, feet curled into claws. Their tailfeathers are black, but dirty grey everywhere else. Except for the naked shafts of their wings, fanned out like tiny ribs. Their beaks are curved and sharp, their eye sockets deep and oval and empty. I don't see how they could have been here when Kelly and I first arrived at the blackhouse, or even when she left more than an hour later, because beak to tail, they take up almost the whole width of the path.

Do you ever get a bad feeling, Maggie?

I set the torch down, go back into the kitchenette, fish out a bin bag from under the sink, and put on some rubber gloves. I try not to look at the birds again as I pick them up, but I can feel the brittle sharpness of their wings, the cool softness of their bellies as I shove them into the bag. It has to have been an animal. A dog, maybe. Or more likely a cat. A big one. In London, I once saw my neighbour's Bengal take down a pigeon.

I stand up, look around at the howling darkness, those little square lights in the east, before backing up the path to the doorway.

I stand inside the mudroom and drop the bag onto the floor. I think of waking up from that nightmare of shadows and rock and grass, the roar of the wind. Mum pushing the damp hair away from my forehead, my tear-streaked cheeks. *People like us, Maggie, we have to listen to our bad feelings. And I'm so sorry that I didn't.*

And then another, older memory – *the* memory: sharp, always so sharp, against a background vague and white and forgotten. The squeeze of my fists; the hoarseness of my throat; the hotness of my tears; the hard throb of my feet as if I'd been standing still a long, long time.

I'm Andrew MacNeil. I'm Andrew MacNeil. I'm Andrew MacNeil!

Mum kneeling in front of me, holding my hands, looking up at me with that same light in her eyes, that serene smile. *Yes, you are.*

And being afraid for the first time – though by no means the last – of that light, that smile. Frightened enough that it sent tremors all the way through me and into her.

I shine my torchlight over the empty path where those birds had been, lying side by side with their wings fanned out and sleek heads touching. Like an arrow pointing straight at the blackhouse.

I'm so sorry that I took you there, baby. I'm so, so sorry.

I switch off the torch. 'I'm not here for you, Mum,' I say into the darkness. But I want to shout it. 'I'm here for me.'

I blink at the night. The smell of the sea on the wind.

I'm here to prove that twenty-five years ago on this island, a man called Andrew MacNeil was murdered.

I pick up the bag. Shut the door. And lock it.

CHAPTER 3

I wake up to sunlight streaming through a gap in the curtains. It's eleven forty-five and freezing cold. I get out of bed, put on thermals under jeans and a hoodie, and open the curtains before shuffling into the kitchenette to make myself a very strong coffee. The sunlight has transformed the large room, turned its varnished pine walls golden-bright.

I feel better after the coffee. Put on my yellow mac and boots. While it's tempting just to hide in here forever, I know I can't. I open the cupboard under the sink, look down at that black bag. The sudden certainty that it's empty is a familiar yet frightening one – far more frightening than finding strange dead birds on your path that weren't there less than an hour before. *Do not allow panic or anxiety to get a foothold*, I think in Dr Abebe's voice. *The first step to trusting yourself is never being afraid to.* And it's this that lets me pick up the bag and open it. I only look long enough to see those brown wing ribs and black underbellies. My relief feels too big, too unwieldy. It reminds me that whatever trust I've had in myself – and I've never had much – is gone.

I hold the bag stiffly by my side as I open the front door. The path is empty. I don't lock the door behind me, if only because I want to. The wheelie bins are beside the house; I open the lid of one and throw the bag in with an involuntary shudder. Two black-faced sheep in grimy, shaggy grey coats watch me from the grass.

I can hear faraway shouts out past the road in the west. The distant drone and creak of machinery. Maybe the archaeologists' diggers. The sheep turn tail and run round to the back of the blackhouse as it starts to rain. I pull up my hood and follow them. I'm not ready for real company just yet.

The wind hits me like a hammer. I can hear the sea; the blackhouse is much closer to it than I realised – there's no more than maybe forty yards between the house and the edge of the headland. I start walking before I've any idea to where, and slow only once I reach the end of the narrow track, and the way grows steeper. The wind and a huddle of cross-looking sheep do an admirable job of keeping me well back from the cliff edge, but the view is staggering all the same. In all directions, the Atlantic Ocean reaches away to the horizon, grey and vast and flat, save for a tiny island in the northeast. I can see nothing at all of the main islands; it's as if Kilmeray is entirely alone in the world. The ground beyond the track is grassy and muddy, swiftly growing muddier, and as I pass the farm, the only signs of life are yet more sheep sheltering next to its barn. I should probably introduce myself to Kelly's *Very Sexy Will*, but, after a moment's hesitation, I keep on walking.

A fog rolls in from the sea as the rain gets heavier, settling in smoky wreaths that soon obscure my view completely. When the track turns, I follow it gingerly until two solid shapes rise suddenly out of the gloom. I swallow, a little shocked by how easily I've become disorientated. The smell of the sea is far stronger; the wind has changed shape and sound, its howl echoing loud and urgent somewhere below me, and I wonder just how close I am to the edge.

The shapes get taller as I creep closer, and when I finally reach them, I see that they're slabs of stone, evenly spaced and rectangular like gravestones. Behind them is the sharp edge of the cliff, and then beyond, a distant cluster of lights that must be Blairmore. Between both headlands is only that howling, urgent wind and murky space – the impression of a drop so sheer that I've no intention of venturing any closer.

I push my wet hair away from my face and hunker down in front of the first stone, weatherworn around its edges, but engraved with intricate swirls and scrolls and inscribed with the words FOR LORNE. And underneath: 9TH APRIL 1994. Its neighbour is taller, sterner, made of hard granite instead of soft sandstone. THE FISHERMAN is chiselled deep and stark across its centre.

I glance back at the sea – where the sea used to be before the fog arrived – and all at once, I see myself standing on a cliff edge – a black dress with white spots and striped tights, above too-big khaki-green wellies. My little hand stretched towards the disappeared sea, finger pointing. *Out there!* My heart stutters, mostly in relief. That memory had first come back to me in the Maudsley's Psychiatric ICU when they started reducing the drugs. Then, it had been a tether, a beacon in the dark. But here, it's real. A real memory of this place. Perhaps not this cliff. But definitely this place. I let out an undignified screech when something suddenly barrels out of the fog to race around me in excited yips.

'Don't mind Bonny. She's too old to keep that up for long.'

Bonny is a black-and-white collie. And sure enough, before her companion even moves into view she settles onto her haunches, head cocked at an angle as she regards me half-kneeling in the mud, my fist still pressed against my chest.

'D'you need a hand?'

I shake my head as I struggle to get up, boots sliding in the mud. The teeth in his smile are crooked, his grey sideburns as thick as the hair that pokes out from under a wide-brimmed tweed cap, his face ruddy and heavily lined. I recognise him from the pub – Kelly's *He's like a hundred and fifty years old. Has an opinion about everything and everyone.* Close to, I realise he's probably only in his late sixties.

'Charlie MacLeod,' he says, holding out a hand that, when I shake it, is unfathomably warm. Like Kelly's, his accent is soft and lilting, sounding more Irish than mainland Scottish.

'Maggie Anderson.'

'Aye.' He nods.

The following silence stretches into awkward territory, and I pull the drawstring on my hood tighter. 'I was just looking at these stones.'

'Aye.' He lets that one sit for an uncomfortable while too, and then he runs a thick-clubbed finger under his nose. 'We've a monument to just about everything round these parts.'

'Who are they for?' Because I can feel another awkward silence looming.

Charlie nods at *The Fisherman*. 'Most of us were fishermen round this coast all our lives. I crewed on my father's boat and then part-owned one of my own, till fishery licences and quotas pushed us out and let the big corporations in. Used to be so much herring, mackerel, salmon, cod, haddock, and hake around these islands you never imagined anyone would've been able to fish them all.' He shakes his head and rainwater runs off the end of his cap. 'Sea out there's taken a great many island men over the years. Rarely gives them back. That stone's to say we remember them.'

He looks out at the curtains of fog. Runs his finger back and forth against the base of his nose for so long I wonder if we're done talking to each other. 'Little one's for wee Lorne. Drowned out there at eight years old.'

'God.' I look down at those weatherworn swirls and scrolls. 'That's awful.'

'Aye, well.' Charlie clears his throat. 'Sometimes, awful's part of living.'

Bonny lets out a low whine, and Charlie bends over, scratches her ears. 'You been down to Tràigh Shearrag yet, Maggie?'

'Where?'

He straightens, points down to that invisible space where the wind still howls and whistles between this headland and Longness. 'Long Stride Beach. I'll take you down, if you like?'

I battle to keep my hood up as the wind changes direction again, shoves me sideways. 'I don't think—'

'Ach, away,' Charlie says, with a bark of laughter. 'No one tell you, if you don't like the weather in the Outer Hebrides, give it a minute?' He turns and heads back into the fog. 'Time and tide wait for no man. And that dog's never come across a stone, memorial or no, that she hasn't fancied pissing against, given half a chance. Bonny, come.'

*

Charlie's right. By the time we round Ardcraig and clamber down the path to the grass bluffs beyond, the rain has stopped and the fog has lifted. Even the wind is calmer. Charlie's surprisingly sprightly; he and Bonny climb up onto the bluff's summit and wait for me to catch up. He reaches down and hauls me up beside him with ease.

The beach below us is deserted. An unexpected paradise of white sand and turquoise sea beneath a vast blue bowl of sky and low-rolling puffs of cloud. There's no evidence at all of the rainstorm we just battled our way through. The sun comes out as we clamber down through grass and then dunes so deep, I sink almost to my knees in places.

Bonny races away with joyful abandon, leaving tracks in the otherwise untouched sand.

''Course, it's a bit busier in the summer,' Charlie says, without a trace of irony. 'You could probably go swimming in a few weeks, if you're so inclined. Gulf Stream keeps the Atlantic pretty warm close to this coast, even in winter.' He nods towards the small island I saw from the headland. 'Eilean Beag breaks up most of the currents and rip tides.'

'It's beautiful here.'

'Aye.' Charlie sits down on the sand and looks across to where Bonny is running towards a white-frothing wave, before taking fright and racing back to dry land. 'Daft dug.'

He reaches inside his anorak, brings out a steel hip flask, and takes a long swallow. When I sit down beside him, he hesitates before passing the flask to me. Despite his interest, there's a coldness to him, a detachment that's not unfriendly, but there all the same. As if he and I were different species and the gulf between us too great to even attempt to bridge.

'Navy rum. Always been a fisherman first and a Scotsman second.'

It tastes marginally better than Kelly's whisky. If nothing else, perhaps it will dilute the hangover I woke up with.

'*Eilean Beag*,' I say, looking at the little island. 'What does it mean?'

Charlie takes back the hip flask, screws it shut. '*Eilean* is "island". *Beag* is "wee".'

'And the Gaelic name for Kilmeray – *Cill Mer*—'

'*Cill Maraigh.*'

'What does that mean?' I'm acutely aware – and doubtless so is Charlie – that I'm making a painfully clumsy job out of trying to ingratiate myself with at least one of the locals. But, for me, perseverance is often starting down a path and realising that it's only going to be more painful to have to turn back.

'Church of Saint Maraigh.' He nods towards a long, narrow headland far distant in the west and still shrouded in dark clouds. 'There's ruins of a thirteenth-century medieval church up on Roeness. 'Course it's also derived from Old Norse. Most place-names around here are. Nearly every MacLeod, MacNeil, MacDonald, MacKenzie, or Morrison born on these islands has Scandinavian blood.'

I start a little at the mention of MacNeil, but I make myself pause, try not to sound too suddenly eager. 'So you've always lived here, then? On Kilmeray?'

'Aye.' He gives me a very narrow-eyed look before turning away.

I smile, frustrated that he didn't take the bait, and unsure how to steer the conversation in the direction I need it to go.

'So,' Charlie says, watching Bonny, now sitting on the sand, tongue lolling as she looks longingly out at the waves. 'This story you're here to write. Why are you writing it?'

And even though this is exactly what I wanted, I suddenly feel nervous. Because I'm a bad liar. I speak before I think. And somehow, I hadn't realised that this would be so hard. Not just telling the lies, but remembering them, *believing* them.

'My boss likes *personal* accounts,' I say. 'Like that American novelist who realised his gran had been poisoning his family her whole life, or the neuroscientist who studied the brain scans of psychopaths and discovered that he was one too.'

I don't have a job any more. I quit the magazine the day I left the Maudsley and booked my flight to Glasgow. I'd lost my mum. My fiancé. Myself. Losing my job barely registered at all. My cover story isn't just a cover story, it's a means to an end. A way to speak to people who were here. To have them speak to me. To find out the truth. About Andrew MacNeil. About me. And I'm still a writer; maybe that's the only part of me I've managed to hold on to.

I risk a sidelong look at Charlie. 'But I think he's going to be pretty disappointed. I don't know that I'm going to be writing anything at all.'

'Why's that?'

'There's nothing to find out, is there? I did a lot of research before I came here, and all of it matched what the film director found in '99 – or didn't. Andrew MacNeil's a pretty common name in the Hebrides. But no Andrew MacNeil has ever been registered on Kilmeray: birth, marriage, death. No Andrew MacNeil has ever registered a croft, peat poll, or fishing boat here either.'

Charlie doesn't reply. Lifts up a fistful of white sand and runs it through his fingers.

'And even if all I can do is write my story, of coming here as a child, it's not as if anyone's going to help me fill in the blanks, is it?' I glance at him again. 'I mean, you were in the pub last night.'

'Well.' Charlie huffs out briefly visible breath. 'People talk, is all. And, in the general scheme of things, not a great deal *new* ever happens here.'

'I'm not going to write anything awful, Charlie. If that's what you think – if that's what everyone thinks – I'm really not. I just need someone to talk to me.'

He stretches out his legs with a wince. 'You know, this place is only beautiful because it's seen centuries of hardship. It's only empty and wild because rich men who owned people as much as the land realised they'd get even richer if they replaced tenants with sheep. And because bloated mainland fisheries emptied that sea of everything but shellfish, forcing men who'd fished here for generations to leave too. Christ, even tourists only think they want splendid isolation, and then, more often than not, complain when they get it. I give those new archaeologists a day before they start whingeing about the lack of Wi-Fi in the bunkhouses and the island price of red diesel.' He slides me another almost-smile. 'Folk come here to take, Maggie. Rarely to give. Always have.'

'I'm not here to take,' I say. Which I manage to sound remarkably sincere about, considering it's the worst lie I've told so far.

Charlie fixes me with a look, a *long* look. And then he sighs and gives a very solemn nod. 'Wee Lorne was Alec and Fiona MacDonald's son.'

'God.' I think of Fiona's pale, freckled face. Alec's narrow and furious eyes.

'Alec's an arse. He's always been an arse – he's a rigger; spends more than half his life offshore on the BP oil fields west of Shetland – but after Lorne died, he became an arse with an excuse. It's not you he has a problem with. It's pretty much everyone.'

'So people *might* talk to me?'

The surf has picked up. Charlie looks out at the horizon just as a big green wave breaks against the shoreline.

'You ever see a *spectre ship*?'

'What?'

'They're famous round this coast. People see them all the time. Lost fishing trawlers, lobster boats, yachts. Old steamships bound for Canada.'

I look out at the flat horizon, as if I expect one to spontaneously glide into view.

Charlie pauses, looks down at the palms of his calloused hands. 'Whole of my thirties, every time I walked west at either dusk or dawn, I used to think I could see a funeral procession walking the Coffin Road alongside me, carrying a black coffin. Always at the corner of my eye; if I looked they were gone. Sometimes I thought I could hear them, like the sound of the wind around the cairn at the top of Ben Wyvis. Got me believing it so much, I stopped going west at all. Thought it meant one day I'd not be making it back to the slipway at Sheltered Bay; one day I'd just be another dead fisherman, another name on a stone with no body under it.' He pauses, clears his throat. 'Because somehow, I always knew that black coffin was empty.'

I shiver a little and think of that noise outside the blackhouse last night. How strange those dead birds had looked. Had *felt*.

'D'you know what a *thin place* is?' Charlie asks.

'No.'

'It's Norse and Celtic. Pagan, and then later Christian. A *thin place* is where they say the distance between this world and other worlds is shortest, the walls thinnest.' He pauses. Scratches the white scruff of stubble on his chin. 'Someone told me a long time ago that a thin place is where *inside the fence* meets *beyond the fence*. Where order meets chaos. Some folk think thin places are where you can know things, do things, see things that you couldn't anywhere else.'

'Ghosts?'

'*Bòcain.*' He shrugs. 'Aye.'

And I'm thinking less about his Coffin Road procession than the bony grip of Mum's fingers, her always furiously certain *I know you can see the darkness.*

'Kilmeray is a thin place?'

'Supposed to be.'

Which, I notice, in spite of his *spectre ship* and Coffin Road stories, isn't really a yes.

We both look at the sand, the sea, the sky; listen to the silence beyond the wind and the waves.

'Mum would've believed it,' I finally say.

'I remember your mum,' Charlie nods. 'She was a good woman.'

Even in the midst of this strange conversation, I almost laugh at that. What Mum would have made of being called a *good woman*. 'You talked to her?'

'Talked to you both. You were like a determined tornado. A tiny wee thing with black wild curls and stick legs that wouldn't stay still for more than a minute.'

'She just died,' I say, finally giving in to the urge to say it. 'Bowel cancer.'

And then there is Dr Lennon again, with his moustache, squeezing my hands between his cool fleshy palms as Mum sits hunched in a chair, refusing to look at either of us. *It's spread to the lungs and brain. Without treatment, we're talking months, perhaps only weeks.*

'Ach, that's . . .' Charlie closes his eyes, shakes his head. 'I'm sorry to hear it, lassie.'

I nod. Unclench my fists. Make my spine and shoulders straight. 'I really do promise that I'm not here to cause trouble, Charlie.' And although this is not entirely a lie, it's not the truth either. I will. If I have to.

When he opens his eyes and turns to look at me, he does it with purpose, as if he's come to some private decision. 'When you came here, you and your mum, we didn't treat you fairly. You were just a wee bairn, and you didn't deserve it. And it's only right that you know why.'

My heartbeat picks up, drumming hard enough that I can feel it. 'I *know* why. I was telling anyone and everyone that my name was Andrew MacNeil and that someone on this island had murdered me.'

Charlie's gaze slips away from mine, and when he shakes his head, something cold turns over in my belly; a frisson of dark excitement. When he takes out his hip flask again and passes it over to me, I accept without comment, drink, and pass it back. The measure he takes for himself is significantly larger, and afterwards, he inhales long and loud before turning to look back at me.

'We lied to you. That was why. Twenty-five years ago, a man did die here. He drowned.' His gaze moves over my shoulder, up towards the bluffs. 'And his name was Andrew.'

CHAPTER 4

End of September 1993

Robert

We're all guilty of something, my father always said. But the biggest sin is fear. And never facing it. That was not his sin, of course. Only mine. This morning, the sun is high. It lights up the occasional sprays of spindrift in silver-white sparks. From this height, the ocean looks endless like the sky. Blue and quiet. But the storms are coming. I can see them in the spray blown from the crests of waves and in the scattered whitecaps out towards the horizon. In the slow steady leaching of light from the sky, a little earlier each day. And I can feel them in the air and against my skin. A prickle. A shiver of old fear.

Today, there are no boats on the horizon, but I can see the red-and-white-striped *Unity* returning to the slip at Bàgh Fasgach. Calum sees it too and races along the shoreline, kicking up water, his high giggles catching and riding the wind. And something inside my chest gets tight with hope.

Once, many years ago, I stood on a headland just like this and looked out at the same ocean. I was alone and afraid and full of despair. But I vowed even then that I would come back again. I'd come back in spite of the storms. In spite of the fear. In spite of the despair. I had hope. Because somehow I knew that one day things would be different. One day I'd stop being afraid. I would come back. And all would be well.

And so, here I am.

On days when I'm less certain – when I wonder why I returned to the islands at all – I walk the length of this headland, to the very limits of my own leased land, and I remember how it was in Aberdeen. That cavernous windowless building, full of noise and blood. Stainless-steel worktops and the stink of fish guts that I could never scrub off, no matter how I tried. The claustrophobia – the suffocation – that I feel when I look out at that ocean is not the same. And it's no match for the feeling I get when I walk Àrd Chreag; when I look at the land, my flock alongside or out in the pasture beyond, their black Hebridean coats bleached brown by the sun.

No son of mine will ever be a farmer.

And maybe that's true, because I don't feel like much of one. Breeding season is less than one month away, and already I'm certain it will go badly; that I'll find some way to screw it up. The summer was wet, and the bere barley and small oat yield too poor; neither will provide enough fodder to see us through winter. Too often when I'm rounding up the flock to move pasture, I find myself looking out at the sea instead. Watching for the high masthead lights of the pelagic and whitefish trawlers out of Steòrnabhagh and Port Nis in the pink-silver of dawn; their radars, stacks, and gantries silhouettes against the horizon. Listening for the rattles and shouts of the smaller, nearer creel boats from Bàgh Fasgach, A'Chàrnach, and Miabhaig. The low diesel rumble of their engines; the high impatient shrieks of the gulls. They are the sounds of my memory, my childhood. Just like my father's voice: low, slow, and always angry.

'Daddy! Daddy! Mammy says hurry up!'

Calum's cheeks are bright as he crests the bluff. He's always looked more like Mary than me: fair and small, with his smile so wide and ready. I wonder if I ever smiled that way.

Mary has already set up a picnic on the beach. Tràigh Shearrag is more sheltered than Tràigh Mhòr further west, but most days a narrow funnel of wind throws the sand into devils. Today though, all is still. Enough that I can feel the calmness move inside me as I climb down onto the dunes. Pushing against the walls of my worry.

'Sit, the pair of you,' Mary smiles. 'Thought I was going to have to eat all this myself.'

She's made sandwiches and pies; packed plastic plates and beakers. She takes a beer from the cool bag and passes it to me. Her hair is loose and wild, the way she knows I love it. She's made a far better effort than I have, and guilt makes me smile harder as I take the beer and sit down.

'You're looking particularly gorgeous today, Mrs Reid.'

She seems startled for a moment, and then she laughs, her cheeks going pink. Mary never wanted to leave Aberdeen. Never wanted to come here. She's an east coast lass through and through; speaks Scots, English and some Doric, but not one word of Gaelic.

A city girl too. Sometimes she tells me that I've brought her to the very end of the world. And yet she came without question.

'Kenny! Kenny!' Calum yells, waving both arms as he chases after the now passing *Unity*. Calum doesn't want to be a farmer either. He wants to be a fisherman. And the thought of that makes my blood boil and run cold at the same time.

You will get on that boat, boy. Dark thunderous brows and sea-grey eyes. Brown-leather skin and ruddy, stubbled cheeks. I've always seen my father in my dreams. Heard him. Felt the sour heat of his disappointment; the sting of his belt or the snood-hooks of his *sma' lines.* On nights when I don't, I still wake up – panicked and vaguely bereft, even though it should only be a relief.

It's not that sly bastard Kenny Campbell who grins and waves back at Calum; he's only a hunched silhouette inside the *Unity*'s wheelhouse. It's the boat's other skipper, Charlie MacLeod. Always with an easy swagger, an easier smile, as if nothing has ever bothered him in his entire life. Maybe it hasn't; maybe behind his winks and grins and quick laughter there is nothing hidden at all.

'Charlie!' Calum cries. 'Charlie!'

Mary is waving now too.

'Come away, Calum,' I say. 'Sit down and eat the lunch your mum's slaved over.'

'It's fine,' Mary says as Calum trudges back to drop down onto the sand.

The *Unity* disappears into the shadow of the headland as we eat in comfortable silence, Calum barely able to sit still and eat his sandwiches in anticipation of the Kinder eggs he knows Mary will have packed into the hamper.

'Stop hotching, Calum.'

He freezes, and then grins wide enough to show the whole beach a mouthful of cheese and bread. 'Sorry, Daddy.'

'There's another meeting in the pub tonight,' Mary says.

'You're joking.'

'Afraid not. Fiona told me first thing in the shop.'

'For God's sake. Meetings about bloody meetings! It's not as if most of us don't have at least a dozen other fucking things to be doing.'

Mary's brow furrows as she looks pointedly towards Calum – although something darker passes over her eyes, and I know she's thinking about Aberdeen.

'Sorry, Calum. Daddy said the bad word you should never say.' I glance at Mary. 'Again.'

'Bad Daddy,' he says in delight.

'Bad Daddy,' Mary says, and then smiles. She strokes my cheek with the cool back of her hand. 'You have to go.'

'Aye, I know.' I wedge my empty bottle in the sand. When we first arrived six months ago, I'd forgotten about this – everyone not just knowing everyone else's business, but being an active participant in it. So be it. I brought Mary and Calum here because they've given me more love and peace than I've ever known. Or deserved. And so it will be worth it. It *has* to be.

Calum laughs when I reach over to grab him, shrieks when I toss him over my shoulder and start sprinting towards the sea.

'Or . . . we could all make a run for it and swim to Canada!'

The shifting sand under my feet and the bite of crushed shells never fails to remind me of Mamaidh. The long days she'd take me paddling or rock fishing and mussel picking; the long adventure stories she'd later tell me by the fire over mugs of steaming chocolate. *You're my good boy. My wee warrior.* Up until the day my father died. The day he went to sea and never came back.

Once, long before we were married, Mary and I got pissed on homemade gin, and had the kind of ill-advised conversation you can only ever have when you're drunk and at the start of love. How many people have you had sex with? How many times have you cheated? What's the worst thing that you've ever done? And even drunk, even already well past the start of love – because the first time I ever saw Mary it was over for me, even before she smiled that open, easy smile – I knew I could never tell her the truth. Not about that. I can no more tell Mary about the worst thing that I've ever done than the real reason I've come back here. Why I've dragged her and Calum to the end of the world. I haven't even told her about the winter – she has no idea what the storm season on these islands is like. So dark and wild and endless that she'll struggle to remember we even had days like these. Or why I'm looking forward to those storms in spite of dreading them. In spite of the nightmares that I always pretend are about something else.

Because facing your fear doesn't mean telling the truth. It means not running away. Not working in a fish-processing plant in Aberdeen, or pretending to be a farmer when you were born to be a fisherman. It's coming back to where it all began. Where it all came to an end. Or as close as I can bear. Only on a clear day can I see the headland of Àrd Shiadair ten miles to the north, or the long, pointing finger of Àird Èinis beyond.

Today, though, I'm grateful for more than just that. Today I'm grateful for the light, the clean thin air. That feeling I get when I walk the land; the green of the grass, the brown and gold of the moors, the purple of the heather and the rose-pink of thrift. The big open sky and the wind that never tastes or feels the same anywhere else. The smells of peat smoke and seaweed and rain. The silence. It feels like Mary. Like Calum. I have never belonged anywhere but here.

And so today, despite all of it: the lies, the secrets, the guilt, the dread, and the fear, I am happy. My heart is light. My mind is quiet. I am here. And it will be worth it. This time it will be different.

CHAPTER 5

When I turn on my laptop and connect to the Wi-Fi, I'm distracted by at least a dozen unread emails. Some half-hearted Happy Birthdays from friends, mostly ex-colleagues to whom I am now, I suspect, only a brief obligation or a pinged calendar alert on their phone – I haven't spoken to any of them in months. Some pdfs from the Maudsley: *Learn How to Manage Your Recovery*; *Understand Your Warning Signs*; *Look After Your Body*. A reminder from Grove Park Funeral Services that I still haven't left a review on *Feefo*. And, last, a Happy Birthday, from Ravi; stilted and somehow disapproving even though it barely says anything at all. I think of his endless *You don't sound right. Are you sure you're okay? Have you been taking your meds?* Towards the end, less concerned than belligerent; enough to drive me to almost feverish weariness. I think of that last day in our kitchen just a few weeks before Mum died. The surprise on his face, and then the anger.

Are you dumping me? Is that what this is, Maggie? And even though it had always been my job to placate, to back down, that day I didn't. Because he wasn't my doctor, and I wasn't his patient. And we hadn't been anything close to happy together for so long it was hard to remember when we ever had been. I'd been proud of myself until I realised it had worked. And he left.

I don't reply to any of the emails. Instead, I sit at the dining table, thinking of Charlie's tight-lipped frown, the quick blink of his eyes against the wind. Excitement still spins cool and dark inside me. I glance at the mood journal on my bedside table, try to imagine what the hell I'd write in it right this minute. I'm fine. To be excited about this is natural. It's *fine*.

'He called himself Robert Reid,' Charlie had said on the beach. 'When he lived here. Told me one night – I'm pretty sure only because we were both three sheets to the wind, we weren't exactly friends – that he'd changed his name ten years before. From Andrew.'

'Andrew what?' And I sat looking at Charlie trying not to look at me, while that something cool and dark kept turning over and over in the pit of my belly.

'He never said. Just Andrew.'

'When did he die? When exactly?'

Charlie turned to face me then. 'Middle of the spring. April, '94. It was the Saturday after Easter.'

And for a moment, the relief was almost as sharp as the disappointment.

'You said, *We lied to you.* Who is we? Who knew his name?'

'Everyone. Just after he died, I told them what he'd told me.'

'So why didn't any of you *say* anything? I mean – Mum said you practically ran us out of town.'

Charlie sighed, shook his head. 'It was a hard time, back when it happened. It . . . no one wanted it brought back up. And we knew, because of his name, because of *Robert*, it wouldn't be.' He held my gaze. 'The dates didn't match anyway. You were born in February. That's what that arse of a director kept telling us anyway. Right?'

I nodded.

'So. The dates don't – didn't – match. And what was in it for us even if they had? We're not a sideshow. Something to poke and point and look down your nose at.'

'That's not—'

'Aye, it was. Maybe not for you, or your mum. But for that smug bastard, and all the other smug bastards who came over here with their vans and cameras and questions, that's exactly what it was.'

I let it go. The reproach, the disappointment that shouldn't feel at all like relief. 'How old was Andrew?'

'Never knew that either. He was a sheep farmer; mid- to late twenties probably – seemed older, looked older, but I don't think he was. His wife, Mary, was a bonnie lassie, a bit naive, younger in mind than him. She and their wee boy, Calum, had this way of looking at Robert like the sun rose and set with him.'

'Where was he from?'

'They came to the island in spring, '93. She and the wee boy were Aberdonian, but his accent was pure Western Isles. Same night he said his name was Andrew, he told me he came from

Ardshader.' I watched Charlie's Adam's apple bob up and down twice. 'It's a coastal fishing village at Uig on Lewis.'

I know how common the name Andrew MacNeil is on the islands. And I know that a man changing his name from Andrew to Robert is proof of nothing at all. But it's a beginning, and that *is* something. I open Safari and then the already bookmarked Scotland's People website, bring up my old search window for the birth certificate of Andrew MacNeil. I replace my initial date-of-birth range of 1919–1976 with 1959–1974 instead, assuming Andrew's age to be somewhere between twenty and thirty-five. When I select *Uig (Lewis)* from the dropdown menu of districts, there's only one result.

Andrew MacNeil, born 1967, in Uig.

'Shit.'

I click on his name, and a pop-up box appears. *If someone was born less than 100 years ago, a certificate must be ordered. This can take at least 15 working days to process.*

I start a death certificate search instead. Realise as I type in Robert Reid and 1994 that my palms are clammy. Excitement is *fine.* Although this is more complicated than excitement. Despite what Charlie said about Robert Reid having died in April and not February.

There are three entries. Portree. Kinlochbervie. North Harris. When I select the latter entry, it disappears behind another pop-up box – *If someone died less than 50 years ago, a certificate must be ordered. This can take at least 15 working days to process.*

'Shit.'

When I'd asked Charlie how and where Andrew had drowned, he'd shaken his head, stood up with a wince. As I'd looked out at the horizon and thought of that black dress with white spots and my finger pointing out towards the sea, I saw that the clouds had turned dark and ominous, and were racing towards us on a rising wind. Charlie whistled for Bonny and we started moving quickly along the sand towards the steep path back onto the bluff.

'Charlie?' I shouted, my hair whipping around my face, sand stinging my skin. 'Where—'

He shouted something I couldn't hear over the now thunderous surf, and swept an impatient arm out towards the angry dark sea behind us. He didn't speak again until we'd reached the top of the bluff and had clambered down to the shelter of the trail on the other side.

'He died little more than a year after he arrived,' Charlie said, reaching down to stroke Bonny's head when she whined. 'He wasn't liked. He was a . . . complicated man. He'd had a bad past. And some folk, they can never shake a bad past. It follows them like a shadow that doesn't need the sun. Robert thought he needed this place, these islands, to be happy. But they never made him anything close to that.'

I didn't answer. Wasn't sure what to say.

'Look,' Charlie said. 'I'll speak to folk, tell them I've told you. See what they say. If anyone's willing to talk to you. But there's a good chance they won't be. What I said before, about it being a hard time, back when it happened . . .' He stopped, looked away as the rain finally started to come down – as hard and fast as earlier, maybe worse – and when he turned back to me, his expression was weary, wary. 'Robert drowned in a storm. Same storm, same night, as wee Lorne did.'

'Oh. God.'

'I'll let you know what they say,' Charlie said, turning left to head back to Blairmore.

'Wait! Where did he live?'

And Charlie had looked away from me again to point up towards the Ardcraig headland. His pause long enough that I realised I was holding my breath inside it. 'The Blackhouse.'

Now, I look around this brightly lit room, breathe its air, cool and still and smelling of pine and coffee and woodsmoke. I get up and run my fingers along the wooden surface of the mantelpiece, looking at my reflection in the wide silver mirror above it. Did Robert once stand in this spot? Did he once look into this mirror? Nothing about the blackhouse feels familiar at all, but still, my heart beats faster.

I remember the trapdoor near the kitchen – Kelly's *earth cellar* – and cross the room to hunker down next to it. The door is big and cut into the pine floor, but it's only when I pull up on its recessed steel handle that I see the small key-shaped hole below it. Locked.

I get up and go into the small box room, but it's literally filled with only boxes, stacked high and taped shut. I pull back the heavy tartan curtain of its only window instead. It's dark outside, even though it's still early. The rain has persisted all afternoon, the wind rattling against the front door and whistling down the steel flue pipe. There's only one light in the gloom, and it comes from the farm. A faint orange glow, rectangular rather than square. And around it, the darker silhouette of stone against the sky. I peer into the darkness and try to imagine Andrew. What he looked like. What he sounded like. A complicated man with a bad past which had followed him like a shadow that didn't need the sun. And then the light winks out.

When someone knocks loudly at the front door behind me, I stagger back from the window, almost taking the curtain with me. I allow myself a few ridiculous seconds to regain my breath and slow my heartbeat. I creep back into the mudroom and peer through the tiny inset window of the door before unlocking it. And am greeted by an icy gust of wind and Kelly's toothy grin.

She looks me up and down, and grins wider. 'Look, Maggie. I know I said it was slim pickings, but I don't think flannel pyjamas are going to cut it even in Am Blàr Mòr.'

*

Kelly's flat is tiny. Little more than a living area, bedroom, bathroom, and a laminate-floored hallway that wouldn't fit two people side by side.

When I follow her into the main room, Jaz is sitting cross-legged on a rug next to an overturned crate of Lego and a little boy with a shock of blond hair.

'Hey, Kelly,' Jaz says before giving me a not exactly unfriendly glance, but certainly one that's miles away from yesterday's generous grin. 'Maggie.'

'Hi,' I say.

'And this wee man,' Kelly says, 'is Fraser.'

'Hi, Fraser,' I say, when he gives me a bashful smile. 'It's very nice to meet you.'

Jaz stands up, goes towards the door. 'When d'you want me back?'

'Maybe a couple of hours, if that's okay?' Kelly says, and Jaz nods, closes the door behind him.

My sigh is very loud in the quiet. 'Maybe I shouldn't go tonight. What if everyone—'

'Ach, don't mind Jaz. In a few days, they'll all have moved on to something else. That's how it goes.' She walks over to the fridge and pulls out a bottle of wine. 'Let's have a drink, I'll make us some food, and then we can go downstairs to the pub. Have a lot more drinks.'

Fraser scrambles to his feet as he looks at me shyly. 'Are you from Glasgow? Did you come on a boat or a plane? Do you live in a house like Jaz or—'

'Give Maggie a chance to answer,' Kelly says.

'I came from London in England,' I say. 'And I got three trains, a plane, a bus, and *then* a boat.'

Fraser's eyes go wide. 'No way.'

'And I'm living in your mum's blackhouse.'

'No *way*.'

'Yes way,' Kelly laughs. 'Now, I need you to tidy away your Lego and go wash your hands for tea, okay?'

Fraser visibly deflates, but heads back to the rug with a muttered, 'Okay.'

'He's very cute.'

'Yeah,' Kelly says, rolling her eyes and pushing a glass of wine across the counter towards me. 'You can say that because you haven't witnessed the bedtime tantrums or the PTSD-inducing three a.m. wake-up calls.' She starts filling a pan with water. 'Pasta okay? Carbonara?'

'Of course. Can I help?'

'You're all right. Although pasta and a stir-in sauce is pretty much the summit of my cooking skills.' She glances at me over her shoulder. 'Sorry if this is rude, but you look a bit weird. Has something happened?'

And because I need to tell someone, I recount my conversation with Charlie, and what I found on the Scotland's People website.

'That's . . . nuts, Maggie,' she says when I finish. 'There actually *was* an Andrew MacNeil? I mean, that's just . . . that's *nuts*, Maggie.' But when she turns round there's something in her expression suddenly that I can't read. Something closed.

'Well. There was a man from Ardshader called Andrew who changed his name and moved here, at least.'

'So, what does that *mean*?' She puts a lid on the pot, tops up our glasses, and sits down on a breakfast bar stool. 'I was going to ask you tonight – if you thought it was true? You know, you being . . .' she waves her hands, half-shrugs, 'reincarnated?'

'It's . . . complicated.' I sit down, give her a tight half-smile.

'My dad used to say that believing in things like ghosts or heaven or reincarnation, all that, was just a fear of dying,' Kelly says.

'Your parents, were they still here in '99 – you know, when I came here? Did they ever mention—'

'No. We moved to North Uist around '95, '96.'

'So they would have been living here when Robert Reid was alive, right? It's just . . . Charlie said Robert lived in the blackhouse.'

'*The* Blackhouse?'

When I nod, her face betrays surprise, even shock, but underneath there's that something else, pinched and still closed.

'Jesus,' she says. 'I mean . . . I didn't know that. That's pretty fucking nuts too.' She shakes her head. 'I know that we lived here above the pub for the first year or so of running it. But I never knew who lived in the blackhouse before we did.'

'D'you think you could ask them? How well they knew him?'

Kelly gets up and goes back to the hob. 'I guess. I mean I can ask, but . . .' She gives an almost theatrical shrug of her shoulders. 'Don't know how much use they'll be. Dad's got a memory like a sieve.' She turns round again, and that shuttered look is gone. 'What about your mum? I mean, you said she was with you – what did she think of it all? Did she believe it? *Does* she believe it?'

'She died,' I say, washing down the *just* with the last of my wine.

'God, I'm sorry.'

I shake my head, look down at my hands. 'Mum believed a lot of things. But the biggie was that she was psychic.' Reflexive embarrassment mixes with anger. 'That she could hear the voices of the dead. That she could predict the future. More often than not, hers. Or mine.'

Kelly leans against the kitchen island, her glass tipping unnoticed in her hand, the wine dangerously close to its lip. 'What did *you* believe?'

'When I was a kid? Her. Later?' I can feel that tight smile pulling at my lips again. 'Like I said, it's complicated.'

She frowns. 'But, the whole *I died as Andrew and woke up as Maggie* thing?'

'It isn't that uncommon. Lots of kids say – insist – that they've been reincarnated; it's been widely documented across the world in all cultures and religions. They can recount names and places and memories that don't belong to them. And then around eight years old, they forget. Sometimes they forget that they ever even had these "memories". Nothing can be proved; the information is generally too vague, too small.' I shrug. 'I used to think it was like seeing ghosts. If you don't believe in them, they just look like shadows. And then, later, I started thinking that if you did believe in them, maybe every shadow turned into a ghost.'

'But, I mean, if Robert Reid *was* Andrew MacNeil, that means he existed,' Kelly says. 'He was real. And if that's true, what other explanation is there?'

I shrug again, feigning a nonchalance I don't really feel. Because the hope that Charlie swiftly extinguished on the beach after telling me when Andrew died has since revived. Kelly's right – Andrew MacNeil existed. Before today – for me – he hadn't. And perhaps that same man came to this island and died here twenty-five years ago as Robert Reid. A man who lived in the very same blackhouse that I am renting. The *same* house. It can't be just coincidence. No matter what Charlie told me, all of that has to mean something. It *has* to. I think of how determined I'd been looking out at that flat sea; the childlike confidence in my *Out there!* I remember the feeling so well because I've rarely felt it since. Absolute conviction.

'Mum believed that we're all reincarnated. But that I only remembered because I was psychic like her.' I never talk about this, not even with counsellors and therapists, because it always makes me feel dirty, *itchy*. Like I'm admitting to something I never did. 'And because she thought he'd died badly.'

'He died badly all right,' Kelly says. 'The sea down on those beaches might look like the bloody Caribbean, but it scares the shit out of me. And have you seen those morbid monuments? I can't bear to even take Fraser paddling out there.' She flinches when the water boils over to hiss on the hob; gives a self-conscious laugh as she gets up to turn down the heat. And I think of how alone and uneasy I'd felt today just standing on a cliff swamped by fog and rain and the sounds of that sea.

'Anyway,' she says, replacing the pot lid and turning round. 'You said that the dates don't match. That Andrew, Robert, whatever his name was, died in April, and you were born, what – in February, right?'

'Charlie could be lying.'

Kelly blinks. 'About the date? Why would he?'

'I dunno. Why did he lie about Andrew in the first place? Or maybe he's just remembered wrong.' *Wanting something to be true,* Dr Abebe says in my ear, *can be a very dangerous road.*

Suddenly all I can see is Mum sitting by my bed, my nightlight illuminating those curly wisps of hair at her temples and the slow half-smile that I grew to hate. Years and years of nights, of her soft and sure mantras like bedtime stories. *People like us, Maggie, we can't deny what we are. People like us, Maggie, we must always be open, we must never be closed. People like us, Maggie, we have to listen to our bad feelings.* I don't want it to be true. But at the same time, God, I do. I do, I do.

I clear my throat, make an effort to smile. 'Anyway, it's going to take at least fifteen days to process the birth and death certificates, but then I'll know the actual dates for sure. And maybe I'll discover something else that I *can* actually write a story about.'

'Did you accuse anyone?' Kelly says, after a long pause. 'Back when you were a kid. When you said you were Andrew MacNeil and you'd been murdered. Did you ever say who'd done it?'

'What?' I'm caught off guard. 'No. I mean – no.'

'I'm sorry,' Kelly says, her cheeks pink. 'That was a bit too tabloid journalist.'

'It's okay. I really don't remember much, to be honest. Mum told me most of it.'

Sobbing hard in breathless hiccups: *I want – to – go – home*, and Mum on her knees, holding my hands. *Okay, my darling, okay. We'll go home.* Knowing even at five years old that she didn't mean it. Knowing that she didn't want to.

Kelly tops up our glasses. 'Rather than wait for the certificates, why don't you go to the town hall in Stornoway instead? They hold civil and parish records. We can ask around tonight; I'm sure someone will be going in the next few days, you could cadge a lift. I'd take you but my car's still in the garage at Tarbert. I think he might have expired, and they're too afraid to tell me.' She flashes me the biggest grin. 'But that doesn't mean you get out of telling me what you find out, okay?'

I've never had many friends. It's mostly by design: I actively avoid having too many attachments, too many relationships that I might not be able to trust. A primary school teacher once told Mum I was 'prickly'. She ended up keying his car. I don't often open up to people because I know where it can lead. And that dirty, *itchy* feeling is something that's always been easier to endure alone. But Kelly's different. I like her. I trust her. And after all our email exchanges before I came here, I feel like I know her. Most of all, I want to talk to her. I want, for once, to be honest. Dr Abebe would be incandescent with pride.

He came to visit me after I'd been in the Maudsley almost a week. I'd been moved from the psych ICU to an open ward by then, and although they'd lowered the dosage of whatever they'd put me on, I still felt like someone else. I couldn't think or sleep. I just shook and itched and stared at walls. When I saw Dr Abebe coming towards me – wearing one of his shiny, ill-fitting suits, black-framed glasses too big for his face, and that solemn half-smile, it was the first time I'd felt anything for days.

'It's Haldol,' he said when I asked. 'They'll take you off it pretty soon. You're doing well.'

'When can I leave?'

'You're not doing *that* well.'

I remember the smell of his cologne as he leaned closer, something sharp and cool; I wondered if it had been a Christmas present. 'This was a psychotic break, Maggie. It's a big deal, and you can't run away from it.'

'I know.' Even though that was pretty much exactly what I planned on doing.

When I told him much later that I was coming here, he knew better than to try to talk me out of it. He spoke to that GP in Stornoway, set up remote support, had me make promises which he knew I always tried to keep.

'You need to tell someone else, Maggie. Someone there needs to know. And you need to promise me you'll tell them.'

And when I hesitated, that solemn half-smile disappeared. 'Promise me, Maggie. After what happened in the crematorium, you have to.'

I'd promised.

'Have you heard of *jamais vu*?' I say now to Kelly. I don't wait for her to answer in case I lose my nerve. 'It's the opposite of déjà vu. I used to get it all the time when I was growing up. It's where something or someone that should be – that is – very familiar to you, like your house or your family, suddenly isn't. You don't recognise them. They feel completely alien. It's a horrible feeling. Like I didn't belong in my own body, my own life.' I pause. 'Sometimes, it makes you *remember* things that have never happened to you. So some people call it postcognition.'

'Of a past life,' Kelly says.

I nod. 'It's actually a pretty common form of dissociation.' I take a low quick breath; I'm horribly nervous, I realise. Because I like Kelly, and want her to like me. I automatically reach for the chain around my neck, the pendant shifting cool against my skin before I let it go. 'When I was fifteen, I finally plucked up the courage to go to my GP. He referred me to a psychiatrist.'

I think of that first psychiatrist, the light that bounced off his shiny bald head. His low, ponderous entreaties to a stony-faced Mum. *Your daughter is unwell, Mrs Anderson. She has been unwell for some time.* And Mum's fury when we were alone, the grief and shame for me – her fearful, gullible daughter. *Mental illness is a tool of repression and ignorance. It's a way for men, for society, to persecute us, to call us hysterical. To keep us witches* – she spat the word – *inside our cages.*

'I have bipolar one. It means that I have manic episodes, followed by depressive ones. The mania usually lasts only a few weeks, if I get it at all. I'll drink too much, spend too much, talk too much, sleep too little. My thoughts race like mad. It feels great. Like nothing bad is ever going to happen again.' I look down at the table. 'And then afterwards, I don't really remember any of it. People tell me what I did or said, and I apologise, like it's on someone else's behalf, you know? I can't describe it. It's the same as the *jamais vu*. As if it's nothing to do with me.

'The depression lasts longer. I just kind of *stop* doing everything.' My smile feels wrong. 'Except sleeping – I do a lot of that.' And a lot of not caring whether I wake up again, although I'm no more going to tell her that than I am what happened in the crematorium.

When I stop talking, the silence is unnerving. My face feels hot, my hands clammy.

'Oh, Maggie,' Kelly says, pulling me into a tight, quick hug. She smells of jelly beans. 'That's awful, I'm sorry. And here's me banging on about reincarnation and murders like we're in *Days of Our Lives*.'

'No, it's fine.' Although I'm grateful when she lets me go. 'I don't want you to feel bad. I mean, I'm all right. It's just . . . someone has to know. I have to tell someone. Just . . . just in case. Because psychosis – you know, delusions or hallucinations – that's a possibility too. So . . . it's just in case, you know, something—'

'Oh,' Kelly says. 'Of course.'

'I *am* all right.' Although I'm not sure who I'm trying to convince. 'I know what to do. I have my meds, I have regular blood tests to check my levels. And there's a doctor in Stornoway who's agreed to see me while I'm here.' I pause, resist the urge to fidget. 'It's just . . . I can't completely relax, you know? I can't completely trust myself.' Any more.

'Then thank you,' Kelly says. For a moment that distant look comes into her face again, and then it's gone. 'For trusting me.'

And as she turns away to dish up the pasta, I'm standing inside that small, airless room in the crematorium again. Furniture polish and the cloying lilies. Mum's coffin up on a curtained dais – open, because she'd always suffered from claustrophobia; would have recurring nightmares about being buried alive. A low hum of conversation, the odd clearing of a throat or creak of a floorboard. And me doing nothing at first but just standing there, looking up at that dais. Looking at the demon squatting next to Mum's coffin – bony, hairless, with too many teeth in his mouth, like bad dentures. Listening to his claws scratching on the varnished floor through all the readings and the songs. And then, at the end, watching as he turned to grin at me before climbing into Mum's coffin and trying to close its lid.

Even though I rarely recalled anything that happened to me when I was manic, I remember all of this. Mum's pale and powdery face, her thin hands crossed over her chest. His smell, like rotting leaves. The shadow he cast over her yellow silk dress when he climbed in. I remember how many people it took to restrain me, to stop me from pulling my own mother out of her coffin. I remember my screams. And I remember the fear. Like nothing I'd ever felt before. Like the end of the world. Or worse, the start of a new one.

CHAPTER 6

There is, I can tell, such a united and palpable effort not to look our way when Kelly and I push through the private door into the pub that it almost makes me want to laugh. And then run. Instead, I return the sentiment by keeping my eyes trained on the paisley-patterned carpet as Kelly marches us towards the bar. By the time we get there, the low hum of conversation has resumed, although I don't doubt for a second that it's mostly about me.

Gillian turns round from the till and gives me a smile that I'm not expecting.

'Kelly said you'd be coming to our wee do tonight, you're very welcome.'

'Thank you.' I can still feel other eyes on me, and my answering smile stretches too wide, goes on for too long.

'What'll you be having?'

'Just a small white wine, please?'

'Same for me, please, Gillian,' Kelly says, handing over a tenner.

I glance at the glossy tiles behind the spirits and optics, reflecting movement in the lounge over my shoulder. 'Are they still looking?'

'Ignore 'em.' Kelly grins. 'Pretend you're on the Central Line.'

When Gillian comes back with our drinks, I pull myself up onto the stool next to Kelly and tap my glass against hers. 'Cheers. So. You and Jaz. Are you—'

'Christ, no! He's like *forty*-something. He's just a good guy. And he's really great with Fraser. He helped me out when I first started working shifts in the pub, and I guess . . . I mean, I'm probably taking advantage now – I do that, I take the piss – but I'm just really glad that Fraser has some kind of decent male influence in his life.' She pauses. 'His dad's a dickhead. He's the reason we had to leave Glasgow.'

'I'm sorry. Is—'

Someone jostles my shoulder hard enough that I spill some of my wine over the bar and the hem of my dress. When I turn round, I find myself looking straight into the angry red face of Alec MacDonald.

'You're not welcome here.'

Before I or Kelly can say anything, Bruce MacKenzie lets go of a beer pump and moves towards us.

'Alec. These days, I'm the one gets to decide who's welcome here or not.'

'She's—'

'Welcome.' Bruce plants his palms on the bar and leans across it. 'We clear?'

I don't look up from my lap until I feel the heat of Alec – of his rage – retreat, and then I take in a breath, look up at Bruce. 'Thank you.'

He studies me with those dark eyes for a moment, and then nods. 'No bother.'

'Don't mind Alec,' Euan says, from a little further along the bar. 'There's not a person in this world that doesn't get on his nerves.'

He's standing next to a woman, impossibly elegant in a silk blouse and linen trousers, and a complicated up-do that has somehow managed to survive the Hebridean wind completely intact. She gives me a smile, less curious than polite.

Euan frowns. 'I suppose by now you know why?'

'Well, I . . .' I blink. Think of that little stone above Long Stride Beach. 'Yes.'

There follows an uncomfortable silence, and Kelly shuffles on her stool.

'So, Cora wanted to meet the new arrival, didn't you, my love?' Euan eventually says, gently coaxing the woman forwards. 'Maggie, this is my good wife, Cora. Cora, this is Maggie.'

Cora smiles again, longer this time, puts her hand out to shake. 'Hello, Maggie. Pleased to meet you.' Her voice is soft, almost husky; her accent English, maybe Midlands. She leans briefly closer in a waft of musky expensive perfume. Her pink lipstick has bled into the tiny wrinkles at the corners of her lips.

'She's come from London, my dear,' Euan booms. 'You Sassenachs have to stick together out here, eh?' His laugh is jolly and far too loud. I think of *You're Andrew fucking MacNeil, right?* and wonder if Euan either doesn't believe Alec about who I am, or doesn't remember that I'm actually from Inverness.

'There you go, Euan,' Bruce says, setting down a whisky and a wine.

'Thanking you,' Euan says, handing over a twenty-pound note. 'And whatever these lovely ladies would like too.'

'That's very kind of you,' I say, but he only nods as he picks up his drinks and holds out an arm to his wife. She takes it with another smile before they walk back through the lounge.

'Another two pinots, girls?' Bruce asks. Kelly nods and he disappears towards the fridge at the other end of the bar.

'Well,' she says, draining her wine. '*That* was weird. Next you'll be getting an invite up to the Big Hoose.'

'The Big House?'

'*Hoose*. You haven't seen it yet? Christ, you can hardly miss it. It's the old Laird's Lodge. Next headland west past yours. Remember I said the whole island was owned by Euan Morrison's family for eons? Some distant, long-dead Euan – why do rich folk insist on giving each other the exact same name, must be a nightmare at Christmas – he was supposedly given Kilmeray by one of the first Lords of the Isles. The Morrisons owned it for centuries, renting out the land to crofters. Everyone still thinks of Euan as the laird, I guess, but he actually sold most of the estate back to the community years ago. His rellies are probably spinning in their great big mausoleums.'

When the front door bangs open, admitting an icy gust of wind, I recognise the stocky blond man who enters, carrying an accordion in one hand and a fiddle in the other, as Donnie MacKenzie, Gillian and Bruce's son. He walks over to where a band is beginning to set up on a small stage next to the pool table. Euan

Morrison is now muttering *testing, one, two* into a microphone on a wobbly stand.

I can tell, although she hasn't said anything at all, that Kelly is dying to ask me more about Andrew MacNeil. But after me telling her about my bipolar, I know she won't pry. Not yet anyway. And tonight I'm tired of thinking about it, about *him*. Of hoping, without really wanting to, without really knowing what it is I'm hoping for.

'It's my birthday today,' I say before I've any inkling I'm going to.

'Are you serious?' Kelly says. 'Why didn't—'

I shrug. 'I don't really celebrate them.'

'Right.' Kelly hops down from her stool. 'Before any more folk from Urbost arrive and it really starts to get busy, I'll get us a celebratory bottle of fizz.' She points a finger at me. 'No arguments. You keep our spot.'

When she heads towards the far end of the bar, I force myself to turn round and finally face the lounge. It's a lot busier than I realised: there are few free seats and even fewer free tables. I recognise some people from last night. The small, steely-voiced woman called Isla – Kelly's *She's a cool dude, tough as old boots* – is deep in conversation with Alec's wife, Fiona, and a younger woman I don't recognise. The latter is frowning, her dark hair pulled up into a severe ponytail, stark against her pale skin. All three of them are staring at me. Alec himself, thankfully, is nowhere to be seen. Over by the big fireplace, there are two crowded tables of what I assume are more student archaeologists, muddy and young and loud.

Kelly returns unexpectedly quickly, an opened bottle of prosecco wedged under her arm, two full glasses in her hands, her eyes wide.

'Very Sexy Will at five o'clock,' she hisses. Sets down the bottle. 'Wait. He's coming over here! Just be – Sexy Will! Hi!' she exclaims, and far too loudly, spinning round from the bar.

Sexy Will *is* sexy. The kind that knows it. That probably uses it. He's tall and broad-shouldered, a green-checked shirt rolled up to his elbows revealing tanned and thick forearms. He needs a shave, his dark hair needs a trim, and his eyes are tired and blood-shot. A startling sky blue. I've time to wonder why I'm noticing all these things, cataloguing them like some kind of bloody check-list, and then he smiles at me – slow and generous – and my heart *thump-thumps* once, twice, as if I'm about to be dropped from the lift-hill launch of a roller coaster.

'Not *Sexy Will*. Will. Just Will,' Kelly is saying. Too fast and still too loud. 'Sexy Will would be weird. Obviously. Hi, Will.'

'Bloody hell, Kelly.' He laughs. 'How many of them have you had?' His voice is low, his island accent soft.

Kelly has gone a very blotchy pink. 'Not enough,' she mutters. And then she swallows about a third of her prosecco.

'You must be Maggie,' he says, holding out his hand to me. 'Just wanted to say hello.' He smiles again. 'And welcome.'

I take his hand, half expecting it to electrocute me. When it doesn't, I'm almost disappointed. And realise that we've both allowed the handshake to go on far too long – enough that it's not a handshake any more – only when Kelly lets out a half-snort, half-cough. I let go and step back against the bar. I'd quite like to down at least a third of my prosecco too, but in the end, I'm saved by the sudden appearance of Donnie MacKenzie.

'Here you go, mate,' he says to Will, handing him a pint of lager. He clears his throat as he looks at me, not quite meeting my eyes. 'Donnie MacKenzie.'

'Hi,' I say. 'Nice to meet you. I'm Maggie.'

There's a short squeal from the pub's speakers that makes everyone wince before looking over to the stage.

'Evening, ladies and gentlemen, and welcome to Am Blàr Mòr,' Euan Morrison says, jowls wobbling. There's a sheen of sweat across his brow and damp patches under his suit jacket's armpits. 'In a few minutes I'll be calling the first dance of tonight's ceilidh.' A grin of his very white dentures. 'The Gay Gordons. So I hope you've all got your dancing shoes on.'

There's a cheer, a few claps.

'Better go.' Donnie looks immeasurably relieved. His smile transforms him; it's open and easy like a child's, infectious enough that I find myself smiling back. 'I'm the piper.'

'So, it's a Scots tradition,' Will says, once Donnie's disappeared into the crowd, 'that every new stranger must dance the first dance of any *ceilidh* with a local.'

I try to look like the prospect of this doesn't seem like both the best and worst idea ever, but my heart *thump-thumps* again, and I can feel my face getting red. My hands have gone clammy.

'I can't. I'm here with Kelly. We—'

'Christ.' Kelly laughs, as the band launches into a very loud 'Scotland the Brave'. 'It's your birthday. Go and dance with him before we all spontaneously combust.'

My face gets hotter when he leads me towards the tiled square of dance floor and the couples already forming a wide circle around its periphery. People are looking again, and it makes me feel even more uncomfortable. When Will takes my left hand in his and reaches behind my back with his right, I can smell his skin, feel his breath against my cheek, and I'm gripped with a terrified kind of adolescent exhilaration, as if I'm about to jump off a cliff. Which isn't only ridiculous, it's alarming. One of Dr Abebe's very many *Warning Signs for Maggie* is disproportionate excitement. And poor impulse control. Although I'm not sure that the latter isn't something I was born with.

'D'you know this one?' Will asks, as I go on standing next to him like a statue.

'I think so.' Mum used to teach me in the back garden on sunny weekends. Dances from her childhood, I imagine: the Dashing White Sergeant and the Military Two-step. Strip the Willow. She would always lead, and we'd invariably end up in a giggling, exhausted heap on the grass.

'If it helps,' Will says, as I furtively glance around at all the spectators and couples, 'pretend it's just us.'

And once we start dancing, pretending is easy. I remember the steps. I remember how great it feels to dance – a feeling that no one could ever argue is not good for me. The pivots and birls spin and blur the room so that Will *is* the only person I can see. I don't think about who's still talking about me, or how I'm ever going to get any of them to talk *to* me. I don't think about Dr Abebe or even Mum. And I don't think about Ravi, who never once made my heart *thump-thump*. I relax. I allow myself to smile, to dance, to enjoy holding someone's hand. An arm tight around my waist. Lifting me off the ground and spinning me dizzy. By the time the music finishes, we're out of breath and laughing, and I don't look at anyone else at all as he leads me to a couple of plastic chairs beside the dance-floor.

'Thank you,' I say.

'What for?'

When I don't answer, he briefly touches my knee with his. 'Everyone's good people here.'

'Okay.'

'I'm afraid I have to go. Got to be up at dawn.' He gives me a slow smile. 'I was already half out the door when I saw you.'

My skin prickles hotter at that, and I'm even more disturbed by how much I want him to stay. And then by how obvious I must have made that look when he touches the back of my hand with the back of his in the space between our seats where no one else can see. I jump. I feel like one long nerve ending.

'Come to the farm tomorrow,' he says, holding my gaze.

'Okay.' I should say no. Or that he wouldn't be asking if he knew anything about me. But I don't want to be so presumptuous. Conceited. Or, more likely, I just don't want to talk about it out loud, this ridiculous feeling. This *warning sign* by anyone's defi-nition. Besides, he has to know at least the one thing about me that everyone else does. And he's still asked.

I nearly jump out of my skin when the band suddenly erupts into what is definitely not a waltz or reel. It drums up from under my feet, clearing both my head and the dancefloor in seconds.

'Is that "Hellbound Train"?'

Will laughs. 'Donnie fancies himself for a Red Hot Chili Piper.' He stands up. 'Night, Maggie. Thanks for the dance.' Another smile. 'See you tomorrow.'

I watch him go, until I realise I'm doing it, and then I make myself get up and fast-march back towards the bar instead. Kelly is perched on a stool, legs crossed and grinning, holding out another full glass of prosecco.

'Oh, girl,' she says, in an American twang. 'You in trouble.'

I take the glass without answering. Swallow half of it as 'Hellbound Train' reaches a crashing crescendo.

'Play "Highland bloody Cathedral",' someone shouts.

Kelly goes on grinning, nudges me as she nods towards the young woman still sitting with Isla Campbell and Fiona MacDonald. Her arms are folded and her narrow face furious as she glares in our direction. 'So apparently, Sheena MacDonald has wanted Will Morrison since the Big Bang. She runs the community shop – better watch out for laxatives in your milk and nails in your Pot Noodle.' She laughs again. 'Oh, boy, have I told you how glad I am that you're here, Maggie Anderson?'

*

'Maggie?'

Charlie smells of the outside: smoke and cold. His shoulders are hunched, and that same wide-brimmed tweed cap is jammed on top of his head.

His eyes slide away to glance up and down the bar, and when

he rubs his forefinger under his nose, I realise that it's a sign he's nervous. 'Come over here a minute,' he mutters.

Kelly raises her eyebrows as he turns away, and I shrug at her before I get off my stool and follow him. He walks to the only red wall not lined with tables and chairs; the one crowded with all those photos of landscapes and people. When he gets there, he turns furtively round as though we're co-conspirators in a crime. He won't look at me, and he doesn't seem to want me to look at him, so I look at the photos instead. The black-and-white ones are mostly of islanders at work: fishing, farming, weaving, and peat-cutting, but the more recent ones are of parties and holidays. Ripped Christmas hats, raised glasses, and grins around these pub tables; group shots taken in the same street beneath coloured bunting and a wide Stornoway Whisky Festival banner strung between two lampposts; windy-looking picnics on a beach that I now recognise as Long Stride. The faces change less than the hairdos and fashions, and when I recognise many of them, including Charlie, it gives me a surprising pang. In Blackheath, I don't even know the names of my neighbours.

'I told everyone,' Charlie says in a low voice. 'And I also told them that you just wanted to write a story, one story, and that would be it. No sideshow.'

'Thank you so much, Charlie. I—'

'The Morrisons are busy preparing for a shooting party on the estate next week, but Isla, Jimmy, Jaz, and the MacKenzies have agreed to talk to you Monday.'

'That's great. I mean . . . so they all knew Andrew?'

Charlie finally looks at me. 'Aye. Much as anyone did.'

'Thank you for doing this, Charlie. I really appreciate it. I was going to ask, if it's not pushing my luck . . . do you think there's a way I could talk to Mary too? What happened to her after Andrew died?'

He pauses for just a moment, and then lets out a low sigh. 'Her and Calum went back to Aberdeen. She kept in touch for a few years: Christmas cards to Isla and my wife, the occasional letter. But they soon petered out, the way these things usually do.' He looks across at the photos. 'Would you want to still be bound to the place that took your husband?'

I glance up at the piece of carved driftwood mounted high on the wall. *The sheep will spend its life in fear of the wolf, and then be eaten by the shepherd.* 'You said that he was never happy. That he'd had a bad past. What—'

'He believed he'd done something terrible. His guilt was like an anchor that one day dragged him down to the bottom.'

My heart stutters, skips a beat. 'What did he do?'

Charlie's tone turns impatient. 'He never said. And I never asked.'

'Why are you telling me all this now?'

He squares his shoulders and turns back to the bar. 'Three o'clock, Monday, at Isla Campbell's house. Last one past Sheltered Bay, 'bout six hundred yards east of Blairmore. You can't miss it.'

He stops after taking no more than a couple of steps away from me, turns around, and comes back again. His eyes are dark, their pupils big and black.

'Because it never sat right with me. Any of it. After he died and Mary left, it was like he never existed. And back in '99, I told you

– and everyone who came with you – that that was true. That he never had.'

'Charlie, I—'

'Maybe it's not your story you're here to write.' He reaches out suddenly, and I step back until I realise that he's untacking a small laminated photograph squashed between two landscapes. He hands it to me. 'Maybe it's his.'

It's a grainy colour photo of a young man standing alone in a grassy meadow in front of a hill, the blue sky and sea behind him. Tall and broad, in jeans and a wax jacket, arms folded over his chest. Brown-haired, with a thick beard, deep-set eyes, and a stoic frown.

'Is that Andrew?'

'It's Robert. He never chose Andrew. You want to write his story, call him by the name he chose.'

After Charlie leaves, I look down at that photo for a long time. Those eyes. That frown.

'Hello, Robert,' I whisper. And look briefly around the pub before slipping the photo into my pocket.

*

I regret not taking Kelly up on the offer of her sofa only when the lights of Blairmore are gone, and I can see nothing but the bouncing circle of my torchlight on tarmac. The night is dry, but the wind has picked up. I can hear it whistling through narrow spaces, howling around the cliffs and Ben Wyvis, and I imagine this little island shrinking slowly, smaller and smaller, scoured and consumed by the Atlantic winds and waves.

I stumble off the single-track road often – blaming the wind over the wine – and invariably into thick sucking mud. I've forgotten where Kelly warned me the worst of the peat bogs are, so am constantly searching for the white fluff of bog cotton with my inadequate light, convinced at any moment I'm about to sink so deep into the mud that I'll never be seen again.

I hear something behind me. A sound gone before I can properly place it, but somehow I know it was a sound that didn't belong. I spin round.

'Hello?'

My torchlight barely penetrates the last few yards of night. My ears rush with the wind and the white noise of trying to hear that sound again. Like footsteps maybe. Maybe. Goosebumps that have nothing to do with the cold shiver along my arms. When I'm caught inside a sudden crosswind, my light veers left in a wide arc that flashes over long grass and stony mountain and the darker shadow of another path maybe thirty yards away. The Coffin Road.

It's just the darkness. The utter *darkness* of it. I'm not used to it, that's all. I feel blind, and it's more than just unnerving, it's frightening. It makes me feel vulnerable in a whole new way, when I thought I'd already felt just about every kind of unsafe there was.

Still. As far as birthdays go, I've endured worse. I barely remember the one I spent in hospital with a fractured skull and broken arm courtesy of that silver Lexus like a roaring wall – I was too young – but a dozen other birthdays flash through my mind. Chaotic, noisy parties always on a razor's edge that invariably ended in tears or parental complaints. The friends who had loved my mum in primary school – the fun mum who sang rude nursery rhymes and sometimes turned up to the school gates in full evening dress or loaded down with bags of goodies – did not love her in high school. Or me. The last birthday that I chose to spend with Mum, I also spent with my only remaining friend, Becca. A far younger sixteen than me, quiet and sweet, her mum had died only two years before, after a long, never-talked-about illness. At my request, we had a quiet picnic in the garden rather than the big party Mum would have preferred; she'd begun sipping large G and Ts that she insisted were only sparkling water, before Becca even arrived.

A creepy clown turned up after an hour – dressed in denim dungarees and a canvas sun hat, face-paint smudged, his left canine more than three-quarters gold. I was pretty sure he was drunk. And then Mum had looked up at Becca, eyes dangerously bright, her smile wide as she glanced beyond her shoulder. *Your mum approves of your new haircut, but thinks you need to lose a few pounds.* I never saw Becca again.

It takes me a long time to reach the blackhouse. So long that I start panicking that I've somehow marched past the headland, heading for God knows where. And then I see it. I must have left the mudroom light on; it floods out from the door's small window, illuminating the path. I leave the road and glance across at the farm, but it's in darkness. I've resolved to only think about that – about *him* – tomorrow.

I can hear the sea now, loud and rhythmic. Insistent. I stop. Wonder if Andrew – if Robert – ever stopped here too, just to listen to the waves crashing against the rocks below.

I take the photo out of my pocket, shine my torch onto his face.

'What was it?' I whisper to the wind. 'What terrible thing did you do?'

Because I know about doing terrible things. I know about guilt. The kind that drags you down like an anchor, all the way to the bottom. And, just like the blackhouse, that can't be a coincidence either. It *can't* be.

'Why did you stop taking your meds, Maggie?' Dr Abebe had asked that first day he visited me on the open ward, his too-trendy cologne battling against alcohol gel and floral air freshener. 'You've always been so careful.'

And I'd thought of Mum's furious, tear-streaked face the day we came home with my first prescription of lithium all those years before. *It's a gift, Maggie! And you're giving it away – you're choking it to death.* I'd thought of looking down at myself through the wrong end of a telescope – a blurry, tiny me sitting at a grey desk inside a grey room. And feeling the worst kind of *jamais vu*. As if I were a complete stranger. Someone I'd never seen before.

Did she tell you the good news? Dr Lennon. Those cool, fleshy hands touching mine. A smile hidden behind his big moustache. *The latest scan shows significant metastatic regression. The last round of palliative chemo worked wonders, despite your mum's reluctance. She'll probably have years instead of months now.*

And I'd thought of Mum's face: thin, white, eaten by shadows. Only that light – that unrelenting light – still bright in her eyes. *It's coming. It's close. They're lying. Trust nobody. They all lie. You have to believe me.* My arms prickling from the memory of her nails. *The pain will send me mad, Maggie. The cancer is coming back and it will send me mad. I know it. I see it.*

But how do you tell a psychiatrist in a mental hospital that you stopped taking your meds, that you suffered the first psychotic break of your entire careful life, because you were no longer able to look at yourself in the mirror? How do you tell him that you want to go to a windy, dark island in the middle of nowhere to prove that a man you never met, never knew, was murdered, because that's the only way that you can see to live with yourself? With what you've done?

Because when I articulate it like this – even in my head – I know it sounds crazy. But when they started taking me off the drugs in the Maudsley, when I started emerging from the fog and back into grief and guilt and shame, this place was what I saw. The memory of me standing on that cliff edge in a spotty dress and too-big wellies, finger pointing out to sea, voice full of certainty. A beacon in the dark.

I wasn't lying to Kelly about what I do or don't believe. It *is* complicated. I know I'm bipolar. But maybe I'm something else too. I might have spent my life disbelieving it, denying it, calling it only dissociation and delusion, but now things are different. Now I *want* to believe it. I want to have once been a man called Andrew MacNeil. I need it to be true. And if what I said as a child about him being murdered was true, then maybe all of it was true. Maybe everything Mum ever said was true.

Charlie is wrong. It's not Robert's story that I'm here to write. It's my own that I want to rewrite. Because if I was once a man called Andrew MacNeil then I *can* live with myself. I can look in the mirror again and not hate who I see. It's selfish, desperate, even ludicrous – and probably the most dangerous of *dangerous roads*, but a drowning woman will grab on to anything to stay afloat.

A sound – that same sound – indefinable but close, makes me whirl round with a gasp. My torchlight sweeps over half a dozen or more silver-bright eyes and I nearly shriek. Until I hear a very baleful *baa-aa*, followed by the muffled drum of hooves.

But once the sheep have gone, faded into the further away night, I can still feel it. Something. Someone. I shiver, remembering Charlie's talk of thin places and spectre ships. I swing my torchlight around and around, seeing nothing at all but road and grass and bog cotton. But I don't say *Hello?* this time. I don't say anything at all. Because suddenly I'm too afraid – too absolutely certain – that someone will answer me. That someone is there, standing in the impenetrable darkness just beyond the reach of my light.

CHAPTER 7

Robert

Islanders will complain about anything. Everything. It's a full-time occupation. The only thing perhaps that gives us any sense of control in a world where the weather is wild, the sea is cruel, and the soil is chalky-dry or peaty-gley. And so we all sit in our homes and our pubs and our churches, week after week, month after month, complaining. And absolutely nothing changes.

'Right, so. We're agreed then that we need at least two more volunteers to cover the pub and shop over the run-up to Christmas. Three would be better; last year it was busier than the Glasgow Fair.' Kenny stands facing us like the wise leader he thinks he is, even though he's younger than Charlie and less than a decade older than me. Broad-shouldered and clean-shaven, always in check flannel and jeans, he looks more farmer than fisherman, but most dawns he marches down to the *Unity* moored at Bàgh

Fasgach like a martyred and grim-faced Captain Ahab never done with the sea. Or his own importance.

'Ask around. I'll put the rota up on the announcement board. If we've no more volunteers by next meeting, I'll pick folk, and it'll be their responsibility to find a replacement.' He looks around the room, flashes a grin. 'So, any other business before we get down to the more serious job of toasting Charlie's big four-O? There's a Macallan behind the bar with our name on it.'

'Just one wee thing,' Euan Morrison says. 'The University of Glasgow has had the extension on its dig confirmed.' He stands up, while pulling his too-tight tweed jacket down over his too-big belly. Anywhere else, Euan Morrison would be chairing these meetings; he is, after all, the one who owns most of the island. I should probably see Kenny Campbell as a welcome alternative.

'We knew it was coming,' Euan says, to quell some half-arsed mutterings. 'But this late in the year, it should only be a limited dig with a small crew. They're still promising to have it wound it up by next summer.'

Beyond the initial noise of the excavation, the Cladh Dubh dig has become just another lazy source of complaint, like the weather. Sometimes I walk out to the ridge and watch the archaeologists – come rain or shine – on their hands and knees in the long trenches on top of Tòrr Dìseart. There's a calm about the place that matches the standing stones beyond on the cliffs of Oir na Tìr. A stillness never disturbed by wind or storm or voice. Fierce and fragile; it reminds me of home.

The pub door bangs open, admitting an almighty gust of cold air. Jimmy strides in, grinning and still in his waterproofs. He works on a creel boat out of A' Chàrnach, though doubtless has an eye on a crew spot on the *Unity*, or even one of the deep-sea trawlers in the north. A fisherman's never more fearless than he is at nineteen.

His grin dies when he sees who's serving behind the bar. Alec's already put in his tuppence worth this evening, and none of it constructive. If complaining is an islander sport, then arguing is his. Men would sooner have a drink with me. I knew plenty of riggers in Aberdeen, and they all had the same kind of feral look about them: as if they left more than half of themselves behind every time they came back from the sea in those rickety Sikorskys. A couple of nights ago, he and Jimmy nearly got into a punch-up over something or other, notable only because for once it was Alec who backed down first.

'Pint, is it?' Alec says, and long, uncomfortable seconds pass before Jimmy nods.

Once he has it, he comes into the lounge, pulling off his wet jacket before he sits down.

'Glad I caught yous. Listen, I know we gave to the funeral fund for the crew of the *Leverburgh*, but I thought we could maybe start another collection for the families, maybe here in the pub?'

'Moira'll be happy to make up a box, Jimmy,' Charlie says. 'Thom, you okay to have it on the bar?'

Thom Stewart looks up from cleaning ashtrays on the other side of the pub. He rarely takes part in these meetings, preferring to loiter on their periphery under the guise of busy landlord, volunteering nothing until directly asked. He's got a wife, Kate, who Mary says won't say boo to a goose, and a one-year-old girl called Kelly, who I've seen crawling all over the pub floor until her hands and knees are black. While Thom just goes on standing behind the bar, smirking and oblivious to anyone but himself, cleaning out his ashtrays and polishing his pint glasses until they shine. He pushes his too-large glasses up the long bridge of his nose before folding his skinny arms and nodding. ''Course, Charlie. No need to ask.'

It's always irrational. The anger. Or perhaps not the anger – it comes, after all, from not wanting to feel anything else. The fear. Shame. Guilt. *They* are what is absurd. To hate fishermen because you hate the sea. Because you hate what the sea does to them. And their endless, pointless, stubborn resilience.

'I've a question for Euan.'

Everyone turns to look at me.

'Last month, I asked if you'd consider selling back some of the croftland under the community right-to-buy.' I try very hard not to react when Euan lets out a long-suffering sigh. 'The Land Fund will be reopening to full applications in a few months. I just want—'

'We've always looked after our tenants,' Euan says. 'We've always been fair. In fact, just last week I called in on you, and Mary said you were both very satisfied with your tenancy, no complaints at all.'

I stand up. 'You were at the blackhouse?'

'You were out at West Point,' Euan says. He squares his shoulders, but doesn't meet my gaze. 'If you've any concerns about rent or the upkeep of either the land or its buildings, make an appointment with me to discuss it.'

'You're not my *laird*, Euan. And what I'm asking for isn't unreasonable. The folk on Eigg have applied to buy the whole island, for Christ's sake! In case you've forgotten what the stone cairns all over the islands are for, we've a long history of rising up against greedy landlords.' I promised Mary I wouldn't do this, that I wouldn't allow my anger to ruin our new beginning. But the want to own my own land is rooted, quite literally, in my need to have solid ground under my feet. Something that is mine. Something that I can rely on. That I can trust. The islands are a part of me, and I came back to be a part of them. And to give Calum something that I never had. A home. Land can never be smashed against rocks and scattered out to sea.

'There were never any riots on *this* island. You haven't been here five minutes, and already you think you're starting a crofters' war? Jesus, man, this isn't the nineteenth century!'

Kenny, always the shark scenting blood, moves forwards. 'Aye, well, Thom's brought it up before too, hasn't he? More than once.'

Surprise makes me glance back at Thom still leaning against the bar, cleaning his ashtrays. He gives Kenny a sidelong look before nodding at Euan.

'And Robert's been renting the blackhouse and Àrd Chreag land now for more than eight months, so he's a right to ask.' Kenny glances towards Bruce. 'Your family's always leased more land from the Morrisons than anyone. What d'you reckon to it?'

'Could be it's time to revisit the idea, Euan,' Bruce says.

He's a few years younger than me; told me not long after I arrived that he took over his father's farm in addition to his own just five years ago, and I've some insight into how hard that must be. At five-eight and lean enough that nosy folk think he's always sickening for something, he nonetheless makes sure he's heard and never has to shout to do it. Never has to get angry. I've admiration for that too. And that he made no comment at all about the price I paid for the flock of Hebrideans before I knew what they were really worth. When he offered to help me with the tupping at the end of October, I didn't even have to swallow my pride to say yes – a sheep farmer's first breeding season has to go well if he's going to survive to a second.

'Well.' Euan has lost much of his bluster. He widens his stance, holds out the palms of his hands. The Diplomat. 'Indeed. Perhaps in the new year?'

'My *mamaidh* always told me better to strike while the iron's hot,' Kenny says with a smile. He could give no more of a shit for the land than he does any of us; his sport is in setting odds and pitting men against each other. 'How about we add it to the next agenda? See which way the wind blows then.' When no one objects, he gives a satisfied nod and starts heading for the bar. 'Right then, we're all done. Let's have a drink.'

When I stand up to leave, Euan blocks my exit.

'I don't know what your game is, Reid, but this is a warning: no one likes folk who stir up trouble.'

I look down at his fat pink fingers where they grip my shirt-sleeve. When he finally releases them, I meet his gaze and hold it. 'I'm not looking to stir up trouble, Euan. I just think a man should own his home, the land he works on. Same way I think a man should own only what he needs and no more.'

There are beads of sweat on Euan's round cheeks. And his jovial laugh is for everyone else's benefit, because his eyes are suddenly narrow-sharp and furious. 'That literally the hill you're going to die on, Robert?'

I turn away from him and walk out of the pub without answering or looking at anyone else. The air outside is bitterly cold, and I breathe it in, relishing the sting in my nostrils, the sharper pain as it hits my lungs.

'Hey, Robert. Wait,' Charlie says, opening the door behind me. 'You not staying for a dram?'

The two MacDonald kids, Lorne and Sheena, are playing down by the shop. Alec's wife, Fiona, must be behind its counter. I think about buying a bottle of whisky, but this isn't Aberdeen. It'll go around like a dose of the clap that I'd rather drink alone than for free.

'I agree with what you said back there, you know. Fact is, men like us always get squeezed by men like him.' Charlie snorts, and it fogs white in the space between us. 'Guess they don't like it when we squeeze back.'

'Never met a fisherman yet who cares more about the land.'

'I have land. Croftland. I'm not Kenny. I don't want to be a fisherman forever.' Something comes into his eyes then. I recognise it. Something haunted enough to make me feel ashamed.

'I don't want to be a farmer forever,' I say. And it's a peace offering, of sorts.

'Maybe we could job-share.' He smiles, and that look is gone. He's just Charlie MacLeod again. Smiling, charming, everyone's friend. The kind of man who sings loudest in the pub, carries women's bags, helps dig a neighbour's peat. Who'd never understand why anyone wouldn't like him. How that might even be possible. And whose wife looks about as miserably unhappy as any wife I've ever seen.

'Thom Stewart's been pushing for a Land Fund application?' I say, to change the subject.

'Apparently fancies being a farmer instead of a publican.' Charlie snorts again. 'And there's a reason him and Alec are closer than peas in a pod; they live for a good fight.'

He claps a hand against my shoulder. 'Listen, I bumped into Mary yesterday morning, and she mentioned you're having trouble with your ATV. I'm more used to inboard diesels, but an engine's an engine, and I'm a pretty good mechanic. I could—'

'I can fix it.'

'Okay.' Still smiling and nodding. Impervious. 'Why don't you come back in for just the one?' he says. 'It's not often Kenny puts his hand in his pocket.'

'Happy Birthday, Charlie,' I say, giving him the smile he wants. And as I start heading for the road, I barely – just barely – resist turning back to tell him to stay away from my wife.

*

By the time the windows of the blackhouse throw gold across the grass, my heart is lighter. The wind is at my back, the autumn air thick with peat smoke and seaweed. I stop and stand inside the dusk, and listen to the fury of the ocean.

When I was a young boy, I would lie on my bed and listen to the same ocean. And then I would drown it out with ghosts and kelpies and gods. Tribes and clans, fortresses and watch towers. Neolithic pyres set above underground caves and chambered cairns; dun beacons warning of danger in relays of fire along headland and cliff. I'd stack books around me like guardians. I'd read them by the white-bright light that always flooded my room in long, slow sweeps. Tales of warring clansmen sailing across sounds in the dark and creeping ashore to massacre their neighbours. I wanted to be Ketill Flatnose, the first Norse king of the Hebrides. Or Magnus the Third, defeating all the local chiefs as *flame spouted from the houses and the king dyed his sword red in blood*. All the gods and spirits and warriors; the epic sagas of battle and magic, love and betrayal, triumph and ruin. They were my only comfort in a world in which I could not fit. And then, after I destroyed that world, they were my only protection against what I'd done.

Mary's bright smile falters in its beginning when I push open the door. She gets up from the chair by the fire, mutes the TV.

'Meeting went that well, huh?'

I watch her walk over to the sideboard. The graceful calmness of her, the straight spine. I remember the first day I saw her: coming out of the Aberdeen City Council building and heading for the Tollbooth, walking fast enough that I was out of breath by the time I managed to catch her. She moved like she'd never ever had to get out of someone's way. That got me before anything else – more than how beautiful she was, alive in a way I had never been.

'Old Thunder was holding court as ever,' I say, taking the offered whisky from her hand. 'With Popeye the Sailor, his second.'

'You shouldn't call them that,' Mary says. Touches her glass against mine.

'You care what I call Charlie?'

This time her smile doesn't dim. 'I care what you call Kenny *and* Charlie. What you call all of them. I care that they might find out. Fiona says some of the men have been talking about how . . . unapproachable you are.' She pauses. 'They're our neighbours, Robert. I want them to be our friends.'

And unspoken is *You wanted to come here. You said it would be better than it was in Aberdeen.*

I drink the whisky down in one. I'd be willing to bet *unapproachable* wasn't the word they used. 'I told Euan I wanted to discuss the land tenancy again, and he said that he'd been round here last week. Why didn't you tell me?'

Mary presses her lips together, shakes her head. Looks at me with a stoic kind of resignation. 'He just stopped by to see if we needed anything. There was nothing to tell.'

'You asked Charlie to fix the quad.'

'I did not. I was making conversation, Rob. That's what people do.' Mary sets her whisky down. Her eyes go flinty. 'Stop it. Don't twist things. Don't do that.'

Mary thinks I've a persecution complex about this place and the men living here, and maybe she's right. Because the closer winter creeps, the darker my dreams and misgivings become. My distrust is born of experience, although I can hardly tell her that. But no one here knows who I am. Who I once was. I'm attacking when there's nothing yet to defend. And that might be how I've lived most of my life, but I've vowed not to do that any more. I think abruptly of my mother. Not the *mamaidh* who took me mussel picking and called me her good boy, her wee warrior. But the mother I was left with after my father died. As if all his rage, his bitter-sour disappointment had been passed on to her, like a *tairsgeir* or a parcel of land. If I do that to Mary, I'll never forgive myself.

I smooth my palm against her hair, her neck. 'I'm sorry.' I step closer, feel the heat of her breath against my skin, the drum of her pulse against my fingers. 'I'm a jealous, grumpy git.'

'You don't care about Charlie or Kenny or Euan Morrison. And the rent's fair, you told me that. But if you really care about owning the land, then antagonising the man who owns the job lot of it is pretty rash, even for you.'

'Pretty rash?' I smile, kissing the corner of her mouth.

'The swear jar's full. I'm trying to practise what I preach.'

I press her against the wall next to the fireplace, and she presses back. I groan when she moves harder against me, and lift her up enough that she has to wrap her legs around my hips and her arms around my neck as she laughs.

'The bed's over there,' she whispers.

'I want you just like this.' I kiss her, my fingers rough against the soft skin underneath her jumper.

She moans against my mouth, starts pulling at my belt buckle, the fly of my jeans, and the noise that comes out of me then is more relieved than eager. When I push her back against the wall again, the wood-framed picture next to the mantelpiece rattles.

Mary whispers *shh* as she stills my hand against her breast. But she's flushed and still smiling as she glances at the closed door. 'Calum'll hear us.'

'No, he won't,' I say. So that when she kisses me again, harder and longer, I can finally give in to all that burning heat. All that comfort offered like an Old Norse saga or a white-bright light. Slow and steady and wild. Full of triumph and ruin.

And afterwards, as she strokes fingers through my hair, long and slow, I press my face into the hollow of her neck and say aloud the words that are inside my head every hour of every day. 'I just . . . I want this to work, Mary.'

She shoves against my shoulders until I have to step back. Her fingers are cool, and yet they make my skin burn.

'Always so serious,' she says, pressing her palms against my face as she kisses me one more time. But her eyes are sharp and dark and unblinking. 'It'll work if you want it to. You don't need to own something to have it, Rob. You just need to believe that it's yours.'

*

Later, when the nightmares wake me up, I get out of bed and go into the mudroom. The door to Calum's tiny bedroom is open, and I lean my shoulder against its frame, watch him for a long time. The dark stars and blue-silver sky of his nightlight moving across his round little face and soft huffs of breath. The love I felt for him when he was born was terrorising, debilitating. The love I have for him now feels big enough to fill the world, the universe, yet still I can only think of it in increments and never as a whole. We none of us get the father we deserve.

I go back into the main room, glance at the sleeping Mary as I creep towards the kitchen. A change in the wind will wake me from the deepest dream, while she could most likely sleep through an earthquake. Still, I open the trapdoor as quietly as I can, the wooden steps icy against the soles of my feet as I climb down into the cellar. I can hear the wind howling around the eaves of the blackhouse, rattling my resolve. It sounds like screams ricocheting around high cliffs and bluffs.

Being afraid of the sea on an island is like being afraid of the fucking air, boy. All those nightmares that I had in the days and months afterwards – drowning, choking for breath through waves of salt and strings of seaweed. Those frown lines like furious scars cut deep into his face. Because he only ever saw my fear, and never once my anger. The rage that grew in me like crop fodder.

I think of lying in bed reading about the Norsemen of the Western Isles as that white-bright light moved slowly across the walls. Sometimes I'd track its comforting progress in seconds— always the same number, never changing. Mary is right. I can destroy everything we have without even trying. The trying comes from knowing that. From seeing it. We need our own white-bright light. To protect us from the dark and from the storms. And from ourselves. So I go over to the workbench against the furthest wall, reach for my cross-cut saw and one of the long lengths of pine I picked up in Bhaltos. And I get to work.

CHAPTER 8

The hangover's a doozy. More mental than physical, which, of course, is one of the reasons I'm not supposed to drink in the first place. I wake up far too early with a ball of anxiety in my stomach, and the first thing I think of is that someone standing in the darkness watching me. The second is of those weird dead birds still in the wheelie bin.

I get up, have a scalding hot shower, a strong coffee. I prop the photo of Robert next to my laptop, and start googling images of crows until I find one with black tailfeathers and a grey body; a sharp, curved beak. *Similar in appearance and size to carrion crows, hoodies or hooded crows are found in N and W Scotland and N Ireland. The hooded crow is often referenced in Celtic and Norse mythology and ritual.* I shiver, pull on a hoodie and go outside. Today, the low sun is bright in a cloudless sky. I glance across at the farm before going round the side of the blackhouse. I open the wheelie bin lid. The two crows lie side by side: black and grey feathers, muddy brown hollow wing shafts, deep dark eyeless sockets. Should I keep them as some kind of evidence? Of what? Are they a threat? A *go home*? A sign? I think of Charlie's thin place. *Where order meets chaos.* And it makes me angry. If it is a threat, and that seems likely given my reception and that I'm still certain someone was watching me in the dark, then I'm giving whoever's doing it exactly what they want. A reaction. But that *is* something I can control.

I slam the lid down, go back around the house. And I make myself walk across the headland to Will Morrison's farm before I can give in to the temptation to put on some makeup or change out of my hoodie. Up close, the cottage is freshly painted white, with a large red door. Next to it is a carved wooden plaque: *Tuathanas Àrd Chreag*. I hesitate, my fist poised in the air. This is just a casual neighbourly hello. It's research, that's all.

And then the big red door opens, and Will is standing inside it. Far too big, far too bright, and *far* too much the same as last night.

He grins. 'You're late.'

I glance at my watch. It's barely eight thirty.

'I've been up since five,' he says, folding his arms and leaning against the door frame. I pretend not to notice his tanned and thick forearms. Again. And when he looks at me just a little too long, that anxiety in my stomach twists into something that's not any better. 'Waiting.'

I clear my throat, ignore the heat I feel climbing up my neck.

'Come in,' he says, moving back to open the door wider.

The farmhouse is surprisingly small. A tiny galley kitchen next to a tinier bathroom. A white-painted living room with heavy furniture and a deep fireplace. It smells of peat and pine.

'Not much to the place. Euan had it built about eight years ago, just before I started farming the land. Front room, bathroom, and kitchen. Only two bedrooms upstairs,' he says, nodding to a narrow, steep staircase. 'Ceilings are low; they're pretty much in the roof space apart from the dormers. Would you like a tour?'

'Ah, no,' I say, and am appalled to realise that the idea of being in any bedroom with him seems more intimate a prospect than even ceilidh dancing. 'It's fine, thank you.'

He moves towards the kitchen. 'D'you want a coffee?'

I don't. My stomach is still recovering from my first, but I'd welcome the space from him it offers. 'Coffee would be great, thanks.'

When he returns, and far too soon, I actually find myself stepping back as he hands me my coffee. Our fingers touch briefly, and this time it does feel a little like being electrocuted.

'So, there's another Scots tradition you might not be aware of, Maggie.' He fixes me with that slow, generous grin again, nods towards the living room window. 'Never waste a moment of sunshine.'

*

We walk west, passing the blackhouse.

'See all those dark scars across the moorland?' Will says, pointing towards the blanket bog beyond the road. 'They're opened peat banks. We'll be harvesting them soon.'

'Who?'

'Whole village, whole island. Early April we'll start turfing, but the real work, the cutting, starts around May.' He smiles at me. 'Hard bloody work, but it's the best time of year. Family comes back from all over to help, and once it's done we have the mother of all parties. Lasts for days.'

I smile back. 'I doubt I'll still be here then, so . . .'

'Never say never, Maggie.'

I clear my throat. 'Those yours?'

He glances towards the half dozen sheep sitting on the road up ahead. 'Yep. Orange and purple dye's mine.' He claps his hands as we reach them and they get up slowly, balefully, before sauntering off onto the grass.

'Should they be here?'

'We don't build fences for the sheep. They run free all over the islands. Makes for better conservation.'

'Charlie said landowners got rid of the islanders and replaced them with sheep because they made more money.'

Will laughs. 'Man, you got the whole exploitation, injustice, and centuries-of-persecution spiel? He usually saves that for the summer tourists.'

As we reach the end of the road, the noises of the dig become noticeable again. The same rattle and creak of machinery that I heard yesterday.

'Okay, so as your official tour guide, I'm now obliged to tell you that you have two choices.' He points left. 'Southwest, which will take us via a very muddy Coffin Road to the equally muddy Sid a' Choin Mhòir and Loch Dubh.'

'*Sid a' Choin Mhòir?*'

He grins, showing his teeth. 'Lair of the Big Dog.'

'Next to Terror Mountain.'

'Oh, yeah, never let it be said we don't warn you. Fucking Miserable Glen would be more truthful. Stretches for a half mile between Ben Wyvis and Tòrr Dìseart, the burial mound the archaeologists are working on, if you fancy seeing that.' He points to the distinctly brighter right. 'Or, we can head northwest, which takes us to *Àite Lurach*, which means Lovely Place, and *Tràigh Mhòr* – Big Beach.'

'I think I'll take Lovely Place and Big Beach.'

'A wise choice, ma'am.'

As we head off the road and onto wet grass, we pass a high plateau enclosed by a stone wall.

'Kilmeray Cemetery,' Will says. 'All graveyards here look out to sea. You're always guaranteed a good eternal view.'

'Have you heard about thin places? Charlie said—'

'Christ, you really got both barrels, huh?' He moves closer, narrows his eyes. 'I'll tell you something Charlie probably didn't tell you about this place.'

'What?'

'The people who live here aren't allowed to be buried here.'

'*What?* Why not?'

He moves closer still, nudges my shoulder. 'Because they're still alive.'

I let out the breath I hadn't even realised I was holding. 'Ha.'

'This is just a *place*, Maggie. It's not mysterious. It's not magic. It's not any more spiritual than Glasgow bloody Airport.'

'Guess you don't think I'm the reincarnation of Robert Reid then?' I say before I realise I was going to.

'I heard about Robert in the pub last night,' Will says. He looks at the cemetery, and then back at me. 'The whole Andrew-Robert thing – and him living in the blackhouse? I mean it's pretty . . . wild.'

'Robert once told Charlie he was from Ardshader in Uig. And yesterday I found out that an Andrew MacNeil was born there in 1967.'

'Shit.' Will shakes his head. 'That's . . .'

My smile is small, my cheeks hot. 'Yeah.'

'There actually *was* an Andrew MacNeil? That's . . .' He shakes his head, briefly betraying his incredulity before schooling his expression again. 'Pretty wild. But anything's possible, right?'

'Yeah,' I say again.

'Look, I know it's not been easy since you got here. That people have been . . .' He stops walking. 'We moved to the island well after it happened, but Mum's always said it was still pretty raw. Lorne's and Robert's deaths both. It took a long time for the island to get over it. I guess you coming here again, it's just stirred it all up.' His smile is sympathetic. 'That's all the hostility is. It'll pass. I meant it last night when I said they're good people.'

I want to tell him about the dead birds. The person watching me in the dark. Even the real reason I'm here, why I've come to this island. But already I care too much about what he thinks. Ravi knew everything about me – he always insisted on that, on knowing every dark and cluttered corner, every urge and thought and want and weakness. And if he ever looked at me the way Will looks at me, I've forgotten it. I'm too used to pity and exasperation and instruction. I'm too used to being judged. And nearly always found wanting.

We walk in silence for a while. As the next headland comes into view, a building appears slap bang in the middle of it. Three-storeyed with dark basalt walls, pink sandstone window surrounds, crow-stepped gables, and a Saltire flying from a pole on its roof.

'Wow. That *has* to be the Big Hoose, right?'

'It's the Laird's Lodge, aye.'

'God. It's huge. No wonder Charlie—'

'Ah Christ, spare me the *Charlie says* on that,' Will says, for the first time sounding pissed off. 'Euan Morrison's done a lot of good for this island, and Charlie knows it. That house and this headland are just about all that's left of his estate after he sold the rest back to the islanders.'

'Sorry. I mean I get it, but *wow*. Look at it.' I shrug, pretending not to be worried that I've annoyed him. 'And the tweed suits. The glamtastic wife. It's—'

'Careful,' Will says. 'That's my mum you're talking about.'

'Shit.' This time, my face flushes hot enough to burn. '*Shit*. I'm sorry. That was so rude. I didn't know they were your parents. God, I'm always – everyone round here has the same surnames and—'

He puts a warm hand on my shoulder, and when I can bear to look, his smile is back. 'Relax, Maggie. She'd probably be very pleased with *glamtastic*.'

He laughs when I close my eyes.

'So you *lived* there?'

'Yep. Ah, crap,' he says, as a figure steps out the massive front door. 'We'd better get out of here before they clock us, or we'll never escape.'

We climb a low sloping hill that moves parallel to the coast, and which, gentle or not, seems destined never to level off. My hangover begins to reassert itself in hot chills and a pounding headache. Until we reach the top.

'This,' Will says. 'Is my *wow*.'

At the bottom of the hill is a vast green meadow stretching as far as the eye can see. It's gorgeous, dotted with silver-still lochans, gold winter heather, and boulders covered in moss and orange lichen.

It opens something inside my chest, precarious and fragile; a sense of longing that I suppose is awe or wonder. At this uncannily beautiful place full of a light and colour so at odds with the bronze desolation of those inland bens and glens. It's a childlike feeling – a thrill unknown but safe – the excitement of Christmas, of Halloween, of a ghost story whispered while tucked up warm in bed. I can feel the sting of ludicrous tears, and blink them away. 'It really is *lovely*,' I manage to say.

When Will takes my hand in his, that sting becomes worse. 'It's machair. Dune grassland formed by sand and broken shells blown from the beach. In a few weeks it'll be even lovelier. Whole place turns into a carpet of wildflowers.'

I let go his hand, self-consciously laugh. 'This is definitely more magical than Glasgow bloody Airport.'

I can hear the sea again once we've crossed the meadow and reached the nearest bluff. Its whole interior flank is punched full of holes, some as small as a fist, others as large as a dinner plate; some shallow, others deep enough to be impenetrably black. And everywhere – absolutely everywhere – jump small brown rabbits.

'Dune systems are magnets for warrens. Though I think this place is probably the rabbit equivalent of Mecca.' Will smiles. 'Or Magaluf.'

The bluff is steep, and close to the top the wind begins whipping around my head, pulling my hair and watering my eyes. Will helps me up the last few feet and I keep holding his hand even though I no longer need to, as I look down at another deserted beach of pure white sand and clear turquoise water, the Atlantic stretching flat to the horizon.

'Big Beach.' Will rubs his thumb over the back of my hand softly enough to make me let go. 'No one comes here much because it's so far west. Swimming's a lot more dangerous with the currents and riptides, but I love it. This way. There's an easy path down.'

The sand dunes are just as deep and soft as on Long Stride, and by the time we reach the harder-packed sand close to the shore, I'm exhausted and sweating. Big distant waves crest and break in roars, rolling inland beneath crowns of spray and white spume whipped high by the wind.

'Two thousand miles of absolutely nothing but ocean until Newfoundland, not even a satellite island.' Will turns from the horizon, reaches out to tug on my completely wrecked hair. 'Gets a wee bit windy.'

I move back out of his reach, pretend I don't see the flicker in his eyes when I do. Because I can't do this; I can't let myself feel this: lust, and worse, *like*. I'm in recovery. This time I can't – I won't – rely on anyone else again until I've relearned how to rely on myself.

'So,' I say, starting to walk along the vast shoreline. 'How did you end up moving here?'

He lets me off the hook, falling into easy step alongside me. 'We were living in Kenilworth after my dad bailed when I was a toddler. Mum met Euan in Glasgow on holiday, clocked he was a man of means straightaway. And when he told her he was landed gentry *and* a widower, that was it, apparently.' He laughs at my expression. 'What? She's very resourceful, my mum.

'A few years after they got married, I was packed off to boarding school with my stepbrother, Iain – hated it worse than Nicholas Nickleby. Euan's first wife died giving birth to Iain. He resented the hell out of me and my sister, Heather. Mum too. Still does.'

'Where are they now?'

'Heather's in Edinburgh. She never wanted to settle here – not enough excitement. Or men. And Iain's down in London. Some kind of financial whizz. He never wanted the estate, or what was left of it, fucked off out of here just as soon as he could.'

'But you didn't?'

Will thrusts his hands in his pockets, looks out to sea. 'I tried. Went to Strathclyde Uni, studied engineering. I had this idea I'd go down to London, live with my dad in Balham. But . . .' He snorts, looks down at his feet and the sand. 'We lasted about a month. So I came back.'

Against my better judgement, I reach out and squeeze his arm. 'I have a shitty dad too.'

He smiles, but for the first time it looks like an effort. 'Probably wouldn't have worked out anyway. Wherever I went. Something about this place, it just got under my skin and stayed there, I guess.'

'You ever think of leaving?'

He gives me a sidelong glance, raises an eyebrow as he grins. 'That an invitation?'

'No,' I say, too fast, like an absolute idiot.

'I would,' he says eventually, with a slow shrug. 'For the right person.'

When I wisely keep my mouth shut, he lets go my gaze and starts toeing off his shoes and unbuckling his jeans. 'Fancy a swim?'

'What?' I try very hard not to stare as he strips down to his underwear in seconds, but it's impossible not to. His shoulders are broad and freckled; his muscles born of hard work rather than the gym, lean and ropey. Hair dusts his chest, follows a dark line down to his belly.

'Come on, Maggie.' He laughs, starts walking backwards into the waves. 'Live a little.'

And I swallow, because I want to. God, do I *want* to. I kick off my shoes, and after just one more moment's hesitation, start clumsily taking off my clothes, face burning. Will doesn't try very hard not to stare; his grin gets wider and his eyes warmer.

The water is freezing. It's so clear I can see the sand under my feet and between my toes. When I wade further in, I let Will take my hand again because those white-trimmed waves are big and high and impossibly loud. I shriek when they get bigger still, and Will catches me around the waist. He pulls me towards him, his hands warm, hair curling wet against his temples.

'Not so bad, right?' he says.

My teeth are chattering as I grin and hold on to his shoulders. And despite my *I can't do this* of less than five minutes ago, the blood fizzes through my veins and my heart *thump-thumps*, like a ridiculous cliché, like I haven't a care in the world. And then it's true. For a moment – just a single fleeting wonderful moment – I don't care about anything else at all.

*

We sit on the highest dune, sheltered against the bluff. I'm knackered and my skin stings. My mouth and cheeks ache from smiling. I look at Will's arms as he reaches into his backpack, the flex of their muscles, the dark ropes of their veins.

'Hair of the dog.' He brings out two plastic cups and a bottle of wine beaded with condensation.

'You brought wine?'

That long, lazy smile. 'I did.'

I'm suddenly acutely aware that if the subject of my research was Will Morrison then I've put in a very good day's work. I already know more about him than I do even Kelly. Never mind Robert Reid. I'm making a study of the veins on his arms, for fuck's sake. His smile when he hands me a cup half-filled with wine is warm and careful.

'Were you here in '99?' I say. 'When I first came to the island?'

He shakes his head. 'I would have been . . . around eight? Already well ensconced in the Scotstoun School for Boys.' He smiles. 'But I heard about you. You were like a Grimm fairy tale. Don't be a bad little liar like Maggie MacKay or we'll banish you from the island, that kind of thing.'

'*Really?*'

'Not really.' He laughs. 'A little bit really. D'you remember it? Coming here?'

I nod, thinking of that cliff, my pointing finger.

He whistles. 'I barely remember what I did last week, never mind when I was a wee kid.'

'I only remember bits, not much that's useful,' I admit. I won't tell him that those memories are just like the nightmares I've had about this place – vague and indistinct but always there. Enduring and indelible. 'What about Robert Reid? What do you know about him?'

Will leans back on his hands. 'Only that he lived on the island for a year or so until he died. That he was a farmer, a Lewisman, who'd left for the mainland years before. That he was apparently not a nice guy.'

'What about how he died?'

'There was a storm. One of those once-in-a-decade jobs apparently. Big swells, dirty sea. He went into the water and was never seen again.' He glances at me. 'That was a far scarier Grimm fairy tale.'

'Someone saw him? Actually saw him going in?'

Will nods. 'Think so.'

'I'm talking to some of them tomorrow. At Isla Campbell's house.'

'Well, hey, that's a good sign. Normally, no one can even agree on who's buying the first round after the bells without voting by committee. And if they've agreed to see you, then they won't mind you asking. I mean, I've always thought it was weird, you know? Why would anyone walk into the sea in the middle of a storm? And why way out here, from this beach? Where the tides and swells are crazy on a good day?'

'Wait.' I lean forwards. '*This* beach? This is where he drowned?'

Will blinks. 'I assumed you knew.'

A chill works its way very slowly down my spine as I look out at the waves, think of those two thousand miles of absolutely nothing until Newfoundland.

'D'you think he could have been murdered?'

Will looks at me for a long moment. 'That what you're going to write about?'

And because I don't want to lie to him, I say nothing.

'This place . . . it isn't a council estate in Peckham or a back alley in Glasgow,' Will eventually says. 'I mean, don't get me wrong, there's plenty danger here. Plenty that'll kill you. But it isn't people. The whole Isle of Lewis and Harris, there's been one murder in over fifty years. What'll kill you here is the land. Or your own stupidity. And more often, the sea.' He leans back on his hands again, looks out at the waves, already wilder than when we were down on the shore. 'Their bodies never washed up – not his or Lorne's – they were just lost out there forever.'

I don't want to look at the sea any more, so I lie back, look up at the impossibly blue sky instead. Mum and I used to spend hours on Southend Beach, staring up at the clouds. She'd say that every one looked just like me. I'd always get mad about it; frustrated that she wouldn't play the game properly, until one day she turned to look at me with an expression so unusually solemn it almost seemed sad.

I see you everywhere, sweetie. On a good day, I even see you in the mirror. Her smile, I remember, had trembled a little, and I'd wondered if she was going to cry. *You are always the best thing, my darling, the most wonderful thing in my whole life.* At eight or nine years old, I'd squirrelled that memory away. Put it in a box that I seemed to know I would need later.

Now I wonder how many times she felt the same debilitating terror as I did watching that demon crawling into her coffin. How often she lost all sense of control, of herself. Because everything changed for me that day in the crematorium. I don't know who I am any more. And if you begin to doubt one thing about yourself, you begin to doubt everything. Coming here, I know, is as much an escape as it is a hope for absolution. It's tempting to start from scratch. To become someone else. Someone with the conviction, the certainty, of that little girl who cried *I'm Andrew MacNeil!* Someone who has a gift instead of a curse. Someone who has nothing to be guilty or ashamed about. Wanting something to be true might be a very dangerous road to go down, but it *is* a road. It's somewhere to go.

'Shit!'

I turn to see Will lunge for the wine bottle as a strong gust of wind roars in from the sea. When I sit up, I catch sight of something beyond his shoulder. Someone is standing on the cliff above the western end of the beach, where the headland of Roeness starts stretching a narrow finger out into the sea. The figure is tall and straight and perfectly still, like the *Fisherman* monument at Long Stride. Watching us.

'Who the fuck is that?'

Will turns, looks up. 'Oh, that's Sonny.' He wipes the sand from the wine bottle's neck. 'Kilmeray's resident hermit. He's been living over there on West Point for years – long as I can remember – in

what's pretty much a one-room bothy. Folk take him food sometimes, but he's pretty self-sufficient, prefers to be left well alone.'

I watch that figure as he continues to watch us, and think of
that someone in the dark. I let out my breath only when he turns
away from the cliff edge and disappears down out of sight.

'Hey, he's fine. He's harmless.' Will touches my shoulder. 'He's
just Sonny.'

The words come out before I can stop them. 'You haven't asked
me yet. If I believe it. If I believe that I used to be Andrew MacNeil.'

'I figure you'll tell me,' Will says, catching my gaze and keeping
it. 'If you want to talk about it.'

I clear my throat. Scramble clumsily to my feet. 'We should
probably get back.'

He nods and stands up, brushes sand off his jeans. 'Kelly
mentioned you needed to go to Stornoway. I'll take you.'

'You'll take me?'

'Sure. I need to go anyway. Tuesday okay?'

And when he grins again and I nod without hesitation, without
any kind of reservation whatsoever, I realise Kelly was right. I am
in trouble.

CHAPTER 9

On Monday, I wake up early, and manage to potter about the blackhouse for a couple of hours before my restlessness gets the better of me. Even though it's threatening rain, I put on my mac and wellies and peer through the door's little window before stepping out onto the path. Every morning, I've been checking that no weird dead birds have appeared in the night; it's in danger of becoming an unhealthy habit. When I reach the road, I turn right, away from Blairmore. I'm tempted to go northwest again, to that valley of machair and rabbits and the roar of the ocean, but instead I turn southwest onto the muddy Coffin Road, heading towards the sounds of the dig.

I assume I've reached the Lair of the Big Dog when the way gets gloomier and muddier, and the sheer face of Ben Wyvis on my left is mirrored by a slow-rising ridge of earth and grass on my right. I've guessed, too, that this is Tòrr Dìseart even before the sounds of machinery and shouting grow louder, but I'm still relieved when the way opens up enough that I'm able to see the diggers and people those sounds belong to.

The ridge is bigger than I imagined. Maybe as much as a hundred yards across, and instead of one mound at its summit, there are two wide and low sloping banks, one significantly larger than the other. I climb up onto a grassy shelf that tracks up the flank of the ridge, growing steadily steeper until it reaches the top.

The summit is a hive of activity. As many as thirty people are milling around the site or hunkered down in long shallow trenches. Close to the larger mound and the low wall of Kilmeray Cemetery in the east, a JCB loader is moving great buckets of earth, although it looks like most of the excavation has been carried out on this end of the ridge.

'Can I help you?'

The archaeologist is younger than me; short and fair-haired and frowning, her waterproof trousers and boots caked in old and new mud.

'I'm sorry. I'm Maggie. I'm staying up the road, and I was just curious to see what you were doing here.'

'It's okay,' another young woman says, moving round the nearest trench. She's wearing jeans and a bulky anorak, her dark hair piled on top of her head in an untidy bun, a streak of grey mud smeared from right ear to chin.

'I didn't mean to interrupt,' I say. 'I'll go if I'm—'

'Really, it's fine.' She smiles, holds out her hand. 'I'm Dr Kumiko Okitsu. Miko.'

As I shake it, the other woman gives me one last unfriendly glare before turning on her heel.

'I'm sorry,' Miko says. 'There's been a lot of . . . interest in what we're doing. It's slowed progress down a bit.'

'She means interference,' someone says in a familiar South London accent, and I turn to see a smiling young man with a shaved head and goatee.

'I mean *interest*,' Miko says, frowning at him. I look at the trench behind her and recognise Jaz crouched next to the JCB, deep in conversation with two archaeologists. 'There's nothing wrong with locals—'

'Checking up on us?' the man says.

'Jaz was on the first dig,' I say.

'Oh, he might have mentioned that,' he says, with a roll of his eyes. 'And what equipment we should be using, where we should be digging, how we should interpret—'

'All right,' Miko says. 'It's still better than the alternative.'

When Jaz looks over, I wave at him. He doesn't wave back.

'Femi Tinubu,' the man says, reaching out to shake my hand. He flashes his teeth, gives me a quick up-and-down glance that feels perfunctory enough that I'm only mildly insulted.

'Maggie Anderson. I'm staying over at Ardcraig.' I shrug. 'I guess I just got nosy.'

'Would you like a quick tour?' Miko asks.

'Are you sure?'

She smiles. 'I could do with the break. Come. This way.'

The three of us walk over wet grass to the flatter, busier part of the ridge furthest from the cemetery.

'An Cladh Dubh is one of the most important Bronze Age burial sites ever discovered in Western Europe. Tòrr Dìseart literally means "deserted mound", but the name was probably derived from the Old Norse word *Dysætr*, for burial place, because they're basically two round barrows raised over graves.' Miko nods at three archaeologists on their haunches inside the first trench. 'Bad weather's been moved up to lunchtime, so make sure you bag and tag, and are ready to cover, okay?'

I follow her and Femi round the end of the trench, where the ground becomes more uneven and boggy. 'This part of the site was never excavated on the last dig. Not after they made their big discovery inside the main mound.'

'Discovery?'

'Please let me tell her, Doc,' Femi says, grinning when Miko nods. 'So, a barrow's just a mound of earth and stones. At their centre are cut graves or, if you're lucky, a stone chamber, or cist, containing bones, cremations; ornaments, jewellery, that kind of thing.'

'And that's what they found?'

'And then some. They found two cists, and inside, two perfectly preserved bodies, one male, one female, buried in the Bronze Age crouch-foetal position.'

'The bodies were mummified,' Miko says.

'You heard of *bog people*?' Femi says. 'Bodies buried in peat bogs keep their internal organs and skin for tens of *thousands* of years. You can see their wrinkles, the fucking expression on their faces. Which can be pretty freaky considering plenty were sacrificed.'

'Wow.' I look over at the unassuming grassy mound. Think of

those black-brown excisions in the moorland between Ardcraig and the Coffin Road – Will's *dark scars* – and fight the urge to shudder. 'But this isn't a bog.'

Femi grins wider. 'And they weren't ordinary bog bodies either. The acidic pH of a peat bog preserves skin and soft tissue, but disintegrates bone. These skeletons were completely intact. Straight after death, they were placed in a bog just long enough to be pickled, maybe a year tops, and then they were dug up again. And then – get this – they weren't buried in those cists for another three to five hundred years.'

'Why?'

'They must have kept 'em somewhere. There are the remains of a Bronze Age settlement about half a mile away, out towards West Point. And if you keep heading southwest to Oir na Tìr, literally the Edge of Land, you'll find standing stones older than Stonehenge. This island, particularly this side of it, is a hotspot for human sacrifice, unusual burial rites, ancestral worship. Who knows what those mummies were used for?' Femi shrugs. 'Maybe they were spiritual advisors, maybe they were guardians to ward away evil. Either way, seems like they played a *very* active part in society for centuries before they were reburied in these barrows.'

I have an immediate and unwelcome image of one sitting at the head of a dining table.

'D'you think they were sacrificed?'

Femi's smile turns even more gleeful. 'We know they were. Skull fractures, stab wounds, you name it. They still have ligatures around their wrists and ankles.'

'Femi,' Miko says. 'Do you always have to make it sound like the plot of a Stephen King novel?'

'More like *Frankenstein*,' he says.

I look over at the three archaeologists still kneeling in the nearest trench, watch them painstakingly putting what look like dried clods of mud into large Tupperware. '*Frankenstein*?'

'They were composites,' Miko says. 'The bodies. They weren't two people. They were six. Radiocarbon dating in early '94 showed that their appendicular skeletons – that's everything but the skull and trunk – dated from around fifteen hundred BC. The trunks, fourteen hundred. And the skulls, sixteen hundred – around the time of Tutankhamun.'

'That's—'

Femi laughs. 'Rad.'

'At the time, it was a major archaeological discovery.' Miko looks over at Jaz, still crouched between the main mound and the cemetery wall. 'I've been trying to secure the funding to come here for years. We're thoroughly exploring all of this ridge for now, but what I really want to do is re-excavate the site of the first dig – the main barrow. It's not unusual to find other cists inserted into an existing mound maybe hundreds or even thousands of years after it was first built.' She frowns. 'We don't need the islanders' permission, but it's always better to get their blessing. Any discoveries on the site will attract new tourists to the island, and new funding for us.'

'*Quid pro quo*?'

'Exactly.' She smiles, and I see the steely purpose behind her friendly patience and politeness. The impressive determination. I think of the meeting at Isla's house later this afternoon, and some of my nervousness retreats. *Quid pro quo.* What's stopping me from trying to do exactly the same? Make them think they want what I want. How hard can that be? It is, after all, what people have been successfully doing to me all of my life.

CHAPTER 10

Isla Campbell's cottage stands alone on grazing land, a ten-minute walk past Blairmore. Miko was right about the weather; I have to battle against driving rain and wind until the road bends southeast. The afternoon becomes so gloomy, I realise I've reached the cottage only when I see its two front windows lit up gold beside the road.

When I knock on the door, it's not Isla who answers, but Jaz. We look at each other for a long awkward moment, while I try not to think about his cool hello yesterday; his snub this morning.

He glances behind himself before turning back to me. 'This is a one-time deal. No one wants to be talking about this again.' The reproachful look in his eyes reminds me so much of Ravi that I have to bite my tongue until the urge to defend myself has passed.

'I didn't realise that you'd been here. Back then.' I clear my throat. 'I'm sorry. I would have told you, when you picked me up in Stornoway. If I'd known.'

And even though I'm pretty sure he sees that for the complete lie it is, he nods and steps back, opens the door wider to let me in.

'Hi, Maggie,' Charlie says, from the gloom of the hallway. It's small and narrow; at its end are steep carpeted stairs. 'Everyone's in the front room.'

My nerves return with a vengeance as I follow him and Jaz into a living room lit by a dim overhead light and table lamps with fringed fabric shades. Isla is sitting in a high-backed upright chair next to the fire. Jimmy, the tall and forbidding prawn fisherman, is slouched in the only armchair. Bruce MacKenzie sits at one end of an understuffed sofa, and Gillian in its middle.

Charlie takes my sodden mac, and I perch awkwardly on the other end of the sofa.

'You wouldn't have thought the sun was splitting the skies yesterday,' I say, far too brightly. The peat fire crackles and smokes.

'This is Jimmy Struthers,' Charlie says. 'And Isla Campbell.'

Jimmy gives me another impressive glower from under his heavy black brows.

'Thank you for inviting me,' I say to Isla instead.

She turns from the fire. 'I'm furthest from the village.' Her gaze is direct and unblinking. Today, her silver hair is coiled into an oversized bun. 'We didn't want the MacDonalds upset. They won't talk to you. They always thought Robert had something to do with Lorne's death.'

'Did he?' I ask before I can stop myself. Remember Miko's *quid pro quo*.

The noise of the fire becomes uncomfortably loud when no

one answers me. Instead, Bruce and Gillian exchange looks I can't interpret and Jimmy's expression grows even more thunderous.

'We'll speak to you here, today, because now that Charlie has told you about the whole Andrew thing, we can hardly say no,' Bruce says finally, turning to look at me with those dark eyes. His expression isn't exactly unfriendly, but it's a lot *less* friendly than in the pub. 'And we'll answer your questions, because Isla is convinced that your coming here now and twenty years ago is for a reason – and perhaps ours is not to reason why.'

'To be clear,' Gillian says with a tight smile. 'We do *not* think that you're the reincarnated soul of Robert Reid. Nor do we think he was murdered. But, for the sake of peace and you going away for good this time, we'll tell you what we know about him.'

I clear my throat again. 'I found an Andrew MacNeil, born in Ardshader in 1967. It might not be the Robert Reid who lived here, but the age fits, the place fits.'

And regardless of anything else, I *do* believe that they were one and the same person. I glance at Charlie, who says nothing. The room becomes silent again.

'But it doesn't matter.' I take a deep breath and offer up the one thing that is not a lie. 'I'm not going to write a story about Andrew MacNeil.'

'Isn't that the whole point of this?' Jimmy growls.

'What about your boss?' Charlie says, his expression inscrutable.

'I'll give him something else. I don't want to become a sideshow again either.' And I absolutely mean that too. 'I'm not here to cause trouble. I'm just going to write a story about Robert. About his life. What it's like to live in a place like this, so remote, so wild;

the challenges, the rewards. The mystery of his death – what you were telling me, Charlie, about the sea, all the people it's taken over the years. People will be interested enough in that.'

None of it sounds remotely convincing. But telling them I wanted to write a story about me, about Andrew MacNeil, was a mistake, I can see that now – it's too confrontational. I can picture Mum sitting beside me at her dressing table in a red silk kimono, showing me how to smile at boys. *You catch more flies with honey, remember that.*

No one speaks for a long moment, and then Isla gets up from her seat. 'I'll get the tea.'

*

'Robert could be . . . hard work,' Jimmy says, brushing scone crumbs onto Isla's carpet.

'He's not the only one,' Gillian says.

'He had troubles.' Charlie shakes his head. 'Like I said, he was—'

'He was a slow puncture of a man,' Isla says.

'Isla!' Gillian says. 'You can't speak ill—'

'Aye, and you can't canonise them either.' Isla folds her arms. 'He complained about absolutely everything. The weather, the sea, the land, the sheep, the rent—'

'Euan Morrison,' Jaz snorts.

'The price of whisky,' Bruce says. 'Man never bought a round once.'

'We fishermen had a special black place in his heart,' Jimmy says. 'Didn't like us one wee bit.'

'D'you know why?' I ask. 'Why Robert hated fishermen?'

Charlie takes a long sip of what must now be cold tea. 'His father was a fisherman. They never got on.'

'You said he'd had a bad past. That—'

'Aye,' Charlie says, putting down his cup. 'Robert was an island all of his own. You couldn't befriend him. Only time he confided in anyone at all was when he was roaring drunk. You can't help a man like that till he wants you to. And you can't ask him questions.'

In the following silence, Bruce leans forwards on the sofa, clasping his knees with his palms. 'We always got on all right.' He looks down at his hands. 'I spent a lot of time over at Ardcraig, helping him with the farm.'

'And come the peat harvest,' Charlie says, 'Robert stepped up same as everyone else, giving a hand to those couldn't cut their own.'

'He was always interested in the dig,' Jaz says. 'Spent a lot of time over at the standing stones at Oir na Tìr too.'

'Wait.' I think of the grass-covered barrow up on the ridge. 'The dig – the first dig – that was going on the year Robert lived here?'

'Aye.' The ghost of a smile crosses Charlie's face. 'He was just about the only one not up in arms about it. Which, if you knew him, was a turn-up. Robert had a poker up his arse for just about everything.'

'Did he ever speak to you?' I ask Jaz. 'Tell you anything about himself?'

'He had an interest in the history of the islands, the Norsemen and early clans,' Jaz says. 'It was his hobby, I guess. He was full of questions, and I was an eighteen-year-old student who thought I knew all the answers. He visited Cladh Dubh almost every day.'

Jimmy sighs. 'Look. None of us liked the man much, but on an island like this, and in a village like this, that doesn't matter. We work and live together, get on together, because it's how we survive. You don't need to like someone to do that, but you do have to respect them. Robert loved his family. He worked hard, and not just for himself. Which counts for a hell of a lot more than a smile and a good sense of humour.'

'Why did you never tell the police?' I say, moving onto shakier ground. 'After he was dead, when Charlie told you Robert Reid's name was really Andrew? Why didn't you tell them?'

Bruce's shrug is almost violent. 'Robert changed his name for a reason, and we had to respect that. Figured the police would find out on their own if it mattered. After he told Charlie, he begged him never to tell.'

'Begged is one word for it,' Charlie says.

'Robert didn't trust anyone,' Jimmy says. 'We figured the least we could do was prove him wrong.'

'And we didn't want trouble.' Gillian frowns. 'Maybe that was wrong too, but we already had Alec screaming murder to the high heavens, and . . .' She shoots me a glare that's only half angry. 'It was a bad *black* time. The whole island was in mourning, and it was enough.' She closes her eyes. 'It was enough.'

When Bruce puts an arm around his wife and squeezes her shoulder, I feel a pang of guilt. That I know is about to get a lot worse.

'Will you tell me what happened? The night Robert and Lorne died?'

For a long-drawn-out moment, the silence is broken only by those crackles of burning peat. And then Isla exhales a loud, resigned sigh.

'There was a storm. A big one. We'd had a lot of bad storms that winter and well into spring, but nothing came close to it. They didn't normally have names back then, but they called this one Òrd na Mara, "Hammer of the Sea". Because it was the sea did more damage than the wind, rain, and lightning combined. It roared over beaches and machair, flooded fields and houses on lower coastlines, swept everything in its path away.'

'A fair few of us were over in Stornoway,' Charlie says. 'That weekend was the annual whisky festival.'

I think of those photos in the pub: years of grinning faces beneath the same wide Stornoway Whisky Festival banner strung between two lampposts.

'The storm wasn't expected out here until late on Sunday, April tenth,' Isla continues. 'But it came fast and hard on the Saturday instead. I was here with Moira, Charlie's wife. Looking after Sheena and Lorne while the MacDonalds were at the festival.' She pauses, takes a breath. 'Trying to entertain them and my son, David, with Hungry Hippos, if I remember right. And when that didn't work, with chocolate left over from Easter.' She stops, and as she pinches the bridge of her nose between forefinger and thumb, I realise her hands are shaking.

'Lorne loved a storm,' she says, staring into the fire. 'Loved the sea. He had a wee dinghy. He knew he wasn't allowed to take it out on his own, and even then, only on the freshwater lochs and lochans, but . . . you could feel the storm coming. It was like a charge in the air, like electricity, and it turned the kids wild.' She swallows. 'We put them all down for a wee nap, and he must have snuck out. Neither of us noticed. I was tired, I always get bad headaches before a storm. It was hours before . . . before—'

'Isla,' Charlie says low, going over to the fire and clasping her face in his big weathered hands. 'It was no one's fault, *a ghràidh*.'

'And Robert?' I ask, my voice small.

'I saw him down on Big Beach,' Jaz says. 'Couple of us volunteered to finish the storm prep at the dig while the others went to the festival. When the storm arrived early, I went out to check on the tarps and tyres around six p.m., and when I heard the waves – they were like mortar explosions – I couldn't resist going over to the bluffs at West Point to have a look. And there he was.'

'Doing what?'

'Just standing there. On the beach. But . . .'

He glances away from me, looks out the window instead, where the rain is tapping against the glass. 'You've been out there? To Big Beach?'

I nod.

'Half of it was gone. Just gone. The sky was black, and the storm clouds were racing inland from the horizon like smoke from a wildfire. And the waves.' He shakes his head. 'Even from the bluffs they looked terrifying. Between forty and fifty feet high in hundred-mile-an-hour winds, they said later.' He looks at me. 'You'd have to have been a madman to go down there. And he was just *standing* there.'

'What did you do?'

'I shouted, but that was pointless. And there was no way I was going down there too. When the wind and rain got worse, I went back to the dig.' He stares out the window again. 'And then I went back to my bunkhouse.'

'Most of the roads, particularly in the west, were flooded,' Charlie says, still crouched beside Isla. 'Rest of us had to stay overnight in Stornoway, till the worst of it passed. By the time we got back the next morning' – he squeezes her fist – 'they were both gone.'

I take a fortifying breath. Think of Will's *I've always thought it was weird. Why would anyone walk into the sea in the middle of a storm?* 'Did none of you ever think that Robert – or Lorne – could have been murdered?'

The atmosphere changes in an instant, and I want to take the question back. But how else can I move forward? How can I even start to prove anything at all if I can't even ask that one question? Or get an answer?

'No, we didn't,' Gillian says, her cheeks pink. 'You already know that we didn't. *Don't.* The sea took them.'

Charlie straightens with an audible pop of both knees. 'She's asking because she has to. It's what the papers latched on to when she was a kid – her saying that Andrew was murdered.'

I give him a grateful look that he doesn't acknowledge.

'If someone wanted to do it,' Bruce says, his face not flushed like his wife's, but cool and still, 'to murder either a wee defence-less boy or an angry fit young man – they picked a black dirty night to do it. They'd have been just as likely to drown themselves.'

'But how do you know for sure that they drowned?' I say. 'Or that they even went into the sea at all? Will said their bodies were never found.'

'If the tides and currents are right, a body can wash up further north on Lewis,' Jimmy says, expression impassive. 'Cliff Beach in Valtos has seen a few over the years. But, more often than not, in storms or high seas, bodies are washed out deep and never seen again.' He shrugs. 'Unless it's in a fisherman's net.'

'We found Lorne's dinghy a few days after it happened,' Charlie says, leaning a shoulder against the mantelpiece. 'Across the sound. Washed up on Hollow Beach.'

'And Robert? Did anyone actually see him going into the sea?'

'My husband, Kenny,' Isla says, looking down at the palms of her hands. 'When the *Unity* wasn't fishing, he'd work on the creel boats out of Carnach. He came back later than usual that day; Moira and I had just realised Lorne was missing and were going spare. I'd tried phoning the police, but the lines were down, and Kenny couldn't even raise the coastguard from the boat. He took our collie out, gave him Lorne's wee hat to scent. But it was too wild, too windy.' She sighs. 'He said later that he saw a man going into the sea on Big Beach, but by the time he managed to get down there, there was no one, nothing. The storm was so black ferocious by then, he wasn't sure he hadn't imagined it.'

'Robert told his wife he was going out to check on the sheep,' Bruce says. 'She didn't raise the alarm until he'd been gone a couple of hours.'

'But *why* did he go into the sea?' I say. 'Did Kenny see anyone else? Is he – could I ask him?'

'You'll have a job,' Bruce says. 'He passed.'

'You pass a bloody bowel movement,' Isla scowls, her small, wide-set eyes almost black. 'My husband died. He's dead.'

Charlie throws me a look of reproach I pretend not to see.

'You pass bloody bowel movements, eh?' Jimmy says. 'Want to get yourself to a bloody doctor, then.' When he winks at Isla and gives her an astonishingly charming grin, her shoulders relax, and she huffs out a low breath.

'Kenny said the man was running,' she says eventually. 'He thought later – we all thought – that Robert went in to save Lorne. That's what we told Mary and the police. Kenny didn't see anyone else, that's what he told me. And whatever else he was, Robert wasn't a man to kill himself. Not that way. If you'd seen the sea that day . . .' She shudders, and her voice loses some of its weight. 'No amount of despair would have driven a person to that.'

She catches Charlie's eye, and I don't miss the nearly imperceptible shake of his head.

'What?' My heartbeat quickens. 'Charlie?'

He frowns. 'It's nothing. Some folk said—'

'Alec said,' Gillian snaps.

'There were . . . we'd had a bit of a run of bad luck on the island,' Charlie says. 'The dig . . . they found some mummified bodies, disinterred them. Stupid superstitious nonsense, but—'

'What kind of bad luck?'

He shakes his head again. 'The weather was bad. Fodder crops failed. The storm season arrived late, but when it did . . .' He clears his throat. 'A few weeks before Robert and Lorne died, some sheep were lost too.'

'Lost?'

The atmosphere in Isla's living room has changed again. It feels opaque and oppressive. No one, I realise, is looking at anyone else.

'Killed,' Charlie says.

'*Killed?*'

'It happens. Dogs or polecats, even feral cats can attack sheep. And Hebrideans are a much smaller breed than the Scottish Blackface.' But he doesn't sound convinced. I think of brown hollow wing shafts, black eye sockets, deep and oval and empty.

'It was a bad time, like Gillian said,' Bruce says. His shoulders as set and tense as Charlie's. 'Tempers were frayed. People were stressed. Relationships were strained. And folk the world over are inclined towards superstition when so much of their livelihoods, their lives, their *survival* depends on the undependable.' His mouth presses into a thin line. 'Everyone needs someone – something – to blame. And Alec – not only Alec – blamed Robert first and the dig second.'

'A curse,' I say. Thinking of Femi's *This island is a hotspot for human sacrifice, unusual burial rites.* That image I can't shake of a mummified *composite* body sitting at the head of a dining table.

The rain is heavier. In the following silence, I can hear it drumming against the living room's windows, the wooden front door.

Finally Jaz nods, his expression blank. 'Triggered when we excavated the bog bodies.'

*

Charlie and I stay behind after everyone else leaves. As Isla and I collect cups and plates, I almost knock over a small wooden photo frame on the coffee table.

'That's my David,' she says, picking it up. 'Twenty-eight next week. I don't know where the time goes.' She wipes the glass with the elbow of her cardigan. 'I'd been told I couldn't have children, so he was our wee miracle.'

In the picture he can be no more than five or six years old. Small and knobbly-kneed, with a mop of blond hair and a toothy smile. I think of Kelly's *David lives in Glasgow. Single and hot as fuck*, and nearly laugh.

'I never forgave myself for that night,' Isla says. Her eyes are sharp and dry, but the frame trembles in her hands. 'For letting Lorne out of my sight. If Fiona had lost David, I would have killed her stone dead.'

'I'm sorry,' I say. And it sounds woefully inadequate, especially as I'm the one who's brought it all back up.

'I believe it, you know,' she says, and when she grips a hard hold of my hand, her own is so icy-cold I can't hide my flinch. 'That your coming back here now is important. Is for a reason.'

I turn round when I hear Charlie clear his throat; he's standing inside the doorway holding my mac.

'Come on, Maggie. Let's leave Isla in peace, eh?'

Outside, the rain has stopped and the sky is no longer overcast. Charlie and I walk towards Blairmore until I can't stand the silence any more.

'Who went to Stornoway with you that Saturday? For the whisky festival?'

For a long moment, he doesn't reply. And then he stops walking.

'I lied back there, Maggie,' he says. 'When I said that you asking if we thought Robert's death might have been murder was because you had to. I think this was a mistake. I chose to help you because I felt like I owed you and I owed him. But you're upsetting people I love. You're hurting them. And a witch hunt is worse than a sideshow.'

'Charlie! I'm not implying that someone here—'

'Well, who else?' he shouts, and I realise that he's furious. His eyes are flinty and his hands are fists. 'This is an island, Maggie! And that night, it was an island cut off from everyone and everything. Why the hell else would you ask me which of us were in Stornoway if you didn't think someone here killed him?'

'I—'

'You can't fit a square peg into a round hole, you know, Maggie. No matter how hard you try to jam it in there.'

'That's not—'

'Aye, it is. I don't know why you want it to be true. But you do.'

And because I'm not about to tell Charlie why – about Mum: *It's coming. It's close*; about the demon and the Maudsley and all the reasons I want to start from scratch, to be someone different, someone new – I say nothing. Maybe he would understand why I need to have been right about Andrew's murder to prove that I was right about once being Andrew himself. But I doubt he'd understand why I *want* that to be true – I can barely admit it to myself – the hope is still too fragile.

'Just leave it alone,' Charlie says as we reach the turning into the village. He looks at me with still-flinty eyes, but perhaps I can see something else behind them, something hiding. 'You got your questions, you got your answers. Just write whatever damn story you're going to, and then leave it alone.'

*

Before heading to the blackhouse, I stop at the phone box and call the bank. My savings have dwindled to almost nothing since Ravi left, and I spent almost the last of it on the blackhouse booking.

'Hi. So, um, my mum just died . . .' I wince in annoyance. 'I sent you her death certificate and a Grant of Probate a few weeks ago to close out her account. I'm just wondering how that's going? Her name was Vivienne Anderson.'

I listen to the distant clack of keyboard keys and think of London, all its noise and lights and people. 'I'm not seeing anything on the system,' the bank assistant tells me. 'Let me just go check. Please hold.'

I think of Isla's dark little living room with its peat fire and fringed lamp shades; everyone sitting around drinking tea and eating scones. Though she didn't hold them often, Mum's parties were legendary – long and loud. The evenings, always a slow-rising tide of people, so many people; the nights, always crowded and chaotic; the early mornings, melancholy and mellow. Portishead meant the end was in sight; I used to lie in bed, having been sent there only a few hours before, and listen to the slow beats of 'Sour Times' while watching the daylight crawl slowly across the ceiling and floor.

I was often the entertainment: plonked on a round leather pouffe, while Mum knelt at the opposite side of the coffee table, shuffling cards. She'd fan them out and have people pick one before turning to me with one of her big party smiles and asking me which card it was.

She must have had boyfriends, but if she did I never knew about them. Sometimes I'd wonder if any of the men at these parties – loud and laughing and swigging from supermarket-brand cans of lager – were more than just her friends. It would give me a hot angry feeling in my stomach; I didn't miss James, my stepdad, and certainly didn't want another.

I remember I'd been worried about the clown from my birthday party. For a while it seemed like he came to every single one of Mum's soirees, and too often I saw the two of them in corners, standing close and laughing.

'You're a clown,' I said once, aiming for mean when Mum sat him down to pick a card.

But he just laughed and winked, flashing that left canine, more than three-quarters gold. 'Only on my days off.'

'He's an actor,' Mum said, cheeks glowing and eyes happy-bright. 'He's going to play Javert in *Les Mis* at the Pavilion next month.'

I rolled my eyes when Mum gave him that smile she practised over and over in her dressing-table mirror.

'It's the eight of clubs,' I said, sullen and resentful. And everyone had cheered and oohed and aahed like they always did. Mum smiling and happy like she always was; getting even brighter under all the applause and wonder.

'See how clever she is, my daughter? How special, and she doesn't even know it.'

'Hello?'

I jump, nearly drop the phone.

'Sorry, yes I'm still here.'

'Your mum died in November? Is that correct?'

'I, uh, yeah. I haven't been well. So . . . there was a delay in me becoming executor. But I've opened an estate bank account now, and I was wondering how long it's going to take to transfer the balance?'

'It's currently being processed. With any luck within the next ten to fifteen days.'

'Okay.' I smile in an attempt to match her cheerfulness. 'Thank you.'

I hang up, and turn round. Even though it's only late afternoon, the phone box's interior light is on, a harsh bright yellow that makes the street and road beyond seem suddenly much darker.

The skin on the back of my neck prickles when I realise that someone is standing across the road from the phone box, staring at me. I'm exposed inside this box of dirty yellow light like a spotlight on a stage. The day has grown too dark to make out who, so I move towards the door, wiping the condensation away with my sleeve. It's Sheena MacDonald, her long dark hair soaking wet and flat against her cheeks. I let out a relieved breath.

When someone starts battering their fists against the phone box's door, I scream. High and wild enough that it scares me more – how alien the scream sounds, as if it can't belong to me. The door is wrenched open, admitting a cold blast of air and a roar of expletives. I recognise Alec's voice before I see his face: puce and gritted, eyes blazing.

'Get out!'

He grabs me by the arm and yanks me from the phone box. For a moment, I wonder if he's going to hit me, and then Sheena is next to us, pulling her father backwards with more strength than I would have expected.

'Dad, stop. Stop.'

And I realise, with horror, that Alec is crying. Great ugly sobs that shudder through his body, bending him almost double.

'Dad.' Sheena half hugs him, half wrestles him away. 'Go on home now. Go home.'

He nods at the ground, suddenly defeated. He turns towards the village, and then stops, turns back to me, his spine straightening. The rage in his eyes is banked but it's still burning. He points a very steady finger at me, his voice low.

'Get. Out.'

Sheena waits until he's gone. Watches me with the same narrowed eyes, her lips pressed thin.

'Losing Lorne almost killed my parents.'

'I'm sorry.'

She violently shakes her head. 'No, you're not, because you're still here!'

'I'm nothing to—'

'You're everything to do with it. Don't fucking lie! You didn't think coming back here would upset anyone, stir up bad memories?'

'Sheena, I . . .' When I move towards her, she steps quickly back.

'You have to leave.'

And when I realise that it's not anger in her eyes, but fear, shining and dark, another shiver runs through me, plucking at my skin.

She swallows, and then turns away. 'You *have* to.'

I wait until she's gone, until I lose sight of her completely beyond the first set of white houses into Blairmore. And then I walk reluctantly back to the road, fumbling with the torch on my phone as I eye the wet gloom of the west with sudden dread.

Something new has occurred to me, something that should perhaps have been obvious before I came here, never mind since Charlie told me about Andrew from Ardshader. I think of his *Why the hell else would you ask me which of us were in Stornoway if you didn't think someone here killed him?*

Because what if that really *is* true? What if someone really did murder Robert? And what if they're still here? Watching me stumble about with my lies and clumsy questions. Following me in the night and leaving weird dead crows on my doorstep. That's not fantasy. It's not projection or overreaction. It's not even trying to fit a square peg into a round hole.

It's not impossible.

I move my torchlight slowly over the dark, impenetrable entrance to the Valley of Ghosts. And shiver again. *Be careful what you wish for.* Because it's not impossible at all.

CHAPTER 11

Robert

I'm on the way to the shop when I hear Charlie shouting my name. I think he's been shouting it for a while; when I turn round he's standing in the road with his hands cupped around his mouth. Some days it's as if Robert was the name I was christened with – I can't remember ever being anyone else. And other days, I completely forget that I'm him.

I'm bone tired. It's barely five o'clock and it's already twilight. In a week it'll be December, and I'll have to start thinking about bringing the sheep into the barn or at least the in-bye land. And with little to no bere barley or fodder oats, more savings will have to go for winter feed.

Charlie beams at me as if we're lifelong mates. 'Saw you passing. I'm just having a wee get-together at mine, thought maybe now you'd fancy that dram?'

It's been weeks since the meeting in Am Blàr Mòr when I last rejected his offer of a drink. For no other reason than his smile, his bloody resilience. I don't think Charlie's a bad guy, but I can't understand him; I'm absolutely nothing like him. And I don't want Mary realising it. What kind of man she could choose instead – cheerful, impervious, *easy.*

'Aye,' I say. 'Maybe I do.'

He looks surprised, but quickly recovers, turning back towards his gate with a grin. Charlie's get-togethers don't happen in the house, but in a large black shed at the edge of his croftland. Many's the time I've passed it lit up gold and loud with laughter. Tonight, it's quiet, most likely due to the early hour, although as we get closer, I hear voices and regret saying yes.

'Look who I found on the road,' Charlie says, as he opens the door. Over its lintel is a wood-carved sign: *Charlie's Bothan.*

'Shut the door, man,' Thom Stewart says. 'It's bloody Baltic.'

The shed is surprisingly spacious. A fuel-burner crackles and glows in one corner, giving out waves of heat. Cushioned wicker chairs are set in a circle around a big wood table covered in pint glasses, cards, and chips. Thom, Jimmy, Alec, and Bruce are sitting around it.

'Hey, Robert,' Jimmy says, turning to shake my hand.

'Pull up a pew,' Bruce says. 'It's good to see you.'

'Don't scare him off,' Charlie laughs, and then turns it into an unconvincing cough.

'What's the game?' I nod towards the table.

'Texas Hold'em,' Thom says, his sleeves rolled up past his skinny elbows, exposing homemade tattoos. READY and RFC in already fading blue. 'But Jimmy here's a born fuckin' cheat.'

'It was a misdeal!' Jimmy shouts, but he's grinning. 'Christ, everyone saw it. A misdeal's a burn card.' He leans back in his seat. 'They're your rules, man.'

'Chancer.'

'Here.' Charlie hands me a pint of red-gold beer. 'Homebrew, but after the first five it doesn't taste too bad.'

'Thanks.' I go to sit down in the empty chair, but Jimmy raises his palm and stands up.

'Here, take my hand. I'm off.' He thrusts his cards at me. 'I'll split the winnings with you.'

'Aye, in your dreams,' Alec says.

'It's only gone five,' Charlie protests. 'Bad enough Kenny's cried off with nothing but a wee cold. What's your excuse?'

Jimmy grins. 'Got a hot date with a lassie in Brèibhig.' He pulls on his waterproofs and claps a hand on my shoulder as he leans in close to my ear. 'Raise more than once in a row and most of them start folding like cheap tents.' And then he disappears out the door in a gust of dark wind.

'Young love, eh?' Thom shakes his head and his laugh has a bad edge to it. ''Course, you'd know all about that, Robert, with a pretty wife like yours, eh?'

I still know Thom Stewart no more now than I did nine months ago when I first arrived on the island, and it's mostly deliberate. He's only in his twenties, but he reminds me of the old men who trawled the islands for work where they could get it, ex-skippers who'd lost their boat to the sea or the bank, or black landers who'd been caught and had their licence taken away. They'd wait on the slip at Na Bàigh for the crews to come down from Àrd Shiadair and Èinis, and whenever my father gave them short shrift, they'd look at him with beady, hungry eyes and the same smirk that's pretending to be friendly. I might not understand men like Charlie, but I understand men like Thom Stewart, all right.

'Okay, Robert,' Charlie says. 'I'm dealer. Thom's opened with the minimum bet of two quid. What'll it be?'

Jimmy's hand is shit: an ace of clubs and nine of hearts against the flop's king, three, and five of spades.

'I'll raise. Two quid.'

'Check.' Bruce frowns, chucking coins onto the pile. 'How's the ewes doing?'

'Good,' I say. 'Great.'

But I don't know if that's true. The vet will be coming over from Langabhat in two weeks, and only then will I know how many lambs to expect in March. The ewes seem tired and listless, but maybe that's what happens when they're pregnant. Since Bruce helped with the tupping nearly a month ago, I've been on a new kind of edge that feels far too fragile. Everything rides on a good lambing season. I don't want to tell Mary how bad it is, how bad it could get, although she can look at the bank balance same as me. And I doubt she'd see much wisdom in raising bets on a shit hand of poker.

'Listen,' I say. 'I've been meaning to bring you round a bottle—'

Bruce holds up a calloused hand. 'Ach, no worries. Happy to help.' But he looks away, as if suddenly reluctant to meet my eye.

'Island life, eh, Robert?' Thom says, giving me that sly, probing look he likely thinks makes him seem clever. 'Quite a change from living in the city, I bet.' As if I haven't been living here for almost a year already; as if he doesn't know that I was born as much a Western Islander as he was.

'Thom was just telling us the Land Fund application's about ready to go,' Charlie says. 'You seen it yet, Robert?'

'No,' I say, and my mood darkens even further at the obvious exclusion. When I look at Thom, he's too busy glaring at Charlie to notice. 'I would have been happy to help.'

'Too many cooks and all that,' Thom eventually says with a cold smile.

Alec snorts. 'And probably best to get it filed before Euan changes his mind.'

Bruce shrugs. 'He sold Cladh Dubh to Historic Scotland thirty years ago.'

'Aye, well.' Alec smirks at Thom. The two of them are thick as thieves. Always leaning against the bar at Am Blàr Mòr, heads together, glowering at anyone who comes close. 'I'm betting they gave him a far better price than he'll get from us or the government.'

'He'll get a better price than he deserves,' Thom says, downing the last of his beer with a scowl. 'Are we playing this hand or what?'

I raise on the turn, and then the river, until only Thom and I are left in for the showdown. He grins at me with tall leaning teeth, pushes his big specs up the bridge of his nose. 'Two pair, kings and threes.'

I put down my cards. 'Three nines and king, ace kickers.'

Thom's curses drown out Bruce's laugh. And Charlie whistles loud, starts pouring drams of whisky.

'You know,' Alec says, giving me a look that instantly makes me feel wary. 'If you're interested, me and Thom run a serious game for a few guys over in *Ùrbost* once a month. You're welcome to join us.'

'Aye. Maybe,' I say, after a pause. Because – Land Fund snub or no, poker game or no – Mary would probably kill me if I didn't at least pretend to be interested. Though I've no intention of playing a *serious* game of cards with anyone. Let alone Alec and Thom. I've gambled far too much already.

*

I don't leave. I've plenty opportunity as the others pull on their coats and head back to their homes, one by one. But by ten p.m., I'm still there, sitting at Charlie's table, drinking his whisky and home brew. Charlie makes no comment on it, even when we're the last men left. Only feeds more peat into the stove and sits back down.

'I should be heading home,' I say, uncomfortable in the sudden silence, and in my strange need to stay.

'Ach, it's early yet. Mary'll not mind, I'm sure,' Charlie says, pouring us both another whisky. 'You work hard enough for two men, Robert.'

Ordinarily, this would make me bristle; I'd find some kind of insult in his words, a smug dig behind his smile. But tonight I can see it for what it is, perhaps even him for who he is. There *is* no insult, no dig. Perhaps there never has been.

'Still, it's never enough,' I admit, and it feels shockingly good to do it. 'Unless nearly all the ewes are pregnant, I'll be lucky to survive this year.'

If Charlie's surprised by my words, he doesn't show it. 'They're a prolific breed, the Hebrideans. Reckon most of them not shearlings will give you twins, no worries.'

I nod and drink my whisky even though I don't share his confidence.

'You'll be less glad of that come March,' Charlie grins. 'Lambing season can be pretty brutal. You'll need help.'

'I'll be fine.' Having Bruce around the blackhouse is one thing; the rest of the village something else.

'No sin in it. No weakness either.' Charlie shrugs. 'One man can't lamb an entire flock, Robert. Not even a man like you.'

That I do bristle at, but Charlie is quick to shake his head, refill our glasses. 'You're a Lewisman, so you know how things are done. Everyone helps. That's all.' He looks at me a little too long. 'What is it you're really afraid of, Robert?'

'The storms.' I say it without thinking, without reserve. Why, I don't know. Perhaps just to say it. To someone. Because the endless toil, the uncertainty and worry, the perceived slights, the dwindling savings, all of it really is just the storms. We're already long overdue, and in Àrd Shiadair that always meant the first one of the season would be a doozy. My father's word; scornful and rolling-eyed. *Let it fuckin' try.* The flash of anger I feel is a reflex too: old and weathered thin. 'A fisherman should know better than me to be afraid of them.'

'Aye, maybe,' Charlie says, but I see the shadow that passes over his eyes. The fear that he pretends he doesn't feel.

He picks up his whisky. Puts it back down, undrunk. 'Why is it you hate fishermen, Robert?'

'Fishermen hated me first,' I say, worried now about the looseness of my tongue. 'Why did you become one?'

Charlie shrugs. 'The MacLeods of Cill Maraigh have always been fishermen. My father worked the pelagic fleet out of Port Nis his whole life.'

I look down into my glass, swirl the brown liquid around and around. 'My father ran three boats. Seventy-foot wooden-hulled herring drifters and whitefish seiners. Just about every man in the area worked for him.'

Some of the whisky sloshes over the rim of the glass, splashing my hand. I was born when my father was at sea and the tide was rising. Both good omens for growing up into a good fisherman. If the tide had been on the ebb, I'd have been doomed to perish by shipwreck.

'I was his only child. And instead of storms and boats and fish, I liked to stay indoors, I liked to read books. I wanted to become an archaeologist, a teacher, a historian – anything but a bloody fisherman.'

I think of that hard, lean face, weathered harder by the sun and the sky and the sea. The contempt in his grey-dark eyes. Sometimes, the sorrow.

'He thought it was a choice. A rejection. But it wasn't. I would've given anything to want the life he wanted for me. To love the sea.'

His belt had been made of thick cured cow hide. Its buckle, Sheffield steel. Sometimes he would cry when he hit me; I'd hear it behind his voice. *There's no salt in your blood. None. You're fuckin' hers, all hers.*

I was eight, the only time I was ever on one of his boats. The *Acair*. We had to go as far out as the continental shelf, some sixty miles northwest. It was a good day, calm and sunny. But the minute we reached the edge of the shelf and the water turned black and deep, I filled up with dread like melting tar. I watched the nets and cookies and floats disappear down into that blackness, their luminous pink swallowed up – *down* – and when the engines started again, I imagined those nets dragging through that dark, over rock and wreck. All those *things* down there, things none of us could see, waiting to grab and yank. And sink.

'I can't explain it,' I say now. 'Where it comes from. Because it's not just fear in me. It's hate. The Norsemen believed in spirits that lived under the sea, the *Sjóvættir*, that could, on a whim, pluck you from the ocean's surface and pull you down to your death. They would make sacrifices to Ægir to keep themselves safe, and carve dragonheads into their bows and sterns.' I shrug, my face hot. 'That day on the boat, I had to be force-fed three measures of rum before I calmed down enough to just speak.'

There had been no sorrow in my father's eyes that day. Only rage. And shame so deep, it turned him to stone: a statue hunched and weighted down. I remember the wind whipping around our heads; wailing echoes through the gantry and wheelhouse. The deck vibrating under my feet as the power block pulley hauled in the net and its lead ropes and neon buoys. Bulging, writhing. Reeking of the sea. I remember my father throwing the first fish he could catch back into the water. The second, he sliced open at the belly, and I willed my stomach to stop churning as he held that dying fish in his fist, sprinkling its blood into the waves. A sacrifice to the sea gods for luck, for a good catch.

I drain my whisky. My swallow burns. 'And then, one day. There was the storm.'

When they left at dawn, the sky was pink and clear and cloudless. I watched them from my bedroom window, tracing their shapes through cold condensation. Three boats rigged for fly-dragging: coils of seine-net rope and cages of headline buoys stacked on the side decks in place of the long wooden rollers for hauling drift nets.

'He didn't like fishing for bottom-feeders like haddock or cod, but this was during the herring ban; no one had a choice. And pretty soon they were having to go beyond inshore waters to find them.'

Charlie only nods. Moves a finger around the rim of his mostly empty glass.

'It was my tenth birthday the day before they left.'

The peat has burned down to smoking embers. A chill has crept under my skin. Mamaidh had baked a sponge and wrapped two weighty encyclopaedias in brown greaseproof paper – one, an archaeological study of Skara Brae; the other, *Norse Mythology and Legends II.* She knelt on the kitchen floor and held the backs of cold fingers against my cheek.

Hide them from your dadaidh. *Tell him I got you that instead.*

A fly-fishing rod and reel leaning against the back door.

That night, after mooring the boats at Na Bàigh, he came back to the house and up to my room. And when he found me reading one of those encyclopaedias, he didn't take it from me, he didn't rip its pages from its spine. He didn't even pull open his buckle and slide the belt from its loops. He just fixed me with that hard, *weighted* look; watched me with it long enough that I started to shake. That next morning, after I'd watched the boats leave, my stomach tight and cold, I went downstairs and found the fly rod still leaning against the back door, splintered into three pieces.

'They went out far. Maybe as far as the continental shelf edge, even though it was late in the season and the storms were coming,' I tell Charlie. 'His crews always trusted him to keep the gear square and hauling speeds tight. He knew the sea depths and fishing grounds, the local tidal streams. No one was a better fisherman than him.'

I look down at the table. At my fingers.

'But the weather turned. Sky went dark like night. The sun was winter-low. Its reflection in the sea made your eyes water.'

It's easy to remember the rain like cold pinpricks, turning the sand black. The wind, high and wild. Fifty and then sixty knots. The sea white with the crests of heavy rolling waves. And that sunlight: a line of bright silver below the black-dark moving sky; above the black-dark rising sea.

'When they came back it was evening. Because of low tide and the heavy following sea, they couldn't put in at Na Bàigh, so they rounded the headland and made for the inlet below the village.'

I stop. My hands have begun to shake. The air, I remember, had smelled like smoke: sweet and sharp. And then it brought lightning: throwing distant spikes into the horizon. I hadn't been scared then, standing alone on the beach. And I was no longer angry. Not like I'd been that morning, tracing their shapes against the window as they left, my father's hunched shape just visible inside the wheelhouse of the *Acair*. But there *was* something in my heart, too big and strange even for awe when I saw that first boat trying to come round Àird Èinis.

'The light on the headland wasn't there. Didn't warn them. And so they came too close. The forward boat smashed against the rocks before they even got around it. The other two didn't ground, but their keels were ripped open and they started taking on water. By the time they reached the inlet, they were already sinking.'

I wasn't alone for long after that. Àrd Shiadair and Èinis would come alive in storms when boats were still out. As if the lightning were touch paper and the thunder a siren. Above the bluffs alarm built and grew to a golden glow, and then was filled with people and torches searching the horizon, the sea, the disappeared light that had become a black tower – a shadow like something burned against a wall. There was a scream, I remember – just one and not loud at all: thin and high and short – when the two remaining boats were spotted close to shore. One was the *Acair*, even in the gloom, I recognised the shape and colour of my father's bloody-minded fury, his determination.

The men came down to the beach then to help bring them in; the women stayed high to watch and shine their lanterns and torches. It would have been different probably, if those boats hadn't almost grounded, if their hulls weren't already stripped raw. Perhaps the fishermen would have made it through the foaming surf and storm unscathed. Instead, as both boats sank by their sterns, the sea rolled in and swamped them a few hundred yards from shore, sweeping every man overboard and taking them back into deep water. None of the shelter-aft life rafts deployed. The canisters had been lashed to their cradles to stop them falling overboard in heavy seas, and they went down with the boats.

The sea stormed up the slipway as a motorboat was launched, only to be smashed against the inlet's southern cliffs and turned around. Another went, with frantic shouts and bouncing lights, to save those in the first. Its engine a low roar, spluttering into smoke once it managed to regain the shore, where it tipped onto its side like a black clock beetle.

A half-hearted smur of sleet began, turning the rain into pins. I stood on the beach, full of that sour-tasting awe, my feet sinking and stuck as I watched those waving arms appear and disappear in quicksilver strokes of torchlight and sea. The fishermen's shouts were distant enough to sound alien, overwhelmed by those on the shore and the storm raging over their heads. But I knew every man in those boats. Knew which village they came from, what family. Some were boys, only a few years older than me. Though none were my friend; both villages sought my father's good will as if he were God. I wondered which of those arms were his – strong arms tanned like hide; it seemed incredible to me that he would ever wave for help at all.

The *Acair* was swept high and southwest, battered mercilessly against the cliff below Àrd Shiadair, until every part of it – every timber and metal beam; winch and drum; net and cage, buoy and grass rope – was gone.

Every boat launched after that, skiffs and dinghies, even the old wooden *sgoths* equipped with only oars and men, all had to turn back or be turned back, most often rescued. Until it seemed as though their efforts were mere distraction from those waving arms, those distant screams, those faces we knew but couldn't see.

The wailing began when the night arrived. It came from those torches and silhouettes high above the beach, standing against the stars like angels in a nativity scene. Over them and the storm, and the desperate shouts of those still down on the shore, I could hear the bell out on the rocks begin to sing of high tide. The sand vibrated under my feet in a nasty hum as though I were back on the deck of the *Acair*, back on the edge of that underwater cliff into nothing but blackness. The air was filled with spume; it washed out my gaping mouth with salt. And the wind raged and raged against all of it – all of us – until it was too late to matter.

The storm blew itself out as quickly as it had blown in. By the time the tide bell had been muted by the sea, the rain had stopped and the wind had died. The wailing had stopped too, and those torches scanned the horizon and low waves in frantic searches. But there was nothing. Not even splintered wood or abandoned netting; the neon-yellow buoys and floats of the drag lines. No evidence at all that there had ever been eighteen men and three boats coming home loaded with catch. Until the gulls and gannets flew from clifftop shelters to gorge themselves on an unexpected feast, their greedy cries drowning out all that eerie silent hope.

And I looked away from the birds and the sea, the men on the beach and the women on the bluffs – and out towards the high dark summit of Àird Èinis where the light should have been burning bright. The moon pushed from behind a cloud to bathe the headland in cool silver, and that was when I finally dropped to my knees in the wet sand. When I finally lost the shine of that strange sweet awe, and remembered what it felt like to be scared. To be sick with a fear so big, so full of sorrow and horror, that nothing else could survive alongside it.

'The Coastguard never came,' I say, glad that my voice betrays nothing. 'There were too many boats in trouble off the western coast that night, and no helicopter could've taken off in those winds.'

'The *Acair*.' Charlie's hands are tight fists on the tabletop. 'The *Marcan-sìne* and the *Darach*.'

That's the problem with fishermen. They never forget. They know every boat, every tragedy, every dead sailor.

Charlie looks at me, blinks shining eyes. 'You're from Àrd Shiadair,' he says, still low like he's whispering.

It's not a question, so I don't answer. Àrd Shiadair. *Am baile gun fhir*, the village without men. And for that whole day – from that morning at my window to that moment before I dropped to my knees on the beach – I'd wished for it. I'd longed for it. Like a Valkyrie choosing who lives and dies in battle, I'd made it happen.

'Your father was Douglas,' Charlie says. His jaw is clenched. 'Dougie MacNeil.'

That isn't a question either. Yet it doesn't feel like a mistake – my terrible secret almost laid bare to someone who's still a stranger to me. Someone I don't trust. Even worse, I want to tell him it all. I'm drunk, but I've been drunk before. And never has it been like this – a terrible freedom that feels too good to stop.

'You're Andrew MacNeil.'

Because Andrew was a fisherman's name. Because I'd been born when my father was at sea and the tide was rising.

'Why did you change your name to Robert?'

'Because I did something terrible. I didn't want to be Andrew MacNeil any more.'

I'm no longer shaking. My hands are steady. But my heart batters against my ribs and pulses inside my throat. I've never told anyone this. I've never come close to telling anyone. Charlie says nothing. Only looks at me steadily, carefully, no trace at all of his easy smile. I look at the dark smoke inside those peat embers instead.

'They used to follow me.' I swallow, and my throat is dry. But I don't reach for more whisky. 'I'd hear them. Watching, following. Muttering. Saying my name.'

'Who?'

Impatience sharpens my shame. '*Them*. The *bòcain*. Sometimes only my father. But, when there was a storm, all of them. All eighteen of them. I'd see their arms in the waves. I'd hear their shouts in the sky. Sometimes I'd lie in bed, watching the light from Àird Èinis as it moved over my bedroom walls, and I'd feel them. Hiding in the dark spaces amid the white.'

Charlie shakes his head. 'There's no such thing as ghosts.'

'Everyone has ghosts, Charlie.' Because he isn't as unaffected as he'd like me to think. There's a reluctance in his eyes, a shadow he doesn't want to acknowledge. When he says nothing more, I get up, stand in front of the warmth of the burner, even though I'm cold down to my bones.

'This is a thin place,' I say. 'These islands, and especially this coast. Where the Nine Worlds meet. Where *innangarðs* meets *utangarðs* – inside the fence meets outside the fence. Order meets chaos.' I close my eyes. 'I know you can feel it, Charlie. This land, this *place*, is like nowhere else in the world.'

'That why you left?'

'I *escaped*. Because I didn't understand that they'd come with me. That this place would come with me. I got married, had a son, changed my name by deed poll, and none of it made any difference. I still heard them; still saw them. I could never . . .' I shake my head. 'I hated it in Aberdeen. I hated the rocks and bitter east wind. I'd swapped light and colour for . . . grey. The Atlantic for the North Sea. And none of it mattered anyway. I'd sacrificed my life here for worse there.'

I turn round, and Charlie is still sitting at the table, his expression unreadable. I can hear the wind howling inside the sea-carved spaces under our feet.

'I can't live anywhere else. I *don't*.' I blow out a breath. 'But I need to tell someone what I did, Charlie. The terrible thing I did.' Because he'll never ask me, I realise. I can see it in that shadow in his eyes. That fear he pretends he doesn't feel.

'You don't, Robert.'

'I do.' My voice cracks, and I let it. 'I *need* to tell someone.'

Charlie's sigh is long and unsteady.

'All right,' he says. But he doesn't look at me when he says it. 'Then tell me.'

CHAPTER 12

My sleep is disjointed and light. I wake often, the darkness an unwelcome escape from acid, jarring dreams of black-tar valleys and angry seas and skeletal birds. A crumbling cliff of rock and grass; the wind trying to snatch me; the sea wild and dark and roaring. My last dream is less reprieve than revision. Mum, raw and loud. Wasted to nothing in her hospital bed. Her face a skull, teeth too wide and too white inside her smile.

And it feels like choking, like drowning in a storm. Her fingers thin and skin bruised, and that terrible smile. *You just have to make the right choice, Maggie, that's all. And you always do.* Because she knows I will. Even when I don't think it's the right choice at all.

I wake up, still choking, mouth open, throat dry. For a moment, I forget where I am, feel like I'm still in that antiseptic hot room, waiting, worrying, trying to sleep on a fold-down bed.

But I remember, even before I fumble for the bedside lamp

switch. I'm in a clifftop blackhouse on the edge of the world. And the sound – the sound that has raised the hairs on my skin and scalp; that has set my heart beating so hard I can feel its pulse in my fingers and toes – is not nurses on night rounds or the swish of fire doors. It is *here*.

I hear it again close to the window. Quick, light taps against the glass. And then muffled, louder taps getting closer. I listen to their progress along the wall towards the fireplace, and I draw my knees up against my chest. I think of the narrow paved path that encircles the cottage. Could it be sheep? But those taps don't sound like hooves. They sound like steps. Light and fast. As though someone is on tiptoe.

I almost scream when something scrapes too loud, too close, against the kitchen wall. It pauses, and I spin round in the bed, ears rushing with white noise as I strain to listen. When it starts up again – a scratching like something pressed against and dragged along the stone outside – I lurch out of bed, my hand over my mouth. The door to the mudroom is open, and I nearly scream again when it reaches the door, starts tapping on the small inset window. Another longer scrape of stone, and then the bathroom window. I think of *bòcain* and thin places. I think of dead birds with empty oval eye sockets. *The hooded crow is often referenced in Celtic and Norse mythology and ritual.* I think of someone watching from the darkness. Worst of all, I think of Robert Reid.

I back into the centre of the room, shaking, shivering, my breath ragged and short. I spin in my own clockwise circle as I follow the resumed fast steps and loud scratching. Round the northeast corner and the box room, the long front of the blackhouse, back towards the west wall and the fireplace. Someone is running around and around the cottage on their tiptoes and tapping the windows, their body pressed up against the stone walls.

I've no idea what to do. So instead I do nothing but continue to spin around and around, my fingers against my mouth as I track the progress of those sounds. Faster, louder. Circuit after circuit, until I can't stand it any more and run towards the door. There I hesitate – my shaking fingers inches from the long curtain hiding the door and its little inset window. The scratching and tapping is at the west wall again, heading for the corner fast. I wrench back the curtain with a breathless *yip* and lurch up onto my tiptoes to look out the window. There's nothing but darkness. The sounds have stopped too, and this I find most unnerving of all.

Until something – someone – knocks at the door so hard, it shudders in its wooden frame.

I do scream then, loud and long. And back away from the door too fast. I end up tripping on my own feet, hitting the wooden floor with a heavy and painful thud. When I get back up again, there's only silence. I can't even hear the wind or the sea. How long I stand there, I don't know. But afterwards, I can't bring myself to get back into the bed. Instead, I turn on every light in the room before curling into a ball on the sofa, where I shiver and shake and stare at the walls and curtains until dawn.

*

When I wake up, I'm stiff and sore. Slices of daylight stripe the pine walls through gaps in the curtains. I think of Ravi's belligerent

You sure you're okays; you don't sound rights masquerading as concern. *Have you been taking your meds?*

'I'm taking my meds, you arsehole,' I say to the ceiling.

The particular roll of his eyes that would make me feel so small, so defenceless. *Yeah, you sound pretty rational.*

But I'm not hallucinating. I'm not imagining things. This isn't a dead man come back to haunt me. And it isn't a demon in a crematorium either; it isn't the dark fear that I now drag around. It's not inside me, it's outside me. And the only danger is in how I react to it, how I choose to deal with it.

That creeping and tapping in the night was not a ghost. It was a person. Perhaps – probably – the same person who left dead birds on my doorstep and followed me in the dark. A person who hopes I will leave. Maybe even the person who murdered Robert. And I will deal with *that* by taking control. By trying to find out who. And why. It's the reason I'm here after all.

The day is cool and still. There are no dead birds on the path, no marks on the cottage walls. No indication at all that anyone was ever here. I open the wheelie bin, look down at the bag containing the two dead crows, warily open it. They look completely unchanged; they don't even smell, and something makes me want to hide them, to keep them as proof of what that person is doing. I pull the bag out and take it back to the blackhouse, where I shove it inside an old canvas rucksack behind the coat rack in the mudroom.

When I walk over to the farmhouse, Will opens the door with a welcoming smile, but whatever he sees in my face is enough to make him blink, frown.

'You still up for going to Stornoway?'

I nod. 'I just – there's something I need to do first. To get.'

'Get?'

I'm fidgeting, and make myself stop. 'I noticed some photos, back at the pub. Of the Stornoway Whisky Festival? Charlie said that in '94, the people who went to the festival couldn't get back until the day after the storm.' When Will only looks confused, I make myself say it. 'So they can't have had anything to do with whatever happened that night.'

'Jesus, Maggie.'

'It's just . . . it'd be helpful to know, that's all. Who they are.'

He looks at me, and I go on trying not to care what he thinks, but it's impossible. When he finally shrugs, the relief I feel is terrible.

'Guess you'll be needing a decoy then?'

*

'We're not open for lunch yet,' Gillian says, when she opens Am Blàr Mòr's big door.

'We're just away to Stornoway,' Will says. 'Maggie needs a pee.'

I try on my most convincing in-need-of-a-pee smile, and Gillian nods, stands back from the door.

'Thanks,' Will says, trailing her back to the bar. He picks up a flier from a table and shoots me a wink. 'Pottery Throw Down? You'll empty the place faster than Donnie doing bagrock.'

I march to the loo, banging its door hard before slinking back into the pub and the long red wall of photographs. I find what I want quickly: a Stornoway Whisky Festival 1994 banner strung between two lampposts. Beneath it, smiling people in waterproofs, waving plastic tumblers of whisky. When I take the photo down, it leaves a very obvious empty space, but I stuff it inside my mac anyway, its narrow frame catching on the zip.

'All done!' I say, probably too brightly, as I march back to the bar.

When we get into the car, Will grins at me before starting the engine.

'We make a good team.'

I take out the photograph so I don't have to answer. I recognise the view: a cluster of fishing boats moored on the opposite side of the harbour from the ferry terminal, Lews Castle and its grounds sprawled behind the narrow corridor of water. The photograph is blurry, water-damaged around its edges. I squint at the faces.

'That could be Charlie, right?'

Will leans close, looks at the grinning face beneath a neon-yellow hood and half-obscured by a full tumbler of whisky. 'Yeah, maybe. Three sheets to the wind, looks like.' He points to the shorter, darker-haired man next to him. 'And that's maybe Bruce?' He peers closer still – close enough that I can smell his skin, see the slow, steady beat of his pulse against his neck – and points at a tall out-of-focus figure at the photo's right-hand edge. 'That could be Jimmy, I guess?' He shrugs.

I look at another man and maybe a couple standing at the left-hand edge of the frame, but here the photo is damaged and their faces blurred perhaps beyond recognition. I stare at them for a long time as if I expect their features to resolve like a magic-eye picture. When they don't, I make myself stop looking, and push the photo inside my handbag.

*

The town hall is a vast building. Red brick and red wood, with tall arched windows, and tiled roof turrets topped with gilt banner weathervanes. Will takes me round to the rear entrance on a busy pedestrian precinct, holds open the door.

'Registration Service is just through there on the left,' he says. 'I need to order some feed in town, but there's a bar and restaurant in the Crown Hotel, down the other end of this street. I'll wait for you there?'

'Okay, thanks.' I need to visit the GP surgery that Dr Abebe has registered me with, and I'm relieved I won't have to explain why. I'm glad to be doing this alone too. I already feel a bit ridiculous. And uncertain about what it is I want to find.

After waiting less than five minutes, I'm shown into a small office, where a middle-aged man with a thin-lipped smile and a small halo of dark hair sits at a desk.

'Hello,' he says, glancing up at me. 'I'm Murdo Black. Pull up a pew. How can I help you today?'

I sit down. 'I'm looking for a death certificate.'

He types something before looking round his screen at me. 'Was it within the last fifty years?'

'Nineteen ninety-four.'

'Then it can't be looked at online. You have to order a copy certificate, I'm afraid, which will cost you the princely sum of twelve pounds.'

'That's fine. I just wanted to check the date and cause of death.'

'All right.' More tapping. 'What was the name?'

'Robert Reid.'

There's a definite pause before the typing resumes. 'Can you confirm the place of death? The district?'

'District? No, um. It was off the island of Kilmeray. He . . . drowned.'

He clears his throat, looks at the screen. 'Right. Here it is. Would you like to order the certificate?'

'How long will I have to wait?'

He props his elbows on the desk and steeples his fingers. 'Normally it's a couple of weeks, but . . .' He flashes neat teeth. 'We're quiet. How about I print you off a copy now? Can be my good deed for the day.'

'Thank you, that would be brilliant.'

He smiles as he gets up, closes the door behind him with a gentle click. And while he's gone, I try not to get my hopes up about Charlie being wrong about the date. I try harder not to think about why he might even have lied about it. I think about the blackhouse instead, and then try not to think about a potential murderer running and scratching circles around it.

Murdo Black comes back in about ten minutes, waving a couple of A4 pages, which he sets down on the desk in front of me. The first says 'Extract of an entry from the REGISTER OF DEATHS in Scotland.' I scan down past Robert Reid's name to When died.

1994 April Ninth
Estimated 1900 hours

Charlie was right about the date after all. Something shifts inside me then. It's a little like panic, but it's diluted, fuzzy around its edges. Maybe for me there is no escape after all, no excuses, no starting from scratch. After all that desperate hope, it's nearly a relief. That I'm just me. The me who stopped taking her meds because she doesn't deserve to be able to look at herself in the mirror.

The cause of death is listed as *Probable drowning or hypothermia* and *Probable hypoxia and acidosis leading to cardiac arrest or hypothermia leading to cardiac failure.*

'I probably shouldn't say, but I remember it,' Murdo Black says. 'I mean, I remember it happening – the storm, him and that wee boy being lost off Kilmeray.'

'During the Stornoway Whisky Festival?'

He nods. 'The festival was a total washout. Òrd na Mara. Worst spring storm to hit the Hebridean west coast in twenty years. Mind you, all we got here on the east coast was about two months' rainfall in one day, but it was enough to send most people home.'

He pushes the other piece of paper towards me. 'Robert Reid's wife and Lorne MacDonald's parents raised separate actions to declare the deaths after they went missing.'

I look down at the paper.

Sheriff Court, 9 Lewis St., Stornoway   15th April 1994

An action has been raised in Stornoway Sheriff Court by Mary Reid, Pursuer, to declare that, Robert Reid, Defender, whose last known address was The Blackhouse, Ardcraig, Kilmeray, is dead. Any person

wishing to defend the action must apply to do so by the 6th of May,
1994, by lodging a minute seeking to be sisted as a party to the action
with the sheriff clerk at the above address.

'Neither death was contested,' he says. 'The decrees were granted,
and the death certificates issued.'

'Thank you,' I say. 'This is really helpful.'

'Can I ask why you're interested?' he says with a shrug, a smile.
'Like I said, we're quiet.'

'I'm writing a story about it. Just wanted to make sure I got
my facts right.'

'Ah! Well, it's a sad story, all right. I knew him. Knew them. Not
well, but . . . back then, there were always community events and
the like out on Kilmeray. I used to go over a few times a year. Got
to know the locals pretty well, particularly in Blairmore. They
were good people. Didn't deserve what happened.'

I take the photograph out of my bag and offer it to him. Ignore
that growing weight in my stomach; the new heaviness in my
chest. 'Would you mind just having a quick look at this, then, see
if you recognise anyone?'

He takes it from me, and gives me a look that is half confused,
half curious. I'd been banking a little more on the latter. 'You want
me to identify the people in this photo?'

'Yes.'

He glances down at it and then back at me. 'Wouldn't you be
best off asking in Blairmore?'

I try an embarrassed smile. 'I think everyone on Kilmeray is
sick of me constantly asking questions. Don't worry if you can't

help, but I'd be happy to include your name in the acknowledgements if you could.'

'Acknowledgements? Your story is going to be a book?'

'Well, maybe. I hope so.' And this time the lie comes so easily I don't have to worry about whether I sound convincing.

'Well. That's something indeed. I'd be more than happy to help.' He looks down at the photo again. 'It's not a very good picture, is it?' He peers at it for perhaps as long as a minute, before putting it on the desk and turning it round to face me.

'Right to left at the front, there is definitely Jimmy Struthers. Next to him I reckon might be Charlie MacLeod.' He moves his finger across the photo. 'That's poor wee Lorne's parents, Alec and Fiona MacDonald, and in front could be Bruce MacKenzie, maybe. Couldn't swear to it, but I'm pretty sure. Right height and hair colour.' He picks the photograph up again. 'Bobby Rankin would probably be a better bet than me; he grew up in Urbost, but he's off on annual leave the next fortnight.' He squints as he holds it closer. 'The man and woman at the end there, I don't know. Looks like water or something's damaged the emulsion on that side.' He hands back the photograph and shrugs. 'And the man standing behind them, no idea either, I'm afraid.'

Which leaves who on Kilmeray? Charlie's wife, Moira, and Isla, who I already know were looking after the children. Jaz, who'd stayed on at the dig to prepare for any storm damage, and had later seen Robert down on the beach. Isla's husband, Kenny, who'd come back from creel fishing, gone looking for Lorne, and said he thought he saw a man going into the sea. Who else? Gillian? Euan? Unless he's the blurry man at the far side of the photo. And

Mary, Robert's wife, who, according to Gillian, had raised the alarm a couple of hours after Robert had gone out to check on the sheep.

I stand up. 'Thank you,' I say. 'You've been really helpful.'

He nods, then cocks his head to one side, frowns. 'You know, library next door's been doing a bit of a hard-copy clearout to microfiche. Why don't you wait here, and I'll just nip over, see if they have any of the original newspaper articles about what happened.'

'That would be really kind of you,' I say, although I've already read everything local in my online research.

He smiles as he opens the door. 'Maybe I'll get top billing in those acknowledgments of yours.'

I sit as I wait. Rub at that tightness inside my chest. I don't why I'm still here, why I didn't leave as soon as I saw that death certif- icate. Why I'm still asking questions about Robert's death. Maybe – even in the face of indisputable proof that I was born nearly two months before Robert died – all that desperate hope isn't abandoned so easily after all.

Murdo Black comes back less than ten minutes later, out of breath and pink in the face.

'Already microfiched and off to storage, I'm afraid,' he says, coming back round the desk. 'Although you can always print from one of the readers for a couple of quid if you're interested.'

'Thanks.' I stand up again to leave. 'I really appreciate—'

'I got this, though,' he says, brandishing a paper. '*Stornoway Gazette*. Strange thing a few years later – a wee girl from the mainland claimed she was the reincarnated soul of a man who was drowned, she said – murdered, if you can believe it – in 1994. Created quite the stir.'

My face heats up. 'Really? That is . . . I did hear something about that.'

'Might be of some use, you never know,' he says, handing it over.

I look down at the photocopy and its headline. 'Child's Bizarre Past-Life Murder Claim'. I wince a little at the large black-and-white photo – a memory that's not quite a memory – me in a plain knee-length dress this time, no wellies, hair whipping around my head; Mum next to me in a tightly belted coat that I remember now was fire-engine red, a strange half-smile on her face. We're standing in front of a dark, narrow corridor between steep rock walls, and I start when I realise that it's the Valley of Ghosts. A shiver pulls at the hair on the back of my neck. And when I glance at the only other person in the picture, a dark-haired man in a badly fitting suit, grinning wide, the hairs on the back of my neck stand up even straighter.

I look at the caption under the photo. *Maggie MacKay, 5, with her mother, Vivienne, and Glaswegian documentary filmmaker Gordon Cameron.*

I look back at Gordon Cameron. His grin, and his left canine more than three-quarters gold.

Remember Mum's cheeks glowing and eyes happy-bright. *He's an actor. He's going to play Javert in* Les Mis *at the Pavilion next month.*

It's the clown from my birthday party.

CHAPTER 13

I find Will sitting in a quiet corner of the Harbour View Bar on the first floor of the Crown Hotel.

'I see you've made a friend,' I say, nodding at the big carved wooden stag head on the wall behind him.

'Aye. Not half as bonny or interesting as you, though.'

I barely resist giggling and then the urge to slap myself as I sit in the sumptuous leather armchair next to his.

'Jack,' he calls over to the barman. 'Can I have a pint of Tennent's, and . . .' He looks at me.

'Just a pinot grigio, please.'

'So.' Will leans forwards. 'Did you find out what you needed?'

'Charlie was right,' I say. 'About the date of the storm, the evening Robert and Lorne died. April ninth.'

'So . . .'

I feel a prickle of embarrassment. 'Seven and a half weeks after my birthday.'

'Are you disappointed?' Will's tone is completely neutral, but I feel that prickle get hotter.

I'm saved from answering by the barman approaching the table with our drinks, and I accept mine gratefully, clinking it against Will's pint before taking a long cool swallow. I look back across the bar, because it's easier than looking at him.

After popping into the GP surgery on the way to the Harbour View, I'd nervously taken advantage of Stornoway's 4G to google *Gordon Cameron + actor + Glasgow*. Found an entry on Mandy, a free job platform for cast and crew. His profile pic showed a dark-haired man of the right age; unsmiling, teeth hidden. His credits were few and far between, nothing I'd heard of, but he'd listed his contact as his agent, JN Entertainment. I'd phoned the number while looking out across the harbour, holding my hair out of the wind. And as it rang out, high and tinny, all I could think was *Don't take this away from me, Mum. Don't.* When it clicked into a recorded message, my relief was far too big.

'Hi, um, my name is Maggie Anderson. I was wondering if you could give me a contact number for Gordon Cameron, please? It's a personal matter. He'd know me as Maggie MacKay, daughter of Viv. I'm available on this number. Thanks.'

'I was in a car accident,' I say now, apropos of nothing but that *Don't.* I look at Will as I touch my right eyelid. 'Anisocoria – a permanently dilated pupil caused by severe head injury. I bull's-eyed a car windscreen when I was four years old.' A face, its mouth a perfect round O. 'Mum always told me that I just let go of her hand, ran into the road. She told me that so many times. But.' I pick up my wine again. 'When I was about fourteen, she got really pissed, and stayed pissed. For days. She did that, sometimes. And she told me that it had been her fault. She'd let go of my hand, *she'd* run into the road. She would have these intrusive thoughts, impulses, and sometimes she'd act on them. And I . . . I'd been trying to stop her.'

Will puts his hand on my arm. I can feel its heat through two layers of wool before I pull away.

'She thought she was psychic. She knew everything about life and death. She saw visions. She received messages. Insights.' My fingers are tapping a nervous and angry tattoo against the table and I curl them into fists. 'She was obsessed with those godawful TV shows; fake mediums wandering around graveyards with earnest faces. Fleecing grieving relatives while they pretended to solve their loved ones' murders. Mum would've loved to be that. To do that. To be *believed* like that.'

I look at Will; finally say out loud what I've been thinking ever since seeing the date on that death certificate and that photo in the *Stornoway Gazette.* Mum's bright eyes, that smile she was trying and failing to hide.

'What if Mum lied to me? What if none of it was ever true? What if she *made* me believe it?'

'You think she made up the whole reincarnation thing?' Will says.

I'm using him as a sounding board, maybe even a confessional. And it's inappropriate, but at the same time, it feels completely normal. Completely natural. And I know I'm not going to stop. 'No. I *don't* know. I was five. I mean, I don't remember all of it, but I do remember believing it. Being sure of it absolutely.'

But I know, too, that for Mum, lying had been like breathing. Made all the more dangerous because she nearly always believed her own lies. And as a child at least, I'd always been ready – far too ready – to run into the road to save her. But what happened here twenty years ago has always felt to me too sacrosanct, too indelible, too big a part of us. It defined us, it was our history – a story told again and again like a mantra, a vow, the biggest tie to ever bind us together. My chest tightens again. The only time when we were the same. A flashback to so many fights, so many tears. All the times I shouted, wounded and ashamed, and always so, so alone. *I hate you! I'm nothing like you!*

'But yeah. What if she did? She could have coached me. It's not impossible.' The squeeze of my fists; the hotness of my tears. *I'm Andrew MacNeil. I'm Andrew MacNeil!* And Mum kneeling in front of me, holding my hands, looking up at me with that serene smile. *Yes, you are.*

'Maybe she read about him, his death. Knew he'd died within weeks of me being born, and realised she could use it.' Because while that one memory has always been white and sharp and never diminished, I don't remember saying *Kill Merry* over and over again until she listened; I don't remember freaking out over a Scottish travel show about the Isle of Lewis and Harris. I don't remember *why* we came here.

I look out the window at the Port Authority buildings and the long piers reaching out into the Minch. Despite the fading light,

I can see ominous black clouds on the distant horizon. 'Or it could have been someone else.'

'Who?'

I think of Gordon Cameron. Even if he is the clown from my birthday party, the grinning gold-toothed actor that came to Mum's soirees, it doesn't mean that he wasn't a documentary filmmaker too. That's possible.

I try to meet Will's gaze. 'I don't know. Maybe the filmmaker, the director, maybe he used Mum somehow. Maybe he had an agenda of his own.'

Will's cautiously dubious expression makes me feel defensive. I know I'm clutching at straws, but everything I learned in the town hall today is too much disappointment – perhaps too much *reality* – all at once. And I feel the need to fight back. 'But how did she know, Will?'

'Know what?'

'How did she know that Robert Reid's real name was Andrew MacNeil? If they were the same person – and I think they were – how did she know?'

'Huh.' He leans back in his chair. 'You're right. She had to have known him.'

'Or someone who did. Maybe even someone who believed he'd been murdered, and wanted to draw attention to it.'

'Okay, so why don't you ask her?' Will says. 'Your mum.'

'I can't.' And this time, along with the grief and guilt, there's anger. Far more than there's ever been before. 'She died.'

'Shit. I'm sorry.'

I shrug, shake my head. Press my lips together as I look back out the window. Because for the hundredth time, I want to tell Will – I want to tell *someone* – the whole ugly truth about why I'm really here. And I can't.

'Christ, though, Maggie. Do *you* really think he was murdered? I mean, I'm trying to imagine any of them actually bumping someone off. Euan'd likely pay someone else to get their feet wet, and for someone who's lived their whole life on an island, Bruce gets freaked out by a spring tide.' Will's smile is pained. 'Alec could shout a person to death, I guess.'

And it's his smile that snaps me out of my selfishness. These are people Will lives with, has known almost all his life. Me using him as a sounding board isn't just unfair, it's monumentally inconsiderate – even for me.

'No,' I say quickly. 'Probably not.' Which is another lie. From what I've learned about Robert, he doesn't seem the suicidal type, and even less, the heroic type. And in spite of, or maybe because of what I've found out today – even if it has nothing to do with me any more – my answer is still yes. I think he was murdered.

'Anyway, there could have been a mistake with the dates, right?' I force myself to smile. 'Or maybe reincarnation doesn't work that way, you know? Maybe there's like a seven-and-a-half-week cooling-off period or something.'

Will smiles a better smile. 'A little celestial R and R before heading back to the coal face.'

I smile back, and I feel the slow, heavy beat of my heart against my breastbone as both relief and reprieve.

'Are you guys eating with us tonight?' Jack calls over from behind the bar, and I lean quickly away from Will. 'The restaurant's pretty booked up, but there's a table free in the next five minutes.'

'I'm up for it if you are?' Will says.

Against all of my better instincts, I nod.

'But then we should probably head back. There's bad weather forecast for tonight.' Will smiles, keeps on looking at me. 'Better to play it safe, right?'

*

'So,' I say, once a waitress has delivered our food and given Will a long, lingering look that makes me bristle. 'Tell me what it was like growing up on Kilmeray. Must have been a cool place to be a kid.'

'David, Donnie, and I pretty much lived outside in the summer. Swimming in lochs and the sea around Sheltered Bay or Long Stride. Racing one another round the island, or playing war games in the Valley of Ghosts. The foothills of Ben Wyvis were good for MG nests.' Will grins. 'Charlie called us the Three Stooges.'

'Must have been pretty lonely sometimes.'

Will shrugs. 'Not when you don't know anything else. Plus there was Heather and Sheena too.' He pulls a face. 'Even if they were *girls*.'

'Kelly said Sheena has always had the hots for you.'

'Well. You can imagine what it's like growing up on a small island. Hormones everywhere and nowhere to put them.' He shifts in his seat, and I'm charmed by his discomfort. 'Anyway, more families started moving into Urbost. And then we were all off to school: me and Iain to Glasgow; everyone else to Lewis. Sheena and David ended up going out for most of high school.'

'Isla's living room is covered in photos of him,' I say.

'Yeah, she thinks he farts sunshine, all right.' Will laughs. 'Last time I saw him was when he came back for Christmas. He's a good guy.'

'What happened to Kenny?'

Will pours me more wine. 'Story I heard was he went out alone on the *Unity*, as far as the shelf, even though he'd mostly been working inshore. And he went overboard in heavy seas. The boat was recovered, but just like Robert and Lorne a few weeks before, his body was never found.'

'Wait.' I still myself, wineglass inches from my lips. 'You're saying that Kenny Campbell died *just* after Robert and Lorne?'

Will nods. 'A few weeks after, I think. Not sure when exactly.'

'That's weird.' It's more than weird. Even if I account for Will's *There's plenty danger here. Plenty that'll kill you. But it isn't people.*

Will shrugs. 'Isla just got on with it, Euan said. Poured all her love into David instead. Grief changes folk, I guess. Sometimes for the better; most times not. Look at Alec. I don't think he's ever tried to get over Lorne's death.' He grimaces. ''Course, what the hell would I know about losing someone? Charlie's wife only left him, and it was like he became a different person overnight.'

'Charlie's wife left him?'

'Aye, maybe fifteen years ago? But I think it had been on the cards a long time. Rumour is Charlie had an affair with someone on the island back in the nineties.'

'*Charlie?*'

Will laughs, but there's little humour in it. 'I know. Maybe it isn't even true, just island gossip. But when Moira left, Charlie just kind of . . . stopped.' He sighs. 'It's like the fun, easy-going guy who'd spent hours chasing us up and down Long Stride when we were kids, or teaching us how to swim in Loch Dubh, never existed.'

We stop talking as the waitress arrives to take away our plates.

'Come on, Maggie,' he says when she's gone. 'This is completely fucking depressing. Tell me something about you. You're always the one asking me questions.'

'I think we've talked enough about me tonight,' I say, my face getting hot.

He looks at me a little too long. As if he already knows all the things about me that I'd rather die than tell him. When the silence between us stretches longer, I resist the urge to fold my arms.

'I'm just not that interesting, Will.'

'I think you are, Maggie MacKay.'

'Anderson.' I can feel my face getting warm. 'I was born in Croy, but we moved to England in—'

'You're Scottish?' When I nod, he laughs, shakes his head. 'You're Scottish and I'm English. Guess you saw right through the whole *It's a Scots tradition to dance the first dance with a local*, then?'

I smile. 'Mum married my stepfather, James, when I was ten, and we moved to Essex, then Hither Green. After high school, I did English lit at UCL, and got a job as a features intern and then writer at a women's magazine you'll never have heard of.'

'You still live in Hither Green?'

'No. I have – had – a flat in Blackheath. Ridiculously overpriced.'

And mostly paid for by Ravi, who'd insisted that if he had to live south of the river, it was there or nowhere.

'That where you lived with the person who gave you that ring?' He touches the faded white band of skin on my finger lightly with his thumb, and I instinctively draw my hands into fists again.

'Ravi.' My voice shrinks. 'We met at uni. Were friends for years. I guess we kind of fell into being something more. He asked me to marry him last year.' I clear my throat. 'And I couldn't think of a reason to say no.'

'Maggie,' Will says, and when I look at him, I'm surprised by the kindness in his eyes. 'You don't owe me an explanation.'

'We had a terrible relationship,' I say. I laugh, and somehow it comes out sounding normal – clean and clear. 'I mean it was *terrible*.' I drain my wine. 'Even by my standards.'

I won't tell Will how long I'd rehearse conversations with Ravi. Practising them in the mirror, so that he wouldn't be able to see some weakness or failing that I hadn't known was there. I'd smile through phone messages, knowing he'd notice if I didn't. Being careful never to sound too high or too low; too upbeat or too quiet. I did anything and everything to avoid his eager concern, his casual condescension, his endless disappointment. And I certainly won't tell Will that sometimes I *still* have those imaginary and profoundly unhealthy conversations. Because even though I hated being with Ravi, hated how small and weak he made me feel, I haven't been able to shake the feeling that maybe he was right. Maybe I do need someone to hold me down. Maybe he really was the only thing keeping me from being snatched up and carried away.

I think of Dr Abebe's *Perhaps you should just be on your own for a bit, Maggie. Try that out for size.*

'Hey.' Will reaches across the table and takes both of my too cold hands in his, unclenches my fingers. 'I shouldn't have asked. I'm sorry.'

'It's fine.'

He keeps on looking at me with that same steady gaze as his warmth spreads into my skin. 'Look. I wanted to say earlier . . .' He shakes his head. 'You know, you can come to the farm. Anytime. I mean, you're welcome anytime. You know, if you run out of sugar or whatever, or just, I dunno, to see me. Anytime. For any reason.' He squeezes my hands, his suddenly clammy, and I can't help the shiver that goes through me, the goosebumps that appear on my forearms.

'Okay.' I don't say anything else. I can't. Because it's not just the heat of him that I miss when I take back my hands. It's *him*. And I don't know what to do about it.

'Are we ever going to talk about this, Maggie?' Will says, pointing first at himself and then at me, those goosebumps on my arms. 'Or are we just going to get closer and closer to doing what we're going to do without ever saying it out loud?'

'I'm sorry,' I say, standing up. 'I need to go to the loo.'

In the toilets, I stand at the sink, run my wrists under cool water. I glance at myself in the mirror. I look like a Maggie I only vaguely remember. Her hair is tangled and her cheeks are rosy and her eyes are clear. My whole life I've wanted to be someone – *anyone* – other than me, and suddenly I'm tired of it. And I'm tired of denying myself everything I want because I'm ashamed or afraid or because I think I don't deserve it. I remember Mum's laughter as we ran along that beach in the rain and roaring thunder, the stretched nylon of our kite snapping back against the wind. I remember that of all the things Mum hated, she'd hated cowards the most.

When I get back to the table, Will looks up at me, his expression worried.

'I'm sorry, Maggie. I shouldn't have said that. Forget I—'

'The rain's not stopping,' I say, still standing.

'Maggie . . .'

I think of the *thump thump* of my heart just because he touched the back of my hand in the space between our seats where no one else could see.

'The receptionist just told me the weather's getting much worse in the west. Better to play it safe, you said.'

Will briefly closes his eyes. 'Right.' He gets up, lifts his coat from the back of his chair.

I pick up my own, look at Will until finally he looks back at me.

'So I booked us a room,' I say.

*

'Jesus, you're shaking,' Will says.

'So are you.'

He laughs, perhaps nervous. 'I guess I am.'

We're standing facing each other in the middle of a tiny hotel room decorated in various shades of brown. Our hands are clasped tight together. I can see tiny red threads in the whites of his eyes, the big black of his pupils. He leans closer still, touches his lips against mine, draws back.

'Are you sure?'

And there's no hesitation at all in my nod. Because although it seems incredible that I should be sure, and although there are a thousand reasons why this a terrible, terrible idea, I'm not going to change my mind. It's been a long time since I trusted myself, since I've been sure about anything, but here and now, I suddenly am.

I touch his face, and another shiver goes through me when he closes his eyes; when I hear his quick intake of breath. And I kiss him with none of his gentleness, clumsy and urgent enough that he loses the last of his hesitation and pulls me hard against him. Kisses me back just the same.

We stumble towards the bed, and Will lets me go long enough to sit down on its edge. He yanks off my jumper and T-shirt, presses his face, his mouth, against the hot skin of my stomach while I wrestle with my bra. When he closes his hands over my breasts, I kick off my jeans while unzipping his. He traces words against my skin, whispers them, but I reach forwards and push him back onto the mattress. I don't want foreplay. I don't want kindness. I don't need them. I just need him.

I straddle him and he swears, arches up against me, grabs me by the hips. His face is flushed; I can see the pulse beating in his neck. I yank and pull at his clothes until he's as naked as I need him to be, tear the condom out of his hands, put it on with impatient fingers. And then I sink back down on him hard enough that it hurts. He groans, pulls me closer to kiss and kiss me, and we move against each other gracelessly; too quick, too fast. It feels like the first time I've had sex in my life, and I become almost panicky with my need to touch him, to fuck him, to be as close as I can be to him. He yells, pushes up into me one last time, and when I start to come, I nearly sob with the relief of it, the release of it. The absolute rightness.

I sag against him, my breath ragged, heart still thundering. And he looks up at me, just as breathless. A dazed smile on his lips. '*Jesus*, Maggie.'

CHAPTER 14

I should feel guilty. At failing so spectacularly to stick to what I'd thought would be the easiest of Dr Abebe's rules: no new relationships and no sex. But I only feel guilty that I *don't* feel guilty. Although as we go back over the sound onto Kilmeray, I do start to feel anxious. And it only gets worse when Will pulls up onto the grass verge beyond the road into Blairmore.

'D'you fancy some lunch?'

'What?' I imagine walking into Am Blàr Mòr together. 'No.'

'Maggie, listen.' He turns off the engine, looks down at my lap where I'm fidgeting, twisting my fingers together. Rain patters against the windscreen. 'I won't say anything. And I want you to know I don't expect anything. If you want, I'll drive you back to Ardcraig right now. But I'd rather go to the pub and have some lunch.' He smiles, warm and careful. 'They'll talk about us anyway.'

I stare at the blurry windscreen. 'I'm not always the best judge of what's good for me.'

Will reaches for my still fidgeting fingers, his thumb stroking the back of my hand once, twice, three times. And I only watch him. I don't pull away.

'I'll be good for you.'

Despite myself, I smile.

He laughs. 'Too cheesy?'

Finally I take back my hand under the pretence of checking my phone. As usual, it registers no signal at all, but a text must have come through on the road back from Stornoway.

Gordon Cameron asked us to pass on his number to you.

It's a mobile number. I save it to my contacts.

'Okay,' I say to Will.

'Okay?'

I nod. 'I'll have lunch with you.'

Because I'm going to keep going, I realise. Despite everything I found out yesterday – the dates, the clown, Mum perhaps having made the whole thing up – I'm going to keep investigating what happened to Robert. I'm not ready to leave. To give up. And maybe that's because I still can't bring myself to believe it's *not* true – that it really is only coincidence that Robert was once called Andrew and that I am living in the very same house that he did. Or maybe it's because I don't want to go back to London, back to my life, back to *me*. And maybe – probably – neither of those reasons are good reasons. But I'm staying anyway. I look at Will again. I'll be careful. I can be careful. I've had years of practice.

*

When we walk into the bar lounge, I realise, with dismay, that the pub is busy. And very interested in our arrival. There are two tables crowded with people I don't recognise, who greet Will with shouted hellos. Two more are full of loud and muddy archaeologists. Euan and Cora are sitting at a small table in one of the dark alcoves, and when Will waves at them, they wave back.

'Hey.' Donnie claps a hand on Will's shoulder before picking up a tray full of drinks from the bar. 'You guys here for lunch? Got the kids this week. Why don't you join us?' He nods towards a nearby table where Gillian and Bruce are sitting next to a little girl with tight black curls and a younger boy, maybe about five, swinging his feet on a low stool.

Will turns to me, an apology in his eyes. 'Do you want to?'

'Sure,' I say. 'I'll get the drinks.'

'I'll go grab us some chairs,' Will says, still looking sorry enough that I make myself smile.

After he goes and I order from a barman I don't recognise, I realise that Donnie is still loitering next to me with his tray of drinks.

'So,' he says, and there's no mischievous grin for me today. 'You decided how long you're sticking around yet?'

His frown is almost a glower, and I've no idea if it's because Will and I spent the night in Stornoway or because his parents have told him what was said in Isla's cottage on Monday. I can't see why either of those things would piss him off, but I'm beginning to suspect there are a lot of things that I don't know or understand, a lot of things that people are not saying, perhaps even hiding. Whether that's more clutching at straws, I don't know either, but the possibility – the suspicion – pisses *me* off enough to glare back.

'Why d'you ask?'

He shrugs, quickly schools his expression into something more friendly as he reaches across the bar to put my drinks onto his tray. 'Just making conversation.'

I look over his shoulder at the wall of photos, and see that Miko and Femi are sitting alone at the table nearest to it. 'I'm just going to go say a quick hello,' I say, returning his lukewarm smile with one of my own before moving away from him.

I skirt the red wall, pretending casual curiosity. Glance quickly over my shoulder at the lounge before pulling the photo out of my bag and hanging it back in its space using my body as a shield. When I turn back round and walk to Miko's table, she greets me with a polite smile. 'How are you, Maggie?'

'I'm fine, thanks. How's the dig going?'

'We're finding some really exciting artefacts,' she says, with a small shrug. 'We haven't found any satellite graves yet like I was hoping, but the main barrow is still producing a ton of Bronze Age pottery. Yesterday we found a gold torc, a kind of high-status bracelet, which could even be Neolithic, so . . .'

Femi snorts. 'I'll tell you what's *really* interesting.' And he's looking at Miko rather than me. 'Ever since we started re-excavating the site of the first dig as well as the southwest ridge, weird things have—'

'Femi . . .' Miko says, and I hear the warning in her voice even if he doesn't.

'Some mornings,' he says, undeterred and leaning closer, 'when the first shift arrives, it looks like someone's been poking around in the night. Muddy footprints or tarps moved. Two days ago, earth looked like it had been disturbed around the most recently excavated part of the main barrow.' He looks at me. 'Now, what I was thinking—'

Miko nudges his elbow hard enough to make him wince. 'I thought we decided that what you were thinking wasn't worth talking about?'

I belatedly realise that Jaz is sitting at the overcrowded archaeologists' table behind us. He sees me looking, and gives an awkward nod.

Femi shrugs. 'I'm just saying, because, you know, the bunkhouses at Long Stride, they're too far away to see anything going on at the dig at night, right?' He turns to me. 'But you said you were up on Ardcraig, right? I'm just thinking maybe you could keep an eye open, see if anyone—'

'Oh my God, ignore him,' Miko says. She hits his arm again, rolls her eyes.

'I'm telling you.' He tuts loudly, shakes his head. 'It's some freaky shit, mate.'

'Well, I'm probably not close enough to see anything.' I think of the impenetrable darkness that falls over the island every night like a curtain. And then of someone running on fast tiptoe around the blackhouse, tapping on its windows. 'But, obviously, if I do, I'll let you know.'

When I head reluctantly over to the MacKenzies, Will, sitting next to Donnie, looks up and gives me another pained smile. Gillian and Bruce are sitting on the only bench; he pulls out a stool from under the table.

'Thank you.'

'No worries,' Bruce says with a smile, one far more genuine than two days ago at Isla's house. 'Good weather for fishes, eh?'

'Not farmers, I'm guessing.'

'Why d'you think we're in the pub?'

Gillian looks at me, expression impassive but shoulders a little too square. 'So, how goes the story? We heard you were busy doing some research in Stornoway yesterday?'

Donnie snorts as he lifts his pint. 'That what they're calling it now?'

Will shoots him a glare so furious that even I flinch, and Donnie puts down his pint without drinking, clears his throat.

'That's enough of that,' Gillian says, although her own disapproval is as clear as a bell.

'Maggie, will you be taking a break from your . . .' Bruce momentarily flails '. . . research, to come to our Friday-night pub quiz?'

'I'm not much good at quizzes.'

'Well, you're welcome to join us,' Gillian says. 'It's our night off, and all this lot know anything about is sheep and football.'

Jimmy comes over to the table, a towel slung over his shoulder. He gives me a fleeting glance. 'Guinness is off, Gillian,' he says. 'And we've got our hands full at the bar.'

'So much for a lunch break,' she says, heaving a long sigh before standing up.

'We want nuggets!' the little boy shouts, before trying to push the girl off her stool and then running full pelt towards the pool table. The girl gives an indignant scream and races after him.

'Rosie! Peter!' Donnie bellows. 'Come back here right now!' He reluctantly sets down his pint before going after them.

'You know,' I say, grabbing for my coat as I look at Bruce and then Will, 'I'm sorry. I've just remembered I've got to get some things from the shop. Maybe we could do this another time.'

Because suddenly I don't feel very equipped to sit through a weirdly cosy lunch, enduring frowns and uncomfortable questions, clutching at my own baseless suspicions. I should be taking advantage, I suppose, and asking questions of my own, but I'm too tired. And yesterday – last night – is enough to process for now. I need to be on my own. I need to think. Regroup. I need to phone Gordon Cameron.

I feel Will briefly touching me – it burns all the way up my arm – but I keep on going and, when the frigid air hits my face as I push open the pub door, the relief is nearly overwhelming. The main street is empty, and I take a few deep, slow breaths. When Will doesn't come out after me, I'm both glad and disappointed. And then mad at myself.

Just go to the fucking shop.

But as soon as I start walking away from the pub, I feel a sudden chill against my skin, just like the moment I found those dead birds on the path or sensed that someone hiding in the dark. This time, though, they don't creep, but rush towards me from behind. And so quickly that I barely have any time to spin round before someone shoves hard against me.

I don't scream, but I do rear backwards, holding up my hands to my face and feeling the warm wetness of spit on my fingers.

'Mum, stop! Stop!'

And it's only when Will manages to pull her away from me that I realise my attacker is Cora. Her face is wild, streaked with tears and black mascara, and her hair – ordinarily so perfect – has escaped in frizzy handfuls that she pulls and twists even as Will tries to restrain her. Her eyes – still looking at me – are dark with fury.

Euan bursts out the pub door and starts fast-waddling towards us, face red.

'I'm so sorry, Maggie. Will. I didn't realise she was gone.'

'It's okay,' Will says, out of breath. 'It's all right, Mum. You're okay. Euan, can you—'

'Of course, of course,' Euan says, putting an arm around Cora's shaking shoulders, stroking her ruined hair. 'Come with me, my love. Let's get you warm and home.'

At once, the anger goes out of her eyes, as if absorbed by Euan's touch or words, and she blinks at me once, twice, in blank confusion before allowing Euan to turn her round and lead her away.

Will waits until they've disappeared into the small car park alongside the pub before turning back to me. 'Jesus, I'm sorry. Are you okay?' He puts out a hand to touch my face; takes it back when I step away from him.

'I'm fine.'

'Mum has early-onset Alzheimer's.' He sighs, shakes his head. 'I should have said something. But she's seemed far more balanced lately.'

'I'm sorry, Will.' I notice that I'm twisting my fingers again, savagely pinching my skin. That bright, wild light in Cora's eyes – reminding me somehow of Mum – has reopened the ugly fear inside me like a poisonous flower. *You can't hide from this, Maggie,* Dr Abebe says. *It will always be a part of you.*

'Let me take you home.'

I can't stand the concern in Will's eyes. The almost irresistible need to reach out and touch him. 'I'm okay. You should go with your mum.'

Euan's huge black Shogun reverses out of the car park and disappears off towards the main road.

'I'll come to the shop with you,' Will says. 'Look, I'm really sorry about the MacKenzies too. It—'

'Will, I'm fine.' I realise that I'm backing away from him, one small step at a time. 'Really. I'd just kind of like to be alone.'

I know I'm being rude. And I know it's hurting him. But my need to escape is far stronger. Perhaps he sees it, because he finally stops trying to follow me.

'Okay. If that's what you want.'

'It is.'

He catches my gaze, holds it for longer than is comfortable. 'Come and see me,' he says. 'If that's what you want too.'

*

When I enter the shop, it's quiet with the kind of hush that has only just stopped being excited chatter, and I realise that everyone has probably seen what happened outside.

Fiona MacDonald, standing behind the counter, gives me an awkward glance before nodding towards the window. 'That was ... Cora isn't well.'

I clear my throat. 'I know.'

'It's a terrible thing.' She sighs, shakes her head, and then turns back to the till and her customer. I belatedly realise it's Isla; she gives me a quick nod before stooping to pick up two full canvas bags. Everyone else resumes their shopping, and the silence is replaced with a lower and better hum.

'D'you want a hand?' Fiona asks, touching Isla's elbow.

'Ach, away, I'm fine, Fiona. *Tioraidh*. I'll see you tomorrow.' She gives me another quick glance as she leaves, and I realise that she looks terrible. Her eyes are bloodshot and the skin beneath them is puffy with dark purple bags. The smile she gives me is thin. 'Cheerio, Maggie.'

I pick up a basket and throw anything edible into it as quickly as I can. When I round the last aisle, I'm dismayed to see Sheena stocking a shelf with tins of soup. She stops as if startled to see me, and I suspect that she's probably the only person in the shop who didn't witness what happened outside. She frowns and squares her shoulders before setting the tins down and turning to face me.

And then she says nothing. I clear my throat, shifting my weight awkwardly from foot to foot as the handles of my basket dig into my palm, and still she says nothing. Just goes on looking at me. I feel vaguely resentful, but after Donnie and Cora I've no desire at all to get into another confrontation with someone else. Instead, I pick something off the nearest shelf without looking, and then turn to go.

She moves so quickly that I almost let out a cry when her fingers close tight on my wrist, spinning me round.

'When I said you should leave, it wasn't only for my mum and dad.' She's talking in a low almost-whisper. There's still hostility in her eyes, maybe even some small measure of that fear I'd seen, shining and dark, on the night Alec attacked me in the phone box. She glances down at my wrist, the skin pinched white around her fingers. 'You're not safe here.'

'What are you talking about?' I shake her off so that she won't know my pulse has quickened.

'I don't know. I just feel it.'

And it's so close to Mum's *People like us, Maggie, we have to listen to our bad feelings* that I gasp and step backwards. 'What does that *mean?*'

But Sheena only shrugs, her eyes glittering. 'It means you should leave.'

Anger finally comes to my rescue. 'Is this about Will?' I say, and I feel a burst of petty satisfaction when her cheeks redden and her hands become fists.

Kelly rounds the end of the aisle, and the expression on her face freezes as she looks from Sheena to me. 'Is everything okay?'

'Fine,' I say, even though the smile I give her feels more like a grimace. 'Everything's fine.'

CHAPTER 15

Robert

It's barely noon, but I'm exhausted. The sheep are ill-tempered and loud, and the rain is cold and unrelenting. I woke to rain like this on the morning of the funerals. That day feels very close today. Has felt very close ever since that night in Charlie's *bothan*. Its hangover hasn't left me either. It bangs at my temples, keeps my temper too short.

I remember standing at my bedroom window as the coffins were carried down the main street. I traced their shapes in the condensation, far easier to outline than three boats rigged for fly-dragging.

'Why aren't you dressed? We have to go down now!'

Mamaidh's face was pinched pale, though anger had given her cheekbones two high spots of red. Her black dress for church exposed bony collarbones and gathered in empty folds around her waist. In just two weeks, she'd become so much *less*. Already, I couldn't remember what her smile looked like.

I stared back down at that slow, wet procession. I couldn't hear the mourners, but I could see their faces: drawn down like melted candle wax, or turned up to the dismal sky, distorted by the rain against the glass. And I could hear the piper, already past and out of sight, playing 'Going Home'.

If ever my father or any of his fishermen had passed a minister on their way down to the boats, they would turn around and go back home. And for fear of angering the Celtic sea gods, he could only ever be referred to as *the man with the black coat*; his church *the bell house*. No prayers could be said on board a fishing boat. Instead, whisky was thrown over the bows and salt over the decks. And every spring, my father would *sain* the boats by setting a bucket full of old rags dipped in diesel on fire and carrying it around the decks, above and below, smoking out every corner. All of it the same as carving Norse runes into a keel, or offering sacrifice to Njǫrðr, the god of fishing and the sea. The same kind of faith, the same hope, in something unseen. A common ground between us that he chose to never see.

'It was my fault.' Because Mamaidh knew why I wasn't dressed. Why I couldn't go down there. Why I couldn't go to the church and sit with all those coffins, all those people. I *couldn't*. They'd see what I'd done. They'd know.

'I told you to stop saying that.' She yanked me away from the window with fingers that pinched. And when they looked at me, her eyes weren't only furious, but afraid. It was the same fear that wouldn't let me sleep – that waved white arms in the light from

Àird Èinis as it swept over my bedroom walls; that muttered in the dark between grey and white-silver.

She pulled me close enough that the fear was all I could see: dark and wild, like the ocean.

'Don't you say that again. Don't you *ever* tell anyone what you did. If they knew, they would hate you. They would hate *us*. Forever. You have no idea what it's like when a place like this turns against you.' The finger that pointed at my face shook. 'And I will no longer have a son. Do you understand?'

And I believed her. I obeyed her. Because I no longer had a mamaidh.

*

Until the rain becomes a merciless downpour and I have to herd the sheep back into the barn, I force myself to keep working. There's still so much to do before winter takes proper hold. It's freezing cold now; I can feel my skin shrink against my aching bones as I push open the blackhouse door. I can hear voices in the kitchen: Mary and someone else. Even before I realise it's Charlie, the beating at my temples has returned.

'Charlie.'

They're standing too close, heads bowed together. Mary springs away from him so quickly, her hip knocks against the oven and she winces.

'Good to see you, Robert,' Charlie says, but this time his too-easy smile can't hide what's underneath. Guilt. I can always recognise it, like an old friend.

I turn to Mary. 'Where's Calum?'

'He's playing in his room,' she says, and her chin goes up like she wants to say something else.

'What brings you here, Charlie?'

'Not much.' Charlie's smile rallies. 'Just wanted to see how you were doing.' He blinks, glances briefly between me and Mary. 'Both of you.'

Something has changed in him. The way he looks at me is different, but I can't work out how. And it makes the cold anger in my belly start to heat.

'Mary,' I say. 'Give us a sec?'

I see the moment she thinks about saying no. But she doesn't. Instead, she gives Charlie her best smile, saying 'It's nice to see you again,' before spinning on her heel and leaving the room without looking at me at all.

'What do you want, Charlie?'

And still that smile won't quit. 'I just . . . wanted to say about the whole Land Fund thing, you shouldn't take what Thom said to heart. He'll be jealous is all. You're a farmer – you're already doing what he's suddenly taken it into *his* head to do. Christ knows, envy can make arses of the best of us – and Thom's certainly not that.'

I nod, annoyed that I've made my hurt at being excluded obvious.

'And I . . . I just wanted to see how you were after Saturday night. You know, after . . .'

Somehow, I'd thought it would help. Telling someone. I thought it would release some of that terrible pressure that's never stopped growing inside me; a gauge long past safe, long past red. But instead, telling Charlie has left a deep hole that hurts more, bleeds more, than any of my secrets ever did.

There's shame too. Shame not just for the why but the *all* I told him. When I'm sober and the day is sunny, I don't feel shadows behind me. It's not *bòcain* that wait in the dark and the drink. It's weakness. That scared, hurt wee boy who ruined my life. I hate Andrew. Every day I wish he'd died instead. That I'd been able to kill him. To smother the fear and hate and *weakness* inside him.

I close the kitchen door. 'What I said to you, it stays between us.'

Charlie folds his arms. 'Robert, I don't—'

I lunge at him probably before either of us knows I'm going to. But it's a relief: the anger that's become a rolling boil; the almost involuntary need to do something about it. I grab him by the shirt, twist it tight inside my fists as I yank him towards me.

'You ever tell anyone my name or what I said to you—'

'A man's business is his business,' Charlie gasps, his face and neck turning an ugly puce. He tries to prise my fingers free, but I only twist tighter as I lean close enough to see my own spit on his cheek.

'You tell anyone, I will kill you, Charlie.'

And then, because I realise I mean it; because I realise the poison in me – the shame, the boiling rage – means it, I let him go.

He staggers away from me, grabs his coat as he retreats to the mudroom and opens the front door. He only turns round again once he's standing halfway along the path, the wind whipping his hair. And the fury in his eyes is easily a match for mine.

'You're an arsehole. You're a fucking arsehole, Robert.'

*

I go to Àite Lurach. Even though the rain is still fierce and the skies over the Atlantic are stormy. Even though there's little that's lovely about the place in December. The meadow is boggy and colourless, the lochans choppy. But still, it calms me, dilutes the fog in my head. There's a peace here. A kind of quiet that even a storm can't disturb or destroy. Like those flat, impassive stones standing sentinel on the cliffs at Oir na Tìr. So tall they can block out the sun.

I climb the bluff almost to its windy summit. Stop at the large flat rock close to the bank and sit in its relative shelter. All around me is quiet. Thin, shivering roots hang down over every dark burrow, large or small, like beaded curtains over a doorway.

I shouldn't have done what I did to Charlie. Shouldn't have said what I said. I look at the wet, grey sky, the fast-moving clouds. I'm fucking it up. I think of Mary's *You don't need to own something to have it, Rob. You just need to believe that it's yours.* I'm fucking all of it up.

Mamaidh's face changed as quickly as she did. She never stopped wearing black, so sometimes that face – no longer thin and pale, but bloated and criss-crossed with red veins – was all that I could see of her. The firelight making wounds in her skin. The lowball tumbler that always shook in her hand.

On nights when storms battered the sea against the beach, and the tide bell's mournful toll echoed inside our cottage, she would stop drinking. She'd look at me for hours instead, and I'd wait for her rage, partly in hope of an end to those unblinking stares.

But I kept my promise. I never told.

And now I have.

Ghosts are just unfinished business. Unspoken truths. Guilt hiding under rocks, inside rabbit holes. They don't need to follow you because they are you.

There's a noise. Loud like a roar. Not from the beach or the sea, but inland and south, beyond the cemetery. When a group of people come running from the direction of Sid a' Choin Mhòir moments later, I stand up, squint to see what they're running from. But the rain has turned the southwest of the island into mist.

The dig. It has to be. I start running too, even though the grass has become slick with rain and the boggy ground untrustworthy. A welcome excitement grips me, one that's forgotten everything else, and that's incentive enough to keep running.

It takes too long to reach the narrow glen. I splash my way along it, towards shouts growing louder. Behind me, people are returning, laid low with rucksacks and rolls of tarpaulin.

Tòrr Dìseart is crowded with people, scurrying left and right like mice. I climb the ridge slowly – nothing can stop you like wet peat if it has a mind to – and once I make it to the top, I see Jaz standing a few feet away, handing out rubber tyres to a line of drenched archaeologists.

'What is it?' I shout, watching them run with those tyres towards the long trench closest to the cemetery, on the edge of the main excavated barrow.

Jaz turns in impatience, then grins wide when he recognises me. The first day I visited the dig months ago, I told him what I knew about the island's history, and in return, he spent hours showing me around the staked-out trenches and plans for excavation. He might be a mainlander and only eighteen, but I know he feels it the same as me: the pull of this land like no other.

'We found something!' he shouts over the wind and the rain and the urgency of those rushing to cover the trenches with tarpaulin. He waves an arm out towards the edge of the trench, where the head of the dig – a Professor Something-or-other who hasn't once given me the time of day – is crouched down and gesticulating wildly.

'Just wait,' Jaz says, as someone shouts his name and he starts heading towards the trench with the last of the tyres. His eyes are shining. 'It's amazing.'

I wait. I stand on the far southern edge of the ridge until the trench is secured, the rain becomes heavier, and the archaeologists start to pack up and reluctantly leave. Jaz stays behind, waits until everyone else has gone before making his way back to me. And even though we're alone, that sense of excitement, of *discovery*, is still palpable enough to raise the hairs along my skin.

'I'll show you,' Jaz says. 'But don't tell anyone I did, okay?'

I follow him along the ridge and round the barrow. Crouch down beside him as we reach the space between the cemetery wall and the covered trench.

'We'll have to be quick,' he says, pushing a couple of tyres off the tarpaulin and fighting to keep hold of it as the wind howls around us. 'It's already been exposed for too long.'

I'm expecting bones. This is, after all, a burial mound. But as Jaz reveals the trench, I see a body, a *person*. I almost recoil, not in fear or disgust, but something else – something I can't name. The body is curled into the foetal position on its right side, hands covering its face. Its limbs and torso are a muddy brown. It has hair, dark and matted against its skull. Its fingers are curled into fists that mirror mine. When Jaz drops the tarpaulin over the trench again, I almost snatch it out of his hands.

'It's amazing, right?' His eyes are still shining. 'Just amazing.'

'How can—'

'The body's mummified. Professor Higgins reckons it was buried in peat before being buried out here.' He grins. 'I mean, it's fucking *amazing*. He looks like he could have been buried a year ago, right? But everything – all the artefacts we've found so far – are late Bronze Age. He has to be three thousand years old.' His eyes widen. 'At least.'

I look down at the rain drumming against the tarpaulin, already forming puddles. My heartbeat is slowing, but my skin is still taut, my muscles rigid. 'How did he die?'

'We don't know for sure. There's blunt-force trauma to his skull. What might be stab wounds to his torso. The bones need to be carbon-dated, and then we can look at definitive cause of death. Find out for sure if he was killed. Find out why.'

But I know why. I think of those brown fists covering his face. The leather restraints around his wrists. I think of all the books I read when I was a kid. This is what people do. What they have always done. To protect themselves and those they love. Anger, rich and deep like sorrow, heats my skin and slows my heart. I think of my father slicing open a fish's belly and sprinkling its blood into the waves. *We sacrifice so that we are not sacrificed.* We offer up whatever we can to be safe. That's what really keeps a white-bright light burning.

CHAPTER 16

'What did Sheena say to you?' Kelly says. 'You seem upset.'

'Nothing really.' I try to shrug, but I can't shake off that look in Sheena's eyes as she'd said *You're not safe here.* 'Just telling me I should leave again.'

'Ignore her. God, she's just so *dour.*'

The sun might be out, but it's still chilly and all the picnic tables behind the pub are empty. We pick one close to the fenced-off cliff edge, overlooking the sound and Lewis.

Fraser runs towards us. 'Look! Look! I found another curly seashell.' He opens his hand and thrusts it towards Kelly. 'And it's still got its thing in it.'

'That's another snail,' Kelly says. 'Just put it back down, and be very gentle, okay?'

She makes a gagging face at me as soon as he does, and I laugh.

I can see the whitewashed cottages of Longwick on the other

side of the causeway and the narrow stone bridge that Jaz and I drove over when I first arrived. Shadows of clouds move slowly over grey rock and brown-and-purple moorland.

'Come on, Fraser, sit down and have your lunch,' Kelly says, opening a Tupperware container. She hands a sandwich to me. 'Bacon, egg, and brown sauce. Complete filth.'

'Where's that?' I point at what looks like another white-sand beach a little further up the opposite coast. It's much smaller than either Long Stride or Big Beach, more like a cove or inlet.

'Hollow Beach,' Kelly says. 'It's nowhere near the road, so a bit of a scramble to get down to.'

The name rings a bell until I remember what Charlie said at Isla's house. 'That's the beach where they found wee Lorne's dinghy after the storm.'

'Was it?' Kelly looks out over the sound. She shivers. 'Kind of creepy, I guess. Bit like those monuments at Long Stride.'

'I've been meaning to ask, have you spoken to your parents since the weekend? Asked them about Robert?'

Kelly stops eating, her sandwich frozen in mid-air. 'No. Sorry.'

'They must have moved into the blackhouse pretty soon after Robert died, I guess,' I say, feeling suddenly like I'm prying, or walking on eggshells like that day in Isla's cottage.

'Yeah. I mean, I don't remember it, obviously – I was, like, two. But yeah, they bought the blackhouse from Euan Morrison some-time in '94, I think. Like I said, Dad was set on becoming a farmer, God knows why.'

'But didn't you say your parents left Kilmeray in '95? Do you know why?'

'Actually, I think it was '96,' Kelly says with a quick shrug. 'I dunno. I mean, they never really talked about it. The storm was the worst to hit the island in decades, even without the deaths. It did a lot of damage.' She shakes her head. 'Maybe they realised they'd made a mistake and wanted to cut their losses. Get out of here.'

I glance again at Hollow Beach and the white-topped waves. *It was a bad black time.* 'I suppose it must have been horrible.'

Kelly nods as she looks away to rummage in her bag. When she turns to hand Fraser a yoghurt pot, her smile is back. 'Or maybe Dad was just a *really* shit farmer.' Her smile becomes a grin. 'So. On to far more interesting things – tell me what you found out in Stornoway.'

I let her change the subject because that closed look has come back into her eyes like it does every time I ask her about her parents, and I don't feel equipped today to wonder if maybe she's hiding something from me too. 'Well, Charlie was right about the dates.'

'Ah. So, no appearance on *Beyond Belief: Fact or Fiction* for you?'

'What?'

'Just some terrible TV show Fraser loves.' She pauses. 'Wait. Have you ever actually seen your birth certificate?'

'Sure.' But my laugh is a little too high as I try to remember if I actually have.

'Can I go on the slide, Mummy?' Fraser says.

'Have you finished your yoghurt?'

His answer is to turn the pot upside down before jumping off the bench and sprinting towards the mini-playground on the other side of the garden.

'So, what are your plans now?' Kelly says. 'Are you still going to write your story? Are you still going to be looking into whether Andrew was murdered?'

I find myself leaning back. Shaking my head. 'I don't know. I don't think so. I mean, the story, yes; the maybe-murder, no.' I like lying to Kelly least of all because of everything that I've already confided in her, about me, about Mum. But it isn't just that closed look or the suspicion that she or her parents might know more about Robert than she's letting on that makes me hold back from telling her the truth. It's because, for the most part, it's always been easier to confide as little as possible to anyone in the first place. Safer.

'So. On to *far* more interesting things,' Kelly says, after I say nothing else. 'You and Will. Spending the night together in Stornoway.' She raises her eyebrows. 'Please tell me you had a sweaty twelve-hour sex marathon.'

When I don't answer, and instead look back out across the sound, Kelly leans across the table.

'What?'

I shake my head, and then stop. Half nod instead.

'*What?*' Her shriek is high enough to momentarily distract Fraser from his ladder climb. 'Oh my God. I mean, I know I was acting like that's what I thought you'd been up to – but I didn't think that's what you'd *actually* been up to.' She grabs my arm and squeezes. 'Oh my God, Maggie! You are officially my hero. What was he like? I mean, I've definitely wondered.'

I can feel the heat rising in my cheeks and cough out a laugh. 'He was fine.'

'Fine? I bet he was a whole lot more than *fine*. But all right, I respect you respecting his honour. I'll just have to stick with my fantasies.'

And something must flash in my eyes at that, because Kelly lets me go to clasp her hands in delight. 'You *like* him!'

I shake my head, press the heels of my palms against my eyelids. 'I just . . . I don't know what I'm doing, Kelly. I mean, I barely know him.'

'Only you know what you should do, but if you need some reassurance, Will's a good guy. He really is.'

'I just. I dunno. I'm not supposed to be doing this. Acting on irrational or impulsive feelings is exactly what I'm supposed to avoid. To *notice*.'

'Maggie. Look. I don't know much. I get most of my life advice from the Kardashians and Dr Pimple Popper, but . . . you seem to have a better handle on yourself than most folk.' Even though she's smiling, her eyes are fierce. 'Plus, you had sex with Will Morrison. And I've got to tell you, there's nothing more fucking rational than that.'

Despite myself, I laugh, and when Kelly laughs back, I feel a burst of affection, of pure gratitude that makes me feel ashamed of my paranoia, my baseless suspicions.

'You're fine,' Kelly says. 'And I'll tell you, okay? If I ever think you're *not* fine. I promise.' She winks. 'In exchange, all you have to do is come back to the shop with me right now, so we can tell Sheena MacDonald that you've seen Will's willy. She'll die.'

*

I lean heavily against the wall of the phone box, watching two gulls chase a crisp packet down towards the ruined church as the phone rings and rings. I keep seeing that newspaper photo in my mind's eye; keep thinking, *What if Mum lied to me? What if none of it was ever true? What if she* made *me believe it?* Keep remembering Mum's tear-streaked face, all the times I heard *I'm sorry, Maggie, I'm sorry*. How little I cared in the end, how rarely I believed her.

It rings and rings. My heart is beating too fast and my throat is too dry; I keep having to swallow.

Don't take this away from me, Mum. Don't. Because – even despite that '9th of April' on the death certificate – I need her not to have lied. If I wasn't Andrew MacNeil in a past life then I need Mum not to have known it. Otherwise, I'll never be able to forgive either of us.

Just like outside the Harbour View, when the rings click over into an automated voicemail, my relief is far too big. But I take the reprieve anyway. I don't leave a message. It's not as if Gordon Cameron can phone me back, and I don't want to have this conversation over email. I want to hear his voice. And I want to hear the tone of it when he answers my questions.

I hang up and let out the breath I've been holding. A gust of wind rattles the phone box door, making me jump. The day outside has grown gloomy, but I jump again when I see that someone is standing in one of the cottage gardens, staring at the phone box. At me. I open the door and step back out onto the street. And I realise, with a sinking heart, that it's Alec. The cottage is furthest from the junction, but I can still see the hostile set of his shoulders and his folded arms. I can still see his narrowed eyes, the open anger on his face. It occurs to me that I don't actually know what he looks like without it. I consider going over to talk to him for only a few seconds; it will do no good. I may not like Sheena much, but I can't deny what she said the night Alec attacked me outside this very phone box. At best, I'm a reminder of what happened to his son, and that's more than reason enough to hate me.

I zip up my yellow mac, turn away from the village, and jog back towards the main road without looking at Alec again. About halfway to Ardcraig the heavens open, and I pull up my hood, lean into the rising wind. I hear something suddenly – a new sound, out of place – and I spin round, searching the gloomy road, the stony foothills of Ben Wyvis. There's nothing, no one. I resume walking, a little faster, and then it comes again. Footsteps, maybe hooves. Something moving and then stopped. Something that definitely doesn't belong to the wind or the rain.

I spin round again, wrench down my hood. The sea fog is back, curling white smoke across the tarmac, obscuring the Coffin Road and the mountain behind completely.

'Alec?' My voice is echoless and thin. I turn again when I think I hear the sound again, this time out towards the west and Ardcraig. I swallow, suddenly feeling as stupid as I feel exposed or freaked out. 'Sonny?'

A kite or buzzard cries loud somewhere over my head and I jump, heart drumming. Look up into the grey-white sky, the rain cold against my skin.

'Screw this.'

And then I don't just jog but run, keeping my head down and eyes trained only on the road all the remaining way back to the blackhouse.

*

Maybe there is someone following me. And maybe the same someone left strange dead crows on my path. And ran around the blackhouse in the dead of night, tapping on its windows. Maybe Alec. Maybe someone else. Maybe – *maybe* – the person who murdered Robert Reid. If Robert Reid was murdered.

But what good does maybe do me? What good does worrying do me? By the time I get ready for bed, I've managed to convince myself that even if there was someone in the fog, even if they're spying or trying to intimidate me, it doesn't matter, so long as that's all they do. I'm trying to take each day as it comes, without falling into old patterns of anxiety. I'm trying to be careful. Besides, the only alternative is to leave. To give up. I think of Will's thumb moving circles on my skin; Kelly's wide grin. That photo of me standing in front of the Valley of Ghosts, hair whipping around my head.

In the bathroom, I open my pill bottle with only a small hesitation, swallow the lithium with water before brushing my teeth. I pick up the town hall photocopies from the dining table, resist reading them through again; I know them almost by heart already anyway. Instead, I fold them in two and go over to the bedside table, reach down to open its only drawer.

And then I let out a shriek that hurts my throat as I stumble backwards, almost falling. Because inside that drawer, next to a couple of rusty keys and a pile of old coppers is another dead bird. It's the same as the others. A crow, black and grey and muddy brown, head turned to one side and feet curled into claws. Its chest is pitted with little black dots.

I shiver, heart thumping. I haven't ever opened that drawer, so I've no idea how long it's been here, but I do know that despite Kelly's *No one locks their doors around here*, I've been locking mine. So either it was here before I was, or someone somehow got into the blackhouse. I'm shaking. I look down at my hands as Ravi says *Are you having tremors? Anxiety?*

I force myself to calm down, to put the bird in the rucksack with the others. But when I slam shut the drawer, get into bed, and switch off the light – despite myself, despite the promise I only just made to myself – I start to think of someone, *something*, stalking me in fog and in darkness. Something bald and grinning with big, crowded teeth. And claws that could scratch black wounds into tarmac.

*

I realise I'd fallen asleep only when I wake up. For a few seconds, I don't know why I have, and then I smell it. See it. Just as the curtain next to the mantelpiece lights up the room in a low whoosh of orange flame. I throw myself out of bed and race towards the kitchen, knocking over dishes and jars in the dark and my panic – too alarmed, too terrified, by that guttering roar and heat behind me to remember where the light switch or the fire extinguisher are. When my hand closes around the latter, I wrench it from the wall and run to the curtain, now consumed by fire, the flames licking along its wooden rail and metal rings. I press down on the lever, and the foam covers the curtain in seconds, smothering the fire in only a few more. I bend over to cough. I'm breathing too hard and too fast; the smoke chokes my throat and scratches at my lungs. When I realise that the rug in front of the fireplace is burning too, I abandon the empty extinguisher, run back to the kitchen to turn on the light and grab the fire blanket. I drop it, stamping over the rug and floor probably far longer than I need to, stopping only when the adrenaline wears off enough that my legs forget how to keep holding me up.

I stay on my knees until my need to breathe fresh air outweighs my fear of going outside. I barely bother to get dressed – simply pulling a hoodie over my pyjamas and putting on my mac and wellies at the door. I grab the keys and Kelly's torch and run out of the blackhouse, stopping only to lock up behind me before sprinting across the grazing grass towards the lights of Ardcraig Farm, flinching from the occasional twin glare of what I hope are sheep's eyes.

*

'Well, it was eh . . . only a wee fire it looks like.'

In the cold light of day, and the colder Atlantic breeze through the kitchen window, it does indeed look nothing at all like the terrifying spectacle of last night. A slightly singed window frame and perhaps a foot of floorboard in front of the fireplace. The rug, tartan curtain, and pole are already in the wheelie bin round the side of the blackhouse.

'Looks like embers from the fire probably set the rug alight first before jumping to the curtain,' Detective Constable Lachlan Scott – 'Call me Lockie' – says, waving around the square leather notebook that he hasn't opened once. 'Heavy-lined curtains can go up like torches if you're not careful.'

He had much the same response to the dead birds in the rucksack when I showed them to him while Will was picking Kelly up from Blairmore, giving both the birds and me a similarly dismissive frown. 'Dead crows,' he said, as if expecting me to argue. 'You never seen 'em before?'

'Not on my doorstep. Not in my bedside drawer.'

'They look stuffed,' he said, giving one a sniff, although I noticed he didn't touch them.

'I think maybe someone is messing with me—'

The sound of a car door slamming had me closing the rucksack and shoving it under the dining table.

'Don't say anything about them,' I said, as Kelly pushed open the door. 'Please.'

And Detective Scott had given me another very long frown that perhaps he reserved only for tourists from London who'd rather invent a crazy local than admit they'd nearly set their holiday cottage on fire themselves.

''Course, neither would've happened if the fire guard had been where it was supposed to be,' he says now, looking down at the fireplace.

This rankles as much as – more than – the *if you're not careful*, because I *have* always been careful. All that wood panelling has made me nervous enough to go without a fire at all, more often than not. 'I put the guard back. I always put the guard back.'

'All right, Lockie,' Kelly says, rolling her eyes, and in a tone of voice that suggests he's not only a detective from Stornoway Police Station to her.

His cheeks flush red to prove it, and he pushes his notebook into his pocket and folds his arms. Looks at me with raised eyebrows.

I shouldn't have phoned the police this morning. Even before he arrived, I knew it. And everyone in the village now doubtless knows too. But I'd done it without thinking. I'd got up before Will, walked down to the phone box in Blairmore, and phoned Stornoway Police Station before I'd even thought about why I shouldn't. Not because I was scared. And not because I was worried that it was all in my mind; that perhaps I just didn't remember not putting out the fire or putting back the guard. I'd done it because I was hopeful. Hopeful that someone really was after me. That someone was trying to make me leave. And that someone – as ridiculous as both the idea and hope was – had been in the blackhouse not once, but twice. Because that hope diluted the *What if Mum lied to me?* It revived the theory that someone like that – no longer content with only hiding in the shadows or leaving behind dead birds – might well have murdered Robert Reid too.

Now, though, in the face of Detective Scott's patronising frown and Kelly's rolling eyes, not to mention Will loitering in silence inside the doorway, I feel mortified.

'Well then,' Detective Scott says. 'I suppose I'll be off. I'll send you a case number. If you need it.' He pauses as he passes Kelly, clears his throat. 'Kelly.'

'He was in my year at school,' Kelly says, when we hear his car engine start up. She gives a theatrical shudder as she pulls another tartan curtain out from a carrier bag. 'Snogged him at the sixth-year Christmas party.'

'Does anyone else have keys to the blackhouse?' I ask.

'No, I don't think so,' Kelly says, blinking in surprise. 'I mean, I've got a spare set, and . . . I guess maybe Mum and Dad, or someone who lived here before. But . . . you don't think—'

'No, no. Of course not. I – I'm just feeling a bit – ' I gesture towards the fireplace. 'I shouldn't have phoned the police, I'm sorry. I panicked. Thought maybe you'd need a report . . . for the insurance or something.' It's unconvincing enough that Kelly cocks her head, gives me a long, considering look.

'Are you sure you're okay?'

I nod. Grab hold of the end of the curtain. And then suddenly I remember what she said to me when she first opened the door to the blackhouse. *The lock's a bit iffy, I keep meaning to get it fixed.* Perhaps keys wouldn't have been needed at all. 'Yes.' I clear my throat. 'I'm fine.'

She finally smiles. 'There's really no harm done, Maggie. I'm just glad you're all right.'

'Maggie . . .' Will says from the doorway. 'I'd better be getting back to the farm.'

I put down the curtain, ignore Kelly's wink as I go over to the door. Will steps down onto the path, rubs a palm against the back of his neck. Last night, I'd lain awake next to him in his bed, having absolutely no idea what the etiquette of fleeing your house in panic versus one night of wild sex was. I'd woken at dawn, the heat of his body at my back, his arm tight around my waist.

'Thank you. You know, for . . . everything.'

'You're welcome to stay again tonight,' he says after a pause, gaze fixed on a point somewhere over my shoulder.

I think of that arm around my waist. His slow breath tickling my hairline. 'If I run out of sugar?'

'Aye.' He relaxes into his smile, and I pretend I don't feel that familiar *thump-thump.* 'If you run out of sugar.'

When I close the door and go back over to the fireplace, Kelly is pretending to be engrossed in threading plastic hooks through the curtain's lining, but when she looks up at me, her grin is wide enough I can see all of her teeth.

'Oh my God,' she laughs, fanning herself. 'I bet he could set a person's curtains on fire any time he wanted to.'

And despite myself – the tiredness, the mortification, the niggling fear, the *hope* – I laugh. Enough that, for a moment at least, I forget to think about anything else.

CHAPTER 17

I'm standing inside that cold light like a silver thread between the end of Mum's bed and the glare of the nurses' station though a small wire-grid window. I know she's awake because I can't hear the grating rattle in her chest and the back of her throat when she sleeps.

It's okay, Maggie, she says. And her smile is serene.

But it isn't.

And still I can feel all those people behind me. Watching. Waiting. Breaths held in expectant horror.

Mum's smile fierce now, with pointed teeth. *It's coming. It's close.*

Air swirls in cold eddies around my feet and ankles, making me shiver and shake. And behind me now, the growing tap, tap, tap of claws against linoleum, against rock. The shatter of glass. Voices, alarms. So much noise that suddenly I have to press my palms hard against my ears until it hurts. Until that light becomes darkness and the silence one long scream.

You have to believe me, Maggie!

'Hey, it's okay. It's okay.'

Will has one heavy arm around me; his free hand moves the damp hair from my face as I blink against too-bright sunlight. I'm breathing hard, too hard at first to speak, to tell him that I am, in fact, okay. Night terrors are nothing new. Instead, I let him hold me, soothe me, until I remember that this was what I'd let Ravi do in the beginning, before both of us accepted my needing comfort being as routine as putting out the bins on a Tuesday.

I think of waking from a nightmare of shadows and rock and grass and the howl of the wind, my throat raw from crying. And Mum running into the bedroom, pulling me onto her lap, rubbing my clammy hot skin and holding me so tight I could hardly breathe. *It's okay, sweetie. You're home. You're okay. You're okay.*

I pull away. 'I'm fine.' I try to smile. 'Sorry.'

Will's own smile is uncertain. His eyes are worried and wary. All the things I hate. All the ways in which I do *not* want him to look at me.

I get up onto my knees before straddling his pelvis, rock myself hard against him. He lets me do it for only a few seconds before he flips me onto my back, his weight warm and new.

'My way this time.'

He moves slowly, his gaze unwavering and intense, his arms a cage, and for a moment, claustrophobia is bigger than pleasure. He kisses me for long paralysing minutes, touching me until my skin is hot. When I feel the thick push of him inside me, almost painful but not quite, almost too much and not enough, I finally reach for him, pulling him close until there's no space left between us. I close my eyes at my name on his breath, hot and unsteady. Give myself up to the need in him that is suddenly wild and only for me. That has no use for any kind of control at all.

When I come, the pleasure takes me as far from pain as I have ever been, and I kiss him over and over, stroke my fingers down his back as he shouts and shudders. He collapses against me, lips moving wordlessly against my neck, and I tighten my hold on him, his weight heavy and hot. Our breaths are ragged. He lifts his head to look at me, and I don't want to look back but I do. Because this isn't just sex. I knew it three days ago; I know it for sure today. This is something so, *so* much more than just sex, than distraction, than *comfort* – and Will knows it too.

When he finally moves his weight away, I close my eyes.

'You should run out of sugar more often,' he says eventually. He's staring up at the ceiling, and his voice is light, smiling. Giving us both the chance to regroup.

I think about the dead crow. The maybe-stalker. The fire. And I know what he'll say. He'll try to rationalise, minimise; he'll try to make me feel better. It won't work. Instead, it will plant a seed in him, small but stubborn, one that he'll remember when I next tell him that something has happened. And he'll start to wonder if it really did.

I smile back. 'I am pretty hopeless at buying sugar. It's a problem.'

Will rolls onto his side and moves closer to me again, supports his head with one hand. The room is warm, the sheets pushed down to our waists. I look at his body, so strong and lean, so familiar to me already; the freckles on his shoulders, the darkness of his hair against the paleness of his belly.

He grins at my scrutiny, reaches out to trace a finger along my jaw, my collarbone. 'Not from where I'm lying.'

'Is that your dad?'

He smiles at me for a few more seconds before turning to look at the small wooden frame pushed up behind his bedside lamp. The photo is of a sun-faded and much younger Cora in jeans and check shirt, standing next to a tall, dark-haired man with Will's striking blue eyes.

'Yeah.'

'He looks like you.'

Will's mouth tightens. 'About all I ever got from him. That, and a phone call once every few years when he remembered I existed.'

'Tell me about Scotstoun School for Boys.'

'It had gargoyles and turrets. We got up at five, played rugby on Saturdays, went to church on Sundays. Best of all, my stepbrother, Iain, was in the same shitty dorm as me, and only stopped making my life miserable when I got big enough to make his worse.'

I reach out to cup his cheek, trace the shell of his ear, the way I wanted to when he talked about his dad. The dad he pretends not to care about, while keeping a photograph of him next to his bed. 'You were miserable there.'

He presses his lips against my palm; I feel his smile as he nods.

'No one's ever realised that.' He pulls back, takes hold of my hand instead. 'We're talking about me again.'

I shrug. 'So?'

'Maggie.'

I sigh. 'Will.'

'Come to the Lodge for lunch. I want Mum and Euan to meet you properly.'

Panic tightens like a belt around my chest as he sits up, glances towards the drawn curtain, still bright with morning sunlight. Perhaps he takes my silence as encouragement, because that smile only gets bigger. 'Come for me. Mum was bad on Wednesday, but it isn't always like that.'

And there it is. The biggest reason of all why I can't.

I shake my head. Look down at our clasped fingers, his thumb moving over my knuckles.

'Hey.' The sharpness of his voice makes me look up. He stares at me, unblinking. 'You can tell me anything, you know.'

'I'm bipolar.'

And when his expression doesn't change, when he just goes on touching me, I keep going. I try to make it worse. I tell him everything I told Kelly and more. About Mum, about me, about what happened at the crematorium, about the Maudsley.

'I'm sorry,' Will says. And when I feel brave enough to look at him again, there's no pity in his eyes. And that suddenly makes me so mad, I want to punch the understanding out of him. He hasn't got a clue.

'I was psychotic that day, Will. I was a crazy person. And it could happen again. You don't need that in your life. Especially with your mum being ill. Trust me. You don't *want* that.'

Because ninety-nine per cent of me knows when I'm high, knows even when it's coming. But the one per cent that doesn't is undeniable. Unreliable. That one per cent is *there*. And especially since that day in Hither Green Crematorium, I can't trust it at all. I can't trust me. I can't even trust the things that I want to believe; that I hope – *need* – to be true.

'I'm sure it's hard,' Will says, shaking his head. 'Bad. But it's not the same. Mum's only going to get worse.' A burst of anger darkens his eyes. 'That's it. That's all. She's just going to get worse.'

'I'm sorry.' It's easier not to look him, so I stare at that bright square of light behind the curtain instead. I see Mum's face – thin, white, eaten by shadows. *It's so close – I know it. The pain will send me mad, Maggie. It's coming back and it will send me mad. I know it. I see it.*

'I killed her,' I say. 'My mum. I helped her die.'

I don't know what's wrong with me. Why I'm saying this – spewing out some awful confession, when I've never wanted to before. I feel stripped down to my bones. Maybe this is the new me I'm trying to become. Or maybe I just finally *need* to tell someone – I couldn't, after all, even tell Dr Abebe. And maybe I need to tell someone why I'm here too. Why I need Robert Reid to have been murdered. Why the things that I hope for are as awful as they are self-serving.

'The doctors said she was improving. The chemo was working. She was still terminally ill, but her prognosis had become years instead of months. But she didn't believe them. She believed she only had weeks. She said she'd seen her future, and the doctors were either lying or wrong. That she would die a terrible, slow, agonising death unless I helped her to beat it.'

And at once, I'm in that room again: the darkness, the silver thread of light, Mum's bed, the small wire-grid window. I can smell her stale, sour breath. Hear those long swinging tubes; the endless drip, drip, drip of fluid in the dark. Heat fizzes through my body, ugly and burning. The bottle rattles as I open it. All the pills she'd stockpiled at home after so many operations. Because she'd known. She'd *seen*. And when I hesitate, when I start to say no again, she presses her cool and steady fingers over mine. The curly wisps of hair at her temples and that serene half-smile.

Please, Maggie. You have to help me. You have to believe me. Make it go away.

And I can feel the wet burn of the tears that run off my chin and soak into my shirt as I shake all those pills out into my hand.

'I did it,' I manage to say to Will now, blinking against that bright square of daylight behind the curtain. 'I helped her. Just because she asked me to. The hospital thought she'd done it herself. I mean, she could have, you know? She could have. She just . . . she wanted us to do it together. She wanted me to be there.'

I finally find the courage to look at Will again, but his expression is very carefully blank. I take in a breath like I've been holding it underwater and it makes both of us jump.

'I need her to have been right about us being psychic, about everything she told me. I need her not to have lied. Not to have coached me. Not to have made any of it up. I *need* to have been Andrew MacNeil. I need that to be true. Because otherwise . . .

otherwise, I helped my own mother to die because of a delusion. Maybe *our* delusion.' I notice I'm twisting my fingers again. 'And because . . . she made me do it, she made me help her, she made me feel like *this* . . . and I need it not to have been just another one of her godawful tests.'

I shake my head, close my eyes. 'All those years ago – here – I *was* certain, Will. I really was. And Mum, her whole life, was always so, so certain of us. I think I've always thought in the back of my mind that maybe . . . maybe at least some of it was real. That maybe we did know what other people forget or can't see. That we come back.' I'm almost whispering; my throat working too hard to swallow. 'Because if Mum – if she was right, if she *was* psychic, and everything she said was true, then what I did was a mercy, a kindness. It was the right thing.'

Will catches my fidgeting fingers, gently straightens them against the sheets. 'And proving Robert Reid was murdered is the only way you can know.'

My laugh is brittle. 'I mean, I know how ridiculous it sounds, I do. And I know that proving it isn't definitive proof that I was once him or that Mum wasn't lying.' Even as that little desperate voice inside me insists, *But you're living in his house, his house.* I look down at our hands. 'But it would be *something.* I'm not afraid of being bipolar. But I am afraid of what happened after Mum died – of that person who became psychotic because she stopped taking her meds for the first time in ten years. I can't lose control like that again. I can't let myself *feel* like that again.' My voice is so hoarse now, I can hardly speak. 'I can't hate myself – or her – like that again. I don't think I'd survive it.'

Because what I felt – what I can *still* feel – in that awful room is bad enough. Mum's laboured breathing warm against my skin as I help her lie back against the pillows. Her fingers no longer steady, her smile no longer serene – no longer a smile – as the minutes tick past in that hot oppressive dark. I feel her fear, sharp and brittle and growing. I see the shine of it in her eyes. I say her name, I whisper it. And when she says mine, I hear the regret in it, maybe even the horror.

'Mum, should I get someone?'

My heart shuddering inside my chest when she answers only with that rattle; that dry choking thing that sometimes I hear in my dreams. 'Should I get someone?'

And because I did – and far too late – she died in the dark, in that room. Afraid and completely alone.

'Maggie.'

I close my eyes. 'I'm sorry.'

'It doesn't matter if your mum was lying or not,' Will says. 'Hey, Maggie. Look at me.'

When I do, his expression is anything but blank. He squeezes my fingers hard. 'You did the right thing.'

'Will—'

'I'd do it too.' His pupils are so wide his eyes are almost black. 'If Mum asked me to. Next week, next year. Tomorrow. I'd do it.'

My nose and eyes burn with the tears I refuse to cry.

'Is that it?' Will says. 'Everything you think makes you a terrible person? Everything you hope will put me off you?'

'You'd be crazy not to be.'

His smile is rueful. 'You've got to stop using that word.'

Crazy *is a word for lazy, stupid people, Maggie.* Eyes always bright, smile always wide as if she knew something everyone else only wanted to. *Don't forget that.* Crazy *is for lazy.*

Will pushes aside the sheets and moves close enough to me that my skin warms and comes instantly alive, my breath quicker in my chest.

'I like you, Maggie. From the moment I saw you I *more* than liked you. And you don't have the monopoly on doubting yourself, you know. On not knowing what's good for you.' He gives me that smile, slow and generous. 'But I *will* be good for you, Maggie MacKay. In whatever way you want me to be. I think this kind of *more than like you* means I don't have much choice.'

The lump in my throat is back, but with it comes a feeling of excitement, of unknown and new. And it's a good feeling. The first real good feeling I've had in so long that I suddenly don't care about careful. Or about *being on my own for a bit.* Or even, for right now at least, about that last night in the hospital.

Perhaps Will takes my silence for indecision because he backs off a little, dropping his hands to his sides. 'We can go slow. As slow as you like.'

I look at the sheets, and then the length of his naked body. 'This doesn't feel slow.'

He grins. 'We can go slower.'

Because I have to touch him, I reach out to press my palm against his chest, the pale muscles of his abdomen.

'Come out in the sunshine with me, Maggie,' he says. 'And have lunch with Mum and Euan. Please.'

I watch the goosebumps rising along his skin. 'That doesn't feel slow either.'

'No.' For the first time his smile is uncertain. 'Probably not.'

'I'm pretty sure Donnie thinks I'm going to break your heart,' I say, too quiet.

'We're talking about Donnie now?'

'I don't want to break your heart.'

He looks at me. 'Then don't.'

I finally give in to my own smile, to that feeling of unknown and new. 'I'll go to the Lodge with you.'

Will laughs and pulls me down on top of him, squeezes me hard enough that for a moment I can't breathe. He loosens his grip and buries his head in the crook of my neck, and holds me like that for so long that I have to feel it: the relief. Both his and mine. And when something like happiness bursts inside my chest, just like that day on the beach, I let myself feel that too. I let myself want it.

And I almost believe it.

*

The Big Hoose is just as impressive inside as out. The entrance hall is cavernous. Dark oak panelling on every high wall, a grand and wide staircase with carved balustrades and green velvet carpet. Large archways branch off into long, gloomy corridors. Painted portraits cover the walls; most look impressively old: men in full highland dress, women in corseted gowns and complicated wigs. An intimidating array of swords and shields are mounted on the largest wall above two cherrywood cabinets displaying a number of shotguns behind thick glass.

Inside an alcove lit by electric candle sconces is a huge framed painting of Cora and Euan standing on a grand alabaster staircase: Cora in ivory silk; Euan in the Morrison tartan: dark shades of green inside square red borders. In the foreground, standing next to a granite pillar topped with marble is a tall, sullen boy in the same kilt and jacket and a much smaller boy in a silver suit and pink dicky bow, grinning widely.

'Oh my God, is that *you*?'

Will laughs. 'And Iain. Mum and Euan got married in Glasgow City Chambers. My sister, Heather, got to stay here, jammy bastard. Chickenpox.' He grins. 'You want to have seen the monstrosity they'd had lined up for her.'

'You're early.' Euan ambles towards us through one of the big wooden archways. He's wearing another too-tight tweed suit, a blue silk tie. I realise Will and I are holding hands, and I drop mine to my side.

'It's lunchtime,' Will says.

'My dear boy, it's barely gone noon. Practically still elevenses.' He cocks an eyebrow. 'She'll flap.'

'Ach,' Will says. 'She's fine. Mum loves feeding folk.'

When they embrace, Euan's laugh is as hearty as ever. 'And how are you, Maggie?' he asks, kissing me on both cheeks. 'Getting the lay of the land?'

'Just about,' I say, when Will winks at me. I feel ridiculously nervous. 'Um, maybe I could help Cora?'

'That would be very kind of you.' Euan points towards the

largest corridor. 'Kitchen is the fourth right. We'll be along in just a jiffy.'

As I go, I hear Euan clear his throat. 'A good day today, son.'

The kitchen is as vast as everywhere else. A beautiful tiled floor, wall-to-wall wooden cabinets and granite work surfaces, a burgundy six-door gas range. The room is dominated by a huge wooden dining table, currently set for four people. Cora is sitting at its end, shredding lettuce into a bowl.

She looks up as I come in, gives me a vague and polite smile as she wipes her hands on a tea towel.

'It's Maggie,' I say. 'Will's friend.'

Her smile remains, but there's no recognition in it, which is perhaps as well. 'Will's here?'

'Yes. He's just talking to Euan.'

I can't quite meet her gaze, and in the following silence, I suddenly realise that I'm behaving towards her the way people have behaved towards me. It's something of a revelation – how automatic it is: the wariness, the awkwardness, the not knowing what to say, or how to separate a person from what they have said or done.

I glance at the counter where there's a chopping board full of sliced peppers and tomatoes, and guess that's what Euan was doing before we arrived.

'I could finish chopping those vegetables?' I say.

'Thank you, dear,' she says before returning her attention to the bowl and the shredding of her lettuce. Her smile is fleeting. 'That would be nice.'

On impulse, I reach out to squeeze her shoulder before thinking better of it and retreating to the counter instead. Because it's not sympathy I feel. Nor empathy. It's anger. Deep-seated and too hot. How fucking unfair life is. How relentlessly merciless. And we're just supposed to go on living anyway.

*

'So how's the story going, Maggie?' Euan asks, leaning back in his chair. 'Will said you were at the town hall on Tuesday. You find what you wanted?'

We're briefly alone. Cora went for a nap after lunch, and half an hour later, Euan sent Will upstairs to check on her. I wonder now if that was because Euan wanted to ask me this question, although I'm glad of the chance to ask my own with no one else around.

'Yes.' I glance at him. 'I just wanted to check Robert's birth and death certificates.'

'Ah.' Euan nods. 'After Charlie spilled the beans about Andrew, eh?'

I think of that photograph. The tall out-of-focus figure at its water-damaged edge that I'd thought might be Euan.

'I think . . . I mean I'm sure Charlie just wanted—'

Euan smiles, pats my hand. 'It's all to the good. These things always come out in the end. Best that those who know are the ones to say.'

I take a scalding sip of coffee. 'Did you like Robert?'

After a short pause, Euan sighs. He stares hard at the china dish of expensive-looking biscuits between us. 'A better question would be did Robert like me? And the answer was not a bit. Was I fortunate to be born a Cill Maraigh Morrison? Of course I was. But birth rights and privilege are never equal; all any of us can do is better than we have done. Which, someone like Robert would say, is very easy for a fortunate man to say. He loved the islands, the land, and we Hebrideans have long had fierce attachments to both, no matter who owns them.' He smiles grimly. '*The man with the house and the steading of his own, and the land closer to his heart than the flesh of his body.*

'Robert wanted to own the blackhouse and the Ardcraig farmland. Or at least, he claimed he did. Over and over. Every community meeting. He had no means to buy them. None at all. But the chip on Robert's shoulder was, I think, as vital to him as his blood or heartbeat. I don't blame him for it. But he blamed me, all right.' He shrugs, and something that he's trying very hard to hide, or perhaps not to feel, darkens his eyes, undermines his smile. 'I'm sorry for what happened to him. He was still a young man. He had a young family. But some people, they just never live. They somehow *can't* live. And that was Robert. There's really no more to know about him than that.'

I glance at him and clear my throat. 'Do you remember anything about the documentary filmmaker who came here with me and Mum?'

Euan looks momentarily surprised by the question. 'Gordon Something, I think he was called. Or Something Gordon. Glaswegian. Slick. Asked questions like accusations, like he thought he was a hair's breadth away from catching you in a lie.' He shakes his head. 'Got just about everyone's backs up in a day.'

I jump when I suddenly hear what sounds like a gunshot. And then another. Euan reaches over the table and pats my hand again just as Will comes back into the room with Cora in tow.

'Mum was awake,' Will says before nodding towards the big window. 'Doubt she would have slept through that lot anyway.'

'Don't worry, my dear,' Euan says to me when another loud crack sounds, closer this time. 'It's just a hunting party out on the estate. Godawful bunch from Edinburgh, wouldn't know their own arse from a pheasant's, but we don't tend to get many bookings this time of year.' He frowns. 'Our days of being picky are long gone.'

Cora turns towards the radio, which has been playing at a low volume, and suddenly claps her hands. 'Oh, it's our wedding song, Euan.'

'I'm too long in the tooth to be dancing,' he says, but he's smiling as he stands up and starts to lead her into a waltz across the kitchen tiles.

The song is old, vaguely familiar. Will rolls his eyes, smiles at me. 'Clannad. Always with the old Celtic folk music.'

Euan laughs. 'Ask Maggie to dance.'

He gets up, holds out his hand. 'Will you do me the honour of dancing to this terrible song with me, Maggie?'

And then that's what I'm doing, dancing around this huge kitchen with a man I barely know and his family, and there's no other place in the world I'd rather be.

'*I will find you, if it takes a thousand years.*' Will grins, his palm warm against my back, his eyes warmer. 'Kinda screams stalker, right? What's wrong with "Don't Worry, Be Happy"?'

Euan's eyes are shining as he looks over at us and then back at Cora, his hand leaving her waist to cup her cheek. 'It's about love.'

And the look that he shares with Will then is full of pain, bittersweet with that same dark anger at its roots. How hard it is to love who we're going to lose. How hard, how strangely unexpected, the realisation that we were always going to lose them. I think of that hot, dark room. How impossible it is to accept that we have always been alone.

CHAPTER 18

In over three weeks, there have been no more dead birds. And, as far as I know, no night-time visitors.

But I haven't lit another fire. And I'm wary of staying in the blackhouse at night, with its *iffy* front-door lock and collection of dead crows, now stuffed back behind the coat rack in the mudroom. Never mind the ghost of Robert dragging my hope around behind him. I still don't like walking alone at night either, hearing sounds behind the wind and waves; seeing shapes in the absolute dark between the Coffin Road and the mountains, the Valley of Ghosts. Knowing and doubting that there is always someone there. Watching.

I've begun meditating every day, faithfully documenting my moods in Dr Abebe's journal. I take long walks to Roeness and Lovely Place, or down to Long Stride to picnic with Kelly and

Fraser. And in these three weeks there have been no dreams, no night terrors. Even awake, I feel calm.

This morning, I can hear the sound of Will's ATV out in the west. At noon, I'll go over to the farm and we'll eat stovies or sweet porridge and drink strong black coffee. He'll try to convince me to stay, and I'll pretend that I need to be convinced. The sun is low in a cloudless sky; it warms my skin through the kitchen window. Frost sparkles on the short grass. I'm trying very hard to live in these moments. To resist the urge to look only forwards, to see only disaster.

I know what I'm really doing. I'm procrastinating because, despite everything, I'm happy. I came here with a purpose – but it was a purpose that was prepared to entertain only one answer. And because I didn't like the one I was getting, the truth that every day I was closer to discovering, I've stopped. It all amounts to the same thing: happiness has always made me a coward.

The money from Mum's bank accounts now sits in mine; enough that I don't need to worry about work – or life – for a while, at least. I look at the photo of Robert still propped up against the wall next to my laptop. Think of Charlie's *You got your questions, you got your answers.* I haven't spoken to him since then, hate that he might still be angry with me. Because every morning I sit down at this table and I pretend to research Robert's life, his death. I pretend that tomorrow I'm going to go down to the village to try to call Gordon Cameron again. I pretend not to be glad that no one's trying to scare me any more – if they ever were. I pretend that I still believe I can somehow prove that Robert was murdered and that Mum was right about us, about me. I pretend that I still want to know. Because if I don't, the guilt comes rushing back in like a tsunami.

When Charlie and his dog, Bonny, pass the blackhouse just a few hours later, it seems like a sign. I look at the picture of Robert again, standing in his meadow; folded arms, stoic frown.

'I know,' I say, getting up from the table. 'I need to say sorry.'

I glance towards the coat rack in the mudroom. And I need to ask him one last question.

Outside, the day is calm, and the island is quiet; I can't even hear the familiar sounds of the dig. I see no one on the short walk from Ardcraig to Big Beach. Even the Laird's Lodge looks deserted. When I crest the hill above Lovely Place, I stop. Overnight, the meadow's grass has been covered in a blanket of short, dense flowers. Pink and purple and yellow, as far as I can see. Will's machair. The sun turns the flowers brighter, the lochans dazzling. Rabbits are running and jumping all around the bluffs. The breeze smells of the sea, warm and westerly, tickling my skin. After the rain and cold and dark, it's magical. It makes me think of lying in bed while Mum read about Hobbiton and the Shire. Another moment to live in.

I skirt the meadow and climb the bluff. The dunes are just as white and deep as before; by the time I make it far enough along the beach to attract Charlie's attention, I'm so out of breath I can hardly muster a shout.

When he sees me, he doesn't do anything for a few seconds, and then gives a brief wave. The way gets easier the closer I get to the shore. I glance up once, towards the long headland of Roeness, and although I realise it's because I'm looking for the solitary figure who watched Will and me, I'm still startled when I see him again, standing on that high cliff edge. Watching. I flinch at a sudden flash, and then another. He isn't just watching. He's watching through binoculars.

The shiver that skates between my shoulder blades is fleeting, but it's enough to dampen my mood, remind me of those after-dark walks.

'Sonny,' Charlie says, with a shrug and a smile that doesn't quite reach his eyes. He's holding a long fishing rod in one hand and a bait box in the other. 'He likes to know what's what.'

'Maybe I should try to talk to him?' I ask before I remember that I'm here to make amends.

'You'd be farting against thunder there.' Charlie snorts. 'Sonny's not a great fan of visitors. Or talking.'

A wet and breathless Bonny runs towards me and pushes her head against my leg, licks my fingers.

'She'll only be a sook to you till she realises you've nothing tasty to offer,' Charlie says. 'We were off to Loch Dubh, but spring has definitely sprung. Bonny was in seventh heaven when she saw all the rabbits.'

'How are you, Charlie?'

He squints in the sunshine. 'All right. You?'

'I'm sorry about that day in Isla's cottage,' I say, when I realise that the awkwardness between us isn't going to thaw. 'When I asked you about who went to the whisky festival. You had every right to be pissed off.'

He shakes his head, looks out at the horizon. 'It was me I was angry with. I'm the one stirred everything up.' He glances at me.

'Stirred *you* up. I shouldn't have arranged the meeting at Isla's. I care about her, she's been through a lot. I was just being a stupid old man with too much time on his hands. I should learn to let things lie. Just relax and enjoy life.'

'I don't think I ever have,' I say. The breeze cools the sweat at my temples as I watch the waves. 'I don't think I've been happy before. I mean, even when I was a kid, I'd watch other kids playing, laughing, and I'd think, why are you happy? One day, your parents will die. One day, you'll die. I've always been scared of being hurt or sick or alone, because I knew those things would happen. That they always happen. *Everyone* knows they always happen, but somehow they can make themselves forget. They can choose living in a moment instead of a whole life. And I don't know if I can.'

I stop, appalled. Snap shut my mouth so hard that I bite my tongue.

'*But pleasures are like poppies spread / You seize the flow'r, its bloom is shed,*' Charlie says.

'What's that?'

'"Tam O'Shanter." Rabbie Burns.' Charlie runs his finger under his nose. 'Now, there was a man knew how to enjoy life. Bit too much.' He reaches into his pocket, brings out his battered hip flask, and hands it to me. 'Heard you had dinner up at the Big Hoose?'

'Lunch,' I say, as relieved at being offered his awful rum again as the fact that he's changed the subject.

He looks at me. 'There's nothing wrong with being happy, Maggie.'

I think of his ex-wife. His dreams about the Coffin Road. The easy-going guy who loved to laugh, who'd taught Will how to swim in Loch Dubh.

'And there's nothing wrong with being scared either. Sometimes, happy can make you stupid. Or blind.' He reaches out to pat my hand, and awkwardly enough that I can tell he's not used to doing it. His eyes darken. 'Be happy. Just don't let it carry you away.'

He stares out at the horizon, and I wonder what – who – he's thinking of. And then he lets out a sigh and gives a sharp whistle for Bonny.

Before he can leave, I shrug the rucksack off my back and unzip it, pull out the hastily wrapped hand towel. I put it down on the sand to unwrap it; brace myself for the sight of empty eye sockets and long, thin wing ribs.

'Jesus,' Charlie says, but when I look up, the sun is over his shoulder, hiding his expression.

'What are they?' I ask, squinting up at him. 'I've kept them in the blackhouse mudroom for four weeks. They don't smell, they don't rot. I thought they might be stuffed, but—'

'Where did you find them?' His voice is still calm and impassive, but something has changed. Perhaps it's *too* calm.

'You know what they are.'

He nods, still looking down at the birds. He moves, blocking out the sun. His face has gone pale. '*Vándr-varði.*'

'Is that Gaelic?'

He shakes his head. 'Old Norse. They're talismans. *Varði* means "to guard against something" and *vándr*. . .' He pauses. 'Means "evil".'

'Evil? What, like spirits?' I search for the word. '*Bòcain?*'

Charlie looks at me sharply. 'Like *bòcain*, yes.'

'But why do they look like that?' I ask, when I realise that he isn't going to say anything else.

Charlie gives the birds another reluctant glance. 'They've been mummified. In peat. That's how you make them.'

'Make them?' I think of Miko describing those bog bodies discovered at the first dig; Femi's glee as he talked about human sacrifices and *Frankenstein*. 'Someone *made* them?'

I look at their skin, the brown shafts of their bones. I think of their wings fanned out and heads touching like an arrow pointing straight at the blackhouse. I think of someone running around the blackhouse in the middle of the night, knocking on its door, perhaps even coming in. Am *I* the evil thing that needs to be guarded against? The thought that someone might think so revives the shiver between my shoulder blades.

'Have *you* ever made them?'

'What? No.' Charlie rolls his eyes. 'Christ, I know life is a wee bit different here, Maggie, but we don't all sit around inside our cottages making thirteenth-century Norse talismans. I didn't even know what they were until—' He stops himself, shakes his head. 'It's just superstition, like nailing horseshoes to a mast or always turning right out of the harbour.' He finally manages to look at me. 'Just like that piece of quartz around your neck that you always rub whenever you're worried about something.'

I look down just as I realise I'm doing it, the pendant smooth and cold against the pad of my thumb.

'You found it here, you know,' Charlie says.

'*Here?*'

He nods. 'On this beach. You ran off, and your mum just about

243

lost her mind. And then we found you down by the east bluffs, holding that piece of quartz like it was a nugget of gold.'

I think of a pink box and white bow. A chain so long, its silver links caught the light as I pulled and pulled it out. It feels as alarming as it does comforting – to realise that I've always had a part of this place with me. *Careful*, that coward in my heart and head says.

'Guess we all need talismans,' Charlie says after a moment, and his voice has lost its steadiness.

And maybe his pause, that unsteadiness, is why I find myself asking the question to which I'm no longer sure I want to know the answer. 'Did Mum . . . did she ever tell you that she knew Robert? Or about what happened to him?'

Charlie gives me a sharp look that I can't read. 'No. What makes you ask that?'

'I don't know. I guess I'm still trying to make some sense of it all.' I look down at the dead crows. And then I catch my breath when I realise what he just said. 'You didn't even know what they were until *what*, Charlie?'

This time, he's quiet for maybe half a minute. Then he takes in a long hard breath and straightens his spine. 'I only ever knew one person who made *vándr-varði*. Who even knew what they were.' When he finally looks at me, I can't read what's in his eyes. 'And that was Robert Reid.'

CHAPTER 19

Robert

As a boy, I ran away when the first storm came – the first after that last. I ran inland, away from the waves at the headland's edge, their screaming thunder and fast shadows. I ran across the peat moor, my feet sinking and sticking, my breath cold and sharp inside my throat. The storm swiftly overtook me: clouds racing black over the way ahead, sheets of rain hiding the road to Uig and Ìslibhig. And I felt fishermen in the wet roaring wake behind me, breathing salty breath against my skin.

And then there was Loch-na-each, its surface wide and choppy; an inlet – an *ingress* – for the angry sea, blocking my escape. Its grassy banks so soft and sodden that I couldn't stop sliding down and down. I screamed when dark water closed over my feet and calves, and grabbed for the grass, coming away with handfuls of only mud. The fishermen laughed inside low rolls of thunder and the rattle of rain against the sea loch. They swam up from its tidal depths, cold fingers pinching at my ankles, trying to pull me out into the deeper water, trying to pull me down. Because they were gods now. Rán, the sea goddess of death, had collected them in her net, and now they lived under the sea like the Sjóvættir. Their names were etched into stone and memory, more vital dead than alive, and righteous with vengeance. And I was the boy who'd traced their shapes against glass and marched towards the light on Àird Èinis with rage in my heart and rocks in my pockets.

But who would help me? Who would save me? My father's hate was heavy and tidal. Just like my mother's. My flailing hands reached and reached for the land – missing, touching, slipping, losing – and then, not grass, not mud, but something cool and sharp and solid. I saw its eye. The hole where its eye should be. The long black beak, the brown sleek skin. A crow.

Suddenly I had the strength to pull myself up out of the loch and onto the bank, where I lay on my side gasping like a landed fish, until the rain stopped and the thunder drew further away. I sat up, wrestled the bird as gently as I could from the peat bank, carried it home tucked safely inside my coat. Put it under my pillow, directly beneath my head.

I knew that I had found a *vándr-varði*. Óðinn, the Raven God, had saved me from the fishermen. From my father. The land had saved me from the sea. I opened the drawer of my bedside table. Looked at the grey metal slingshot, its flat band looped inside a knot. I hadn't used it – hadn't even looked at it – since that terrible day, that terrible night. But now I could use it for good. I could use it to save myself.

I reached under my bed for the heavy *Norse Mythology and Legends II*. Turned to chapter 3, 'The Process of Mummification'. Because I would need more. A lot more.

*

When the first of the big storms finally arrives, I'm not expecting it. Still not ready for it. The skies over the headland have been growing darker for hours, and I've watched them as I round up the flock. Waiting for the clouds to turn north or south, to go out to sea or towards Lewis as they have every time before. But instead, they grow only darker and closer, and when the rain starts, the thunder isn't far behind.

The sheep are spooked, disobedient. For more than a month it's seemed like they're less tired and listless than actually sickening for something, even if the vet can find no cause. When Bruce suggested I use a different feed supplier than the one he'd always recommended, his smile was more apologetic than worried. 'No point trying to save money, Robert, if it ends up costing you more.' During our now regular end-of-week drams in the blackhouse with Mary, he's given me much the same advice regarding Thom and Alec's Ùrbost card game. I value the advice over those drams, though I'd never admit it.

I pretend not to be relieved when I get the sheep back into the barn; pretend not to be dismayed when I notice one is missing. The storm's fury is louder, wilder as I drive the ATV back towards the grazing land; the tyres' grip far poorer. When I arrive, I have to turn on my torch – it's barely three in the afternoon but the world is black as night. And it feels as if there's no one in it but me.

And then I see her. In the lee of the cemetery hill. A pale round shape with glowing white eyes. I kill the engine and circle towards her slowly, despite the rain, the brutal and still rising wind. She must have got lost and sought shelter, although it's unusual for any sheep to separate from the flock. I lower my light as I get closer, but she makes no move to run when I get to within her flight zone. She doesn't acknowledge me at all.

The fear in me is old enough that it should be diminished. Neglected enough that it should be rusty and forgotten. But it has woken up in me as if the roiling Atlantic and the blazing sky are its alarm clock. The darkness makes me feel dizzy and disorientated, as if I'm somewhere else entirely. Somewhere far beyond the fence. In the *utangarðs*.

What shelter the hill offers is poor. The wind and rain are hardly lessened at all as I crouch to get within a couple of feet of the pregnant ewe. She's lying down, front legs splayed. Her cheeks are tight and concave and her ears point down and back – she's in pain. Her eyes flinch from the torch as she turns to look at me and her eyelids droop.

I set the torch aside as I touch her head, and then feel down each leg for breaks or swelling. When I press my palms against the soaked coat of her flank and swollen belly, she flinches, curls her lips. 'Easy, girl.'

The rain gets heavier as I shine the torch back towards the ATV. Maybe fifty yards. But when I force her rump down against my braced knees to lift her, she goes rigid and lets out a *baa*, harsh and high and distressed. I let her go, sink down into the mud on my knees. She barely moves, barely registers my proximity, makes no sound at all as the sky bellows and lights up the island white and bright like a flare. And then all I see is red. In the following blackness, I pick up my torch and turn it onto us. Blood. Thick and wet and everywhere. Covering the ewe's coat from shoulder to flank. All over my hands, my sleeves, my thighs.

I don't need to put either of us through trying to find out where it's coming from because it's already far too much to matter. When she *baas* again, low-pitched and weak, I take the battering, panicking fear inside me and squeeze it down tight into a box, close its lid. I lift her head onto my knees, and she opens an eye long enough to look up at me.

'It's all right, girl,' I say, stroking her head, those flat down ears. 'It's all right.'

She closes her eye again, her breath puffing shallow and fast, and I stay with her as the storm rages all around us, the rain streaming off the end of my nose, my chin; the lightning turning the land into a hellscape of dark shadows and silver-bright plains. The sea louder than even the thunder: a pounding roar that longs to grind us into sand and dust. I stay with her as her breathing slows, until I can only see the fog of my own exhalations. I reach down to feel for a pulse at the top of her back leg, but there's none. I stay on my knees, stroking her head and ears for a few minutes more. Just to make sure. Dying alone is my greatest fear – greater even than being seen for what I am.

When I am sure, I lay her head back onto the ground, and get up slowly, my limbs stiff with cold. Another boom of thunder makes me flinch; the lightning that follows fast on its heels throws the towering Beinn Uais into stark relief against the white sky.

The fear burns inside me like poison. It revives the need to run away, across pasture and bog and road until I'm anywhere but here. Instead, I return to the ATV, make myself drive as slowly as I can back towards the road. When I reach the blackhouse, I make myself keep driving eastwards, finally coming to a stop alongside Loch Tana. Standing inside Beinn Uais's vast shadow does nothing to alleviate the hackles on my neck, the shudders chasing up and down my spine. But I keep going. Across the Coffin Road and then into the darker V between the mountains. Gleann nam Bòcan, the Valley of Ghosts.

My boots sink into the saturated peat; my torch creates as much gloom as light as I head deeper inside that narrow valley. I see the spot just as I become certain that I'm never going to: a deep, old fissure filled with spongy green moss at the base of the mountain's eastern flank. I drop back onto my knees again, start digging down into the mud with my hands.

I find the first quicker than I'm expecting to, and as I pull it free the relief is almost nauseating. The crow is covered in mud, but I can tell that its skin is too soft, too pliable. It hasn't been long enough yet, weeks rather than months, but needs must. I excavate three – one for each of us – and leave the rest. The last is in the worst shape. One wing is very brittle, broken in at least three different places. My aim isn't as good as it once was.

I run back to the ATV, drop the birds into a plastic bag that I wrap around one handlebar. When I press the start button, the engine catches once, twice, and then dies. On the second attempt nothing happens at all. Another scream of lightning turns the blood on my jacket and skin to black, and in the return to darkness, fear climbs back onto my shoulders, wraps its arms around my chest. My torchlight shakes over mud and rock and bog. I can see the distant gold lights of Blàr Mòr, the further away lights of the blackhouse. I can feel the *bòcain* in the darkness. I can smell them: wet rope and net; the pungent brine of their breath.

No. Ghosts are just unfinished business. Unspoken truths. They don't need to follow you, because they are you. I turn off my torch. Look into the darkness of the west. This morning, when the storm was only black clouds on the horizon, there was someone up on the ridge behind the cemetery. I saw them on Tòrr Dìseart. I saw them, and just like those clouds, I forced myself to see no threat in them. Watching me. Watching my flock. They're always near now. Watching. Waiting. Never near enough to recognise. Sometimes not even near enough to see; only a shiver down my spine or a prickle on my skin. There is threat in everything. In everyone. No matter what Mary believes. No matter what I've promised her.

I'm not a man that men like. I've never tried to be. I think of Euan's smug superiority; Thom's snide asides. I think of the deep and angry wound my confession has left inside me. The expression on Charlie's face when he called me an arsehole.

I grab a tighter hold on the swinging bag as I lean forwards, turn the key back to neutral, and press the start button again. Finally the four-stroke engine rumbles into life, and I accelerate fast away from that shadow between the mountains. I take the corner back onto the road too tightly, momentarily rocking the ATV onto two wheels. And I keep going, splashing west through mud and freezing water, and throttling off only when home is in sight, its light and warmth spilling over my skin.

I *will* protect myself and my family. And I will trust nothing – no one – that isn't mine. That's what people do. What they have always done. No one is going to chase me away. No one.

CHAPTER 20

The ruined church outside Blairmore always looks less benign in daylight than it does at night; mean and peremptory, even without a roof or windows. I flinch when two bickering crows launch themselves off a stone corbel to fly across my path, reluctantly reminded of Charlie's *vándr-varði*; the three mummified birds inside my rucksack in the mudroom.

I haven't spoken to Charlie since that day on Big Beach almost three weeks ago now; Kelly, for nearly as long. Will and I have been living inside a bubble of sex and sleep and little else, and I feel guilty. It's the only reason I'm heading into Blairmore. I glance across at the blanket bog ahead of Ben Donn. The careful piles of heather-and-moss turf stacked beside the road. The peat harvest has begun to loom very large in my mind. I was never supposed to still be here now, in April, never mind May. But the dread that grabs hold of me every time I think about leaving, about going back to London, looms even larger.

When I get to the village, there's no answer at Charlie's cottage, so I start making my way towards the pub. Fiona MacDonald is on her knees in her small front garden. When she sees me, she stands up.

'Maggie.' Her smile is warm; today there are no anxious lines creasing her forehead or the skin around her eyes. 'Going to see Kelly?'

'Yes, I thought I'd—'

'I think she's working in the pub today. Restocking the cellar.'

'Oh.'

'Can I maybe offer you a coffee? Tea?'

She's nervous, I realise. Not anxious, but definitely nervous. She's taken off her gardening gloves, and her fingers wind restlessly around one another.

'Um . . . I really should—'

'Alec's not here.' Her cheeks flush pink. 'He went back to the rigs a few weeks ago. And Sheena's in the shop until six.' She blinks twice. 'Are you still writing your story?'

My nod is automatic, if only because it's easier than saying no.

'I'd . . . like to apologise to you for the way we've been,' Fiona says. 'And I'd like to explain. To help.'

For a moment, I hesitate. But one of Dr Abebe's rules is that I should never shy away from facing what should be faced. Confronted. Because I've always given myself an easy out and called it caution. Or in this case, perhaps happiness.

Fiona walks back towards her open front door. 'Come in. Please.'

There's someone watching from the neighbouring cottage's window. As I follow Fiona down the path, they move back out of sight.

'Coffee or tea?' Fiona says, as she leads me into a surprisingly spacious open-plan living area that leads to a small kitchen and French doors.

'Coffee, please. Just black, no sugar.'

I sit on the sofa. There are a couple of framed photos on an otherwise empty pine sideboard: one a landscape studio shot of Fiona, Alec, and a teenage Sheena – Sunday best and awkward grimaces – and a much smaller, older photo of a boy in school uniform: a dark cowlick and a gap-toothed smile.

'That was taken about a year before,' Fiona says, coming back from the kitchen with a tray. She briefly closes her eyes as she sets it down. 'I've never been able to stop doing that. It's like the night Lorne died, time reset to zero. And everything became before or after.' She hands me a steaming mug. 'How Alec's been with you ... is unforgivable. I could say grief made him that way, but it would only partly be true.' She looks at the photos again. 'He's always had a temper. Been too quick to judge. Sheena too. She's her father's daughter, all right.'

'You don't need to apologise.' I think of Alec's blazing eyes when he wrenched open the phone box's door. The rage in them when I thought he was going to hit me. The ragged sobs that shuddered through his body, bending him almost double. And then Sheena's *You're not safe here.*

'You must find me pathetic.' Fiona's eyes fill with tears, and she presses the backs of her hands against her pale, freckled cheeks. 'But it's . . . this is always a very bad time of year for me. For us.'

Because it's April. I suddenly realise that the anniversary of Robert's and Lorne's deaths is in just three days.

'I'm sorry. I didn't—'

'Lorne was hyperactive. Couldn't sit still for even a minute.' She clasps her fingers together briefly and then lets them go. 'The GP on the mainland diagnosed ADHD, tried to prescribe him some pills, but I never let him take them.' Her smile is thin. 'I remember you, you know, back in '99. You were just like him – a whirling dervish. It was terrifying, looking after him. Especially when Alec bought him that bloody dinghy. Every day, Lorne would come home full of wild stories and the battle scars to prove them. My blood pressure got so high at one point, the GP tried to use *that* as the best argument for medicating Lorne.'

She closes her eyes. 'But he was a good boy too. My best boy. Some nights he'd have tired himself out so much during the day that he'd crawl onto my lap like a cat and just conk straight out. And he never stopped saying *I love you, Mummy.*' Her voice breaks a little. 'One day, he would have, I'm sure. If he'd had the chance to.'

'I'm so sorry.'

She clears her throat. 'And I'm sorry to go on. It's just that there are so few opportunities to talk about him. Alec won't. And Sheena barely remembers him.' When she looks at me again, her pale blue eyes are clear, their gaze steady. 'Lorne isn't just a wee dead boy. He was a person who deserved to grow up. Who deserved to have a story of his own.'

When I nod, she sits up straighter. 'So. Ask me what you want about Robert, and I'll try to answer.'

I think back to that afternoon in Isla's house and her insistence that the MacDonalds had always thought Robert had something to do with Lorne's death. But after all that Fiona's just said, I can't bring myself to ask. 'Did you like him?'

'I think I mostly did. There was something reassuring about him. Noble, maybe. He loved his family. He was good to them.' She looks across at the sideboard again, and her expression becomes pinched. 'But you never know, do you? What goes on in people's lives. Behind closed doors.'

'What did you think was—'

'Did Charlie ever tell you about what Robert said he'd done? Back when he was growing up in Ardshader?'

I shake my head. 'He told me that Robert said he'd done something terrible.' *His guilt was like an anchor that one day dragged him down to the bottom.* My heart stutters a little. 'But that he never told Charlie what it was.'

Fiona narrows her eyes. 'Well, you'll have to take that up with Charlie. Because Robert told him, all right. And when Robert died, Charlie told us.'

I try to shrug off my confusion. Try harder to ignore the squeeze of hurt inside my belly. And worse, the curiosity. The bad hope that suddenly makes my heart stutter again. Why would Charlie volunteer a truth, but wrap it in a lie?

'What did Robert do?'

Some of the hardness goes out of Fiona's face. 'Ardshader is – was – a fishing village. Robert's father ran most of the boats out of that stretch of west coast. Charlie knew him. Had crewed a few early seasons on the *Acair* before the herring ban.'

'Wait.' My heart starts beating so hard I have to curl my hands into fists. 'Charlie knew Robert's father?'

I think of Charlie standing on Long Stride Beach all those weeks ago, trying not to look at me when I asked *Andrew what?* His emphatic *He never said. Just Andrew.*

'All fishermen know one another,' Fiona says with a shrug. 'In the spring of '77, when Robert was ten, there was one of those once-in-a-generation Atlantic storms. Sank more than half a dozen island boats. Including the three out of Ardshader. All hands lost.

'There's a permanent light up on Aird Einish, which protected boats coming into the Bay's harbour from the rocks and headlands. But that night, in that storm, there was no light. The boats were ripped up on the rocks and sank in the surf, yards from shore, while the entire village watched. Everyone lost someone.' She looks at me. 'Robert told Charlie that he broke the light. That he was angry with his father, and so he went up to Aird Einish when the boats went out on the morning of the storm, and he hit the light's lamp with a slingshot and rocks.'

'*What?*' I think of Robert standing in a grassy meadow, arms folded and alone. That sad, stubborn frown.

'And it weighed so heavily on his conscience that it ruined his life.'

'God.' I realise that my hands are still tight fists only when my nails dig into my skin enough to sting.

'You don't know the whole story, Maggie. Not yet.' Fiona's lips curve up into an abrupt and humourless smile that makes me want to shiver. 'If you really want to write Robert's story, go to Ardshader and see what kind of a man he was.' She stands up so suddenly, I almost drop my coffee. 'In fact, I have time. Why don't I take you?'

*

'Hey, Fiona, Maggie,' Jaz says, as we walk back down the path. He's hauling a canvas sack filled with branches and leaves towards the neighbouring cottage's front gate, and I realise he must have been the shadow in its window. 'Where are you two off to?'

'Ardshader,' Fiona says, after a pause.

Jaz pauses almost as long, and then puts down the sack. 'I can take you, if you like?'

'Don't worry,' Fiona says. 'We can just as easy get the bus from Longwick.'

'It's no trouble.' Jaz's smile is brief. 'I was going to burn these, but I can take them to the recycling yard at Timsgarry instead.' He swings the sack over his shoulder and opens the gate without looking back at either of us. 'Come on.'

I hesitate, suddenly reluctant. I don't want to go to Ardshader. I don't want to know the whole story. Not any more. But because I can think of no way of explaining why – that I'm happy and I'm afraid of anything that might take that away – I follow them anyway.

CHAPTER 21

The sun is blinding as we crest a steep hill and Jaz brings the car to a stop.

'See those houses?' he says to me, pointing towards a flat and grassy headland to the southwest of a huge bowl-shaped bay of wide white sand. 'That's Ardshader.'

Fiona gets out of the car. There's been a very strange atmosphere between her and Jaz all the way here. Nothing that I can define, but nonetheless, like static electricity, an undercurrent of tension. Although part of that might be down to me. Because I can't deny that, despite my reluctance, some of the old excitement is back. I've been certain for months now that Robert Reid and the Andrew MacNeil born in Ardshader in 1967 were the same person. The same Robert Reid who made Norse talismans to protect himself from something or someone. Norse talismans that someone has been leaving for me. And Charlie has been lying to me about him.

'I'll pick you up on my way back,' Jaz says, leaning across the passenger seat as I get out too.

'No need for me,' Fiona says. 'I have to go to Ardroil. I'll get the bus back.'

'It's fine,' I say, when he looks at me instead. 'I'd like to walk. There must be a shorter route on foot?' Ardshader is fewer than ten miles north of Kilmeray, but the winding inland roads, negotiating hills and mountains, lochs and lochans, have taken us easily double that distance.

Jaz looks at me for a long moment, his expression inscrutable. Perhaps I'm still smarting from Charlie's lies, but something in Jaz's eyes, his demeanour, the weird near-silent car journey from Kilmeray, has made me feel less uncomfortable than uneasy. I watch Fiona as she marches away along the road, and think of her bad smile, *You don't know the whole story, Maggie. Not yet.*

'There's no direct path back along the coast, but there's the Old Glen Road,' Jaz finally says, pointing towards some foothills maybe fifty yards to the northeast. 'It's a narrow pass between two mountain ranges. But it's six miles, at least. And then you still have to get back to the coast and Longwick. You'll have no phone signal, and the weather could turn.' He shakes his head. 'Be safer if I just pick you up.'

'Honestly, I'll be fine. I could do with the exercise.' I step away from the car. 'Thanks for the ride.'

'Locals call the Old Glen Road *Beul na Bèist*,' he says.

'*Beul na Bèist?*'

'Devil's Mouth. From an old proverb: *tilg mìr am beul na bèist.*

Cast a bone in the devil's mouth, and it will save you.' He shrugs. 'Maybe keep a look out. Better safe than sorry.'

And then he pulls the door shut and drives off in a shower of gravel.

I walk along the main road around the bay, to where Fiona is standing next to a brown sign, *Aird Einish, 1 km.*

'He can be a right fussy busybody when he wants to be,' she says, with more heat than I would ever have expected from a woman who's always seemed so timid.

I look down at the long dunes of sand and then the wide-curving bay beyond. The tide is in, but still the beach is impossibly vast, way bigger than any on Kilmeray. The sea is a shallow, hypnotic wash of low waves frilled white. I try to imagine a storm; what it must have been like to stand up here or down there and watch your husband, brother, or father drown. Did Robert watch? Or was he too ashamed, too afraid, of what he'd done?

'The memorial is just here,' Fiona says, climbing over a wooden stile into an overgrown grassy meadow. She offers me her hand as I make a far clumsier dismount.

The memorial – polished grey granite, a little over four feet high – sits on the border between the meadow and the rocky cliff down to the bay. The waves, many feet below, sound suddenly loud. Beneath '21st of October 1977' and the names of the boats – the *Acair*, the *Marcan-sìne*, and the *Darach* – there are eighteen names etched into the stone, many with the same surname. The oldest and the first is Robert's father: *Douglas MacNeil, 48*; the youngest, *Malcolm MacKenzie, 18*. But what makes my eyes sting, makes those waves seem suddenly deafening, are the addresses listed alongside. There are only two streets, simply Àrd Shiadair and Èinis: 2 Àrd Shiadair, 4 Àrd Shiadair, 5, 6, 7, all the way down to 10 Èinis – and those numbers carved deep into the granite make it suddenly very real. This terrible thing that happened. That spared no one at all.

'This way,' Fiona says, her voice too loud in the windy silence.

'Where are we going?' I say as she starts marching away across the meadow.

She slows only to look over her shoulder. 'The Aird Einish light. It's why we're here, isn't it?'

The headland on the opposite side of the bay is far longer and steeper. The way quickly goes from flat and boggy to steep and rocky. I'm sweating and out of breath by the time I manage to catch up to Fiona at its summit. The Atlantic wind is bitter cold as I stand and look across to the exposed cliff edge. At Fiona's 'Aird Einish light'.

'Shit.' I shake my head, close my mouth.

I'd been expecting a wooden or skeletal beacon tower, something easily reached, easily sabotaged. Instead, this is a lighthouse in every sense of the word. A white cylindrical stone tower with ochre trim that must be at least one hundred feet, with a balcony and huge metal cage around the black lamp room at its summit. A long, single-storey building sits alongside it and a high stone wall encloses both.

'It's a Stevenson lighthouse,' Fiona says without looking at me. 'One of the best examples. Built in 1899 by Robert Louis Stevenson's uncle, no less. A hundred and seventy-one steps to the lamp room.'

'*Shit,*' I say again. I can't stop looking at it, this huge tower, its shadow almost reaching us on the edge of the headland.

Fiona's answering laugh is more of a bark, short and humourless.

'Did they ever find out?' I finally say. 'Why it failed the night of the storm?'

Because nobody could have sabotaged that lamp, that light. Much less a ten-year-old boy with a slingshot and some rocks.

'A technical fault. My dad was from Islivig, just up the road. He said it had only been automated a few years, so they sent engineers from Glasgow. Replaced the lamp and the lens.' She looks back towards the bay. 'Most folk round here thought it was for show. To be *seen* to be doing. No one was ever told exactly what went wrong.' There's another bite to her voice then, and I recognise Sheena in it. In her. Fiona MacDonald seems like a completely different person away from Alec. I wonder if this is the Fiona MacDonald that comes to life whenever he goes back to the rigs.

'Anyway.' She turns round abruptly. 'I'm dropping in on a friend in Ardroil, if you fancy coming?'

'No, I—' I make myself look at her instead of the lighthouse. 'I think I'll go to Ardshader since I'm here, have a look around.'

Fiona shrugs, looks across the bay towards the houses on the flat and grassy southwest headland. 'That storm killed Ardshader. Einish too. Even closed the harbour. It's why Dad left. After the storm, there was nothing here for anyone. Most people went to family on the mainland. Some went to Canada.' She turns back to me, struggles to hold my gaze for more than a few seconds before she swallows and looks away again. 'It's just a place of ghosts.'

When she starts to march away, I can feel, so strongly, the tower and its shadow at my back that my 'Wait!' comes out as a shout.

Fiona stops, turns around.

'Why did he do it?' I say. 'Why did Robert lie about breaking the light?'

'Why do any of us do anything?' she replies after a long silence. 'Perhaps he believed it.' There's a kind of grimly determined look to her tight smile. 'Or perhaps he just wanted someone to write a story about him.'

And that look makes me finally brave enough to ask her what I couldn't in the cottage.

'The night they died, do you think that Robert tried to save Lorne?'

Fiona squares her shoulders. Finally looks me unflinchingly in the eye. 'No. I don't.'

*

The village of Ardshader is really just a road. Lined with perhaps twelve houses, a small stone church at its end. All are modest white houses, with the occasional ruin of a blackhouse alongside. Many of the white houses themselves are abandoned. A rusted Land Rover minus its tyres and number plates sits in a small garden; behind it, net curtains in the two upstairs rooms billow in the breeze, the glass in the windows gone. Its neighbour has a boarded-up front door.

I've never thought about why or even when Robert left Ardshader for Aberdeen. But I wonder now, why did he come back? Even though the sun is piercing the low clouds in spears, turning the beach white-gold and the sea turquoise clear and every stretch of grass or meadow a deep warm green, I still wonder. Because Fiona's right. There's a bad feeling here; something that twists at the stomach and constricts the chest. Maybe it's Ardshader in its ugly dereliction, its *bòcain*. Kilmeray isn't here, of course. It doesn't feel like here – empty and oppressive. But it's close. You can probably see this headland from Ardcraig. And almost certainly the higher, longer Aird Einish. And the lighthouse itself. I might not know why Robert told Charlie what he did about the lighthouse, nor even why Fiona brought me here to see it, but suddenly I feel a burst of acute pity for Robert, perhaps forever trapped by duty and self-loathing and guilt. We're the same. It makes something burn inside my chest, a dangerous feeling close to hope again. Like looking into someone's eyes and recognising yourself.

*

I regret turning down Jaz's offer of a lift back to Kilmeray within an hour of setting off down the Old Glen Road. It's less a road than a stony – mostly muddy – track. Away from the coast, the air is thicker and colder. The mountains either side of the track blot out the sun entirely. Every few yards large boulders sit ominously across my path, and I try not to think about where they came from. There are no blankets of deep warm green down here. The only vegetation is either orange-grey lichen or moist dark seams of moss between rocks.

I've brought the heaviness of Ardshader with me. It sits on my shoulders, making the road seem darker, even more oppressive. I take out my phone, and sure enough there's no signal of any kind. It's already four o'clock. Six miles of this now seems like a ludicrous undertaking, and I've no idea how many I still have to go. I try to pick up my pace; my boots disturb loose stones and gravel, making too much noise in the airless space. I don't like that I'm unsettled – afraid – for reasons that I can't explain, can't rationalise. And I don't like that I've suddenly started thinking of Mum again – the Mum with a wild light in her eyes. I don't like that I can almost feel her panicked breath against my clammy skin. *Do you ever get a bad feeling, Maggie?*

More than once, I stop to look behind myself. Pretending that it's only because I'm disconcerted that I can't see the road's beginning or end. But the hairs on the back of my neck are making me shudder. And the echoes of my own steps have begun to sound like someone else's.

As the day grows darker still, I let out a startled yelp when loose scree rattles suddenly down the mountain inches away from me. I look up at the grey sky above, at the towering dark summits of the cliffs. My heart thunders hard enough inside my ears that I struggle to hear anything beyond it. There are no bones here, animal, bird, or otherwise, but that doesn't stop me thinking of *Cast a bone in the devil's mouth, and it will save you.* It doesn't stop me imagining dark silhouettes standing on top of those mountains and throwing bones down like *vándr-varði,* to protect against evil, against the *bòcain* that live in these shadows.

But, strangely, the worst thing is neither the claustrophobic dark nor the sense that I might never reach the end of it. It's the almost silent *silence*. I'm too used now to wind, to waves, to *wild*. This dark, close pass punctuated by nothing other than falling scree – not even birdsong – is more than unnerving. It makes me flinch every time I hear anything at all.

And then I *do* hear something worse than silence. A scuffling rush like shoes or boots surfing a slide of loose stones. Followed by a curse. Loud enough to echo around the grey wet walls.

This time, I don't stop. I don't look back. I run. So fast and so hard that I immediately start sliding against the ground too, my ankles turning over rocks. My breath is too loud. I keep my head down, force my eyes onto the dimming path, so that I can see nothing else but the obstacles in my way.

I don't know how long it takes to reach the end of the Old Glen Road. When I finally see grey light up ahead, my breath has become little more than ragged sobs, my running sprint a shambling fast-walk. I can feel someone so close behind, it seems impossible that they haven't yet caught me. Haven't yet reached out to touch me. I scramble up onto a sparse patch of grass, stumble towards the sudden sound of waves, any moment expecting to be yanked back into the dark. I slow only once I see the wide loch ahead of me, swerving instead onto a sheep track between it and the sloping edge of the western mountain range.

The rain comes out of nowhere. Heavy and icy-cold. I keep on running, slipping through mud, entirely disorientated. I follow the sound of the waves, and when I see the small inlet less than fifty yards from the track, I pick up speed, sliding down to its sandy edge more on my backside than my feet, palms soaked and studded with stones.

I can barely see the sea at all in the gloom. But suddenly, I do see lights. High on a dark headland too far out to be here on the main island. And suddenly I remember sitting in Am Blàr Mòr's beer garden with Kelly and pointing out this very place. I'm on Hollow Beach. Where Lorne's dinghy washed up.

I have an almost visceral urge to reach those lights, to reach Kilmeray – the pub, the people, the place – so strong that I find myself running towards the choppy surf. It washes icy cold over my boots and jeans, far higher and faster than I'd been expecting. And then I see closer, brighter lights. Hear a diesel engine.

I grab for my phone and turn on its torch. Start waving both arms high above my head as I shout into the wind. The boat is far enough out that I'm sure they won't see me, but within seconds they slow and start to turn. I look back at the growing dark, the mountains behind me now little more than darker shadows. I can see nothing. No one. My light, I realise, is probably the only one for miles.

The boat reaches the edge of the inlet in minutes. Two large masthead lights are turned on, momentarily blinding me, and then I see a dinghy being lowered into the water out beyond the surf. I watch as it powers towards me – its outboard engine high and loud like a chainsaw. I'm overwhelmed by so much noise after the ominous suffocation of the Old Glen Road. Now that most of my fear has diminished, I've time enough to feel slightly embarrassed about my situation, until the dinghy pulls up onto the sand, and I recognise the big dark-haired figure that starts to climb out.

'Jimmy!'

He squints, wipes his eyes. '*Maggie?*' He shakes his head. 'Quick, get in before the waves get any higher.'

I wade awkwardly through the icy surf, and Jimmy presses a neon-orange lifejacket over my head before helping me clamber into the dinghy. He turns it round quickly, and we roar out against the waves, reaching the fishing boat in what feels like seconds. My climb up onto the boat is made even harder by the bone-deep cold of the water, and by the time Jimmy pulls the dinghy in after us, all the strength in my body seems to have left through my legs.

'Here, come into the wheelhouse,' he says before half-hauling me there himself.

Inside the small, cramped space, another fisherman – younger than Jimmy and dressed in the same dirty yellow waterproofs – swivels in his chair away from a crowd of computer screens and electronic controls. He looks just as startled to see me as Jimmy was.

'Got ourselves a wee drowned rat.' Jimmy grins. Although he also looks fearsomely pissed off. As well he might, I suppose. Now that I'm no longer in any danger – if I ever was – I've the luxury of being more than a little mortified. When he inevitably asks why I was trying to flag down a passing fishing boat, I'm definitely not going to tell him it's because I thought I was being stalked by either person or *bòcain* along the Old Glen Road.

My teeth are chattering. Jimmy pulls the lifejacket back over my head and replaces it with a barely warmer wax waterproof.

'Why the hell were you waving a torch about on Hollow Beach?' he says.

I don't miss the tiny smirk at the corner of the other fisherman's mouth as he turns back towards the wheelhouse window, one hand taking hold of what looks like a giant joystick, the other adjusting the small ship's wheel between his knees.

'I'm sorry,' I say. 'I was hiking and I got lost, and then the weather . . . it got dark, and . . .' I look up at him through wet noodles of hair. 'I panicked.'

'Hiking.' If anything, Jimmy's expression becomes even sterner, and then his whole face relaxes into a wide, delighted grin. *'Hiking!'*

His bellowed laughter makes me jump, but when the other fisherman joins in, I start feeling resentful.

'Dear God, woman. If you want to go hiking around here, the very least you need is a weather forecast, a map, and,' Jimmy looks my bedraggled state up and down, 'some decent walking gear.'

'Well, I know that now.' What I want to say is that I hadn't planned on hiking anywhere today, but then I'd have to explain about Jaz and Fiona and Ardshader and that seems like an infinitely worse prospect. Luckily, Jimmy seems to take pity on me, handing me a steaming black coffee before moving back out on deck and leaving me in peace. The other man says nothing to me at all, although I occasionally catch his reflection staring at me, and then quickly sliding away.

Jimmy comes back in to get me as the lights of Kilmeray get closer. I stand shivering on deck as we turn slowly towards what must be Sheltered Bay: a small and stony cove with a concrete slipway along one flank. I look up at the high lights of Blairmore on Longness, the comforting gold squares of the pub's windows, the more muted glow from houses beyond.

'This'll do, Billy,' Jimmy shouts, when we're about fifty yards from shore.

It's only when he and I are in the dinghy and heading back towards land that he turns to look at me again. This time, his smile is surprisingly warm. He has a deep dimple, I notice, in his left cheek.

'That look on your face,' he says. He glances towards the shore. 'It's how I feel every time I come back here too.'

I don't know what kind of look is on my face, but I do know what I felt standing on Hollow Beach, looking across at those lights. How much I longed for their safety and familiarity – and badly enough that I almost walked straight into the sea.

'I'm glad to be back,' I say, smiling through still-chattering teeth. And I only just manage not to say the last word, still on the tip of my tongue. *Home.*

CHAPTER 22

Robert

The storm is no calmer by the time I stumble up the path to the blackhouse. I flinch from the figure I see suddenly moving away from the barn door. And then I drop my plastic bag and run towards it, storm and dread be damned.

But it's Jimmy. I stop, confused enough to lose what impetus my anger gave me. When I shine my torchlight over his face, he blinks and looks away, but not before I see the flicker of guilt in his eyes. He's in his fisherman's waterproofs, neon-yellow in the gloom, so hardly hiding, but still. I think of that someone always watching me, watching my flock. I think of the slow-pulsing heat of the ewe as she died.

'I was out at West Point, got caught in the storm,' he says – half-shouts – over the wind. 'Just wanted to see if you'd got the sheep in okay or needed some help.'

I can hear the sheep in the barn – even over the roar of the waves and thunder – their *baas* are discordant and afraid.

'I'm fine, Jimmy.'

'Aye.' He shifts his weight from foot to foot. Glances at me and then away again. 'Look, I just wanted to say . . . I know what it's like to be the outsider. Places like this, they . . .' He shakes his head. 'I just wanted to say, you've a friend in me. If you ever need one.'

And this time when I shine my torch towards him, he looks suddenly every inch of only nineteen, embarrassed and earnest, a frown on his lips as if ready to take it all back if I laugh. I don't.

'Thanks.' And I wonder, briefly, if I'm going mad. If I really am as paranoid as Mary says I am. When another bang of thunder shakes the grass under our feet, Jimmy ducks and turns back for the path and road, raising a hand in goodbye.

I stand for a few seconds longer until Jimmy's own light disappears, the rain starts drumming down harder, and another roar of thunder sets my heart beating too fast again. I check the barn door, and then I turn and run for the blackhouse, picking up the bag before shoving my shoulder against the front door. Calum, wearing Spider-Man pyjamas and holding a sippy cup of milk, freezes inside the kitchen, his mouth a round O.

'Hey, wee man.' I try to slow my breathing, but I know my smile is not a good one. A convincing one. 'D'you want to come down to the cellar? Come on, let's go down to the cellar.'

'I'm having my milk.'

'I know. You can have your milk down in the cellar.' A crack of lightning sounds overhead, shaking the front door inside its frame. I flinch. 'Come on, Calum.'

His hand is warm and sticky inside mine, and it's all I can do not to pick him up and run. There's a loosening inside me and it scares me. I know I have to resist it. Fear is good, fear is what keeps us safe. But blind panic is a different beast. That's what fucks everything up.

I open the trapdoor and turn on the cellar light, keep hold of Calum's hand as he goes down the narrow stairs painfully slowly, his warm milk sloshing left and right inside the cup. At the bottom, I stop long enough to pull the three *vándr-varði* out of the plastic bag and spread them out on my worktop.

'Crow.'

'That's right.'

Calum's brow furrows as he screws up his nose. 'Yeuchy.'

'It's just mud. Remember when we went up to the standing stones and it rained so hard your wellies got squelchy stuck?' I turn back towards the stairs before he can answer. 'I have to go and get Mummy now, okay? I'll bring Mummy down, and we can all stay here until the storm has gone away, okay?'

He frowns again. And this time when another crack of lightning sounds overhead, he flinches too.

'It's just a storm, Calum,' Mary says. 'It's just noise. Nothing to be scared of, remember?' She's standing halfway down the stairs, one hand on the banister, the other on her hip. The look she gives me is furious.

'Mummy's right, sport,' I say, crouching down into a squat. I don't want Calum to be afraid of storms. Not because of me. 'It's just fun to come down here and play, isn't it?'

He gives me a dubious look worthy of Mary before his chubby

cheeks widen into a delighted grin as he points at my jeans and jacket. 'Ket'up!'

I remember the blood only in the instant Mary reaches the bottom of the steps and comes up alongside me.

'Rob – my God.' Her hand comes up to cover her mouth.

'It was a ewe,' I mutter, pulling her away from Calum by her elbow. 'I just found her up on the pasture.'

'Why the hell did you not change your clothes before . . .' She gestures towards Calum, but she's still staring at the blood in barely disguised horror. 'Jesus, get *changed*, Robert!'

'Okay, okay.' I jog over to the workbench again, where I've left a T-shirt and some overalls hanging over a stool. I pull off my coat and shirt and jeans before Mary can take Calum upstairs again, my panic like a bird inside my chest. Hurry up. Hurry up. Did Jimmy see the blood too? Surely the gloom and rain weren't camouflage enough, and yet he said nothing. Sour suspicion returns, and with it that fear I *am* going mad. How could it have been Jimmy? Why would Jimmy want to kill my sheep?

Calum giggles. 'Daddy pants.'

I zip up the overalls, kick my bloody clothes under the worktop before I turn round again. Mary has gone quiet; she's looking around the cellar with that pinched, worried look I haven't seen in weeks. I know she's been down here before. She just hasn't talked to me about it. Yet.

'Calum,' she says finally. 'Why don't you sit over there on Daddy's stool and drink your milk before it gets cold, okay? Ask Daddy to help you up.'

I lift him onto the stool and ruffle his hair before walking back over to Mary.

'What are we doing down here, Robert?' She's being very careful with me. I can tell she wants to shout, but she won't.

'It's safer.' I can't quite meet her eye.

'It's just a storm. Nothing will happen to us inside the house, you know that.'

I can't tell her how afraid I am. The dread certainty that we can't stay upstairs while thunder rattles the windows and lightning tries to strike its way down through us and into the boggy ground. While the storm and sea lash at the walls trying to get in, and the sheep cry together in fear. Mary doesn't know about Andrew MacNeil or Àrd Shiadair. She doesn't know about the storm. I told her once about my parents – enough that she understood I wanted the very opposite for Calum. The kind of childhood I'd never had. But I never told her anything more.

'I told you,' I mutter. 'Storms are different here.'

I think of her accusing me months ago of having a persecution complex about this place. Maybe I should tell her that the ewe was butchered. Maybe I should tell her about that someone up on the ridge behind the cemetery this morning. Watching me and the sheep. Or about Jimmy loitering in the dark outside our barn.

She narrows her eyes and takes hold of my hands, even though they're still streaked with dried blood. Mary's never been squeamish, never afraid to confront anything. Maybe that's why I was drawn to her in the first place. 'Rob. Please. It's cold. The boy needs his bed.'

When I don't answer, her fingers tighten enough to sting. She draws back, traps me inside her gaze, her disapproval. And still unspoken, always unspoken, is *You said it would be better here.*

In Aberdeen, the darkness hadn't just descended, it had crashed down on top of me like a tsunami. And while I was trying to surface, it swept me so far and so fast that when I finally stopped, I hardly knew who I was any more, never mind where. Mary is who saved me. Who dragged me back to land. And I could never explain to her where it had come from, what seismic event had caused it. Because there had been none. Just a deep, hollow hole inside me that wanted – needed – to come home.

'Fiona said something bad's going on between you and Charlie, but he wouldn't tell her or Alec what. Charlie's been nothing but nice to us, Rob, and you *promised* me. You promised you'd try.'

'I know.'

And that's why I can never tell her any of it. She won't understand about the land. About the Sjóvættir and the Landvættir. She won't understand why, after I watched my father's boats leave at pink dawn, I marched to Àird Èinis. The rage – the fury – inside me growing bigger, wilder when every shot, every stone, was repelled by the metallic *no* of the lamp room's steel cage. She won't understand that truth abides in thin places. And some things that should never be possible can never be undone. That the weight of will, of want – of hate – can be bigger than rocks inside a slingshot; bigger than glass or metal or might. Or *no*.

I think of all the *vándr-varði* I've buried in that dark V between the mountains. My mother's eyes, black and wild like the sea. *Don't you* ever *tell anyone what you did.*

So I can put up with anger and worry, and even mistrust.

Because underneath them, Mary still loves me, she still respects me. She looks at me with those lochan-calm eyes and still sees mostly the man she wants to see.

'Daddy, I need a weewee,' Calum says. But it isn't true. I can tell what he needs, what he wants, what he's feeling, often before he can. Mary says it's uncanny, but it isn't. I've trained myself to know my son completely, so that I will never once misunderstand him, or neglect him, or make him feel like he isn't the most important person in my world. He just wants the attention that Mary's arrival has robbed him of.

'Let me put the big light off,' I say, going back towards the workbench. 'I have special lights. You'll love them, Calum. They're very cool.' I haul an old blow-up mattress into the centre of the small space, turn to look at Mary as I go back for the pump. 'I've got snacks, the old portable TV. An electric blanket in case we get cold.'

'Put the lights on, Daddy!' Calum says, wriggling about on the stool. 'Put the 'pecial lights on!'

I go to Mary, take hold of her hands. 'Come on, Mummy,' I say, and I resist kissing her only because she's still mad. She hasn't thawed all the way out yet. 'It'll be fun.'

She sighs. And although there's a small smile at the corners of her mouth, that worry, that *pinch*, hasn't completely gone either. When a louder, nearer roar of thunder sounds overhead, I force myself not to wince, not to acknowledge it at all.

'Just this once,' she says.

'Yeah!' Calum shouts.

Mary goes to lift him back off the stool, and I'm too relieved to join them straightaway. I look down at my hands instead and watch my fingers until they no longer shake.

'Robert.' Mary's voice is as weary as it is sharp. It reminds me of my mother again. 'Why the hell are there three dead crows on the workbench?'

CHAPTER 23

'Yello?'

'Hi, hello, um . . . this is . . . this is Maggie. Maggie . . . MacKay.'

'Ah.' There's a long pause. 'Yes. The agency gave you my number.'

Through the phone box's dirty window, I watch a couple coming out of Am Blàr Mòr, holding hands and laughing. 'Do you remember me?'

There's another pause, longer this time. 'I do.'

But it doesn't matter, because I already remember him. I saw his wink, his grin, his left canine more than three-quarters gold the minute I heard *Yello*.

'I was sorry,' Gordon Cameron eventually says when I don't reply. 'To hear about your mum.'

I've no idea how he knows; he wasn't at the crematorium, that's for sure, or he probably wouldn't be speaking to me at all.

'You came with us to Kilmeray. Back in '99. You were the documentary filmmaker?'

'That's right.' He sounds only a little surprised that I'm asking.

'So.' I swallow and hope he doesn't hear it. 'You were a filmmaker then . . . as well as an actor.' I deliberately don't make it sound like a question, and close my eyes against his answer.

This time the pause is so long I wonder – almost hope – that we've been cut off. 'No. I wasn't.'

My stomach squeezes, and the ballast inside it lurches. The only thing I manage to say is 'Mum', choked and hot.

'She tried for a long time to drum up interest, you see,' he says, oblivious. 'But there was none. Your mum, she was always so sure about you – both of you – you were only a wee kid but you must remember. Man, all those parties, and you never picked the wrong card once. It was incredible. She just wanted the world to see it too. Plus, you know how she was about all those psychic TV shows. I think she hoped if we filmed it, someone would want to buy it.'

'Are you saying that she organised it all? That you didn't fund it? That it was nothing to do with you?'

'Well, I agreed to it, of course. But she paid *me*. She paid all of us. I don't know where she got the money from, perhaps she'd been saving it. It just meant so much to her, you know? It always did.'

And I know he's telling the truth. I remember saying to Kelly how desperate the filmmaker must have been. How much he'd gambled on the unreliability of parish records, and the spectacle of it. Of me. Only he hadn't been the desperate one after all. And I remember that night with Will in the Harbour View Bar; telling him why I was so sure Mum hadn't been lying: *How did she know that Robert Reid's real name was Andrew MacNeil?*

'How did Mum know someone called Andrew MacNeil had lived on Kilmeray?'

This time, the pause is long enough that I become almost panicky with a need to fill it.

'Because you told her.'

That old memory, so sharp. The squeeze of my fists; the hoarseness of my throat; the hotness of my tears. Mum holding my hands and looking at me with that light, that smile.

'Viv was special, Maggie,' he says. 'And so were you. She just wanted the rest of the world to see it.'

'Thanks.' And I've hung up before he can say goodbye.

I lean against the phone box. Think of all those times I'd sat in bed as the dawn crept in under my curtains. Mum leaning close in the light of the bedside lamp, close enough that I could smell the rose hand cream on her skin.

Hold still. Nearly done. There! All out.

How radiant she'd always looked at those times. How beautifully alive as she smiled and stroked my hair. *I'm so proud of you, baby. Did you see how impressed they all were! Well done!*

And I'd look at those infrared contact lenses back inside their case on the bedside table. I'd think of those marked cards in the coffee table drawer. *But Mummy, it wasn't true.*

Yes, it was, sweetie. Of course it was. That same light. That same smile. *But sometimes even the most special of us need a little help.*

*

When I get back to Ardcraig, the pasture is empty. Perhaps Will's taken the sheep out west towards the beach. The sun is high, the wind for once low. I can hear someone hammering a fence post with a wooden mallet: its echo is the only sound apart from the birds and the waves. Spring is truly here. Ben Wyvis has lost its burnt orange in favour of bright green, and as far as I can see, the machair is covered in a riot of colour: purples and whites and pinks and yellows. The island is beautiful, bright and alive in a transformation that I could never have imagined back in those first dark and oppressive weeks in February. The metaphor isn't lost on me; when Will took me for my first blood test in Stornoway last week, the GP said I was 'positively blooming', as if we'd already met, as if he could see what weight was being lifted from my shoulders.

I could wait for Will at the farm, but I go to the blackhouse instead. I stand inside its main room, the sunlight turning the walls pale gold, and I think about Mum. I think about me. I think about Robert. And just as I glance at that trapdoor near the kitchen, I remember those two rusty keys inside the bedroom table drawer.

I open the drawer with some trepidation, but there are no new dead birds. The keys feel cool against my palm as I walk across the room and hunker down next to the trapdoor. The first key fits perfectly, and needs only a few hard rattles to turn and click open the cylinder lock.

I hesitate for just a moment before I pull up on its recessed steel handle. Maybe on a day like any other, I wouldn't look. I wouldn't dare. But today isn't a day like any other. Today is the 9th of April, the day that Lorne and Robert died. And today is also the day I've finally accepted that Mum lied. Her tricks, her marked cards, all those years of cheating, and all those people – just like Gordon Cameron – always so ready to believe in that fantasy, in any fantasy. Of course he would believe Mum. *I* believed her. I don't remember saying *Kill Merry*, because I never said it. I don't remember why we came here, because I wasn't the one who wanted to. All of my life, I've danced to her tune one way or another, even when I knew it was a lie – when I could see it with my own eyes. I never forgot that I knew, I just pretended to.

The trapdoor opens up onto a steep and narrow wooden staircase disappearing quickly down into darkness. I've already taken out my phone before I see the switch set into the brick wall. The resulting light isn't just unexpected, it's bright like daylight, enough that it makes me flinch. The cobwebs tickle my skin and get caught in my hair as I go slowly down the steps, trying not to lose my grip on the rickety old banister.

The cellar is bigger than a root cellar, but not by much. Its floor is packed earth and its walls white-painted brick, cracked and dirty. It's cool and smells musty like peat. When I feel a slight breeze against my face, I glance up to where a vertical steel pipe disappears into a hole in the wall close to the ceiling. Strangely, it's that hole – dark and ragged – rather than the tight windowless space that makes me feel most claustrophobic.

I wander slowly around the room, touching the walls, which feel dry and scaly against my skin. There are long wooden shelves the length of one wall and a workbench against its opposite, covered in tools and jars of nails and screws. I drag my fingers through the thick dust of the workbench, touch the long-rusted tools: a hammer, a wood saw, a yellow-and-black-striped screw-driver.

Despite the brightness of the room, I've almost reached its last corner before I see the large solid shape against it. I step back less in fright than surprise – although there's no denying that, under layers of blue-weave tarpaulin, the shape is the height and width of a tall man. My heart is beating a little too hard as I reach out and pull that tarpaulin free. The dust makes me cough.

It's a lighthouse. Made from plywood and soldered metal, the large bulb of what looks like a spotlight torch at its summit. When I step back again, look at it a little longer, my stomach squeezes. The tower has been painted white. With ochre trim. The lamp room is black. Surrounded by a large metal cage. It's the Aird Einish lighthouse.

The back of the cage hangs open. I reach behind it to find the torch's switch. When I slide it left and right nothing happens; the battery doubtless died a long time ago. Something on the white ceiling above it catches my eye: a pale-yellow shape that jogs a memory from my childhood. Mum reading me all those stories while I lay warm in bed.

There's a second light switch at the bottom of the stairs. I hesitate only briefly before I press it and plunge the space back into darkness.

The breath catches loud inside my chest, my throat. The whole ceiling is covered in glow-in-the-dark stars. Hundreds of them. Enough in constellations that I recognise for me to suspect that this was the night sky above Kilmeray twenty-five years ago. My eyes prick and sting; the lump inside my throat makes it suddenly impossible to swallow. *Robert.*

I sit down on the second-from-last cellar step and look up at those stars, their glow dim and fading. Was this place meant as some kind of memorial? Or confession? Maybe even penance? Or was it like his *vándr-varði*: a talisman against ghosts? Because this forgotten, windowless, dark room – this is where Robert is; this is the place that *he* haunts.

I think of him looking out at the world from his meadow, unsmiling and inscrutable. I think of the Ardshader memorial and those mournful net curtains billowing in the breeze like ghosts. Fiona was right. To understand Robert's life – his death – is to understand who he was. A boy – eventually a man – who believed that he'd caused those boats to sink, those men to die. A boy who'd been angry, who'd hated his father, and so had fired rocks at a one-hundred-foot-high lighthouse. Maybe Robert *did* believe that he'd broken that light on Aird Einish, or maybe it only mattered to him that he'd wanted to. Isn't that what guilt amounts to, after all? Less what we do than what we *want* to do? What we know we *would* do?

Maybe I'll never know how Mum knew about this place, about Andrew MacNeil. I can't ask her. I will never be able to ask her. But I no longer have to dance to her tune either, and there's liberation in that. Because it *doesn't* matter any more. I was right all those weeks ago: the story has never been about Robert. It's about me. Not the me that came to this island twenty years ago, schooled in another lie, another trick, just like those marked playing cards. Not even the me who saw a demon trying to climb into her mother's coffin. But the me who sobbed as I shook all those pills out into my hand. The me who believed that living in the same house as Robert had to be a sign I was reincarnated, and not just coincidence in a tiny village. The me whose need to be absolved made her desperate to believe. Because I was taught to lie. And I was taught to believe it was the truth. And that's something that a tortured and long-dead man can't fix. Because it's pathetic. And it's time to stop.

When I phoned Gordon Cameron, it was only because I'd managed to convince myself that finding out the truth – about Mum, about Robert, about me – didn't mean having to lose the happiness that I've found here. But there's no denying the relief I felt behind the disappointment, the shame. I am not special. I am not absolved. I did not *make the right choice.*

And I am not the reincarnation of Andrew MacNeil. We are *not* the same. Or at least we don't have to be. Guilt made Robert. Perhaps it even killed him. And maybe that's the real reason I came here. To discover that I can live with mine.

I stand up, climb the cellar steps. Stop at the door and look down at the stars, the dark loom of the lighthouse. I think of the bright spring light above: green and white and pink and yellow.

'Goodbye, Robert.'

And then I leave him in peace.

*

Will barely gets through the farmhouse door before I launch myself at him. He closes both arms tight around me even as he protests my kisses, my impatient fingers at his jacket buttons.

'Hey, I'm filthy – Jesus.'

He says the last as I yank his jacket off over his head, taking his jumper with it. When I move on to his belt buckle, he laughs loud and pulls me up against him harder than before. Hard enough that for a wonderful moment I can't even breathe.

'Christ, Maggie,' he says against my mouth. 'If it's *eau de ewe* turns you on, I'll be enjoying my days in the fields a lot more from now on.'

I lean back and laugh – perhaps the first real laugh in a very long time. Cup his beautiful, warm face in my hands. I feel hot and awake and alive. And I know instinctively that none of it is bad. None of it is frightening. None of it is a harbinger of mania or delusion or psychosis. None of it is bad hope.

'I'm going to help Charlie with his peat harvest.'

Will's eyes widen. 'You sure? It's tough work.'

I shove against him; feel his laughter in the pit of my belly. 'You think a city girl like me can't hack it?'

He smiles, presses his forehead against mine. 'I think you can hack anything.'

I kiss him once, fierce and quick. 'I don't want to go back.'

Will's smile disappears and he goes very still.

My heart hammers a little harder. 'I can freelance. Once Mum's money runs out. I want to stay. Here. With you.'

Because whatever the truth was behind Robert's ugly fate, it's not going to be mine.

'If you want me to?' Because still, *still*, I'm too afraid to be happy.

'If I want you to?' Will shakes his head, his expression suddenly so stern that I wonder, with alarm, if I've read all of this completely wrong. 'Maggie. It's taken everything I've got not to ask you every day to stay.'

I press my palm to his chest, where his heart is hammering harder than mine. 'I'll be good for you too.' My eyes sting. 'I promise.'

All that sternness vanishes inside one of his slow, easy grins. 'I love you, Maggie MacKay.'

And although it's not the first time he's said it, it's the first time I let myself believe it.

'I love you, Will Morrison.' It's the first time I've said it back.

CHAPTER 24

One month later, the first day of the peat harvest dawns clear and sunny. I walk down towards Blairmore without Will; the Morrison peat banks are out towards the Lodge and Big Beach. The bogs either side of the Coffin Road are already filled with dozens of distant figures, bending and rising, shouting across the otherwise still morning. The whole of Kilmeray is alive with people and activity, and although it feels strange and new, it also feels good, exciting.

I spot Charlie across the road from the church, Kelly beside him as they both wave at me. Even the church seems brighter today, its empty windows and lichen-covered rookeries less threatening than weary. This has a lot to do with the two life-size papier-mâché figures propped up against its main door: pink-faced and rosy-cheeked, sporting kilts, waterproofs, and tam o'shanters; one holding a pair of bagpipes, the other an accordion.

The bog is surprisingly firm under my boots. I reach Kelly and Charlie in less than a minute, and realise that Miko is there too – hunkered down in a narrow trench and already covered in mud.

'On the verge of sending out a search party, weren't we, Kelly?' Charlie says.

'Yup.' Kelly grins, wiping her forehead with a shirt sleeve.

I've seen Charlie plenty of times in the last month, but I haven't once asked him why he lied to me about Robert confessing his full name and what he thought he'd done in Ardshader. People lie for many reasons, not all of them bad. And most of them have nothing at all to do with the person they're lying to. Charlie has given me so much. A few months ago, that wasn't enough. Now it is.

'Excuse me, but this is the earliest I've been up in weeks,' I say. 'Hi, Miko. How are you?'

'Good,' she says, although her smile is a little dim. 'Time's pretty much up on the dig, and most of the students have gone back to Glasgow. Femi and a few others have stayed to close up the trenches, get the equipment ready for shipping, so I thought I could make myself useful here.'

Which means that there have been none of the finds she'd hoped for – on either the southern ridge or in the original mound. 'I'm sorry.'

She shrugs, gives me a better smile. 'That's archaeology. We're off to North Ronaldsay in the summer, maybe we'll have better luck out there.'

'Hi, Maggie,' Donnie shouts, from a neighbouring peat bank that's already been significantly dug out. Since Will told him I was staying, Donnie's attitude towards me has thawed enough that we've even enjoyed a few drinks together in Am Blàr Mòr when Will hasn't been around.

Bruce is the one doing the digging. He looks over and waves before cutting free a foot-square slab, which Gillian picks up and throws to her son, who stacks it onto an already crowded bank on top of the trench.

'You do what Donnie's doing,' Charlie says to me, helping me down. 'I'll cut, Kelly'll toss, you can help Dr Okitsu stack.'

'Yes, sir.'

'When are you going to give me a go on the spade, Charlie?' Kelly says.

'Spade?' Charlie growls. 'This here is a *tairsgeir*, as well you know. Belonged to my father and his father and his father before him, same as this peat poll.' He leans forwards, plunges the angled steel blade deep into a dark layer of peat. 'And if you think you're getting any kind of *go on it*, you've another thing coming.'

'What are they for?' I ask, pointing at the two papier-mâché figures in front of the church.

'That's Shug and Hamish,' Kelly says, reaching down to lift a thick slab of peat the same colour and consistency as chocolate fudge cake. 'They make an appearance every peat harvest.'

Charlie looks over at the MacKenzies. 'Maggie wants to know what they're for,' he shouts, pointing a thumb towards the church. Their laughter echoes loud around the space, trapped against Ben Wyvis's steep and stony foothills.

'Okay,' I say, catching the peat slab from Kelly. It's surprisingly heavy and smells like old wet leaves. By the time I've thrown it onto the edge of the bank, my arms and hands are covered in a layer of thick brown mud. 'But what *are* they for?'

Charlie squelches his way across the trench towards me, expression stern.

'You here to help or just to ask stupid questions?' he says before handing me a pair of elbow-length rubber gloves.

'Hey,' Kelly shouts. 'How come she gets gloves?'

He presses them into my hands, briefly squeezing my fingers. His smile is as fleeting. 'Thanks for being here, Maggie,' he mutters, so low I barely hear it.

*

For more than five hours, we dig and cut and toss and stack. Miko and I copy Donnie's technique, filling up the top of the trench with one layer of cut peat, and then laying the next in diagonals over the bank's edge like the backbone of a dragon. Once the MacKenzies have finished they come over to help, and in the end, Charlie and Bruce cut so much, we have to throw the last slabs out beyond the ends of the banks.

Finally, Charlie wipes the peaty blade of his *tairsgeir* on the heather. 'That's a good day's work all right.'

'To the pub!' Kelly says, as Donnie helps her out of the trench.

I ache all over. And feel unbelievably filthy. A late afternoon breeze has started cooling the sweat on my skin, making me itch. I take off Charlie's gloves before Donnie reaches down to help me up too.

'Thanks,' I say. 'Guess I'll go have a shower and see you all there.'

'No showering allowed,' Kelly says, linking her arm through mine. She shrugs. 'Straight from the banks to the party, them's the rules.'

'Why is the party now anyway?' I glance back at the stacks of peat. 'We're not finished yet, are we?'

'No,' Gillian says. She has a thick brown smear of mud running from her hairline to her chin. 'But it takes a few weeks for the peat to dry enough to be gathered and taken back for stacking. And for some folk who've come over to help, this is the first time they've visited in a year.'

'The final gathering of peats is a whole different kind of cele-bration,' Donnie says before giving me another of his catching grins – mischievous and round-cheeked. 'This way, we get to have two.'

'Plus, you're going to hurt like hell on a highway tomorrow,' Bruce says, giving me a wink. 'And the only thing can help you with that is a lot of whisky.'

*

The pub is standing room only. I've never seen it so busy. I recog-nise far fewer faces than usual, and assume that much of Urbost and their extended families must be here too. Everyone looks like I feel – sweaty and tired and manky – and the whole lounge smells like a peat bog.

'Large white wine, is it?' Charlie says to me, lip curled in disap-proval.

'Thanks, Charlie.'

'Aye.' He nods towards the pool table. 'Your man's over there.'

When Will sees me and gives me a wave and that sexy grin, I grin straight back, not even caring that I probably look worse than I feel.

'I'll help Charlie,' Miko says with a smile.

'Shit!' Kelly says, gripping my elbow. 'There's David Campbell. Now that you've nabbed the only eligible bachelor on this whole island, he's my last option. Come on.' She's already pulling me along in her wake. 'He's *so* hot. First time he's been back in God knows how long and look at the bloody state of me.'

I laugh. 'You look great, Kelly.'

David is standing with Cora, Euan, Will, and a woman I don't recognise. When we reach them, Will steps forwards to put an arm around my shoulders.

'Guys, I'd like you to meet Maggie. My girlfriend.' He winks at me. 'Maggie, this is my sister, Heather, and my good mate, David.'

I can feel my cheeks burning as Heather pulls me into a tight hug and squeezes my hands. 'Oh, I've heard all about you, Maggie. Will won't shut up. It's like a miracle: the eternal bachelor finally lured out of his hermitage. For a moment there, I was worried he'd end up with one of his sheep.' Her laugh is as fast and high as her voice, her smile generous. She's like a female version of Will: pale skin, dark hair, and bright blue eyes.

'Maggie, can we get you a drink?' Euan says.

Will's already told me that the Morrisons always hire workers from Lewis for the harvest, but the immaculate Euan and Cora stand out like sore thumbs in the dirty, jubilant pub. The absence of Euan's son, Iain, is also obvious, and when I look at Euan, always so genial, so doggedly affable, his arm around his smiling wife, I only just manage not to give him a hugely inappropriate hug.

'I'm fine, thanks. Charlie's getting me one.'

'It's a good thing you did, you and Kelly,' Euan says. 'Helping Charlie out today. No one ever wants to ask for it.'

'Especially if they're Charlie MacLeod,' David says. He laughs and offers his hand before kissing me on both cheeks. 'Very pleased to meet you, Maggie.'

Kelly wasn't exaggerating. Isla's golden child is just that: tall and broad, with thick fair hair and a jawline so chiselled I immediately want to give a teenage giggle.

'I'm glad you're making my main man here happy,' David says.

'Oh, very good, Campbell,' Kelly scoffs. 'Is that what passes for smooth patter around Charing Cross these days?'

'Actually, I'm in the West End now.'

'That's a shame,' Kelly says. 'I was hoping to move back to Kelvinbridge in the next couple of months. Now I'm going to have to rethink the whole thing.'

'It's good to see you, Kelly.' He laughs, moving closer to pull her into a hug. 'You look fantastic.'

Kelly valiantly tries to maintain her cool, although when he lets go her cheeks have gone a very obvious pink. She clears her throat. 'You coming back for the gathering as well?'

'Jimmy and Jaz have offered to help Mum.' He nods to where Isla – in muddy dungarees and the largest, floppiest sun hat I've ever seen – is sitting with perhaps half a dozen other women around a long oval table. 'But yeah.' David gives her his wide-dimpled smile. 'I'll be back.'

'You're just full of bad news today,' Kelly says. She glances towards Charlie and Miko coming back from the bar. 'And I'm not particularly looking forward to another day of being bossed around by Antonius Proximo here either.'

'What are you gibbering about, girl?' Charlie says as he hands over our wines with a frown.

'*Gladiator*, Charlie.' Kelly rolls her eyes, making me laugh. 'Even an old dinosaur like you *has* to have seen *Gladiator*.'

*

As the evening wears on into night, a buffet of hot rolls is laid out in the lounge. Even though it's nine p.m., the sun streams through the pub's windows, making it feel like late afternoon. A few hours of solid drinking have given most people a second wind, and there's plenty of enthusiasm when Donnie and the rest of the ceilidh band set up in the corner of the bar.

I, however, am exhausted – a pleasant bone-weariness that makes me long for bed. As people start getting up to dance, I look towards the bar, where Charlie is hunched over on a stool.

'I'm just going to go see how Charlie's doing,' I say to Will, before gladly turning away from the dance floor.

Jimmy is leaning across the bar, an empty whisky glass in his hand. He straightens when he sees me, nods at Charlie.

'Maybe you can cheer this morose old bastard up,' he says. Which seems vastly hypocritical, but I'm still grateful for his rescue from Hollow Beach and that he's never once rubbed my nose in needing it. Besides, he might have a point. Charlie's shoulders are hunched and low, as if he has the weight of the world on them. And while my cheeks ache with hours of smiling, his mouth is flat, fixed into a mean, tight-lipped scowl.

'It's Maggie!' he says, with more of a grimace than a smile. He grabs hold of my hands in his cold calloused fingers, and I realise that he's drunk – *very* drunk. His eyes are red-rimmed and un-focussed. 'Did I say thank you for the cutting today? Because Moira says I don't say thank you.' He shakes his head. 'And I'm . . . I'm—'

'It's fine, Charlie. You did.'

'I'm grateful to you, Maggie. I am.' He knocks against the bar with his knuckles. 'Jimmy, another Talisker over here.'

'Hey,' I say, managing to catch him by the shoulders before he overbalances and falls off the stool. 'Why don't we go sit at that table over there for a bit?'

'Aye. Okay.'

By the time I've managed to get him off the stool and over to the table, the band has launched into a very loud, very fast 'Baba O'Riley'. I glance over to see the unlikely figure of Isla, now minus her floppy hat, playing the piano with as much vigour as Donnie is playing his bagpipes.

'I was a shit husband,' Charlie says, as if there's been no break at all in our conversation. He balls his hands into tight fists. 'I treated Moira like shit.'

'Charlie—'

'It was my fault.' His gaze focusses briefly on mine before sliding away again, and he takes in a hiccupping breath. 'I had an affair, you know. Right here. Right under her nose.'

'I don't think you should be telling me this.' Because his agitation is palpable, and even before he raised his voice, too many people were looking over at us.

'I'm sorry. I'm sorry, lassie.' He makes a visible effort to sit up, square his shoulders. 'Maudlin old bastard.' He sighs, runs his forefinger under his nose. 'The peat harvest, everyone coming . . . coming back . . .' He drifts off for a few seconds before blinking. 'Makes the place feel different, you know? Makes the past, everyone who's gone, feel that wee bit closer.'

I think of our first long-ago conversation on Long Stride below those sad stone memorials. 'A thin place.'

The change in Charlie is immediate. His distress is so palpable that it straightaway infects me, a cool, ringing alarm that raises the hairs on the back of my neck. The tears in his eyes make me feel even worse. 'Shit. I'm sorry. What did I—'

'I haven't been telling you the truth, Maggie. I haven't told you the truth.'

'I know.' I take hold of his hands and squeeze. 'But listen, it doesn't matter.' I think of Mum's smile. *Trust nobody. They all lie.* And then she's gone. Like a whisper I didn't hear. 'The truth isn't everything, Charlie. It isn't even the most important thing. The past is the past, no matter how close it is. You helped me see that.' I try to smile. 'And I guess, so did Robert.'

'I knew the truth,' Charlie says, as if I haven't said a word. 'I wanted you to write that story – I wanted to help you to write that story – because I knew the truth.'

'Charlie,' I say, and I'm squeezing his hands too tight, but I can't help it. I need him to stop. I need him not to tell me anything that might risk what I've only just found here. What I've only just chosen. Behind us, 'Baba O'Riley' is reaching a deafening crescendo. 'Please don't—'

He yanks me hard towards him without warning. His breath is warm and sharp with whisky.

'I know who did it, Maggie,' he says. His eyes are suddenly very clear. 'I know who murdered Robert.'

When the door of the pub bangs open, loud and sharp like a gunshot, Charlie flinches and lets go of me. My chair rocks backwards on its legs. The music stops; Donnie's bagpipes cut off with an indignant squeal, and in the ensuing silence, Femi stares back at us all from the windy, sun-filled doorway. Instinctively, I know something's wrong. He's lost all of his London bad-boy swagger. His face is drawn, almost comically agitated; he searches the room with a kind of desperation.

'Femi?' Miko says, moving to stand between him and the bar.

He looks at her with some measure of relief. 'Miko.'

'What is it? Are you okay?'

'No. I – we . . .' He shakes his head.

'What *is* it?'

Femi takes in one long, shuddering breath. And then another. 'We found a body,' he says, in a low almost-whisper that I still manage to hear. Charlie goes still beside me, his knuckles suddenly white against the table. 'At the dig. We . . . we found a body, Miko.'

And I can tell that he doesn't mean a three-and-a-half-thousand-year-old bog body.

Robert. I see him standing and unsmiling against a green hillside.

'It looks like a . . .' Femi seems to register for the first time that everyone is looking at him. He appears to shrink, hunching down as if bracing himself for whatever he thinks is coming his way. His gaze flickers over Charlie and me, and then he looks only at Miko. 'It's a child.'

CHAPTER 25

Will and I go back to the pub two days later. The rain is cold and heavy, the sky and sea a battleship grey. We hold hands but we don't speak. The road is otherwise empty. The opened peat banks with their dragon-scale spines look like fortified earthworks, as if the island is under siege. We've certainly spent the last two days holed up at the farm as if it is. Having a lot of sex. Mostly, I suspect, because it takes away the need to speak. And, if I was feeling less miserable, because it's a way of saying *I love you* or *I'm here*, without having to say why it needs to be said. Without having to mention out loud the dead child.

But I *am* feeling miserable. All of the air has been let out of my happiness, and, selfish as it is, I feel cheated. Disappointed at its fragility, when I'd thought it was finally here to stay. I used to see signs in everything; it was, ironically, one of Dr Abebe's *warning signs*. Probably because I rarely saw them when

I was content, when I was in control. Today, as we walk through the low wet clouds and the miserable cold, I see those signs everywhere, and not just in the peat banks. I see them in the weather and in our silence. In the dark shadows of Terror Mountain and the Valley of Ghosts, the violently flapping blue-and-white police tape strung across the road into the cemetery and Cladh Dubh, and in the shrill alarms of the crows returned to the ruined church. It feels like the end of something that was just beginning.

The pub isn't as busy as I'm expecting, which is a relief. Euan nods at us from behind a long table set up opposite the bar. It was his summons that forced us out of isolation, and judging by the low and unsettled grumbles, we're not the only ones. Beside him sits a policewoman in black trousers and a bulky black jacket with POLICE SCOTLAND printed in white below the lapel, while two other men in grey suits loiter against the wall behind them. One of them is Detective Constable 'Call me Lockie' Scott – who came to the blackhouse the morning after the fire.

There's no one from Urbost or anywhere else here, I notice. Nor any of the relatives who helped out with the peat harvest. Will said Heather and David left for Stornoway Airport as soon as the police gave the okay on Sunday. There are no archaeologists either. I wonder if they've been asked to stay away. Because we're the only ones who might know something, I consider, as I look around the grumbling room. Before realising that the *we* doesn't actually apply to me. The disappointment instead of relief that I feel at this is a measure of just how much this place has come to feel like home.

Will waves at Cora, who's sitting next to Euan and the long table, her hands clasped tight in her lap. We head towards the MacKenzies, sitting at their usual table. I don't see Kelly; perhaps she's upstairs with Fraser. Bruce nods as we sit down; Gillian offers us a brief smile. The MacDonalds aren't here. That seems ominous in and of itself. As if reading my thoughts, Donnie leans over, a deep frown line between his eyes. 'Alec's on his way back from the rigs.'

This is unspoken. The conviction that the dead child must be Lorne. It's an obvious assumption. He's the only child to have ever gone missing. I think of that little memorial above Long Stride.

I look across the room, where Charlie is sitting with Isla, Jaz, and Jimmy. He must have seen Will and me come in, but he's staring resolutely across at the long table, at the police-woman's black-and-white chequered hat and the sheaf of papers alongside it.

Euan clears his throat. 'All right, let's get started.' He turns to the policewoman. 'This is Inspector Lynn Urquhart. I'll . . .' Euan looks pale, tired. He sits down heavily without finishing his sentence.

Inspector Lynn Urquhart is in her late forties, with sensible short-cropped dark hair and a round, friendly face. 'I've met most of you before, of course. I'm very sorry to be here in such difficult circumstances, but I'm sure you understand that we need to ask you some questions.'

Jimmy stands up. 'Is it Lorne MacDonald?'

She presses her lips together, puts her hands on the table, and leans forwards. 'Yes. DNA analysis has shown that the body we recovered from the Cladh Dubh dig is that of Lorne MacDonald.'

The room doesn't erupt, but releases its collective breath. Isla presses her hand against her mouth, stifling a sob.

'I know this is hard,' Inspector Lynn Urquhart says. 'But obviously we need to establish how Lorne died and why he was buried on this island when he was supposed to have drowned at sea.'

She comes out from behind the table and walks to the centre of the room. 'Initial postmortem findings have failed to establish a cause of death, and although we're waiting on lab results, there's a chance that no COD will be established forensically. That means we have to speak to everyone who was living here in April 1994. In a few minutes, my colleagues, Detective Sergeant Munro and Detective Constable Scott, will start to hear witness statements. That will take some time, so we'd appreciate your patience. And if you could not discuss any specifics with one another while you're waiting, we'd appreciate that too.'

She looks around the room. 'Anyone who wishes to speak to me in confidence is welcome to do so. Phone Stornoway Police Station and ask for me by name. Anything you say will be treated as completely confidential.' She leaves a long silence before folding her arms and moving back towards the table. 'Anyone who was not living here in '94 is free to leave.'

Will sighs. 'I'm going to stay with Mum,' he says. 'She doesn't look great today.'

'D'you want me to stay too?' I ask, praying he says no. Although the rain is now lashing down hard against the windows, I suddenly want to be anywhere but here.

He gives me a brief smile, shakes his head. 'You should go back to the farm. I'll come as soon as I can.'

Charlie walks by our table, heading towards the toilets, and I spring up.

'Charlie.'

He half-turns, wards me off with the flat of his palm as he keeps on walking, his gait shambling and unsteady. I can feel the anxiety radiating from him.

'Charlie!' But I let him go because I can't bear to see his distress. I can't bear to add to it. To ask him about what he knows, what he's been hiding all this time. Because I haven't been able to forget how clear his eyes had been that night in the pub; *I know who murdered Robert.*

*

It's barely four p.m. by the time I get back to the farm, but the sky is the colour of dusk and there are shadows everywhere. The rain has relented to a fine damp mist that blurs and shifts like muslin curtains. I stop, for a moment, on the road looking west. The police tape has come away from one of the old gate posts ahead of the cemetery; it waves and frantically flaps in the wind like a tethered bird.

Femi said that the north end of the main trench collapsed as they were filling it in, exposing the body. I remember him telling me way back in February that it looked like someone had been poking around in the dig at night. Muddy footprints and moved tarps. Earth disturbed around the recently excavated part of the main barrow. Which suddenly makes sense, if someone was afraid that the dig might uncover what they'd buried there twenty-five years ago. If they were trying to find it first.

I shiver and step onto the wet grass. If Charlie was telling the truth the night of the peat harvest and someone really did murder Robert, then maybe they murdered Lorne too? Maybe Lorne saw them kill Robert, or maybe Robert saw them kill Lorne. And if Charlie knows, then doesn't it stand to reason that *he* saw something too? Maybe he's protecting the person responsible, and that's why he's blown so hot and cold. Or maybe, *he* . . . I think of his weather-beaten face, the wild tufts of hair that poke out from under his tweed caps, the finger he runs under his nose whenever he feels uncomfortable, uncertain. The awkward but determined way he patted my hand when he was telling me that it was okay to be happy. Charlie wouldn't kill someone.

I open the farm door and step inside, close it quickly against the wind. I turn on the light, sit down on the sofa, pull a tweed blanket over my legs. I feel cold and ill at ease. Because if any of that is true than the *person responsible* isn't just a theoretical possibility that weeks ago I decided probably didn't exist. They're not even some formless, nameless stranger. It's someone Charlie would protect. It's someone here. Someone I know.

*

I wake up suddenly from a nightmare, forgotten but still squeezing the breath inside my chest. I realise that it's dark. Cold. Will isn't back yet. I look at my phone. Eight p.m. Sunset isn't for another two hours, but it already looks like night outside. I think of the sun that streamed through the pub's windows just forty-eight hours ago. I get up. I should eat. Instead, I start restocking the fire grate before going on the hunt for matches in the kitchen. I freeze in front of its only window. There's a light on inside the blackhouse.

I shouldn't go. The old me would *never* go. And I can already feel her creeping back. I'm having bad dreams again. And I'm letting everything I've begun to love about this place become warped and poisoned.

Face it, I think in Dr Abebe's voice. *See it and confront it.*

Maybe I left the light on. Even if I know I didn't.

I grab Will's heavy-duty torch, pull open the door. When I step outside, I struggle to pull it shut again. The wind is ferocious now, battering against me from all directions, its echoes howling and trapped in the spaces between cliffs and the sea. I walk quickly towards the blackhouse before I lose courage. I test the door and its *iffy* lock, and when it swings open I step back. My heart trips. I can't see anything through the little inset window, so I make myself switch off the torch and hold it high like a club. And go in.

There's no one there. Everything looks the way I left it a few days ago. Except the light that's coming from the standard lamp next to the sofa. I can hear the cheerful tick-tock of the cartoon Highland cow on the mantelpiece behind it. On the other side of the room, the bed and wardrobe are in darkness.

I venture further in, still brandishing the torch, still trying to keep hold of my courage.

'Hello?'

Nothing but the wind.

I go over to the dining table, pick up my laptop and tuck it under my arm. I snatch up the photo of Robert too, push it inside my mac pocket. The hairs on my forearms are standing up. I can't shake a feeling of *jamais vu,* as if I'm watching myself through the wrong end of a telescope again. It feels like sitting alone in bed while someone runs around the outside of your house, or waking up to find that house on fire and a mummified bird in your bedside drawer. And then deciding to forget that any of those things happened. Because they don't belong in your life. Because you have no intention of ever facing anything at all.

And then I hear a metal click – familiar and loud. The bathroom door swings open on a long, low creak. The bathroom beyond is in darkness. All I can see of the person standing motionless inside its doorway is a vague outline against the shadows. I'm standing in the light, but they're hidden in the dark.

I step back again. Once. Twice. It feels like I'm falling, the ground rushing up to meet me. Too fast to stop.

'Who are you?' My voice is tremulous. My chattering teeth are the loudest thing in the answering silence.

When the figure moves, I shriek. When something flies out of the darkness towards me before hitting the floor in a sickening wet thud less than two feet away, I shriek louder. It's a dead crow, bloodied and slick with rain.

'*Leave me alone!*'

The click near the standard lamp is my only warning before the room is plunged into blackness. I drop the torch and laptop and run for the door. Because I can feel that second someone else in the darkness, closer than the standard lamp now – close enough that I can hear their too-loud intake of breath before they hold it. The hackles on my neck send shudder after shudder down the length of my spine as I battle to pull open the latch, but I don't stop, I don't look behind me. I wrench open the door, run out onto the path and back towards the farm so fast that my legs start to seize and my body pitches forwards. Only the panic of falling, the terror of being caught, keeps me going, keeps my legs moving.

When I reach the farm, I sprint inside, slip on the doormat as I spin round to slam the door shut behind me. Only when I've locked the mortice do I stop to draw breath, go back over to the kitchen window. I can't see anything at all. The blackhouse is in darkness.

I look at my own silhouette in the glass. And see Mum's face instead, thin, white, and eaten by shadows.

It's coming. It's close.

*

When Will comes back, I'm sitting in the dark at the kitchen table. I flinch from the sudden glare of the ceiling light.

'Maggie?'

'Where have you been?'

He shuts the door, comes towards me. 'The statements took hours and then I decided to walk back instead of getting a lift with Mum and Euan. Get some fresh air. Check on the sheep. Why are you sitting in the dark?'

'There's someone in the blackhouse.' I know I don't sound right. I know I need to at least try to sound right, but I can't. And I certainly can't tell him that I'm sitting in the dark so that I don't have to see faces of dead people in the windows.

'Stay here,' Will says, running back out through the door, leaving it open to swing wildly in the wind.

I don't get up. I don't look out the window. I don't close the door. I close my eyes instead, tighten my fingers around the cool planes and sharp edges of my pendant, knuckles digging into my breastbone. And when Will finally comes back, I let out the breath I hadn't known I was holding.

'There's no one there. Nothing looks disturbed.' He closes the door against the wind, puts his torch and my laptop down on the kitchen table. 'Except I found these on the floor.'

'There was someone there. There were *people* there.' There's a dangerous lump inside my throat. I think of the dead crow in the middle of the room, bloodied and slick with rain. There's no way he couldn't have seen it. Which can only mean that it's gone.

Will crouches down next to my chair, takes my hand in his. 'Baby, it's okay,' he says, in a new and careful voice. 'It's been a hard few days. Anyone would be jumpy. Maybe—'

I wrench my hand back. 'Don't speak to me like that!'

'Okay. I'm sorry.' He stays on his knees looking up at me. His gaze direct and very clear. 'I believe you.'

And I think of looking down at that thin, white face eaten by shadows; the purple moon-shaped welts her nails left in my skin. *I believe you, Mum.*

I feel all the fight go out of me, and when Will pulls me towards

him, I slump against his shoulder, try to let go of the tears that
the dark kept at bay. They won't come. I feel cold and empty.

'It's all right,' Will says, and his arms are around me again,
absorbing my shudders. 'It's all right.'

But it isn't.

I think of Dr Abebe the last time I saw him: shiny suit, too-big
glasses, sharp cologne. 'You've had bipolar since puberty, Maggie.
You know how to manage it better than anyone. There's no reason
to believe that you will have another psychotic episode ever again.'
That always solemn smile. 'Not if you're careful.'

'They were there,' I say against Will's skin. 'I didn't imagine it.'

But you might have, a spiteful whisper in my head says. Because
maybe you got too happy. Maybe you stopped being careful. Maybe
in letting go of Robert and your mum, you forgot to hold on
quite so tight to your own flying lines.

'There are birds . . .' I say. 'There's a canvas rucksack in the
mudroom. Please, there are—'

'You want me to get it?'

When I nod, Will lets me go, tries not to show the concern in
his face as he cups my cheeks in his hands. 'Lock the door behind
me this time, okay?' He opens it and I try not to wince at the
howling wind. 'I'll be back in a minute.'

I lock the door, sit back down at that wooden table inside that
wooden room. I don't shake. I don't think of Mum. I don't think
of anything. When Will calls my name, I get up on aching legs,
let the wind back in, cold and punishing. There's nothing in his
hands. There's no expression on his face, but he doesn't know that
I can see what's in his eyes. Because I've seen it many times before.

'There was someone there,' I whisper. 'There was . . .'

Will closes the door and lifts me up. Carries me towards the couch without saying a word.

Help me, I think, as I let him. As I hold on to his solid warmth. *Make it go away.*

CHAPTER 26

Robert

There are two more dead ewes less than three weeks after the
first. I find them in almost the same place; in the shelter of
the low cemetery wall. It's late afternoon, the skies are fast-
moving and dark. I can smell the sea on the wind – another
winter storm blowing in from the Atlantic to batter its rage
against rock and stone and sand. I can smell the blood too, so
much of it, turning the ewes' sun-bleached coats black and
slick. They died the same way as the first; a deep ugly wound
above their pregnant bellies. I'm too tired and despairing to
be angry. More than three healthy ewes, I've lost at least three
lambs, an entire winter's feed and vaccines. The claustrophobia
is back; a weight that I feel in every step. The fear too, taut
and debilitating. Because until I know who is doing this, how
can I stop it?

I think about dumping the carcasses in the same place as the
first: up on the empty moorland beyond the standing stones at
Oir na Tìr, but at the last minute decide not to. Some small spark
of anger bursts finally into life inside my stomach, and I haul

them onto the back of the ATV instead. Ignoring the blood, the stiff and unyielding weight, the punishing wind.

The lights are on inside the blackhouse, but I drive up to the barn. I park at the back door. Sheep might be simple animals, but they're not stupid. I go marching past them carrying two dead ewes and there'll be hell to pay. The chest freezer is just inside the door. There's not much in it. Mary has used most of the meat and fish over the last few months; we're due another trip east to restock. I put the dead sheep inside binbags before stacking them at one end of the freezer. I strip off my coat and wash the blood from my hands before going back outside again.

The day is darker, the storm closer. It squats like a spreading bruise over the horizon, and for a moment, I'm almost paralysed as the wind whistles around my head, howls inside the fissures and caves in the rock under my feet.

I shake it off, hurry for the blackhouse's welcoming light. As I get there, the door opens and Charlie steps out. Mary is smiling inside the doorway, and just like that, the spark of anger catches, goes up like kindling.

'Came by to check on you all, Robert,' Charlie says, although he has the good grace, at least, to look caught. 'Going to be a bad one, they reckon. Already force ten and fifty-foot waves out in Bailey and Rockall.'

'Maybe it'll change direction,' I say.

'Aye, maybe so.' He stops on the path. 'We can hope.'

'Thanks for coming, Charlie,' Mary says. Her smile has gone.

I go inside, close the door behind me. A boy is sitting on the living room floor. Older and sullen-faced as he reluctantly helps

Calum finish an oversized jigsaw. I realise it's Euan Morrison's son, Iain, just as Euan bangs open the bathroom door and marches into the mudroom.

'Robert!' he says, fat cheeks wobbling. 'You've a full house, eh? Just popped round with some spare wood and peat.' He glances out the window and frowns. 'Going to be a bad one, looks like.'

When I say nothing, he clears his throat. 'C'mon, Iain, best get back before the rain comes on.'

'Thank you, Euan,' Mary says before looking pointedly at me.

'Aye, thanks,' I say, opening the front door as he pulls on his coat.

'Not a problem.' He flashes a smile that reminds me of that meeting in the pub last year when I first asked about the Land Fund. 'Just being a good landlord.'

'He and Charlie only wanted to help,' Mary says once they're gone. 'There's no shame in accepting it. You said that's what living in a place like this is like.'

I don't reply because I don't trust myself enough to know what I'll say. My tiredness is gone now, burned completely away.

'Daddy!' Calum says, abandoning his jigsaw to run towards me in clumsy excitement, headbutting my legs.

'Hey, wee man,' I say, scooping him up, trying to smile. 'Shall we go down to the cellar and turn on the stars?'

''Pecial light,' he shouts, clapping.

'Aye, we'll turn on the special light too.'

'Robert.' Mary grabs me by the elbow, but I shake her off as I open the trapdoor and start heading down the cellar stairs carrying Calum.

She follows behind. Says nothing as I sit Calum down on the mattress and turn on the lighthouse's lamp – a slow-moving arc of white-silver against the brick walls. She folds her arms when I turn off the main light to reveal all those hundreds of stars.

'Night stars!' Calum grins, clapping his hands again as he stares up in a wide-eyed wonder that's never tired, never disappointed. It helps douse some of my anger, enough that when Mary pulls me back towards the stairs, I go without protest.

'Rob. We can't stay down here again.'

'How many times do I have to tell you? You haven't seen a proper Atlantic storm make landfall. We have to—'

'Charlie says those kinds of storms are once in a—'

'*Charlie* turns on the charm and lies through his teeth to anyone stupid enough to listen. I don't want you letting him in this house any more.'

Mary folds her arms again. 'He also said that these cellars are one of the worst places to be in a storm. Even at this elevation, if the sea surges, if it comes up onto the land, this place could flood in minutes.'

I remember, the day after my father died, I found a dead seal high on the headland close to Loch nam Each. Sleek and big, one baleful black eye staring up at me. I imagine green-dark sea rushing down the cellar steps – icy-cold with limbs of seaweed and crowns of yellow-white foam. I know I'm not hiding down here because I'm afraid of a storm. I'm afraid of losing the people I love. Even if they don't always love me.

I look at Mary, the fire in her eyes and colour in her cheeks; at Calum still staring up at the stars on the ceiling. I want to keep them safe. I want to keep their love down here with me in this sanctuary I've created. This world that has no one else in it. Nothing but us, the stars, and a sweeping white light, constant and certain. It will always stay bright. It will never become a black tower – a shadow like something burned against a wall. I will never let it.

'Why don't you just ask what you want to ask me, Rob?' Mary says, her eyes dark.

The sharp lines in my father's face. *You're feeble, boy. Weak like a woman.* I should tell Mary the truth.

'Are you fucking Charlie?'

Wine-red spots blossom on her cheeks even as the rest of her face pales to waxy white. 'No. I'm not fucking Charlie,' she says, low. 'And I'm not fucking anyone else. Not here, not in Aberdeen. Not once. But I don't think that's what you really want to hear, is it?'

I close my eyes. Sometimes it feels like I'm choking. Like I'm drowning inside the words I want to say. 'Someone's killing the sheep.'

'What?'

'I lied to you. When I said I didn't know what happened to that ewe last month. She was butchered. And today, there were two more.'

Mary presses her fingers against her mouth, sends a terrified look towards Calum. 'What kind of animal could have—'

'I've put them in the freezer in the barn. And I'm going to phone the police tomorrow.' I look at her. 'It wasn't an animal.'

She steps back against the wall. 'What do you mean?'

'Someone's been watching me. Watching us.'

'Who?' She shakes her head. 'You're scaring me, Rob.'

I glance across at the workbench. 'D'you remember the dead crows?'

Mary's eyes are wide. 'Did someone – *God*, did someone kill . . .'

'No. Yes.' My hands are fists. 'I did.'

When her eyes grow wider, I force my hands to unclench. 'You don't understand this place, these islands, because I've never told you. I've never been able to. The crows are *vándr-varði*. I made them to protect us.'

Mary snatches a piece of paper out of her jeans pocket, unfolds it to reveal a clumsy Viking rune pattern drawn in black felt-tip. 'Calum's been doing these. I'm finding them all over the house. He even drew one on the wall. The Helm of Awe and Terror, he tells me. To protect us from evil.' She shakes her head, and I understand that she's furious. 'I will not have you make Calum as paranoid as you.'

'That's not what – it's no different to touching wood or never putting shoes on a table. When I was a kid, whenever a storm was coming, Mamaidh always told me to put a poker and tongs in the fire to protect the house. These islands are thin places. And you have to be careful – so careful – what you do in thin places.'

'For God's sake! What does that *mean*, Robert? Fiona told me you were acting strange in the village last—'

'Christ! I couldn't care less what Fiona bloody MacDonald told you.' I make myself stop. I feel desperate. She has to understand. She *has* to. I hold out my hands. 'I'm sorry. It's just I have to make sure that you and Calum are safe.'

'Robert.' The anger goes out of her and she comes towards me. There are tears in her eyes.

I tuck a loose strand of hair behind her ear, let my palm linger against the softness of her cheek until the ground feels a little more solid beneath my feet again. And I finally say what I should have said the minute we drove off that ferry from Skye. 'You have to trust me, Mary. Mamaidh was right.' I rub my thumbs against the warm wet of her skin. 'You have no idea what it's like when a place like this turns against you.'

CHAPTER 27

'I said you don't have to come.'

'And I said I want to come,' Will says, quickening his pace to match mine, trying to take my hand.

'Why? You don't believe me.'

'Hey. Wait.' He grabs hold of my hand, forces me to stop walking. '*Wait.*'

I try not to look at him even when he turns me around.

'I said I believed you,' Will says. His lips are pressed thin, his eyes dark and intense. 'Because I believe you, Maggie.'

I feel different today. I woke up feeling better. Stronger. Calm rather than desperate. A little angry. I regret the weakness of yesterday. I can still feel its contamination in Will's *I believe you;* in my lingering need to hear it. But I'm not that person any more. I face things.

The birds are gone. My canvas rucksack is gone. But even if

I'm still reluctant to lean too hard against my own judgement, both Detective Constable Scott and Charlie saw them – saw the *vándr-varði*. And someone took them.

'I get why you're doing this, all right?' Will says. 'I get why you want to find out what happened.'

Yesterday, I finally told him what Charlie had told me, that he knew who'd murdered Robert.

'Robert Reid went missing on the same night as Lorne, there's no way one isn't anything to do with the other. And I mean, Jesus, whatever happened to that wee boy, however he died, someone – probably from this island, this village – buried him in the ground and left him there for twenty-five years.' Will's expression tightens. 'I know these people, Maggie. I've known them pretty much all my life. And if one of them . . .' He shakes his head. 'If they were waiting for you last night . . . if that's what . . .' He takes my hands again. 'We need to talk to the police.'

'They won't believe me, Will. Especially when they hear the whole bloody saga about me coming here as a kid, what I said. It'd be pointless.' I start walking towards Blairmore. 'I just need to get Charlie to speak to me again. Then maybe I'll get some answers.'

And this time, I'm not asking because of that person in the blackhouse. I'm not asking to salve my own conscience or to grieve my mother. I'm doing it because I owe Robert. I never wanted to prove that he'd been murdered for his sake – and when trying to prove it threatened my happiness, I threw him away like rubbish. Somehow Mum had known who he was, that he'd changed his name, even that he'd been murdered – but when knowing that didn't get her what she wanted, she abandoned him too. So I have to see this through. I have to find out what happened. Not for me this time, but for Robert.

*

No one answers when I knock on Charlie's door. I peer through the letterbox and see only a dark empty hall. 'Charlie. Charlie!'

'Well, if he's in there, he's clearly not in the mood for visitors. Come on,' Will says, turning back for the gate. 'If he won't help us, we'll go to Stornoway. Do what you said.'

When we push through the doors of Am Blàr Mòr, the pub is empty even behind the bar. We still creep towards that red wall of photographs like furtive thieves, and as soon as I find the photo, I quickly take it down.

'What ya doin'?'

'Jesus,' both Will and I say in unison, springing away from the wall and each other.

'Caught rotten.' Kelly grins in delight, folding a bar towel over her shoulder. 'Well, come on, you have to tell me now.'

Feeling something between embarrassed and defensive, I hold out the photo of those smiling people in waterproofs standing under the Stornoway Whisky Festival 1994 banner. 'Everyone in this photo was in Stornoway the night of the storm – the night both Robert and Lorne died. So . . .'

Kelly's smile disappears. 'Fuck, Maggie.'

'I need to do something. I just *need* to do something.' I hold out the photo again, but she doesn't take it. 'D'you recognise anyone?'

She frowns, shakes her head, though I notice that she hardly looks at it. 'Why don't you ask Charlie?'

'Charlie isn't talking,' Will says.

'I can't ask anyone in Blairmore about this photo without having to explain why. But last time I was in the town hall in Stornoway, they said there was a guy from Urbost who worked there and who knew everyone back then.' There's a restless sense of urgency in me; a feeling that if I stop moving even for a moment, it's going to be too late to ever catch up with the truth.

Kelly unfolds her arms. 'I'll take you.'

'What?'

'Jaz'll lend me his ridiculous Chelsea tractor.' She smiles a very un-Kelly-like smile. 'I have to talk to you anyway. There's something I need to tell you.'

*

Kelly drives fast. The Range Rover roars across the flat bleak inland moors, still gold, still empty, still fierce with whistling wind.

'You won't tell anyone about this, will you, Kelly?'

'Of course not.'

'I mean, someone *must* have killed Lorne, right? And I've been thinking that Robert knew who and that's why he died, but what if Robert was the one who did it? And what if someone saw *him*? I mean, Christ, if Alec saw him . . .' I endure a flashback to his blazing black eyes. To Sheena's *You're not safe here.*

'Or maybe Isla's husband, Kenny Campbell, killed Lorne? I mean, it's pretty coincidental that he died a few weeks later, right?

Maybe he killed them both and the guilt was too much for him? Or what about Jimmy? I mean—'

Kelly brings the Range Rover to a squealing halt at an empty T-junction, and I shut up. Try to ignore the abrupt panic at my overexcitement; the sense of urgency I still feel in my chest. 'Sorry. That was too much.'

Kelly turns to look at me, my flaming cheeks. 'I get it. Wanting to know. Needing to know. I do.' She shakes her head. 'God, it's just that . . . everything feels so weird all of a sudden, doesn't it? I keep looking at Fraser and thinking of that poor wee boy alone all those years without even a headstone apart from that lie out at Long Stride, and it just – Christ, the one thing you can always rely on around here is that nothing ever happens. I used to think that was a bad thing.'

She turns on the windscreen wipers as rain starts coming down hard and fast, low cloud turning the moorland into sprinting shadows.

'The police have been to North Uist to speak to Mum and Dad,' she says, her voice suddenly different, not sounding like her at all any more. 'Mum said a major crime unit from Inverness is taking over the investigation.'

I close my eyes, force myself not to say anything more, not to ask her about the police speaking to her parents. 'And I'm banging on about suspects like I think I'm Poirot,' I say instead. 'I'm an insensitive shithead. I'm sorry.'

'Hate to break it to you, but you've got more of a Miss Marple vibe,' Kelly says with a smile, but her voice is still flat. I look at her until a car draws up behind us, flashing its lights, and then she accelerates through the junction and onto the Stornoway road.

*

Bobby Rankin is in his sixties. Tall and lankily thin, he stands in the office doorway with what looks like a permanent stoop, his grey eyes tired.

'Aye, Murdo told me about you. Your book about the Kilmeray deaths in '94.' He comes round the desk and sits down with a wince. 'What is it I can do for you?'

'Um, I was just wondering . . .' I take the photo out of my bag. Its frame makes too loud a clack against the desk as I set it down. 'Mr Black, he couldn't identify everyone, and he thought you might be able to?'

'Ah. The famous photograph.' He picks it up. 'It's in bad nick, all right. Let's see.' He brings it close to his eyes, squints for a couple of seconds, and then moves it a few inches away.

'Mr Black thought the ones at the front were Jimmy Struthers, Charlie MacLeod, and maybe Bruce MacKenzie?'

'Aye.' Bobby Rankin nods. 'I think he's right at that. And behind them is the MacDonalds, Alec and Fiona.'

'He didn't recognise anyone on the left-hand side of the photo.'

'Can't say as I blame him. Not much of it left, is there?' He squints for a few seconds more before setting the photo back down on the desk. He points to the man and woman at the very left edge of shot. 'I can't tell who they are, I'm afraid, but standing behind them is Euan Morrison. Definitely.'

'Thanks.' I'm inexplicably disappointed. Mainly because I don't know how this helps. Or even how I thought it *would* help. I shove the photo back into my bag as I stand up and hold out my hand to shake his. But he's no sooner let mine go than he shakes his head abruptly and comes back around the desk.

'Wait a wee minute. Can I see that again?'

I hand him the photo, and he stares at it for perhaps a full minute. 'I'm afraid someone's told you wrong.'

'Told me what wrong?' Something in his certainty quickens my pulse.

'That photo can't have been taken on the day of the festival.'

I go still. 'Why not?'

He holds out the photo. 'See that fishing boat moored up behind them? CY415? It was a scalloper, out of Castlebay. Belonged to a Malcolm Sinclair. His brother, Alan, ran a Stornoway creel boat, which sank out past Ness during the storm on Saturday, ninth of April. Day of the festival. Coastguard managed to get the crew off, but Alan didn't survive the trip to hospital. Malcolm came up from Barra to register his brother's death on the Monday.'

'The Monday?'

He nods. 'Registered the death myself.' He points at the photo. 'That boat didn't arrive in the harbour until Monday the eleventh of April.'

I look down at the photo as if it's going to disagree, come up with some kind of counterargument.

He shrugs. 'Maybe they decided to stay on a few days, ride out the storm. That's what a lot of folk did. Those banners generally stay up at least a week.' He smiles. 'Doesn't need to be a festival to enjoy whisky, after all.'

Except that Charlie told me they all headed back to Kilmeray the very next morning.

*

Outside, it's still only early afternoon, but the ferry terminal is practically floodlit, and the deep curve of the harbour and marina beyond is studded with lights from fishing boats and yachts, piers and pontoons. I walk past pubs, cafés, and hotels painted white and yellow and blue, glowing gold at their windows. The sky over my head is ominously dark, the wind against my face cold and damp.

I feel numb. I feel confused. I'm starting to feel afraid again. Because if Charlie lied – and I don't see how he couldn't have – then it can only mean one of two things. That Bobby Rankin is right: they came for the festival and stayed at least two days past the storm. But Lorne died on the Saturday, on the *day* of the festival; surely there's no way that Alec and Fiona MacDonald wouldn't have been told – for another two days – that their son was missing. I take out the photo frame, smear rainwater across its glass, blurring those faces more. Which leaves only the second possibility. That maybe the eight people in this photograph were never here in Stornoway on the night of the storm after all. That they were on Kilmeray. And that they came here, days after Robert and Lorne had died, and posed for a photograph to set up a lie. To make anyone think, like I had, that they were the only ones with a sure and certain alibi. I look at their relaxed and easy faces. All except Alec and Fiona, I realise, who are standing like frozen and unsmiling waxworks behind everyone else. And then I look at Charlie, brandishing his whisky, grinning inside his neon-yellow hood. *I haven't been telling you the truth, Maggie. I know who murdered Robert.*

I was right. He's been protecting someone all this time.

They all have.

And I have no idea who. Or why.

CHAPTER 28

Robert

The sheep have gone. All of them.

When I first found the barn door wide open, I was more pissed off than concerned. Assumed it was my fault. My inattention. Because I'm not sleeping. And I'm drinking too much at night to make me sleep. To escape the storms that are always on the horizon now. The blackness of Mary's moods. And sometimes, the way she looks at me, with a kind of tired and detached curiosity. As if I'm a bug on a slide; something to be dissected and studied. As if she's forgotten I'm still her husband.

Just after dawn, I rode out towards the village looking for the sheep, and then past Bàgh Fasgach and Loch Tana. Even down to Beinn Donn and Ùrbost. On the way back, I saw Charlie and Jaz watching me from their gardens. It's been a fortnight since I reported the dead sheep, and still no one has come out from

Stornoway Police Station. Not that the carcasses in the freezer are likely much use to anyone now.

When the flock wasn't out on the croftland or even down on the beach, that was when I started to get concerned. And now, after searching all the western moorland, I'm reduced to peering over the edge of its cliffs to see if I can glimpse any bodies on the rocks beneath or in the loud white surf. When I finally turn my face away from the wind and look across at those tall standing stones on the hill, for the first time they don't soothe me at all. Because there's no way an entire flock of sheep has fallen off these cliffs or any other. Sheep are less stupid than most people; they only blindly follow when they know it's safe.

Someone has done this. More probably, someones. They've stolen my sheep because they can. Because I'm not like them. Because I'm not a man that men like. Because I'm not a fucking fisherman. I'm barely a farmer. And because I won't beg for their help, their fucking approval. I've tried. All my life, I've fucking tried, and it's never enough. *I* am never enough.

But they won't get away with it this time. They won't drive me back to the bitter wind and rocks of the North Sea. They won't take away the peace – the *right* – that only this land can give me. I won't let them.

Because I won't hide any more. Not from storms. From *bòcain* that whisper saltwater hate into my ears. I don't need Norse talismans to protect me. I don't need a cellar full of light and stars. I just need my family. And my will to survive. That's always been enough, after all. I just need to use it. To fight for what is mine.

But when I get back to the blackhouse, it's empty. Mary and Calum have gone too.

CHAPTER 29

I struggle to make much conversation on the hour-long journey back to Kilmeray. I catch Kelly giving me curious looks, despite my insistence that Bobby Rankin had nothing interesting to say, but I'm not about to tell her what I've started to suspect about the people in that photo. She seems jumpy again, and it makes me more nervous. So much so that when she swerves abruptly into the lay-by before the Blairmore junction, my heart actually skips a beat.

'Kelly?'

She pulls up on the handbrake. Turns to face me and sighs.

'D'you remember I had something to tell you?'

'Shit. Yes. Sor—'

'I'm leaving. One of David's friends has a flat to rent in Hillhead. Fraser's school is happy to take him back, and I can get waitressing work until college starts after the summer. Jaz has offered to manage the blackhouse.'

'David, huh?' I say, trying to smile.

'This just doesn't feel like home any more. Finding Lorne, it's the final straw. I think I've just been hiding out here because I'm too afraid to restart my life, you know?'

And I do. I know exactly. 'When are you going?'

'There was a cancellation on the first flight to Glasgow tomorrow, so we're going to stay over in Stornoway tonight.'

'*Tonight?*'

'The weather forecast isn't good.' She looks out the windscreen. 'I'm sorry. I didn't want to tell you, because you're pretty much the only reason I don't want to go.'

'I'm going to miss you.' I reach across the space between us to give her a hug. She hugs me fiercely back, and when she lets go, her eyes are watery, her nose red.

'There's . . . There's something else.' She looks out the window again.

I see her swallow, and it revives my earlier unease, my long suspicions about what she's been holding back from me. That closed expression she always wears when I ask about her parents.

'We're friends.' She glances at me. 'We *are* friends. But, um . . . a few days after you arrived, I was speaking to my dad on the phone and I mentioned who you were, you know the whole Andrew MacNeil thing – and he got really pissed off. Wouldn't tell me why. But he asked me . . .' She blows out a breath. 'He asked me to keep tabs on you, tell him what you were, you know, doing, writing, whatever.' She turns in her seat to face me. 'I promise that first night when you arrived, I didn't know. That Robert had even existed. That he lived in the blackhouse before my parents bought it. I didn't know about any of it until Dad told me. I don't know anything about what happened back then either, he and Mum have never talked about it. And I mean, it's not like there's been anything to tell *him*, not really. But I shouldn't have done it. I should have told him no.'

I look out the windscreen. Think suddenly of that face behind the wheel of the silver Lexus as it hit me. That mouth a perfect round O of shock. More a feeling than a memory. Like the returned and restless panic that all is suddenly changing, ending, and I'm powerless to stop it. That it's already far too late for me to even try to catch up.

'Don't be mad at me, Maggie. I couldn't bear it.'

'I'm not mad at you.' I smile, briefly squeeze her wrist. 'I promise.'

She smiles back, but her hands curl into fists. 'There's something *else* else.' She pauses, shaking her head. 'I don't know why I lied about it, why I didn't tell you.' She glances down at my bag and frowns. 'My parents. They're in that photo.'

*

The sky grows ominously dark as I trudge down the road away from Blairmore. Inside the shadow of Ben Wyvis, the rain begins in earnest, icy and determined, heavy enough to soak through my mac in minutes. The wind howls around inside my hood as I battle to keep hold of it while trying to take heed of the frantic waves of bog cotton warning me not to veer off the road. I should have let Kelly drive me back to Ardcraig, but Will might be at the farm, and I need this buffer, this time to process both the photo and Kelly's confession. And that she's going to leave. Tonight.

I remember asking her months ago why her parents had left the island so soon after buying the blackhouse from Euan Morrison. Her answering shrug; *Maybe they realised they'd made a mistake and wanted to cut their losses.* Or perhaps Robert's ghost had haunted them too. Perhaps that *mistake* had been a bigger one than Kelly knew. A mistake that had them leaving for North Uist barely a year after Robert's death.

I glance across the grazing pasture to the low row of bunkhouses ahead of Long Stride. They look so small, so fragile in the darkness. I know pretty much all the archaeologists have already left, and I wonder if Miko and Femi were among them. I suddenly feel very alone. As if I'm the only person left on the island. The only person left in the world.

I actually shriek when the ATV roars out of the southwest, swiftly decelerating when they see me, my yellow mac probably the only thing visible in the gloom.

It's Bruce, bundled up inside a huge black anorak, his face wet and red.

'You shouldn't be out in this,' he says by way of greeting. 'There's a storm coming.'

'Have you seen Charlie today?'

He frowns, shakes his head. 'If he's any sense, he's battening down the hatches. You want a lift to Ardcraig?'

'I'll be fine.'

He presses his lips together, his dark eyes unreadable. I think of that photo in my bag. And then he's gone, the roar of the wind and his ATV swallowing any goodbye.

When I get back to the farm, its lights are off, and I can't hear the sheep in the barn. I can maybe hear the rumble of another ATV out towards Big Beach. I should go inside, start a fire, wait for Will. But still there's that restless sense of urgency in me, the feeling that I can't stop moving. I know I'm okay. I know I'm not manic. But I suspect now that I'm grabbing on to what happened to Lorne and Robert because it's something to grab on to. To feel in control of.

And then I see the birds. Four dead crows lying in a straight dark line, joined beak to tail, in front of the blackhouse door. My leg muscles tense and burn with the need to run. But I don't. I pull out my phone and take a photo instead.

'Fuck you.' I don't shout it, but I mean it.

I turn away from the blackhouse. I don't look at the birds again. Instead, I start climbing the hills west towards Lovely Place. Probably because I associate it with safety. With Will. Even with Mum. In my mind, its riotous flowers, sparkling lochans, and bustling rabbit city will somehow be immune to the weather. An oasis of calm.

It isn't, of course. It's less lovely than it is a muddy quagmire that I struggle to negotiate without losing my balance, slipping into boggy puddles that climb wet up my jeans to the knees. By the time I manage to clamber halfway up the bluff, I'm exhausted. I have to grab fistfuls of tall, scratching grass as I pull myself up towards the summit, my ankles twisting over rocks and hidden rabbit holes. I stop for a moment and lean heavily against a flat rock close to the bank. Take the Stornoway photo out of my bag again. Look at those blurry faces. Try to see anything in them – any lie, any guilt. Jimmy, Charlie, and Bruce. Alec and Fiona. Euan. Kelly's parents.

I should have gone to the police in Stornoway. I should have taken this to Detective Inspector Lynn Urquhart. And I should have told her what Bobby Rankin told me. It's proof of a lie. And perhaps – probably – it was one that was told to them as well as to me. But instead, I came back here. I'm *stuck* here. I think of the birds. And all at once I wish I were anywhere else.

The beach below is a dark grey blur of sea and whipped-up foam. Waves batter the sand, the headland cliffs. The wind tastes of salt. The noise is incredible; a barrage of exploding shells. I think of Robert standing down there in a storm far worse than this. The rain is like hailstones, blurring my vision, but when I look across to West Point, where Jaz had been standing that night he saw Robert, I see someone else. Standing on that cliff above the western end of the beach. And looking. Just like the last time, straight at me.

No.

Because it's enough. I don't want to run. I don't want to hide. I look at that figure looking at me. *See it and confront it.* I shove the photo deep inside a large but abandoned rabbit burrow, the corners of the wooden frame dislodging old earth. Dangling grass roots tickling my skin like spiders' legs.

And then I start walking along the bluff towards that western cliff. And Sonny.

*

My courage lasts until I reach the beginning of the Roeness headland. I can see stony ruins some hundred yards away. Perhaps the remains of the medieval church that gave Kilmeray its name. It looks murky out there. Less a headland than an island, long and narrow and shrouded in gloom and sea spray.

Sonny is gone. But less than twenty feet from the cliff's edge is a small stone bothy. It has one square window. A low wooden door, dirty grey and scarred with jagged cracks. Its corrugated tin roof is rusted brown and orange.

I approach the building slowly because suddenly I feel dizzy, unbalanced. I don't know what I'm going to do when I reach that grey door. And then I'm spared the decision when it swings open with a nerve-jangling shriek.

In the roaring wet silence that follows, we look at each other. He's tall and broad. When he crosses his arms, his shoulders span the doorway. His beard is thick, rusted brown like the roof, amid bigger patches of grey. His hair is short, his dark eyes stony, his mouth a mean pressed line.

'Robert?' And I'm appalled when it comes out as a choked whisper.

Those eyes narrow. That mouth gets meaner. When the door bangs hard inside a gust of wind, I flinch.

He smiles. 'Suppose you'd better come in, then.'

CHAPTER 30

Robert

Everyone is inside the pub. Bright gold windows at the end of the village road. And as I'm standing outside in the gloom looking in at them all, I feel such sorrow and shame that it has to become rage before it crushes me.

I barge through the door, angry enough that it slams loud against the wall and then tries to hit me back. Everyone stops and turns, and it's so much like the nightmares I used to have – all the widows and fatherless children standing in the street below, staring up at me with hate, the long light from Àird Èinis moving over my skin – that I step back.

'Where are my sheep?' And I regret, too, that my shout sounds more like a scream.

'You're drunk,' Euan says, in that fucking voice of his, like he thinks he's still king of all that he surveys.

Although he's not wrong. I am drunk. Horribly drunk. Because I can't lie when I drink. I can't tell myself that shadows don't follow me. I can't tell myself that if only I try harder, if only I can be a better man, then my luck will change. My life will change.

I'm so drunk, in fact, that everyone looks the same: featureless blurs pretending to be people. Except for Mary and Calum. Sitting alone at a table close to the bar. Mary is half-turned away from me, but her foot is tap-tapping a tattoo against her chair leg. She's holding on to Calum with a white-knuckled fist. Her eyes are squeezed shut.

What have they told you? I look at her hunched shoulders, always so strong, so square. *How have they turned you against me?*

'The police know,' I say to all those faces. I draw my hands into fists. 'I told them.'

Thom Stewart comes round the bar, that perpetually smug almost-smile fixed to his face. 'I think you need to calm down.'

Behind him, Bruce shakes his head and looks at the floor.

'You killed my fucking sheep,' I say, and I'm saying it to all of them, every last one of them, because they all know who. And they all know why. Because islanders stick together; villages stick together. And they always protect the wrong people. 'But you're not taking my family.'

I march further into the lounge, steady myself against an empty table when the floor briefly tilts. 'Calum.' I try to blink my eyes clear to see him better. 'Come over here, son.'

'Stop it!' Mary says, and her voice is high and thin like I've never heard it before. 'Just stop it. Go home, Robert.'

'I told you not to fucking listen to them!' Because I did. I told her so many times that I can hardly believe any of this is happening at all. 'I'm your husband, Mary!'

But she looks away again. And her tears only make me more furious. I look at Calum, my boy, clinging to her side like a limpet. A baby. 'Calum! Get over here. Now.'

'You're frightening him,' Moira MacLeod says. Calm and soft like I'm a child needing to be talked down from a tantrum. Next to her, Charlie gets up, palms held out. Always the peacemaker.

'You know your husband wants to fuck my wife, Moira?' My heart is thundering inside my ears; the blood is pulsing inside my fists. 'I mean, I know you go about pretending that the sky is always blue and the sea is always kind, but even you can't have—'

'That's it.'

And it's not Charlie that starts coming for me, but Alec MacDonald. Any excuse to swing his fists, to get out whatever kind of rage it is he always brings back from the North Sea. Perhaps it was him. I can see a man like Alec butchering defenceless live-stock just for the hell of it. Jimmy gets up too, and that stings a little, almost as much as Bruce's shaking head, until I realise it's only to grab hold of Alec and pull him back against the bar.

But Jimmy doesn't look at me either. And instead of remembering him telling me I had a friend in him if ever I needed one, I remember that flash of guilt in his eyes when I found him outside my barn.

No one is really looking at me, I realise. As if, to them, *I'm* the featureless blur pretending to be a person.

'Son,' Kenny says. He gets too close too quickly, blocking out everyone else. 'Whatever's wrong, you can tell us.'

Son! As if there weren't less than ten years between us. I let the indignity of that override his outstretched hand, until I blink and his expression comes into sharp focus. It's not smug or superior, but warm and maybe even concerned.

Charlie comes towards me then, palms still up like I might be a dangerous dog. 'We want to help you.'

And I almost believe him. Until I think of Mamaidh's face, pinched pale and blotched red with fury. *If they knew, they would hate you.*

So instead of answering Charlie, instead of answering any of them, I turn round and march back towards the door. When no one stops me, when no one even calls out my name, I yank it open.

'Mary. Please.' My voice is too weak over the wind, the rain. 'Come with me?'

And although she hesitates, although she finally, *finally*, looks at me, in the end she only shakes her head.

CHAPTER 31

It's dark but surprisingly warm inside the bothy. Aside from the fire, the only light comes from a squat half-burned candle. There's one chair. A mattress and sleeping bag lie on the other side of the room; in its opposite corner, a small camping stove. The air is smoky, thick with the heavy sweetness of peat, but underneath is bitter, metallic. I notice the dead rabbit at the same time as the shotgun, lying side by side on the table.

'A man should kill what he eats.'

My stomach squeezes a little – either at the gun or rabbit, perhaps both – and I fold my arms and square my shoulders. *Do not allow panic or anxiety to get a foothold.*

'Why have you been watching me?' It's not the question I want to ask, of course. But everything is happening too fast and I can't keep up. I need some space to regroup.

'It's what I do,' he says.

'Why have you been watching *me*?'

He smiles, so fleeting if feels like I imagined it. 'I think you know why.'

'You know who I am?'

'Aye.' He walks over to his chair and sits down. Leaving me standing in the centre of the room. 'Folk from the village bring me food, news. The women mostly.' A scowl. 'Charlie, if I'm unlucky.'

'I thought you were dead. They said you drowned at sea.'

He lets out a sudden roar that I recognise as laughter only when I see that fleeting grin again. 'So they say. But that's just a story. And stories can be dangerous, girl. Mostly for those telling them.' Dark, almost black eyes stare at me from under bushy grey eyebrows. 'Or writing them.'

My gaze keeps sliding back to the table, the gun and the blood. 'Why did you change your name?' I ask, skirting closer to those questions I really want to ask.

He cocks his head, stretches out his legs. 'It was the name my mother gave me as a child. I wanted it back.'

'But surely Andrew was—'

'Not Andrew.' He's impatient again. 'Sonny.'

'That's not what I meant. I'm asking—'

He makes a low growl in his throat like an animal, and I snap my mouth shut, take two steps back.

'You really want to know why?'

I try not to cringe. I try instead to think of the young man standing alone in a grassy meadow in front of a hill. 'Yes.'

There's a pause. Long and far from silent. Above us, the rain drums and rattles against the rusty roof. When he looks at me again, his cold scrutiny makes me shiver. 'Have you ever been asked to swallow a lie, girl? To stomach a secret so rotten, that the only way you can keep it down is to become someone else? To pretend it's not inside you?'

And I want to say yes. I want to say yes so badly I say nothing.

He snorts and turns back to the fire. 'They told you I drowned at sea because lies – *stories* – are like sandbags.' A flash of lightning through the only window lights the room bright white. He doesn't even flinch. 'You need to keep stacking them up, over and over, until eventually there's none left.' A disconcerting flash of teeth. 'And the water comes in anyway.'

A sudden and terrible suspicion strikes me. And at once I'm so utterly certain of this realisation that has come out of nowhere, out of nothing, that I retreat backwards again, my heart suddenly battering itself against my bones.

'You're not Robert.'

I flinch from the roar of his laughter; that hard, joyless bark.

'You're Kenny Campbell. You're Isla's husband.'

He rears up from his chair with such speed, such fury, I let out a shriek, stagger backwards against the door.

'Kenny Campbell left this island because he couldn't – wouldn't – keep a secret so rotten it infected his blood, his dreams, his own wife,' he roars. 'My name is Sonny. And you'll use it.'

'I'm sorry.' And I marvel that I manage to say anything at all.

'You better ask your questions, girl. 'Cause your time's almost up.'

My heart is still drumming away, like an echo of the torrential rain. 'What was the secret?'

'Stop asking questions you know the answer to.'

'It was who killed them. Right? The secret was who killed Lorne and Robert.' I think of the tears in Charlie's eyes, his breath warm and sharp with whisky. *I haven't been telling you the truth, Maggie.* 'Do they all know who?'

A pause. And then the firelight throws black shadows across his face as he nods.

'Do you know who?'

Another nod, sharp and short. I can see a muscle pulsing inside his temple. The air between us feels thin and tight.

'You only get one more question.'

'Who killed them?'

'That's two questions.'

And before I can process that, he's moving even closer to me, and there's a cold light in his eyes that really does look a lot like madness. I'm afraid of him in the same way that I used to be afraid of Mum. The way I'm still sometimes afraid of me. I have no idea what he's going to do.

'Who murdered Robert?' The door handle digs into the small of my back, and I only barely resist the urge to reach behind me and turn it. The wind rattles the wood, it chases shudders the length of my spine. 'That's my question.'

'You sure that's what you want to know?' He's close enough now that I can see and smell the rabbit blood on his skin, his squeezing fists. Lightning flashes half of his face silver. 'Because once you do, girl, no amount of sandbags will keep all that water from coming in.'

CHAPTER 32

Robert

I run west. I don't know why. I don't even know why I'm running. Except that it feels like the only thing left to do. The road is flooded with rainwater, flowing downhill back towards the village. The wind slaps at my skin until it burns. When I finally reach Oir na Tìr, it howls around the standing stones. I fall down at the grassy centre of the cross, and the world spins as all those tall stones pull away from me towards the dark north, south, east, and west. I take the whisky out of my pocket and drink, let it warm my throat. And I wait. For those stones to put Robert back inside me.

Because Robert isn't weak. He isn't *this*. And Mary was only ever supposed to see him, never Andrew. If I can't stop her from leaving, from taking Calum with her, what do I have left? If I can't survive here, where do I go? This land, these islands, are the only place I can live. But I'm always someone I don't want to be. So what is there left for me to do?

*

When I wake up, the moorland is wet and sucking like a bog. And the sky is as heavy with approaching night as rain. My dream crouches at its edges, hides behinds rocks. Now it's only blood and fire and the briny taste of seawater; whatever else it was is gone. But I feel strange and dislocated. As if I'm awake inside another dream.

I'm stiff, frozen to the bone. When I try to get up, my legs are dead weights. I fumble for the bottle, drink until I choke. Dread squeezes at my stomach. My heart beats a loud staccato.

I hear fishermen shouting. And an engine, deep and coughing. The *Acair*. My father. And I try to get up again, panicked now, scrambling around in the muddy grass. I need to hide. From their shadows like the cold tar black of the Atlantic beyond the continental shelf. Like nets dragged through a darkness alive with rock and wreck and death.

'Leave me alone!' My eyes blur; the tears feel warm. This is why I shouldn't drink. Because I only pretend that I want to know the truth. Here, on these islands, in this thin place, there are no fences. There have never been any fences. Everything has *always* been beyond and never inside. And I've always known. What weight of will is inside a thought, a want, a rock. And what weight you must always carry after that will – that want – is done. And a lighthouse has become nothing more than a black tower; a shadow, like something burned against a wall.

I manage to get onto my hands and knees. Begin crawling away from the stones, back towards the dig. There's safety there. A different kind, less spiritual than hopeful; closer to Norse talismans and putting a cat's claw under the foundations of a house. But any port in a storm. The dark is lower. Closer. And I can hear them behind me now. Louder. Closer. The fishermen. Panic returns feeling to my legs, and I get up, the mud sucking at my boots as I run across the moorland. I slip and slide; fall and get up. The wind from the western cliffs roars through me. At Loch Dubh, I stop, my breath wheezing, icy cold, from my lungs.

There. Standing close to the loch's eastern edge. A figure. Staring. Darkness all around him as if he is its centre, its source. My father.

He shouts. Words that are swallowed by the wind before they can reach me. But too loud, too angry. I can see his teeth. He moves closer, and still I can't move. The loch water froths and churns like the sea; I barely feel its icy spray against my skin. My legs prickle and shake. And still he comes closer, closer. Until it's too late to run. Until all I see is him.

Not my father.

Andrew. Weak and small. And never gone.

He shouts again. Andrew has haunted me my whole life. He's the only *bòcain* I've ever needed to be afraid of.

I pull him down into the mud, where we slip and slide and he shouts and shouts. I put my hands over his mouth – wet and sharp with those teeth – and I press down. Still he struggles against me, flailing arms and legs, nails and teeth piercing the numbness of my skin, sending hot spikes of pain up into my wrists and elbows.

But I don't stop. Because I'm a Valkyrie choosing who lives or dies over a loom of blood. I'm a vengeful ghost that lives under the sea. I'm a goddess of death that collects spirits in a net so wide it will never be full.

'You told,' I whisper against his ear, the sodden mess of his hair. 'You were never supposed to tell.'

His struggles grow weaker. I can feel his ragged breath against my skin. Slower, slower. His eyes are like black shining marbles.

'It's all right.' I stroke his head. 'It's all right.'

Because I love him too. I've dreamed of watching him sleep. Always inside a nightmare of waves and endless sea. Where no one can see him. Or save him. And I've dreamed of watching that white-bright light sweep around us as I pick up a pillow, put it over his face, and press down hard.

We sacrifice so that we are not sacrificed.

I choose to sacrifice Andrew. And all of his nightmares. So that I can finally just be Robert.

CHAPTER 33

'I'm sure.' I try to breathe, to sound like I mean it. 'Who murdered Robert?'

'I saw you with Charlie,' Kenny says, nodding towards the rain-lashed window. 'Down there on the beach. You think he's your friend?' His smile gets wider. 'Charlie just has a dose of what I have. And I don't think guilt is going to save you, Maggie. If you keep poking around inside old wounds, I don't think *he's* going to save you.'

'Why are you trying to scare me? Why won't you just tell me the truth?'

That smile disappears. 'Because a storm is coming. You think it's already here. But it isn't. Not yet.'

'Ken – Sonny—'

'The Norse name for this island is Great Protector, and that's what it does all right. This island protects its own. Always has.'

His voice drops to a conspiratorial whisper. '*That's* why you need to be scared.'

'Tell me why, then. If you won't tell me who.' I push myself away from the door and walk towards him. 'Why was Robert killed?'

He throws up his arms. Gives me a frighteningly ordinary look of exasperation out of eyes that are still black. 'Because he killed Lorne, of course.'

'*Why?*'

He answers me with only a grim, thin-lipped smile.

'Who killed Robert? Just tell me. Please.' But I'm already backing towards the door again, even before he sidesteps to the table and picks up his shotgun. This time, his laughter sounds like the sea.

'I think you should run, wee Maggie MacKay.'

I flail behind me for the door handle, too terrified to turn my back on him for even a second. I shake as I wrench it back and forth until finally the door flies open out of my grasp and the wind and rain rush in.

But I get no more than ten feet from the bothy before I stop, turn round. Kenny is standing inside the doorway's bright rectangle, surrounded by nothing but darkness.

'Tell me. Please, Sonny. Please!' I can't go without knowing. Even though I'm every bit as scared as he said I should be. *Because* I'm every bit as scared as he said I should be.

He barks out another laugh. 'You sure, girl? You sure even now?'

'Yes!' I have to shout to be heard over the rain rattling against the roof and the wind howling around the headland, and after the stifling closeness of the bothy, it's almost a relief. 'Who killed Robert? *Please.*'

My heart drums faster than the rain as he walks towards me, still holding the shotgun, still wearing that humourless smile. He stops.

'We all did.'

'What?' I take one step back. And then a second.

'We killed him.' Another flash of teeth as he brings up the gun against his shoulder, aims the muzzle at my chest. 'Every last one of us.'

When he pulls the trigger, I let out the scream that's been trying to batter its way out of my chest. And when nothing answers but a dull metal click barely audible over the storm, I stagger backwards again, tears stinging my eyes, bile choking my throat.

Kenny doesn't lower the shotgun. He grins at me along the length of its barrel. '*Bang.*' And then he winks.

And I run.

CHAPTER 34

I run back towards the bluffs. It's the easiest route and affords the best view. The rain and wind have changed direction, barrelling westwards in rising gusts, trying to shove me back towards the bothy. Dusk is coming; the stormy skies are heavier with it – an oppressive gloom that blurs and hides the edges of what I can see.

Just get back to the farm. I put my head down and press forwards, looking only at my feet until the bluff widens and starts to slope less steeply down to the meadow. Get back to the farm, get back to Will, and then work out what to do next. I can't think about *We killed him*. I can't think about all those dead birds in front of the blackhouse door. Because it feels like something might break inside me if I do. Something crucial that's barely managing to function as it is. I just need to get back to the farm.

I glance left only once, out across the furious Atlantic, when I realise there's someone on the beach. Not Kenny, it can't be –

although my heart does an unpleasant flip all the same. My second thought is of Robert.

I shield my eyes from the worst of the wind. They have their back to me, whoever it is, and they're wearing a cobalt-blue cagoule; it flaps and ripples like a flag on a pole, its hood pulled tight around their head. They aren't moving. Just standing in the middle of the sand, and staring out at the wild surf and wilder ocean beyond. Something about the *way* they're standing makes me shiver. So still, so decided, despite those gale-force winds that can be no less brutal on the beach. I think again of Jaz watching Robert from the top of this bluff. *You'd have to have been a madman to go down there.*

And then they start walking – marching – towards the sea.

I step forwards and then falter. I shout 'Hey!' and even I barely hear it. But still I don't think that they're going to just walk into the sea while I watch. Until they do.

My second 'Hey!' is far more horrified. And when they're briefly pushed back towards the shore by a particularly high wave, and that hood is wrenched free to reveal long silver-blonde hair, I stagger backwards too. It's Cora.

'Shit. *Shit!*'

There's no time to get to the easier path down to the beach. Instead, I start climbing backwards on my hands and knees, scrabbling for purchase as I slip and slide and drop far too quickly, grabbing hold of clumps of long grass that straightaway break or tear out at their roots. I fall the last few feet, landing hard on a dune.

The sand is no longer a soft white Caribbean arc, but hard and wet. Deep twisting channels have been carved from the sea to the grass, filling up with swirling, frothing water. The sea is no longer a brochure-perfect clear turquoise either, but an angry, choking mass of white spray and dark seaweed. I run through streaks of yellow-grey foam, shouting Cora's name. I can still just about see her, that flapping blue cagoule. In between breaking waves, the water has reached as far as her chest.

I jump backwards when the first wave hits against my calves, splashes up past my knees. It's freezing cold, shockingly so, but that's not what makes me hesitate. I can swim, but not well. Up close, the size of the surf is terrifying. Before they break, the waves have to be close to fifteen feet high. And when they do break, cresting white and far too fast, the roaring crash of them is almost deafening. I don't see how to get past one, never mind how to reach Cora. I think of that polished granite memorial at Ardshader and I suddenly understand how a whole village of fishermen could die within yards of home and safety.

'Cora! *Cora!*'

But I can no longer see her at all. And that's what decides me. I can stand here and shout and pretend that might work, or I can go in. There isn't enough time to do anything else.

I take off my bag, my boots, my mac, throw them back onto the beach as I start wading into the sea. Almost straight away the sand is sucked from under my feet and then a wave slams into me hard, dropping me backwards, roaring over me like a stampede. I scrabble to get up again, salt water washing out my mouth, rushing up my nose, making me choke and panic. But I've no sooner got onto my feet than another wave pushes me back, pushes me down, chokes me some more. I get up again, and when I see another dark wave rising, rising, barrelling towards me, I manage to spin back towards the shore, and to stop panicking long enough to jump upwards when the wave is almost on top of me. It still hits me hard enough that for a few seconds I'm propelled along with it, before its peak passes and I'm able to regain my balance and my breath.

I go on like this for what feels like an eternity. Paddling frantically between waves, turning my back on them as they hit, trying not to lose too much ground or choke on too much water. I struggle against a rising panic that has as much to do with watching the beach retreat further and further away as it does the dread of the next wave arriving. The moment I realise that I've made it past the worst of them, the worst of the surf, I look for Cora.

Out past the breakers, the sea is rolling, heavy and high. Endless. I struggle to tread water as battling currents push me left and right, toss me up and down. The sea stings my eyes and slaps against my skin. I'm cold now. My jeans feel like a lead weight, my legs and feet are completely numb.

'Cora!'

For a moment, I can't see her and I'm scared. The sky is low and dark, the sea is icy. And alive. I'm out of my depth, quite literally – I could be ten feet or a hundred feet from the bottom, I have no idea; the water below me is viscid and black. I imagine stone memorials lining every coast and headland that I can no longer see, and I feel dizzy. I could die out here. *Everyone* dies out here.

When something brushes my leg, my arm, I scream – thin and

high – and I try to get away, kicking out with my legs, trying to turn back towards the shore. Until a hand grabs hold of my shoulder and spins me round.

Cora's face is waxy white. Her hair hangs in thick wet ropes around her cheeks and ears.

'Jesus. Thank God you're all right.' I pull her towards me. 'We have to get back to the beach.'

She lets go of my arm, shoves me away. Her face is expressionless. Her eyes blank.

'Cora, please. It's not safe out here. We have to get back to the beach. Will and Euan are waiting for us. They asked me to come and get you, okay? It's Maggie, remember? Please come back with me, Cora. I promise you'll be safe.'

When she grabs hold of me again, my relief is short-lived. The fingers that squeeze my arm are blue with cold. But the rage in her eyes is white-hot. And then I'm fighting off slaps, as panicked as they are frenzied, aided by furious splashes of water.

'Cora, stop!' I put up my hands to restrain her. I don't want to hurt her, but I can hardly move my arms or legs any more. They no longer feel numb but as if they're on fire, and spasms of electric pain shoot up into my chest and pelvis. My thoughts – even my panic – feel slow and disordered. I'm running out of time more quickly than energy. 'Cora. *Please.* You have to trust me. Let me help you get back to Will.'

And then she stops. The wind shoves us briefly apart as the rain starts again in earnest, pricking holes in the sea, drumming hard against my skull. Cora stares at me. Blinks once, twice, her breath cloudy white between us. Her eyes spill over with tears, and my panic changes, quickens. Forgets entirely about the sea, the storm.

'Cora—'

'Where am I?' She makes a sound, low and distressed, as she spins round in the water, looking out at all that sea.

'Cora—'

'I don't know you. Do I?' she says. Her voice is high and afraid. Her eyes dull and unfocussed. And there's something else. Some other change in her – alien and brittle – that I can't put a name to but understand enough to want to run from. To swim from.

But I can't. Because it's Cora. It's Will mum. And it isn't her fault that she's sick, that her brain is slowly destroying itself. It isn't her fault that she doesn't know she needs help. And if I save only myself instead, then I'm still the same person who fed my mum enough tramadol and morphine to kill her twice over. I'm still the same person who pretended she didn't know why she saw a demon climb into her mother's coffin.

I reach for Cora, pull her towards me with what's left of my strength. My vision keeps blurring; I'm sinking lower in the water. But to my relief, Cora doesn't resist this time; she clings to my arm and sags against me as I turn towards the shore. I push forwards, pulling her behind me. As the waves get bigger, the edges of their crests begin to break into spindrift. I have no idea how I'm going to keep hold of her once we hit the breakers, but there's nothing else to do. Spray stings my eyes, foam blows across my face in streaks. One wave pushes us high, and then together, higher. Cora's nails dig into my skin, her breath hisses briefly hot against the back of my neck. And then she lunges with a terrified scream – 'Help me!' – her hands clamped heavily on my shoulders.

The bubbles of my own scream tickle my face as I struggle to push back up to the surface. Cora's fear makes her surprisingly – horrifyingly – strong. Her fingers are still digging into my shoulders. In my panic, I keep trying to push up, even though there's no strength left in my arms. When she lets go for an instant, I give one last shove, and then I'm free again, gasping for air, lungs burning, heart thundering, arms thrashing.

The waves are much bigger now, tossing us around like a giant whirlpool. I can see spinning flashes of the beach, closer now, but still impossibly far. And Cora's hold on me is even stronger than the sea as she grabs at me with wild-eyed terror. I see her teeth snap together before she opens her mouth to scream again.

I choke as a wave smacks against my chest and I swallow yet another mouthful of icy seawater. 'Please, Cora.' A cough wracks my already burning lungs. 'Stop.'

I feel a flailing fist smack hard against my temple, sending me backwards into another wave. And then Cora's whole weight is on me, pushing me down, deeper this time; the icy water closing over my head fast. And I can hear my screamed gurgle in the instant that I realise I could drown like this – *am* drowning. I can see the dark shadow of Cora above, surrounded by churning, tireless water. And then I look down into all that darkness below, all that black nothing, so calm, so still. So quiet after all the rage and noise.

How can this be happening? I think of laughing with Charlie and Kelly. I think of Will; our hands touching bright and sharp in between chairs where no one else could see. I'm so tired. I long to breathe in. Just once. Once would be enough. And underneath that is relief. Bone-deep and undeniable relief that finally it's all over.

Will, I'm sorry. The bubbles of his name escape upwards, leaving me behind. *I'm sorry.*

*

The pain is less of a shock than the noise – so much of it, all blended together into a muffled, booming mass of sound. I try to fight it off, to turn back to that blessed empty silence, but then something pops inside my ears, and all that sound rushes in, loud and suddenly clear.

I rear up, choking, coughing, trying to turn myself over, trying to pull air into my lungs. They don't burn any more; instead, they feel full of blood, cold and thick, and every breath I manage to take hurts so badly I almost want to stop.

'She's okay. She's okay!'

I can feel hands on me, but that's muffled too, as if my body no longer belongs to me. And I can't see. Everything is grainy and black, shadow and vague light. I lie on my side, just trying to breathe. I can smell the sea. I can taste salt in my mouth, can feel the grit of sand on my tongue, against my teeth, my skin. I can hear the waves now, not close, not quite as wild. I can hear the wind howling around the headlands, whistling in and out of their shallow dark shelves. And I can hear voices. Shouting.

I want to shout too. I want to let go of the shriek inside my head and inside my mouth. I want to run. I struggle to sit up.

The sand gives way under the heels of my palms, cool between my fingers. Hands touch me again, push at my shoulders, and I slap them away.

'It's okay, you're okay, Maggie.'

Charlie. Charlie's voice. Charlie's eyes, wide and dark. His shaking palm against my cheek.

I try to speak but only manage another cough, hacking its way out of my aching lungs. Charlie's kneeling in the sand next to me. He leans me against him until I can breathe again.

Will is on the other side of me, his shaking hands on my hair, my arms.

'Are you all right? Baby, are you all right?'

'She's okay,' Charlie says again, in that unsteady voice.

Someone wraps me in a blanket.

'We were looking for Mum when we . . .' Will's voice breaks. 'I saw you. I saw you going into the sea, and I . . .'

Some feeling has come back into my skin. It prickles and fizzes hot when he presses his face into the space between my neck and shoulder. I realise that he's just as wet as I am.

'I could have lost you. Jesus, Maggie. I could have lost you both.'

And then more than just hearing or seeing or feeling returns. Awareness comes back to me like another electric shock, so fast, so *at once*, that it makes me jolt. I look around at the beach, dark with approaching night. It's full of people. Alec and Fiona and Sheena. Jimmy, Isla, and Jaz. And next to Euan, soaking wet and sobbing on the sand, wrapped inside another blanket, is Cora. Gillian crouches alongside her, an arm around her shoulders. But Gillian isn't looking at Cora. Instead, she's looking at me.

I think of those bubbles tickling my skin, the last of the air in my lungs.

I struggle up onto my hands and knees. Because there's something bigger behind my panic – something I found in the storm, in the sea, that I can't remember yet. And then suddenly I remember Kenny, grinning down the barrel of his shotgun. *We killed him.*

'Maggie, what's wrong?' Will says. And I long to lean against all that concern, to lay my head on it and go to sleep.

'Maggie?' Charlie says.

Trust nobody, Mum whispers in my roaring ears.

When I manage – finally – to get onto my feet, I'm sobbing. Even though the wind is calmer now, I stagger against it. Against Will's hands and concern. The sand gives way under my feet, pitching me forwards.

'*Maggie?*'

Miko is standing ahead of the path down to the beach. She's holding a small, bright torch and wearing a neon-green-and-yellow anorak. I stare at her, all that colour and light, and stumble towards it, letting her catch me before I fall.

'Please.' I try so hard not to cough I almost forget to breathe. 'Get me away from here.'

'Maggie, what—'

'*Please.*'

'She needs to go to hospital.'

I cringe away from Charlie's voice. Too close. I grab hold of Miko's sleeve, so tightly she winces.

'You weren't breathing. Jesus. *Jesus,* Maggie,' Will says, reaching for my hand. 'You didn't have a pulse.'

'I'll take her back to Long Stride,' Miko says. And something inside me finally loosens at the resolve in her voice. The authority. I feel so relieved that my legs almost forget to keep holding me up.

'Come on,' she says, putting an arm around my waist. And if a slight tremor comes into her voice, I can hardly blame her for it. Not when my heart is still hammering so hard inside my chest, I can hear it. I'm aware enough to know it's panic. Panic and shock. Hypoxia and probably hypothermia. But it's not only that. It's the briny dread that still clogs my throat. That makes me think of those tickling bubbles of air and Kenny's smile, his teeth. *A storm is coming.*

Because suddenly I'm so, so afraid that he's right.

CHAPTER 35

'Here.'

I take the coffee mug, wrap my still numb fingers around it.

'There's some brandy in it.' Miko smiles, sitting down on the narrow bed opposite mine.

The bunkhouse is small and warm. A tiny kitchenette and toilet at one end, a fold-down desk next to the door, the two beds in between. It smells of pine and the perfume Miko wears, jasmine maybe. I close my eyes and take a deep breath, try to stop shaking.

The knock on the door isn't loud, but I cringe all the same, spill coffee over my lap, the baggy jumper and leggings that Miko had me change into as soon as we got back here.

'It's Will. I just want to talk to you, Maggie. Are you okay?'

I close my eyes, and Miko gently prises the mug out of my hands.

Will knocks again, hard enough this time that the doorframe shakes. 'I'm not going anywhere. Tell me what's wrong. For God's sake. I just need to know you're all right. Please.'

I can't listen to his voice. I can't see his face. I can't answer his questions. I only want to hide inside empty and undemanding quiet. I only want to try and *think*. When I'm with him, I can't.

'It's okay,' Miko says, as she goes towards the door. 'I won't let him in.'

When she comes back, I jolt as if I've been sleeping. Maybe I have.

'Charlie's out there too. He wants to talk to you.'

I shake my head. 'I can't. Not now.'

Miko sits down next to me, takes my swollen fingers inside her cool hands. 'I don't know what's happened, and you don't have to tell me. But I don't think you need to be scared. Anyone can see that they're both just worried about you.' When I don't reply, she sighs. 'At least let me take you to Stornoway. Charlie's right, you need to go to hospital. Hypothermia can—'

'I'm not going to Stornoway. Not yet.' Then I remember Kelly is leaving tonight, and almost change my mind.

'Maybe you should talk to Charlie. Hear whatever it is he has to say. He says it's important.' She holds my gaze. 'He says he saved your life, Maggie.'

I take another painful breath. I don't think I need to be scared either. Not of Charlie. And I do need to talk to him. I need to know what I *am* actually afraid of.

'Okay.'

Miko gets up, opens the door, and slips outside again.

Charlie comes back in alone. 'Are you all right?'

His voice is shaking, and that makes me feel steadier. I nod. Absently rub at my breastbone, at the slow-radiating throb there.

'I'm sorry,' he says, looking briefly down at his hands. 'It's been a while since I . . . you're probably lucky I didn't break a few ribs.'

I feel another jolt then. I died. And Charlie brought me back. I try to imagine it – lying on the sand with everyone else standing, watching, while he tried to beat my heart into starting again. I can't remember dying. I can't remember coming back to life.

Charlie exhales in a long, low rush. Closes his eyes. 'You know.'

'I talked to Sonny. Kenny Campbell.' I make myself look at him. 'He said you killed Robert.' And then I have to look away. 'All of you.'

Charlie lets out another breath, shakier, and when he sways on his feet, I have to fight the urge to go to him. When he looks at me again, his eyes are shining wet. 'You're safe here. I promise.'

But I don't believe him. 'I died, Charlie.'

'Christ.' He rubs his forehead. 'What a fucking mess.'

'You lied to me. About everything.'

Charlie drops his hands to his sides. Squares his shoulders. Eventually looks at me. 'We found them out at Loch Dubh. Robert and Lorne. It was late. The storm was blowing itself out, the moon was bright. And . . . there they were. We thought they were both dead at first. But Robert had just passed out. The drink, the cold.' He rubs his hands over his face again. 'The shock of what he'd done.' He shrugs. 'Christ knows. Probably all three.'

'He'd killed Lorne.'

'Suffocated him.'

'*Why?*'

'He – it . . . Robert . . .' Charlie makes a frustrated sound. 'It was our fault. We knew, all of us, that something was wrong, and we did nothing.' He pauses. 'Or maybe we *should* have done nothing. Instead, we made a bad situation worse, and—'

'What are you talking about?'

'We stole his sheep. Just before it happened. Rounded them up, hid them in Bruce's barn.' He shakes his head. 'That was it. That was the tipping point, I've always been sure of it. If we hadn't—'

'Why the hell did you steal his sheep?'

Charlie presses his palms together as if he's about to pray. But when he looks at me, his gaze is unwavering. 'Because he was killing them.'

*

Robert

I wake up in bed and know immediately that something is wrong. I don't move, but I can tell that I'm still wearing my clothes. And there is pain. In so many places it's hard to name one. Sharp and dull; deep and shallow. Cold and hot. Light burns my eyelids gold, but I don't open them. I'm too afraid to; they throb and ache. There are two men in the room. Discussing me in hissed whispers.

'This is insane and you know it. When the lines are back up tomorrow, we're phoning the police.'

'We have to wait.'

'What for?'

'We need to think.'

'What the fuck is there to think about?'

It's Kenny and Charlie. And the more I lie here listening to them talking about me, the longer I pretend I'm still asleep and not vibrating with pain, that sense of dread in my belly gets bigger. The real pain that I know is waiting for me to move gets louder. A flash of water. Great towering stones and eyes like bright shining marbles. The warm weight of a ewe's head in my lap, her breath puffing shallow and fast as I stroke her flat-down ears. *It's all right.* Except it isn't.

'We *need* to phone the police.' Kenny isn't talking in a hissed whisper any more.

'It's still like a bloodbath in the kitchen,' Charlie says. 'The last thing we need is the police sniffing around until we've—'

'Aye? And how long exactly do you think you can hold Alec back from finishing him off?'

A flash this time of rage – teeth-bared and black-eyed. Sobbing, spitting roars of pain and flailing fists. Coughing, slipping. A tiled floor slick with my own blood.

I force open my swollen eyes. Cringe, when instead of seeing the sun coming through Mary's net curtains I see only white-painted brick and a bright overhead bulb. I'm in the earth cellar. My head aches, full of rocks with sharp edges. I sit up.

Kenny curses and Charlie flinches. Both of them stand at the foot of the old blow-up mattress, staring down at me as if I'm someone they've never seen before.

'Where are Mary and Calum?' My voice is hoarse, my throat sore.

'They're fine,' Charlie says. 'They're with Bruce MacKenzie.'

'Why?' The room is cool, but I feel hot. Kenny is like a statue. He glares at me without blinking; he opens and closes his mouth without speaking.

'What do you remember, Robert?' Charlie says. There's no cheerful smile for me today. Only thin pressed lips and purple-dark shadows under his eyes. 'What do you remember about last night?'

I shake my head. 'I don't . . . I don't . . .'

'This is bullshit,' Kenny shouts, his big hands curling into fists. His glare becomes narrow and measured, and I cringe when he moves suddenly, reaches into his pocket, brings something out. 'You think you can do what you like, Charlie, and we'll all just fall into line?' His mouth flattens, then turns into a sneer. 'You're an arrogant son of a bitch. Always have been.'

He turns for the stairs, the banister squealing its protest as he grabs hold. And then he stops, his shoulders briefly sagging. 'You think I don't know? About you and Isla? You think Moira doesn't know?'

When Charlie says nothing at all, Kenny brings his head up and turns around, throws what is in his hand too fast and hard at Charlie for him to catch. It hits the earth floor with a muted thud, and I realise that it's the trapdoor key.

Kenny stands on that bottom step and looks only at the wall. 'We need to phone the police.'

And then he thunders his way up the stairs and into the blackhouse.

I look up at the kitchen through the open trapdoor. I look at Charlie. The rocks inside my head grind against bone and nerve and each other.

'Why are you here?' My voice is slow and faraway. It doesn't sound like my voice any more. Black crouching shadows creep closer. 'What did I do?'

*

'You kept him *prisoner?*'

Charlie shakes his head, then stops. 'It wasn't supposed to be – it just . . . happened. After we found them . . . after the MacDonalds found out about Lorne – Alec went berserk. We'd taken Robert back to the blackhouse, and Alec damn near knocked the door down trying to get at him. Took five of us to get him off Robert; lucky he didn't kill him. Fiona begged us not to phone the police – didn't want to risk losing her man as well as her child. And I . . . I felt too much guilt to say no. Because I'd known things weren't right with Robert for a long time. I'd known they were getting worse.'

'*Why* did he kill his sheep?'

'One morning, back in January, while Jimmy was up on Tòrr Dìseart, he saw Robert with his flock in the nearby croftland. Saw him crouch down behind the eastern cemetery wall for a few minutes before taking off on his ATV. Jimmy didn't think anything of it till he was walking back a few hours later and found a ewe in that exact place, with what looked like a deep knife wound to her belly. When he realised there was nothing he could do for her, he found me and Kenny. But when we went back up there, she'd disappeared.'

Charlie closes his eyes. 'Robert . . . he had all these . . . interests. Obsessions really. Norse mythology mostly. I don't know if he believed in all of it, deep down, but . . . he was a man who needed to feel in control because he never did. He needed his superstitions, his rituals. His talismans. It was Mary who told me about the *vándr-varði*. She was worried about him. He'd had some kind of breakdown in Aberdeen. But we didn't listen to her either. Not really.'

'He told you about the storm in '77, that he thought he'd killed all those fishermen.' I try and fail to keep the anger out of my voice. All the lies Charlie has told me while dangling tiny crumbs of truth over my head. 'I saw the lighthouse, Charlie.'

He gives me a look then, desperate, as if needing me to understand something I can't. Or won't.

'People are complicated, Maggie. I know you know that. I think that as a boy he believed he'd killed those men because he thought that his mother believed it. Maybe she was afraid of what might happen to them if their friends and neighbours heard his wild claims, because the only way people get through these kinds of tragedies is if they stick together, help each other. Or maybe she was just mad with grief. I don't know. But whatever the reason, I think it was why Andrew invented a thin place full of gods and ghosts where it *could* be true. Where you could fire wee rocks at a one-hundred-foot-high lighthouse and have it break – just because you wanted it to.' He sighs. 'But she died when he was eighteen, and maybe then he felt like he could finally be free. He left. He found a wife who loved him. A life. A future. Robert suffocated Andrew.'

'You think that he murdered a little boy because he hated *himself*? Because he believed in gods and ghosts and thin places?' But I can't summon much outrage, because I know exactly what hating yourself feels like. A thick and impermeable skin you can't ever fight your way out of; endless vicious circles you can't think your way free of.

Charlie nods. 'He *told* me that's what happened. I think that when Robert revealed his real name, his real history, he brought Andrew back.' His gaze is suddenly calm, unblinking. 'And I didn't do anything. I was the only one who knew about him. I saw Robert get worse, and I didn't do anything. So when Lorne died, I wanted to *do* something.'

'You wanted to help him?' Because I've no idea what he means. I think of that cool and musty windowless cellar, and I shudder. 'To help Robert?'

'Yes.' He shakes his head hard. 'No. I . . . We were in shock. The whole village. It was just a week. We kept him in the blackhouse for a week. But it was . . . a long week. And then . . .' Charlie's expression changes. All that calm vanishes like the sun behind a cloud. 'And then Robert started to speak.'

My heartbeat is one slow thud after another, heavy enough that I can feel the pulse beating in my neck. 'What do you mean?'

Charlie swallows. The look he gives me is almost pleading. 'Sometimes what we do *is* far worse than anything we believe in.'

And I know he isn't talking about a ten-year-old boy firing rocks at a lighthouse while wishing his father dead.

'Charlie.' I press my palm against my neck, feel my heartbeat in my fingers. 'What did you do?'

*

Robert

I don't remember killing the sheep, but I know that I did. Because there were the overalls stiff with old blood under that workbench in the cellar. And because I don't remember killing all the birds either, but there were always so many of *them*, hidden deep inside that old stone fissure filled with green moss. And so I have to believe that I killed Lorne MacDonald too. Not just because Charlie told me so in a voice that shook, tears running down his face. But because I can feel the terrible truth of it, even if I can't remember.

I sleep, I wake. Once to the sharp smell of bleach and the sounds of people in the kitchen; once to the clatter of metal and plastic, the whisper of voices. I sleep, I wake, the stars bright above me; the Àird Èinis lighthouse a dark shadow in the corner; a memory of slow white light moving across walls, constant and safe. And through it all I'm trapped under the sea; the darkness sweeping over me like a tsunami again, and all I can do is try to surface, try to breathe. But still, I see his black shining gaze like the ewe's baleful eye, her breath freezing in the air; I feel the strength in rage that I've never found in peace. And I know that it's true. All of it.

Mary comes to see me on the third day, and I'm so glad, I feel some of that darkness lift. Because Mary is who saved me from that last tsunami. She's the one who dragged me back to land.

She doesn't come over to the mattress. Instead, she sits on the stool next to my workbench, and looks across at me as if I'm a stranger. She looks like my mother. After. Hunched and small. And full of wrath.

'Why?' Her whisper is small too. Her tears are quick, they run off her chin and into her lap. I put those shadows under her eyes, those lines around her mouth. I put that dark tired fury inside her voice.

'Is Calum okay? Can I see him?'

'Can you see him?' Mary stands up, and enough of her comes back to square her shoulders and set her jaw. 'No, Rob, you can't see him.' Her eyes still shine but her tears stop. 'You killed a wee boy.'

I close my eyes as all that water fills my lungs again. And when I open them, Mary is gone and above me is only black dark sea.

I surface slowly. So slowly that at first I don't notice, until I realise that I can breathe again. I can feel and see and hear again. So much pain and noise that I almost long for the weight of water. Lorne is all I see. A wee boy who hadn't even started to live. I find that I can't look at my hands, can't look at my skin. Can't look at any part of me at all.

'Charlie.' I can't look at him either. I stare down at the food he's brought me instead; a thermos of broth that I know Mary has made, and fresh white bread. 'Please don't tell the police. Please don't let them take me away. I'm begging you. Please.'

And Charlie just holds his head in his hands as he shakes it.

'I know what I did. I know no one can ever forgive me for it.' I fight to hold back all that pain and noise, to make it wait at least until Charlie is gone. Until I've said what I want to say. 'I need to be punished. But not like that. I can't . . . I can't do that, Charlie.

Please.' I think of a windowless, cavernous building, full of noise and blood and steel.

He looks down at me, eyes red. 'Just tell us why, Robert. Why did you do it?'

'You know why.'

But he goes on shaking his head. Pretending that he doesn't. Pretending, too, that he doesn't know why I'm really still here. Why he locks me in this cellar every night.

'Tell us for Mary's sake. She loves you. She wants what's best for you.'

I stare at the tray, the soup, the bread until my vision blurs. 'No. She loves Robert.'

When Charlie doesn't reply, I stand on stiff legs. Walk over to the bottom of the stairs, look back at the Àird Èinis lighthouse. There is too much to comfort me down in this cellar; it's a stronghold instead of a prison. I look up at the bright pine walls of the blackhouse instead. The sunlight from above is warm against my skin, my hands. My *hands.* I've poisoned it all. Everything – everyone – I've ever loved. And I have to atone. We sacrifice so that we are not sacrificed. That is what I've done. I've killed – I've murdered – a wee boy who hadn't even started to live because I wanted to kill Andrew. I've always wanted to kill Andrew.

'Truth abides in thin places, Charlie. Eye for eye, burn for burn, wound for wound.' I look up into the blackhouse and feel my lungs expand, fill up with so much air. 'Life for life.'

'Suicide,' I say. 'Robert meant suicide.'

Charlie nods once. His hands are clasped so tightly they've turned white.

'He needed help, Charlie! There's no way he was in his right mind. Not when he killed Lorne MacDonald, or when he decided he wanted to kill himself. And instead you said okay? You didn't tell the police, you didn't tell a doctor? You locked him up for a week, and then you just said *okay*?'

And the horror, the outrage, that I feel isn't only for Robert, I know that. It's as much for Mum and her own myths and thin places. And it's as much for me, pulled forever in two directions, neither of which I wanted to call home.

'He would have gone insane in prison, Maggie. Or in some hospital. A bad thing happened to him when he was too young, and he could never get over it, no one helped him get over it.' Charlie looks at me. 'Just going back to the mainland would have . . . He needed this place, this land, this sky, even this sea. It was a part of him. It's a part of all of us.' He lets out a long breath. 'I wanted to help him. And that's the truth. The truth I never told anyone because he'd just murdered an eight-year-old boy.'

'If you did that – if you allowed that – then what Kenny said was right.' There's a dull throb inside my throat. 'Robert was murdered. *You* murdered him.'

The look Charlie gives me is suddenly fierce, hot. 'Robert Reid wanted to atone for what he'd done. He wanted to be punished. To be forgiven.'

'And did you tell everyone else what he wanted to do? Or did you just let him do it?'

'I told everyone. Of course I did. I told them everything that he had told me, about his real name, about Ardshader, about why he'd done what he did to Lorne.' Charlie looks down at his hands. 'We had to decide.'

Everything inside me goes quiet. Even my heartbeat. 'Oh my God.' I remember Will's *Normally, no one can even agree on who's buying the first round after the bells without voting by committee.* 'You voted.'

Charlie winces a little, looks away.

'You voted to kill him.'

'We voted to help him die. It's not the same.' But there's no fire in his words this time. No conviction.

And my outrage, my righteousness, turns to ash in my mouth too. Because I'm inside that silver thread of light stretching thin across the floor, listening to the rattle of Mum's breath. The rattle of that pill bottle inside my fist. *Make it go away, Maggie.*

'We're a community,' Charlie says. 'We're a family.' He draws his hands into fists again.

'Everyone said yes?' And I loathe myself a little for both the hope and the anger I can hear in the question.

'Everyone but Kenny,' Charlie says. 'For the MacDonalds – Alec, at any rate – it was about revenge, but for everyone else, it was for justice.' He gives me that pleading look again, desperate to be understood. 'And what's justice but the middle ground between compassion and revenge?'

He stands up, paces the bunkhouse end to end and then back again. 'I thought it was the right thing to do. For Robert. For everyone.' He stops. 'But you're right. Kenny was right. And I was wrong.' When he looks at me again, I flinch from the haunted horror in his eyes. And all the hope and the anger drain out of me.

'Christ, Maggie. I was so, *so* wrong.'

CHAPTER 36

Andrew

Mary won't see me. She won't say goodbye. My brave and wonderful wife who has never been afraid to confront anything. Until I dragged her here to the end of the world. When Charlie leads me out into the mudroom, I can still hear her inside Calum's bedroom. Low deep sobs that make my own throat ache. All the tears I've made her cry. Our goodbye was endured without once saying the word; both of us trying too hard for Calum – hard enough that it was no real goodbye at all. I can hear Calum too. His little voice, confused, trying to comfort her, probably trying to hold her hand. He always wants to hold your hand.

Charlie opens the front door. Outside, the breeze is cool. It smells of the sea. The road is empty, the headland deserted. Bruce is standing on the Coffin Road alongside my grazing sheep. He looks over at me and freezes still, so I give him a nod, and after a long moment, he gives me one back. I'm glad they're safe now; I'm glad he's the one looking after them.

Charlie starts heading west without looking back to see if I follow. The wind gets higher, colder, as we get closer to Àite Lurach. I'm limping, and my bruised ribs ache as my breath gets quicker. I feel a fleeting regret that I'll never see the machair again – all that colour and light – but it's only dull, distant. We climb the bluffs, and I ignore the stutter in my heart when the Atlantic appears before me, flat and featureless. The late afternoon sun is low like the tide; its reflection glitters over all that endless grey like diamond stardust.

We take the path down. Charlie curses when he loses his footing close to the bottom and sinks into the banked sand dunes. It doesn't take long to reach the shoreline – even at its lowest tide, the sea stays close to the land. When we finally stop, my heart stutters again, louder this time. And when Charlie turns to look at me, he senses it.

'You don't have to do this.'

I breathe, low and slow. 'Yes, I do. I can't go back.'

Charlie's trying to maintain that careful blankness, but it doesn't fit his face. I realise that I miss the easy smile I so despised, now that I know I won't be seeing it again.

'Then we can do it a different way, Robert. Not *this* way.'

'No.' The calm inside me is like a cocoon. 'It has to be this way.'

But still, I hesitate. I can't quite take these last few steps. I look out at the sea, down at the white-frilled waves around my boots.

'I'm not afraid of pain, Charlie. I'm not afraid of dying. I'm afraid of fear.'

Charlie swallows. 'Everyone's afraid of fear.'

'Will they all come? Will they all be there?' My voice is too small. The stutter in my heart too big.

'It'll be the way you wanted it to be. I gave you my word.'

I glance back at the beach and headland one more time. 'Goodbye, Charlie.'

And as his mask finally starts to crack, I turn away quickly and begin walking into the sea.

The cold feels almost hot. I take in gasping breaths as I march fast and hard through the waves. Everything hurts: my knee, my ribs, my jaw, but I feel very sure that I can't fall – that I must not fall. Because my cocoon is getting smaller, its walls bowed inward by the growing weight of water. As the surf gets higher, I start trying to swim. There's a rock out past West Point, just below the Roeness headland and the stony ruin of its church, and that's what I head for. I'm determined to do this right.

It takes a long time. When I finally escape the waves and reach the rock, half-submerged and slippery with seaweed, my arms are dead weights, and everything below my waist is numb. I half-pull myself onto the rock like a fat seal, breathing hard and fast, coughing out seawater. When I look back at the beach, there is Charlie, standing on the shoreline. He's looking my way, and I wonder if he'll raise his arm to wave. But he doesn't. I look behind me at the ocean, so impossibly vast now that I'm inside it. The relative shelter of the western headland is welcome, but its shadow is not. I look back towards Charlie and the sun, and try not to wish I was there instead of here.

I rest for a while and look up at the sky, see strange half-aware visions of black towers and white-bright lights, beacons of fire along headland and cliff. When a wave washes me off the rock, I come awake with a shout, and the panic I feel as I struggle to reach it again finally rips a hole in my calm, my resolve. The current has changed, it's stronger, sharper. The sun has dropped halfway below the Atlantic horizon, turning the sea the colour of blood, and scudding grey skies have chased the white clouds away. I'm cold. My teeth are chattering and pins and needles prick my skin. I feel impossibly tired, as if I could sleep forever, and any relief I feel about that, about how painless and easy it might be to just slip into sleep again, is shattered when I look back at the beach and see only Charlie.

But he promised. He *promised*. And so I have to wait. I have to keep holding on.

*

And then it's dusk. Dark. But I finally, finally see the figures up on the bluff. Their silhouettes stark against the fading grey of the inland sky behind. All of them standing and watching, their torches spheres of yellow-gold light. There are men down on the beach too – now just a darker strip of land between the bluffs and the sea.

I'm thrown up and down by rising waves. High tide must still be three or four hours away, but the wind is up – icy cold and north-westerly. I feel suddenly awake, even though I can barely force my hands to go on clinging to the rock, the muscles in my legs and arms won't work, and my wet clothes are pulling me down. When I look up at the sky, those clouds are one amorphous dark mass now, so low it feels like I could reach up and touch them if I wanted to. I feel pressed between the two: the heavy sky and the angry sea, and then a rumble of thunder, deep and close enough that I can feel it inside my chest. Fear – sharp and hot – floods what's left of my resolve. To do this right.

This was what I wanted. This, exactly this. To die like my father died. Like a fisherman dies. On rocks in a storm, watched and mourned from the shore. I wanted atonement. Forgiveness. Peace. A wave slaps hard against the rock – now at least two-thirds submerged – sending up sprays of water that sting my eyes. I cough as another slams my shoulder and flank against the rock, scraping its sharp edge along my cheek and bruised chin. I scream when I can, when I finally stop choking – and the heavy rolling sea yanks me backwards and spins me around. I cling frantically to the rock, filled up with that old and paralysing dread of being swept out into the soulless sea, never to be seen again.

I taste blood. And the black shadows are all around me, Sjóvættir crouching inside the merciless waves; *bòcain* with their nets and knives. The horror that has always been fathomless – that I will be drowned by this ocean, by its cruelty that is as cold and vengeful as a boy tracing boats against a window. Because somehow I've forgotten. That the one thing I'm more afraid of than fear is dying alone.

Lightning tears open the sky and throws the sea – the chaos all around me – into stark relief. A white frozen snapshot of hell. Waves suddenly like mountains; the spaces between them black and bottomless chasms. When the light is gone again, I look up at the dark sky, down at the dark sea. Back at those spheres of yellow-gold. I was wrong. There is no peace in this.

I push away from the rock and start to swim for the shore, but I only sink. The water sucking me down like a peat bog. Terror takes the last of my strength and pushes me to the surface, where I flail and choke until my knuckles smack hard against rock again. I start to scream. To wave. To try and pull myself up onto what's left of the rock, so that they can see me. So that they know. I don't want this. I want to come back. I want to come home.

For long and terrible seconds, I think that they can't see, that they don't understand. And then, for longer and more terrible seconds, that they can and they don't care. But then I see Charlie running across the sand. I hear his voice, clear and clean, above the rising storm, the furious sea.

'He wants to come back!'

And then those lights are no longer still.

Kenny and Charlie put a skiff – a big one, at least six-man – into the sea close to the headland. But the surf is too high; even with the help of two others – I think Jimmy and Bruce – they can't keep it steady, they can't gain any ground.

Most of the figures have come down from the bluffs now. The beach comes alive with dizzying lights like directionless fireflies. But some remain stationary; lone fixed points against the skyline that anchor me, keep me focussed; remind me of my mother.

The wind becomes more ferocious. Howling and ricocheting around the cliffs and headlands. The waves batter me, washing over the rock in endless punishing assaults. More people help to push the skiff into the sea. So many I can't recognise them, so many that I can no longer see the boat at all, but finally it gains momentum, and I can see figures climbing aboard, frantically trying to row their way free of the surf. For one moment, it looks like they will – the skiff rides high once, twice, but then the wind changes again, and the next wave slams into its port side, tipping its crew into the sea. I can hear their shouts, see their frantic efforts as they try to control the upturned boat, but the sea hurls it back onto the shore, washing those figures back with it.

Thunder rumbles, heralds icy quick rain that pounds against my skull. Lightning cracks and flares, and the sea swells higher. High enough that in the white-bright light, those waves look like the sky. Like the world. Salt stings my eyes, my throat. Spasms shudder through me, chattering my teeth, stopping my heart in longer bursts.

Figures crowd around the skiff again, pushing it back into the waves. But two run for the bluffs, climbing fast before heading east. I recognise Jimmy in front; he must be going for his creel boat, or maybe the outboard dinghy pulled up on the slip at Bàgh Fasgach. I don't know who's following him, only that it's not Charlie. Because he promised me he wouldn't leave. I see him climbing into the skiff again with three others, rowing and rowing against the sea and the tide. And I hold my breath inside my chest as the wind and current push them closer, closer.

But not close enough. Less than fifty yards from my rock, the wind throws them westwards, into the shadow of the headland, the sea there surging higher and threatening to smash them against the cliffs. And then I let out a sound, high and thin, when it does just that, spinning them around once, twice, before launching them against a cliff face. I don't hear the sound it makes, not over the wind and the thunder and the hard-drumming rain, but I hear the shouts and screams on shore. In another flash of lightning, I see the boat splinter, see the bodies thrown free and frantically swimming. Finally spat back onto the beach.

When they all get up, I let out a breath, gasping quickly for another. I look at those bobbing frantic lights, those sodden and defeated figures on the shore. The skiff is gone. Even if Jimmy does manage to get a boat around Eilean Beag and all those headlands, it'll take too long. Above me, the rain becomes sleet, and then hailstones, hard and relentless. Those mountainous waves pound and choke. I've become so heavy, I can't hold on to the rock. I can't tread enough water to stay afloat. I've swallowed too much of the sea; my belly feels hard and full, and still somehow empty. My exhaustion is like nothing I've ever felt before – leaden and hopeless, like a starless black sky.

And then I look back at the beach. All the torches have gone, except for one lone gold circle that shines out across the furious waves. A sob rises up in my throat: afraid and helpless like a child's. For a terrible moment, I can't see anything but that solitary light – my vision is too blurred and the dusk has too many shadows – and then I can. I can see them. Wading into the sea, into the wild surf. A long thin line of people holding hands. Charlie at the front, waving, shouting at me to hold on a little longer as they head towards my rock. Towards me.

And then I understand. *This* is what I wanted. Not to suffer atonement for the terrible things that I've done. Not to suffer a fate that should have always been mine. Not to be seen, or to be sacrificed. I've never understood anything, or anyone, at all – least of all myself. I watch that line waver and stretch, but it never breaks. Even as the wind howls and the sea roars and the sky screams, it keeps reaching for me. They want to save me. They know me. They see me. And they *still* want to save me.

I think of Mary. All that burning heat beneath cool and calm. Slow and steady and strong. I think of Calum, his round little face and eager smiles. My wee boy. Who I have loved more than life, more than anyone else I have ever known. We none of us get the father we deserve.

Instead, I'll become just another soul lost to the sea. One who battled so long and so hard to come back again. Because ghosts are just unspoken truths. And the weight of my fear will no longer be a millstone around my neck, but an anchor. A memory of home.

The end is never the end.

I let go of the rock. Look up into the starless sky. And I finally let the sea have me.

CHAPTER 37

'*The Fisherman.*'

I think of that tall stern memorial above Long Stride, looking out at the sea. 'It's for Robert.'

Charlie wipes his eyes. 'It's what he wanted it to say. So it's what it says.'

I look out the bunkhouse's only window. I can see a narrow run of stars overhead, solid and linear like the lintel of a door. And below them the sea. I don't know what to say. I don't even know what to feel.

'After . . .' Charlie rubs a forefinger under his nose, and then dangles his arms between his knees. 'Nothing was ever the same. The Stewarts – Kelly's parents – they voted yes, but they didn't come down to the beach. Afterwards, Thom bought the black-house, took over the lease for the land. And stood it for little over a year before he took his family away to North Uist for good.' He shakes his head. 'And Kenny. He might have been the only one to vote no, but he was on the beach that night anyway. And when I realised . . . when I saw that Robert wanted to come back, Kenny was the first one to go for the skiff. He'd left it pulled up against Roeness. Maybe he'd planned to use it all along.' He sighs. 'Alec never forgave us. When we started trying to put the boat out to sea, Bruce had to knock him out cold.'

Charlie stands up, looks out at that line of stars. 'The guilt we've always felt over what we did is our cross to bear.' He turns back to me. '*My* cross to bear. I suppose that's justice too.'

'The dig. That's why Femi thought someone had been poking around, moving tarps, after Miko switched the dig back to the old barrow, isn't it? Why Jaz became their shadow? Because you were all worried about Lorne's body being discovered?' It's easier to ask Charlie questions. To seek out more things to accuse him of instead of having to think about what he's actually done.

Charlie nods, sits back down. 'Robert had been the one to suggest burying Lorne there.' His smile is awful. 'We couldn't bury him in the cemetery, not without . . . not without explaining what had happened, but Robert said that the whole ridge up to the moorland and standing stones had been sacred ground for millennia.'

'But *why*, Charlie? Why couldn't you just explain to the police what happened? I don't understand.'

He opens his mouth, closes it. Shakes his head. 'Maggie, I can't – it's hard to explain. We—'

'And the whisky festival?' I say. 'I know you faked that photo. Why?'

He sighs. 'Robert had reported us as being responsible for killing his sheep. He'd told the police in Stornoway we were all against him, out to get him.' He shakes his head again. 'We didn't trust Kenny, or Mary's silence. And Alec thought that if the police found the blood – I mean, we'd cleaned it up, but you know, they can still find it, can't they, if they want to, and there was *so* much of it – he thought they'd think he killed Robert.'

Charlie closes his eyes, and his voice gets quiet, small. 'And we were still waiting to hear back about the Land Fund application. We were up against at least six other communities for the money. None of us ever said it, not outright, but if it had got out – the truth, never mind Alec being accused of Robert's murder – we would never have been awarded the funding to buy Euan out.'

'Christ.'

He winces. 'It was a mess, Maggie. And we did what guilty people do. We made it worse. We made *us* worse. We became paranoid. We made up lies for questions no one had asked. We decided that those of us Robert had probably accused needed an alibi. Just in case. Day after the storm, we tried to get out to Stornoway to take the photos while Isla reported Robert and Lorne missing, but the roads were flooded, impassable. We had to wait until Monday. The phone lines were down, they nearly always went down in big storms – so no one ever questioned why we didn't contact the police until then.

'Jimmy dumped Lorne's dinghy in the sea north of the sound, and we made up a story for what happened that night. We're a community, a family. There can be no secrets among us. That's what caused this mess in the first place.' He sighs. 'When Jaz decided not to leave the island, we had to tell him the truth too. He agreed to give a false witness statement that he'd seen Robert going into the sea alone. Kenny agreed to say the same, but . . .' Charlie glances away. 'He walked out to the bothy on West Point less than a week after we spoke to the police. And that's where he stayed.'

'So it all worked out,' I say.

The look Charlie gives me is half-stony, half-anguished. 'When Robert changed his mind, we were all glad, Maggie. All except Alec. We'd thought we were doing what was right. What Robert wanted.' His hands draw into fists. 'And we did everything – *everything* – we could to bring him back.'

'Who's been following me? Creeping around? Watching me from the dark?'

'Alec.' Charlie's expression becomes even more pained. 'As soon as we realised what he was doing, we convinced him to go back to the rigs early. As much for his sake as yours. You have to under-stand, it's himself he hates the most. Always has been.'

When I give him a disbelieving look, he heaves another sigh.

'He and Thom Stewart were always thick as thieves. And Thom had taken it into his head to become a farmer. He'd planned to rent the blackhouse and Ardcraig land from Euan long before Robert beat him to it, though I don't think Robert ever knew. Thom wanted him out from the start. He and Alec put rock salt and glyphosate in the soil of Robert's fodder crops. They blackmailed Bruce over money he owed them in a poker game; forced him to recommend the wrong feed, give Robert bad advice. They even wanted him to screw up the tupping and lambing until Bruce found the money to get them off his back.'

He looks at me. 'I didn't know. None of us knew. Not until Alec drank himself into a stupor about a week after Robert had died. Then it all came out. Lorne and Sheena *were* at the Campbells for a sleepover the night he died, but Alec blames only himself for Lorne's death.' Charlie's expression hardens. 'And can't say as I disagree with him.'

'Then who followed me back from Ardshader?' I say. 'Alec was gone by then. Who—'

'Jaz,' Charlie says, gaze sliding away. 'We were keeping tabs on you, that's all. We just wanted to know what you were doing.'

'*No.*' I think of those scuffling boots surfing a slide of loose stones inside the dark corridor of the Devil's Mouth. 'He was trying to scare me, Charlie.' And my anger roars back because I know I'm right.

'Maggie, everyone was scared. *Is* scared.' He reaches out his hands towards me and then thinks better of it. 'And no matter what I've said to you since you came back, so am I.'

I try not to look at him then, because I don't want to feel sympathy for him. I don't want to remember standing inside a peat bog as he squeezed my fingers and muttered *Thanks for being here.*

'Alec left the dead birds?' I say. 'And the fire? Was that him too? Christ, Charlie, he could have killed me!'

When Charlie says nothing at all, my anger gets bigger. Brighter. 'He was in my *home*. He terrorised me while I was sleeping. How can—'

'God.' Charlie weighs his head in his hands, stares down at the floor for long seconds. 'What a fucking, *fucking* mess.'

And that's what finally snaps me out of it – my pointless inter-rogation that's more like a tantrum. The sight of Charlie holding his head in his hands; the tremble of his fingers against his hair. Because, I realise, this is the one question he was hoping I wouldn't ask. Unease wakes up inside my chest again, sending nervous shivers down my spine.

'That wasn't Alec.' I look at the crown of Charlie's bowed head. 'Was it?'

I think of drowning. Looking down into viscid blackness and feeling nothing but the bubbles of my last escaping breath. I think of Charlie's *It was Mary who told me about the* vándr-varði. *She was worried about him. He'd had some kind of breakdown in Aberdeen.*

The why that I found in the sea, the why that made me think of Kenny's smile. *A storm is coming.* The why that was a change in Cora – alien and brittle – that I couldn't put a name to. It had been her voice. Her accent. No longer English but Scottish. Aberdonian.

'Oh, God,' I say. 'Cora is Mary. Cora is *Mary.*'

Charlie's shoulders sag. 'She never went back to Aberdeen. When the Stewarts bought the blackhouse, Euan insisted that she move into an unused wing of the Big Hoose. Her and Euan, they got . . . closer over the next few years.' His shrug looks heavy. 'And eventually, they married.'

I swallow. 'She's the one who was creeping around outside the blackhouse, who came *into* the blackhouse, God knows how many times? Who set a fucking fire in – did you know? Did you know that she—'

'No. No, of course not. We all knew she was getting worse, even before you came back. But after . . . maybe she did it because someone was living in the blackhouse again, and she could see the lights at night. Or maybe, I don't know, maybe it was because it was you – the wee girl who'd once said she was Andrew.' Charlie's sigh is bone-deep.

I think of her spitting fury outside the pub all those months ago. Those cracks of gun fire across the Morrison estate that day in the Big Hoose, and those shotguns inside two cherrywood cabinets. Spindly black wings like ribs and feet like claws, and a cool soft belly pitted with birdshot.

'She made the *vándr-varði*, didn't she? You said that she was the one who told you about them. She left them outside the blackhouse. *Inside* the blackhouse.' Those talismans to protect against evil. To protect against me. The me who'd once said she was Andrew.

'I only found out what she was doing after that day you showed me the *vándr-varði* down on Big Beach,' Charlie says. 'I went to tell Euan and he said that sometimes she'd slip out at night, and he'd find her outside the blackhouse, or on her way there. But he didn't know about the *vándr-varði* – not until I told him.'

'Someone took them,' I say, something a little more complicated than anger quickening my heartbeat again. 'Someone knew where I'd put them, and they took them.'

Charlie has the grace, at least, to look both sorry and guilty at the same time. 'I told Euan that you'd been keeping them in a rucksack in the mudroom.'

I think of that figure hidden inside the dark bathroom doorway, looking at me in the light before throwing that dead crow, bloodied and slick with rain. Cora. And then I think of the standard lamp's click in the instant before everything was plunged into blackness; that someone else in the dark, close enough to me that I could hear their too-loud intake of breath before they held it. Euan.

That something more complicated than anger flashes brighter, tries to gather more outrage.

'Did Will know? Did he know what—'

'No. No, he didn't know, Maggie,' Charlie says, his head shaking violently and his mouth a tight line. 'He didn't know what Cora was doing. He didn't know any of it.'

And then, of course, I get it. Far too late. 'No. Oh no.' Because all I can think of is Will. *Will.* I find myself squeezing Charlie's arm hard. *'No.'*

He looks at me, grabs hold of my hand. 'Maggie. Robert made us promise to look after them,' he whispers. 'We couldn't do anything but that.'

I snatch back my hand, press it shaking against my hot face. 'Does he know?' I'm whispering too. 'Does Will know that Cora is Mary? That he . . . *he* is Calum?'

Charlie shakes his head, eyes red. 'When Cora started getting sicker and all of . . . this started, we knew we'd have to . . . Just – I know I've no right to ask – but just give us the night, Maggie. Let us tell him. Please.'

When Miko comes back in through the door, I flinch.

'Sorry,' she says. 'I . . . Will said you'd need these, Maggie.' She holds out a pill bottle. It's my lithium.

Exhaustion suddenly swamps me. My heart doesn't just ache, it hurts. 'I need you to go now, Charlie.'

He gets up without objecting, and walks over to the open door. Where he pauses.

'We decided,' he says, but he only looks ahead, at the night outside the bunkhouse. 'All of us. Down on the beach, after you left with Dr Okitsu and Will followed. That if you knew the truth . . .' I hear his laboured swallow. 'Whatever you decided to do – to say – we'd agree with it. No matter what.' He turns back towards me. 'We'll all be in the pub, tomorrow lunchtime.' His expression is pure Charlie: stern and sorrowful. 'I promise, Maggie, you're safe here.' He holds my gaze. 'No matter what.'

CHAPTER 38

The next day I get up while Miko is still sleeping. Sneak out after leaving her a grateful note that explains very little. It's less than she deserves, but if it allows her to leave, to feel released of any concern or responsibility, then perhaps it isn't. I'm still wearing the jumper and leggings she gave me, and I hope she won't mind that either. I take only my mac; I can't even look at the clothes I almost drowned in. The clothes that I *did* drown in.

Outside, the air is clear and fresh; the storm's oppressiveness has gone. The sky is pale blue and purple, the clouds solitary and white. I glance east towards Blairmore, but head north instead towards Long Stride. Everything aches and twinges. My skin is salt-sore and red; it burns. But I feel bizarrely refreshed. My head is as clear and clean as the air.

The beach is less recovered. The sand is grey rather than pristine white. Marred by tidelines of seaweed and broken shells, and deep jagged gouges filled with seawater that make me shiver. My chest aches. I rub my breastbone, wince when I remember the bruise that the heel of Charlie's hand has left. I think of his face, stony and distraught, and that ache gets bigger.

I walk west slowly until I reach those two standing stones. THE FISHERMAN, tall and stark and granite-stern, and its neighbour, with all its swirls and scrolls of softer sandstone. FOR LORNE. It makes me think of *forlorn* – pitifully sad and abandoned, or a hope unlikely to succeed. I suppose that choice is mine.

I don't want to make it. I *want* to do nothing. I want to forget all that I've fought so hard to know. I want to feel safe and quiet. I don't want the responsibility of deciding anyone's fate ever again.

But Robert killed Lorne because he never took responsibility. He never asked for help. He never escaped that lighthouse, nor the long shadow it cast over his life. Alec, Thom, Bruce, and Fiona never took responsibility for sabotaging an already damaged man. And the rest of the villagers never took responsibility for helping him to die.

I look up at the sun as a fine mist of rain moves in from the sea, cooling my skin and speckling the sand darker. I look across at the empty western cliffs of Roeness wreathed in cotton-wool clouds. I'm not inside a goldfish bowl, looking out at a world I'm not part of. Not any more. I'm here. I'm part of this place, these people. And they are part of me.

I think of lying in bed, the dawn creeping under the curtains as Mum read to me about Hobbiton and the Shire. My nightlight illuminating those curly wisps of hair at her temples. *You are always the best thing, my darling, the most wonderful thing in my whole life.*

Mum never took responsibility for our life of uncertainty and chaos. For running into the path of that silver Lexus, and still – still – refusing to accept that she was anything but special. She never took responsibility for lying to me. For asking me to help her. For asking me to believe her.

Because she knew I didn't. From the moment I took myself to the doctor's at age fifteen and ever after, I never believed her again. We both knew it. And she asked anyway. I fed her those pills one after another anyway. Because in my heart – I rub the ache there, the deep spreading bruise – I just wanted it to stop. I wanted it all to be over. I think of sitting on that second-from-last cellar step, looking up at Robert's stars and thinking, isn't that what guilt amounts to? Less what we do than what we *want* to do? And I have never even come close to taking responsibility for that.

I look at that tall stark stone. Trace the swirls and scrolls of its neighbour with numb fingers. Guilt brought me here. To this island. To Robert. To this decision.

You just have to make the right choice, Maggie. And you always do.

*

Blairmore is deserted. The shop is shut. Pinned to the door of the pub is a hastily scribbled sign: *Private Party.* I hesitate, have to take one deep breath and then another before I find the courage to open it.

The dull hum of already muted chatter goes silent. Everyone turns to look at me. Just like they did on that first winter day three months ago. How long ago that seems now.

The MacKenzies are sitting at their table. Bruce looks worried, but Gillian looks defiant. Donnie is more solemn than I've ever seen him; he won't look me in the eye. I wonder if he knew the whole story all along; if he'd known his childhood friend had once been Calum. Alec stands at the bar alongside Jimmy, and even though both of them are giving me the same kind of glower, I can see Jimmy's hand hovering behind Alec's shoulder, ready to grab hold. Isla, Fiona, Sheena, and Jaz are sitting at the long table that Inspector Lynn Urquhart had stood behind. On the other side of the lounge, Charlie sits alone. There's no Euan, no Cora, no Will.

I don't venture any further into the lounge. I wait for someone to speak, until I realise that they're waiting for me. I swallow, throat dry. I can feel my nails digging into the flesh of my palms. I look over at that red wall of photos: landscapes of sea and cliff and beach; portraits of men, women, and children. And the mounted piece of varnished driftwood above them. *The sheep will spend its life in fear of the wolf, and then be eaten by the shepherd.* And I remember that day in the Big Hoose's kitchen with Cora and thinking how fucking unfair life is. How relentlessly merciless. And we're just supposed to go on living it anyway.

'I won't say anything,' I say, still looking at that wall.

There's a sob, loud and short, and Fiona slumps against Isla before covering her face. Isla looks at me with those steely stern eyes, and then looks away.

'Robert killed Lorne,' I say, wincing a little as Fiona sobs again. 'If the police come to any conclusion, it'll be that one.'

I look at Charlie, his head bowed low, his forefinger rubbing the space between his mouth and his nose over and over again. I think of holding his hands and telling him that the truth isn't everything. It isn't even the most important thing.

'I had no right to come here. Not the first time. Not this time. I'm sorry.'

And then I look around at them all, unable to say how much I will miss them. How much I will miss this village. This island. How much I will miss the life I'd thought I could have.

'Maggie.' Bruce stands up. Fixes me with those dark eyes. 'Thank you.'

I nod. Swallow past the growing lump in my throat. 'I'll leave tomorrow.'

And then I turn away and open the door. Step back out onto the street without once looking back.

CHAPTER 39

I go west. I pretend it's because I need to retrieve the photo of the whisky festival, so that I can put it back on the red wall where it belongs, but it isn't true. I give the farm a wide berth, although I see no sign of Will. He's normally up and working by now, but today the curtains are shut. I don't look at the blackhouse at all. That's why I'm going west. I need the space and the comfort that Lovely Place gives me. I need to process my own hurt before I can take on anyone else's.

The sun is out as I climb the bluffs again. I sit on the warm flat stone, breathe in salty air. Look down at the meadow, the resilient machair, pink and purple and yellow and white. The rabbits chasing one another from burrow to burrow. My breaths are unsteady, the ache in my chest returned. It's happened so fast. The end of this. When I'd just been at the beginning. But I can't stay, knowing what I know. I don't have the right to do that either.

To be a permanent reminder of Robert, of what they did. I had my chance to stop looking, to stop digging, to choose happiness instead, and I didn't take it.

I stand up, go over to the abandoned burrow. Reach inside past the grass and trailing roots, feel the sharp edges of the photo frame before I pull it out. I sit back on my heels for a moment, brush the earth from the glass, from those blurry, smiling faces. I wonder what they were thinking when that picture was taken. All that horror, all that guilt. Despite the enormity of what happened to me yesterday, I'm ashamed of the way I shut down. The way I ran and hid. I think of Miko holding my meds. *Will said you'd need these.* He's probably feeling more confused, more alone, than he's ever felt in his whole life, and I'm still hiding. I remember that first day down on Big Beach when I asked him if he'd ever thought of leaving the islands, and he answered with that grin. *I would. For the right person.*

I get up, seized suddenly with purpose again, with hope.

'Maggie.'

I turn, slap a startled hand against my chest.

Charlie looks tired, his ruddy face grey and stubbled white. 'It was a good thing you just did. Thank you.' There are dark shadows under his eyes as he glances down at the photo in my hands.

I thrust it at him, feeling vaguely ashamed. 'It was the right thing, that's all.'

He doesn't reply, but he looks down at it for a few seconds before swinging an open rucksack off his shoulder and pushing the photo inside.

'You going to Will?' He doesn't look up.

'Yes. Is he okay?'

Charlie sighs – an exhausted, shaky sigh that makes me feel uneasy, back on unsafe ground.

'I can't keep lying to you,' he says. 'I can't keep telling you the truth mixed with so many lies it may as well not be true at all.'

He reaches into his rucksack and brings out a wide wooden box.

'Charlie . . .' I realise that I'm shaking my head, backing away from him towards the bluff. 'No more.'

But he holds it out to me until I take it.

'It belonged to Robert,' Charlie says, when I don't ask. 'I found it here, years ago. Inside one of these old burrows.'

I look down at the box. There are three words etched clumsily across its lid in what must be Gaelic. *Tha mi duilich.* That sense of creeping unease has become paralysing; I can't do anything but read those words, over and over.

'Open it, Maggie.' Charlie's voice sounds strange, changed.

The hinges of the box's lid squeak enough to make me wince. Inside are two black bags. The larger is heavy and made of tightly woven canvas. I hold my breath as I pull out the object inside. It's a Y-shaped metal frame attached to a flat black rubber band. A slingshot. I glance at Charlie as I set it and the box on the ground, and take out the smaller bag, velveteen-soft and rattling. I pull its drawstring wide with still shaking fingers, spill the contents out into my hand. Half a dozen pink quartz stones. Just the right size to fit into the slingshot's cloth pocket. The same planes and sharp edges as the pendant I can feel pressing against my bruised breast-bone. And my heart – the heart that stopped beating less than one day ago – starts drumming so hard and so fast that I let out a gasp, drop the bag and the stones onto the ground.

'Maggie.'

I shake Charlie's hands off, back up against the bluff. When my knees finally buckle, I'm glad to give up trying to stand.

'Maggie!'

I think of that day on Big Beach with Charlie at the beginning of spring when the island was coming alive again, just like I was. *You found it here, you know. On this beach. We found you down by the east bluffs, holding that piece of quartz like it was a nugget of gold.*

'We were in shock,' Charlie says, in that same strange voice. 'I told you that. But I didn't . . . that doesn't explain how . . . it was like time had stopped. After Robert did what he did, after we did what we did and he was gone, it was like everything just . . . stopped.'

I can hear him move closer, but I don't look up.

'We couldn't decide what to do, none of us. And then it was too late – we'd waited too long, we couldn't tell the police anything even if we'd wanted to. We'd cleaned up the blackhouse; we'd buried Lorne.' Charlie's voice breaks. 'The storm woke us up. *The Hammer of the Sea.* The worst spring storm to hit the west coast in two decades. And we . . . God help us, we saw the opportunity in it. Robert had never come back. He'd never washed up anywhere. He'd just gone. So. We decided to say that both he and Lorne had been lost to Òrd na Mara.'

I squeeze my eyes shut, try to grab hold of the calmness of this place, the peace, but it's like trying to grab hold of smoke. Belching up from a fire that's burning everything I own.

'Robert died on a different night,' I whisper. 'A different storm.'

I can hear Charlie swallow. 'Aye.'

'How many days before the festival?'

When he doesn't answer me, I make myself look at him. He looks back – tired, beaten. Old.

'Charlie. How many days before the festival did he die?'

He closes his eyes. 'Fifty-three.'

'*Fifty-three?*' Something halfway between a sob and a laugh comes out of me. My fingers are numb when I press them against my mouth. 'What date?'

Charlie lets out a long, shuddering breath. He reaches his hands towards me but doesn't move closer. 'The fifteenth of February.'

My birthday.

I scramble backwards, push myself to my feet. 'No. No.' I start climbing, half-crawling up the bluff towards its summit, ignoring Charlie shouting my name.

At the top, the wind is as fierce as ever, and I welcome its fury. I look down. The storm hasn't only carved deep wounds into the sand of Big Beach, it's changed the topography of its dunes and shoreline – so much so that it no longer looks like the same place, the same beach. As if it's an imposter. A replacement. I look out across the Atlantic. Quiet and flat beneath white puffs of cloud. Clear and turquoise blue. I think of that sharp memory against a backdrop of white. The squeeze of my fists; the hoarseness of my throat; the hotness of my tears.

I'm Andrew MacNeil. I'm Andrew MacNeil. I'm Andrew MacNeil!

Mum, with that light in her eyes, that serene smile. *Yes, you are.*

And then I look west towards Roeness, that low grey shadow of Sonny's bothy. Did he know? Had they *all* known?

'You knew,' I say, when Charlie climbs up beside me, breath wheezing. '*You* knew.'

He winces, holds out his palms. 'When you first looked at me as a five-year-old kid, I knew.'

There should be questions. So many. But I can't ask them. I can't even think them. It's too much. Too much to accept. That Mum hadn't lied. That the five-year-old me hadn't lied; hadn't believed a lie. That when Robert died, I was born.

'I didn't know how to tell you,' Charlie says. 'I knew I should tell you the truth this time. That if I didn't, you would just keep coming back. Like a fishing boat to port.' He stops. His eyes are bright with unshed tears. 'So I tried to help you see. But it was so hard, just another terrible mistake. It . . .'

I feel suddenly exhausted. I look back down at the rabbit burrows, that flat warm stone. The pinks and purples and yellows and whites. 'What does *tha mi duilich* mean?' My voice is shaking, but I feel completely numb.

'"I'm sorry". It means "I'm sorry".'

I think of Will's name in my mouth as it escaped upwards away from all that black water, leaving me behind. *I'm sorry.* And the sob that breaks out of me sounds more like a howl. I drop hard onto my knees, one hand over my mouth as another and another shake through me. *Will.*

'Maggie. Maggie.' Charlie's arms come around me and he pulls me against his chest. He holds me so hard I can barely breathe. His heartbeat thunders against my ear. His tears dampen my skin. 'I'm sorry. I'm so, so sorry.'

I cry like I've never cried before. Kneeling in the grass and mud, surrounded by the Atlantic waves, a carpet of colour, and a blue sky clouded white. I cry even when my voice gives out and my lungs burn as if I'm drowning. I cry for Robert. For me. And for the five-year-old child for whom there had never been a difference.

CHAPTER 40

I stop on the edge of the grass, look up at the white stone cottage with its red door and carved wooden plaque. *Tuathanas Àrd Chreag.* When I look across at the blackhouse, I see that someone has taken away the birds, and wonder if it was Will.

Face it, I think. Confront it.

The door is ajar, so I open it, step up into the narrow hall. Will is sitting at the kitchen table, his shoulders slumped, long legs sprawled out in front of him. He looks up at me, still standing in the hallway.

'Maggie.'

I can't move. I've forgotten so quickly. How it feels to look at him. To have him look at me.

'I didn't know about Mum.' His voice is hoarse. His eyes red-rimmed. 'I promise you. I never knew.'

'I know. It's okay.' I make myself go into the kitchen.

'It's not okay.' He stands up. 'None of this is okay. It's crazy.'

He comes towards me, and it takes everything I have not to run, not to look away.

'Are *you* okay?' The concern in his eyes is fierce. He reaches up a hand to touch my face, perhaps my hair, and then hesitates, curls it into a fist. 'I was so fucking scared. When I saw you . . . when I saw what Mum had . . . I'm so sorry. I don't know what I would have done if—'

'I'm okay,' I say, trying to smile and not even coming close to managing it.

'She's much worse than I thought. No wonder Euan has been stressed out. He's probably been shitting himself that she was going to tell the truth, expose all their fucking lies.' He shakes his head. Gives me a pleading look. 'In her own fucked-up way, she was trying to protect me.'

'I know.'

'I'm so fucking sorry, Maggie.'

And this time he does touch my face. His fingers are warm. When he moves closer, he is all I can see and smell and feel. And I have to back away. I have to back away so fast and so far that I find myself inside the narrow hallway again, gripping hard at the kitchen doorframe.

The grief in Will's eyes sharpens. 'What's wrong?'

I don't know what to say. How to answer. How to tell him. That Cora was right to protect him. That once I was someone else. Once I was Robert Reid. Once I was Andrew MacNeil. His father. And because I'm resolved to see it, to confront it – to confront everything I want to run from, there's no hiding from that. There's no pretending that nothing has changed. Or that what Will and I have – this connection that I've never come close to having with anyone else – isn't murky now. Knowing what I know – what I have no choice but to believe – will always make it murky. Wrong. I look at Will, and the love I feel for him is agonising. Impossible. 'You're Calum.'

He flinches, turns away from me to run his fingers through his already messy hair. His voice is furious, but so unsteady. 'They came round last night, Charlie and Euan. They told me everything they'd already told you. That Mum . . . and I . . . were from Aberdeen. We'd never lived in Kenilworth; Mum never met Euan in Glasgow. That my father . . . my father was Robert Reid.' His voice cracks briefly as he looks down at the table, and I recognise the photo that had been beside his bed: a young Cora standing next to a dark-haired man with Will's eyes. '*That's* mum's brother, my fucking uncle. No wonder he crapped himself when I turned up on his doorstep in Balham.' When he spins back to me, all that anger runs out of him and I want to hide from the way he looks at me. 'Everyone lied to me. My whole life. My first memories of this island are of the Big Hoose and that's it. I don't remember anything else. I swear I would have told you if—'

'I know.'

He looks at me. 'Nothing's changed. I'm *Will*, Maggie. I haven't been Calum since I was three years old.'

'Everything's changed,' I whisper.

He moves closer to the doorway, and I grip hold of it tighter. 'Please don't go.' His voice is low. 'Please don't leave.'

And then he isn't just touching me, he's kissing me. He's holding me so tight that my chest remembers how to hurt. And all of it feels unchanged, undamaged, and so, so *right* that I can't bear it. I can't survive it.

'No. Will, stop!' And the sheer panic in my voice makes him let go of me straightaway.

I wrap my arms around my torso. My throat throbs and my eyes sting. I can feel my flimsy defences start to crack. The pain that's waiting behind their thin walls and towers. 'I can't do this if you touch me.'

'Then don't do this. Stay.'

'I can't, Will. I can't.'

'Then I'll come with you. We can build a life together somewhere. Anywhere else.'

I'm shaking my head before he's even stopped speaking because it sounds so tempting. So possible. 'This is your home.'

His smile is bitter. There are tears in his eyes. 'Don't you get it, Maggie? You are my home.'

And it takes what little reserves I have left not to go to him, to comfort him, to comfort *me*. But I don't. Because I know that I will never ever be able to do this – say this – again.

'I don't expect you to understand. But this is the right thing. For both of us.'

Because I'd rather he hated me for the rest of our lives than burden him with knowing why. What *I* know – what I can barely accept – is too new, too raw. But it's also never going to change. His *father*, the word runs through my mind like a train on a circular track. It doesn't matter that I don't remember it, it doesn't matter that I love him now only as Will, the man I thought I'd spend the rest of my life with. It doesn't even matter that soulmates the world over were doubtless once something else to each other too: a brother, a mother, a son. It will still be true. And I can never *unknow* it.

When he starts shaking his head and closes that last remaining space between us, I hold up my hands. 'I need to go. This isn't my home. This isn't my life. I need to find out what is. And I can only do that on my own. Please.' And I try to make myself mean it – to at least sound like I mean it. That this is what I want. '*Please*. Just let me go.'

And maybe he sees something in my eyes then. The determination, the resolve. Because he bows his head and closes his eyes.

'When are you going?' He wipes impatient fingers across his cheeks and they come away wet.

'Tomorrow.'

He winces. But when he finally looks up at me, he doesn't look defeated at all. 'Stay here tonight.' He comes back towards me and pulls me close, his fingers digging into my skin, his eyes dark. 'Maybe you're right, and we both need to be on our own for a while. Maybe I need to find out who I am too.' He leans close enough that I can see the blurred threads of red inside his eyes. Cups my face inside his hands. 'But you and I are meant to be together, Maggie MacKay. And nothing you say, nothing we do, is going to change that.'

I don't reply. I don't resist when he kisses me again. Or when he leads me down the hallway towards the bedroom. Or when he pulls me down onto the bed and I feel the *thump-thump* of my heart once, twice, as if I'm about to be dropped from the lift-hill launch of a roller coaster. This last time belongs to me and not to anyone else. It belongs to us, to what Will and I might have been. I love you, I say to his skin, his tears, the whisper of my name in his mouth. I love you.

CHAPTER 41

I wake up early, when the light through the bedroom curtain is grey and the room still full of shadows. Will is lying on his side, facing away from me. I listen to him breathing, watch the rise and fall of his shoulders. I want to touch him so badly that I make myself get up. Get dressed. Open the bedroom door. Leave without saying goodbye. I know he's awake, but he lets me do it. He spares me the pain of having to say no again. The pain of having to pretend I mean it.

The morning air is biting enough that I can blame it for my stinging nose, my blinding tears. And the icy Atlantic wind for having to stop, to lean heavily against the farm's smooth white wall for too many minutes just to breathe. But when I start to waver, to think about going back, I make myself move again. To cross over the pasture to the blackhouse. I make myself go inside and pack my bag, and I don't stop, don't look, don't think.

But as I open the door to go, I have to turn around. I have to pause and look back at the brightly lit pine walls, the tartan curtains and Harris tweed cushions. The driftwood mantelpiece and the Highland cow clock; the wide silver mirror and the standard lamp. The earth cellar trapdoor and its recessed steel handle. I have to take one last breath of pine and coffee and woodsmoke. I have to say goodbye. And then I have to leave.

I walk slowly back along the main road, partly because I want to commit every part of this place to memory – the overgrown Coffin Road; Loch Tana, Ben Wyvis, and the Valley of Ghosts; all those peat slabs drying in the sun like dragon scales. Everyone will be coming back soon, for the gathering and stacking. That last big party in Am Blàr Mòr. I push away the pain I feel at that. It can't belong to me.

An old green jalopy is parked next to the ruined church. Charlie is dozing in its driving seat. When I open the door, he blinks and curses.

'Sorry.' I get in, dump my bag in the back seat. The car smells of paint thinner and coffee. 'Thanks for doing this.'

He nods. Hands me a steaming thermos cup. 'You okay?'

I nod back. 'Let's go.'

'You don't want to stop at the village?' I can feel the weight of his scrutiny.

'No.'

'You don't need to do this, Maggie. You don't need to go. That's not why I told you.'

I turn to face him, try to smile. 'I think it was, Charlie. And you were right.'

He looks at me a little longer, and finally turns on the engine, which coughs into rumbling life. I stare up at the imposing slopes of Ben Wyvis as we round the corner southeast, and then Charlie makes a sound low in the back of his throat and I turn away from his window.

Everyone is waiting at the junction into Blairmore. Jaz and Euan. Isla and Jimmy. Bruce, Gillian, and Donnie. Fiona and Sheena. Even Alec. All standing side by side in a line. Charlie doesn't stop driving, but he slows as we approach them, and I hear him swallow once, dry and loud.

'You *all* knew,' I say. 'When Mum and I came with the film crew. You would have known then. The day I was born. The day Robert died. You would all have known it was true.'

'We knew.'

'But when I came back, you were kind to me.' I watch them get closer, press my palm against the window. 'And when I decided to stay, you welcomed me.'

Charlie's voice is gruff. 'We thought you'd come back home.'

My eyes blur as we pass the junction and that silent, solemn line. Jimmy nods and Isla smiles. Bruce raises a hand. And I know that they're not there to see me go, to be sure I've gone. Instead, they're like lights on top of a headland or bluff shining down onto the sea. They're saying goodbye. They're making sure I know that I haven't been alone.

I turn round in my seat, watch them and Blairmore get smaller and smaller. 'Like a fishing boat to port,' I say.

'Aye.' Charlie looks at me and smiles. 'Just like that.'

*

After Kilmeray, the lights and bustle of Stornoway feel almost claustrophobic. The terminal is bright with floodlights and car lights. The ferry sits low in the water, its wide ramp rattling and creaking as cars and vans roll off onto the tarmac. Seagulls shriek and swoop around the harbour and the road beyond. Something clenches tight inside me when I think about the mainland. The future. When I get out of the car, Charlie follows me, retrieves my bag from the back seat.

I can't look at him. The silence between us that had been comfortable now feels strained and awkward. My heart hurts. Every breath hurts.

'What will happen to Cora?'

'We'll look after her,' Charlie says.

My phone beeps with a text, and when I see it's from Will, I thrust it back into my pocket unread. I watch the last of the cars disembark before I turn back to Charlie again. The wind whistles around us, snatching at his thick sideburns, the wiry grey hair that pokes out from under his tweed cap.

'Will doesn't know,' I say.

Charlie nods. 'And he won't.' He looks at me, his eyes sharp and grey, face ruddy and lined. I remember when I first met him, thinking that there was a coldness to him, a detachment, as if he and I were different species and the gulf between us too great to even attempt to bridge. Now I see more than just the kindness in him. I see all that he's hidden. All that he's sacrificed. All that he's suffered.

'What am I going to do without you, Charlie?'

He puts down my bag, takes hold of both of my hands, squeezes them tight between his own, calloused and warm. 'I think it's me should be asking you that, lassie.' He squeezes my hands tighter. 'You'll be right. That's what I've learned during my time on this earth. You're always as strong as you need to be. You'll be right.'

But his eyes have turned haunted, and the grip of his fingers falters. And something like anger cuts through my numbness, my melancholy, because I realise why. What Charlie believes about himself – what he's always believed about himself. That he's weak.

'You know what I've learned?' I say. 'Guilt is like a cancer. And the only way to make it right is to cut it out.'

When Charlie finally looks up again, his mouth trembles and his eyes are shining wet. 'I'm sorry,' he whispers. 'I am so sorry. There's not a day has gone by that I haven't wished I'd said no. Or told you I could see the lie, plain as day, in your eyes when you said you weren't afraid of dying.' His voice breaks. 'Or that I didn't reach out and hold on to you when you turned away from me to walk into the sea.'

I let go of his hands. Cup his face in my mine, watch his tears pool against my skin. And I think again of telling him that the truth isn't everything. Because this I can do for Charlie. I can give him peace.

'I forgive you.'

CHAPTER 42

I stand on the stern deck and wave, until not just Charlie but all of Stornoway is gone, swallowed inside the rocky inlets and headlands of the east coast. The wind howls around my head. The deck is empty, its rows of red plastic seats deserted. Metal rattles and bangs, waterproof covers slap and flap. My trainers slide on the deck as I lean against white-painted railings.

When I first arrived, curtains of fog had rolled across the Minch. And a storm-dusk had hidden the horizon, any hint or shape of the island that was off the bow. Now, even as that island gets further and further away, I can still see its grey cliffs and brown moorlands; the fiery golds and purples of its glens and summits. The lonely gold lights dotted along its coast like a chain of beacons. The white encircling surf. Where inside meets outside. That's where I am now. Where I will always be. Outside.

My phone rings, and I jump, surprised I have a signal. When

I see that it's Kelly, some of my melancholy lifts, and I'm already smiling even before I hear her familiar voice, always so fast and full of laughter.

'Where are you? Tell me you've left the island at least, or I'll have to murder you. I've been waiting patiently since last night to dive headfirst into a vat of blue WKD and a family pack of cheesy balls.'

I laugh, and it sounds so strange – so alien – to me, that I immediately stop.

'I'm sorry. I got waylaid.' I look at that surf, those lonely gold lights. 'But yeah, I've left the island now.' I turn away from the worst of the wind. 'Listen, I just wanted to say thank you again. For offering to put me up, for being so—'

'Are you kidding? I can't *wait* to see you. I mean, Fraser's great company and a big fan of cheesy balls, but he can't help me out with vats of blue WKD. You'll love it here. You're going to find the writing job of your dreams and stay with us forever if I get my way.' She snorts. 'And you know I'm pretty good at getting my way.'

'Thanks, Kelly.' I will never tell her about Robert. About any of it. Not for me. Not even for her dad. But for her.

'All part of the service.' Some of the smile goes out of her voice. I can picture her expression, the concern that she's always been so careful to hide. 'Are you okay, Maggie?'

I turn back to the wind, the strait, the disappearing island. 'I think so.'

I don't put my phone away after I end the call. Instead, I open Will's text.

Don't Worry, Be Happy x

And something changes inside me. Suddenly and without warning. Like a switch, dark to light. All that sadness, all that resignation, vanishes like rain clouds blown inland on an Atlantic wind. I think of Euan and Cora dancing to Clannad in their kitchen. *I will find you, if it takes a thousand years.* I think my anger – at how hard it is to love who we're always going to lose. But no one ever really loses anyone. I know now how love should feel, because of Will. Because of us. And the life that I choose now without him will be different, but he will always be the reason I chose it.

Maybe we are all just composite bodies, sitting at dining tables inside houses. Maybe what we sacrifice is only who we once were and what we once knew. And it's others who remember. Who build monuments and tell stories about who we used to be. Because Mum was right. Who I am has never been a curse. I know who I once was. And I know what I once knew. I think of Euan's *Some people, they just never live. They somehow can't live. And that was Robert.* Because Robert could never see that the only forgiveness he needed was his own.

When I fed Mum all those pills, one after another; when I watched her die – it was my choice. And I forgive myself for making it. Just as I forgive myself for never seeing either of us as anything more than a diagnosis; more than a few words in a file or on a prescription. I think instead of her eyes always bright, smile always wide, as if she knew something everyone else only wanted to.

And then it's easy, so easy, to reach into the neck of my mac and pull the chain free over my head. To rub the cool quartz of the pendant between nearly numb finger and thumb. To lean over the railings and drop it into the water, its long silver links catching the light before disappearing under the waves of the ferry's wake. I reach into my pocket, take out that photo of a young man standing alone in a grassy meadow in front of a hill. Tall and broad, arms folded over his chest. A thick brown beard, deep-set eyes, and a stoic frown.

'Goodbye, Robert.'

I let the photo go. Watch it flutter and flap, buoyed briefly by the wind before it vanishes into the same waves. I'm not Robert Reid. I'm not Andrew MacNeil. I don't believe in talismans or Norse myths. I don't believe that people are cursed. I don't believe that they deserve to be.

I'm not my bipolar. And I'm not my mother. I'm not Maggie MacKay. I'm not the Maggie Anderson who lived in London, pretending to be happy with so little.

I'm not even the person who stood on the deck of this boat three months ago. Who stood on a beach and told Charlie that she'd always been afraid to be happy. That she didn't know how to live in a moment instead of a whole life. Because she died. And I was born.

I look west, as those headlands and summits slowly disappear behind wreaths of sea mist and sun. That has been its gift to me. This thin place. This beautiful and wild place that will forever be a part of me.

It's never too late. Because the end is never the end. There will always, always be time.

To love, to forgive. To live.

EPILOGUE

End of September 1993

Robert

We're all guilty of something, my father always said. But the biggest sin is fear. And never facing it. That was not his sin, of course. Only mine. This morning, the sun is high. It lights up the occasional sprays of spindrift in silver-white sparks. From this height, the ocean looks endless like the sky. Blue and quiet. But the storms are coming. I can see them in the spray blown from the crests of waves and in the scattered whitecaps out towards the horizon. In the slow steady leaching of light from the sky, a little earlier each day. And I can feel them in the air and against my skin. A prickle. A shiver of old fear.

Today, there are no boats on the horizon, but I can see the red-and-white-striped *Unity* returning to the slip at Bàgh Fasgach. Calum sees it too and races along the shoreline, kicking up water, his high giggles catching and riding the wind. And something inside my chest gets tight with hope.

Once, many years ago, I stood on a headland just like this and looked out at the same ocean. I was alone and afraid and full of despair. But I vowed even then that I would come back again. I'd come back in spite of the storms. In spite of the fear. In spite of the despair. I had hope. Because somehow I knew that one day things would be different. One day I'd stop being afraid. I would come back. And all would be well.

ACKNOWLEDGEMENTS

Thank you, as ever, to my brilliant editor, Carla Josephson, and my equally brilliant agent, Hellie Ogden, for their generosity and expertise, absolute faith and endless patience! I'm grateful to you both more than words can ever say.

Thank you to the hugely talented team at Borough Press and HarperCollins, who have been so enthusiastic and supportive from day one. Thank you to Suzie Dooré, Ore Agbaje-Williams, Ann Bissell, and Margot Gray. Thank you to Claire Ward for her terrific artwork. And thank you to Izzy Coburn, Sarah Munro, Maddy Marshall, Jaime Witcomb, and Alice Hill for always working so tirelessly to bring authors and our books to as many readers as possible. Words can't express how grateful I am. I've loved working with you all.

Thanks to the Janklow & Nesbit UK team, especially Ellis Hazelgrove, Maimy Suleiman, Ma'suma Amiri, Megan Browne, and Kirsty Gordon.

I also owe a huge debt of gratitude to the people of the Isle of Lewis and Harris. Open and generous, and as unique as the islands themselves, the warmest of welcomes is always guaranteed, no matter the weather! Although the island of Kilmeray is entirely fictional (and loosely based on the uninhabited island of Scarp off the west coast of Harris), many of the places mentioned in *The Blackhouse* are very dear to my heart, due in no small part to those who live in them.

More specifically, I am incredibly grateful to Police Sergeant Donald John Macleod of Stornoway Police Station, for very patiently answering all of my questions about island policing. Thank you, too, to Marlene and Fraser Ralley, for kindly lending me their wonderful house in Cliff, where much of *The Blackhouse* was conceived. It was a magical few months.

The Ardshader storm in 1977, and the subsequent loss of three fishing boats and fifteen fishermen, was inspired by a real-life tragedy that happened on Lewis in March 1885. When a sudden gale forced the fishing fleets of Ness to return home, two boats decided to make for land on the northwest coast at Eoropie. When they became grounded on rocks instead, the villagers were forced to watch as every rescue attempt failed. All twelve fishermen drowned. Known as the Cunndal Drowning, a memorial now stands on a cliff above the bay where the boats tried to land. Every man who died was from the village of Eoropie, their names, ages, and addresses – from 1 Eoropie to 36 Eoropie – bring home just how devastating such a tragedy must have been for this small fishing community. This book is also dedicated to all the Hebridean fishermen who have lost their lives at sea over the years, and to the families that they left behind.

Thank you to Gillebride MacMillan and Eileen MacDonald for their considerable help with Scots Gaelic translation, and their patience in the face of all my fictional place names! Thank you, too, to Alison Lang and the wonderful Gaelic Books Council. Any and all mistakes are completely mine.

Thank you to the mental health charity, Mind, for all information and advice. I'm also especially grateful to the people who were kind enough to talk to me about their own personal experiences of living with bipolar 1 disorder.

Thank you to all the booksellers, reviewers and bloggers for their endless enthusiasm and kindness. I am forever indebted and would name every one of you if I could!

Thanks to my friends and family for their fantastic support, especially my parents, Muir and Louise Johnstone, my sister, Lorna Booth, and my godmother, Susan McEwan. Thanks also to Nina Allan, Chris Priest, Priya Sharma, Sarah Pinborough, Lorna Waddell and Shona Van der Wolf.

And thank you to my husband, Iain. The Isle of Lewis and Harris might be our place, but you are, and always will be, mine.

Last but never least, thank you to readers everywhere. I thank you most of all.

CAST OF CHARACTERS

Maggie Anderson (Maggie MacKay)

The Campbells:
Isla Campbell
Kenny Campbell
David Campbell

The MacDonalds:
Alec MacDonald
Fiona MacDonald
Sheena MacDonald
Lorne MacDonald

The MacKenzies:
Bruce MacKenzie
Gillian MacKenzie
Donnie MacKenzie

The MacLeods:
Charlie MacLeod
Moira MacLeod

The Morrisons:
Euan Morrison
Cora Morrison
Iain Morrison
Will Morrison
Heather Morrison

The Reids:
Robert Reid
Mary Reid
Calum Reid

The Stewarts:
Thom Stewart
Kate Stewart
Kelly Stewart
Fraser Stewart

Ejaz 'Jaz' Mahmood
Jimmy Struthers

The Archaeologists:
Femi Tinubu
Doctor Kumiko ('Miko') Okitsu

GLOSSARY OF TERMS AND PLACES

<u>Kilmeray Island</u>

Eilean Cill Maraigh
Kilmeray Island [translation: 'Church of (St) Maraigh' Island]
Pronunciation: **ay**-lan / **keell** / mar-**aye**

Eilean Beag
Wee Island
Pronunciation: **ay**-lan / b**aik**

<u>Villages on Kilmeray</u>
Blàr Mòr
Blairmore [translation: Big Battle]
Pronunciation: b**laar** / m**ore**

Ùrbost
Urbost [derived from Old Norse meaning New Dwelling]
Pronunciation: **oor**-bost

<u>Places on Kilmeray</u>
Gleann nam Bòcan
Valley of Ghosts
Pronunciation: gl-**aun** / nam / **bow**-can (as in bow-tie)

An Droch Chadha
Wicked Pass
Pronunciation: an / dr**och** (-ch as in loch) / **ch**-aa-huh (ch as in loch)

An Cladh Dubh
Archaeological dig on Kilmeray since the 90s [translation: The Black Burial Ground]
Pronunciation: an / **clou**-ch (-ch as in loch) / **doo**

Tòrr Dìseart
meaning: burial mound/ deserted mound;
derived from the Old Norse word *Dysætr*, for burial place
Pronunciation: **torr** / **jee**-shirsht

Sid a' Choin Mhòir
Lair of the Big Dog
Pronunciation:
she-**ch** (-ch as in speech) / uh / ch-oin (-ch as in loch) / **vohr**

Àite Lurach
Lovely Place
Pronunciation: ach-eh (-ch as in speech) / **lur**-ach (ah as in loch)

Àrd Chreag
Ardcraig [translation: High Cliff]
Pronunciation: **aa**-rd / ch-**raik** (ch as in loch)

An Rubha Siar
West Point
Pronunciation: an / **roo**-ah / **sheer**

Oir na Tìr
The Edge of Land
Pronunciation: or / nuh / **cheer** (ch as in cheer)

<u>Bodies of Water on Kilmeray</u>
An Cuan Siar
The Atlantic Ocean (West Ocean)
Pronunciation: an / **coo**-an / **sheer**

Loch Dubh
Loch Dubh [translation: Black Loch]
Pronunciation: loch / **doo**

Loch Tana
Loch Tana [translation: Slender Loch]
Pronunciation: loch / **tan**a

Glumag a' Bròin
The Pool of Sorrow
Pronunciation: **gloo**-mack / a / br-oihn

<u>Beaches on Kilmeray</u>
Tràigh Mhòr
Big Beach
Pronunciation: try / vore

Tràigh Shearrag
Long Stride Beach
Pronunciation: try / **sha**-rack

Bàgh Fasgach
Sheltered Bay
Pronunciation: **baa**-gh / **fass**-gach (-ch as in loch)

<u>Mountains on Kilmeray</u>
Beinn Uais
Ben Wyvis [translation: Terror Mountain]
Pronunciation: bay-hn / **oo**-wish

Beinn Donn
Ben Donn [translation: Brown Mountain]
Pronunciation: bay-hn / donn

<u>Lewis Mainland</u>

<u>Villages</u>
Àrd Shiadair
Ardshader [translation: High Dwelling/Settlement (from Old Norse sœtr)]
Pronunciation: **ar**ds / shi-a**durr**

Èinis
Einish
Pronunciation: **ain**-ish

Àird Èinis
Aird Einish headland [translation: High Einish]
Pronunciation: **ar**ds / **ain**-ish

A' Chàrnach
Carnach [translation: Rocky/Stony]
Pronunciation: uh / ch-**aarn**-ach (-ch as in loch both instances)

Bodies of Water
Na Bàigh
The Bays
Pronunciation: ne / **bye**

Bàgh an iar
West Bay
Pronunciation: **baa**-gh / an / **ee**-ar

Loch nam Each
Loch Naich [Translation: Loch of the Horse)
Pronunciation: loch / na / **eh**-ach

Beaches
Tràigh Lag
Hollow Beach
Pronunciation: try / **lack**

Tràigh Shiar
West Beach
Pronunciation: try / **sheer**

Non-fictional places

Steòrnabhagh
Stornoway
Pronunciation: sch-**torn**-o-vai

Port Nis
Port Ness
Pronunciation: porst / **nish**

Brèibhig
Brevig
Pronunciation: **brae**-vig

Miabhaig
Miavaig
Pronunciation: **mia**-vaig

Bhaltos
Valtos
Pronunciation: **val**-tos

Langabhat
Langavat
Pronunciation: langa-vat

Islibhig
Ishlivig
Pronunciation: **eesh**-lavig

General Gaelic Terms
Òrd na Mara
The Hammer of the Sea (historic storm in 1977)
Pronunciation: **or**dst / na / **ma**ra

Tilg mìr am beul na bèist
Cast a bone in the devil's mouth. From Gaelic proverb:
Cast a bone in the devil's mouth and it will save you
Pronunciation: ch**illig** / meer / am / **be**-al / na / **bey**-ge-t (-ge as in
   a**ge**)

Am baile gun fhir
The village without men
Pronunciation: am / **bal**-uh / goon / eerr

Acair
Anchor (name of a boat)
Pronunciation: **ach**-ker (-ch as in loch)

Marcan-sìne
Spindrift (name of a boat)
Pronunciation: **mar**can-**sheen**-uh

Darach
Oak (name of a boat)
Pronunciation: **dar**-ach (as in loch)

Tuathanas
farm
Pronunciation: **too**ah-hanas

Tairsgeir
peat cutting tool
Pronunciation: **tar**ash-gir

Sgoth
boat, a clinker built skiff
Pronunciation: sk**aw**

Tìoraidh
goodbye, cheerio
Pronunciation: **chee**rie

a ghràidh
my dear, my love
Pronunciation: oo / gir-**aye**

<u>Old Norse terms</u>
Vándr Varði
Norse talisman: Vándr meaning evil / Varði meaning to guard against
Pronunciation: **van**-dr / **var**-thea

Sjóvættir
Sea spirits in Norse mythology
Pronunciation: **sjo**-vat-tear

Landvættir
Nature/land spirits in Norse mythology
Pronunciation: **land**-vat-tear

Dysætr
Burial Ground
Pronunciation: **doo**-satr

Innangarðs
Inside the house/fence
Was often interpreted in early Medieval Paganism as the enclosed human
world of order, law and security, which must be protected from the
outside
Pronunciation: **innan**-garthz

Utangarðs
Outside the house/fence
Was often interpreted in early Medieval Paganism as a wild and chaotic
world beyond the human, inhabited by monsters and giants
Pronunciation: **ootan**-garthz